P9-DNV-620

CHAPTER & HEARSE

CHAPTER & HEARSE

Suspense Stories About the World of Books

Edited by
Marcia Muller & Bill Pronzini

William Morrow and Company, Inc.
New York

"The Missing Shakespeare Manuscript," by Lillian de la Torre. Copyright 1947 by Lillian de la Torre; copyright © renewed 1974 by Lillian de la Torre. First published in *Ellery Queen's Mystery Magazine.* Reprinted by permission of Harold Ober Associates Incorporated.

"The Man Who Collected Poe," by Robert Bloch. Copyright 1951 by Popular Publications, Inc. First published in *Famous Fantastic Mysteries.* Reprinted by permission of Scott Meredith Literary Agency, Inc., 845 Third Avenue, New York, N.Y. 10022.

"The Penny-a-Worder," by Cornell Woolrich. Copyright © 1958 by Davis Publications, Inc. First published in *Ellery Queen's Mystery Magazine.* Reprinted by permission of Scott Meredith Literary Agency, Inc., 845 Third Avenue, New York, N.Y. 10022.

"Clerical Error," by James Gould Cozzens. Copyright 1935 by The McCall Corporation; copyright © renewed 1963 by James Gould Cozzens. Reprinted by permission of Harcourt Brace Jovanovich, Inc.

"Murder Walks in Marble Halls," by Lawrence G. Blochman. Copyright 1942 by Lawrence G. Blochman. First published in *The American Magazine.* Reprinted by permission of Anita Diamant, agent for the estate of Lawrence G. Blochman.

"Reflections on Murder," by Nedra Tyre. Copyright © 1958 by *Sleuth.* Reprinted by permission of Scott Meredith Literary Agency, Inc., 845 Third Avenue, New York, N.Y. 10022.

"The Adventure of the Spurious Tamerlane," by August Derleth. Copyright © 1964 by Fiction Publishing Company. First published in *The Saint Mystery Magazine.* Reprinted by permission of Arkham House Publishers, Inc., Sauk City, WI 53583.

"One Thousand Dollars a Word," by Lawrence Block. Copyright © 1978 by Lawrence Block. First published in *Alfred Hitchcock's Mystery Magazine.* Reprinted by permission of the author.

"QL 696. C9," by Anthony Boucher. Copyright 1943 by The American Mercury; copyright © renewed 1971 by Davis Publications, Inc. First published in *Ellery Queen's Mystery Magazine.* Reprinted by permission of Curtis Brown Assoc., Ltd.

"Murder at the Bouchercon," by Edward D. Hoch. Copyright © 1983 by Edward D. Hoch. First published in *Ellery Queen's Mystery Magazine.* Reprinted by permission of the author.

"Seven Types of Ambiguity," by Shirley Jackson. From *The Lottery* by Shirley Jackson. Copyright 1943, 1944, 1947, 1948, 1949 by Shirley Jackson. Renewed © 1971, 1972, 1975, 1976, 1977 by Laurence Hyman, Barry Hyman, Mrs. Sarah Webster, and Mrs. Joanne Schnurer. Reprinted by permission of Farrar, Straus and Giroux, Inc.

Library of Congress Cataloging in Publication Data
Main entry under title:

Chapter and hearse.

1. Detective and mystery stories, American.
2. Detective and mystery stories, English. 3. Books and reading—Fiction. 4. Authors—Fiction.
I. Muller, Marcia. II. Pronzini, Bill.
PS648.D4C45 1985 813'.0872'08 84-16497
ISBN 0-688-04184-1

Printed in the United States of America

First Edition

1 2 3 4 5 6 7 8 9 10

BOOK DESIGN BY JAYE ZIMET

CONTENTS

INTRODUCTION

The bit of advice most often passed down to new writers is that tried-and-true maxim, "Write what you know." Of course, this advice is not always followed to the letter, nor should it be. In the case of suspense writers, it is fortunate that we do not feel compelled to experience the dark passions, murder, and mayhem that fill the pages of our work.

However, when the crime-story writer combines research and imagination with a subject he truly understands, the results can be exceptional—as we believe you'll see in the stories contained in this volume. After all, what does a writer know better than the world of books? Where is he more at home than in the confines of a library, a bookstore, or a publishing house?

More than a few writers are collectors—of rare books, research volumes, anything that happens to strike their fancy. Among the well known are Frederic Dannay, half of the team that created Ellery Queen, whose large library of rare and important mystery fiction now resides at the University of Texas; renowned critics, authors, and Sherlockians Anthony Boucher and Vincent Starrett; Wisconsin writer and publisher August Derleth; and, of recent vintage, your editors.

Bookshops also tend to draw writers, not only as patrons

but as employees. Just a few of the literary practitioners who have been or still are booksellers: Phyllis A. Whitney, Nedra Tyre, Roy Harley Lewis, Art Bourgeau, and Georges Simenon (who has said that he enjoyed his stint as a bookstore clerk because it gave him plenty of time to read).

Other writers have had careers as librarians, notably Carolyn Wells, Dorothy Salisbury Davis, and Charles Goodrum. Still others were editors: Frederic Dannay was founder and, for forty years, editor of *Ellery Queen's Mystery Magazine;* Anthony Boucher was cofounder and coeditor of *The Magazine of Fantasy & Science Fiction;* Clayton Rawson edited both a hardcover mystery line and *EQMM* for many years. And still others worked on the staffs of literary magazines (Edgar Allan Poe) and/or developed important avocations as book reviewers (Anthony Boucher, Helen McCloy, Brett Halliday, Dorothy B. Hughes, Robert Wade).

Above all, writers are readers. Their shelves overflow with volumes new and old, read, and as yet unread. Books and magazines are stacked in every room of their houses, covering table tops, spilling over on the floors—publications that seldom gather dust because they are constantly being picked up, leafed through, read, and reread.

It is no wonder, then, that writers often employ, in their own fiction, themes involving the world of books. Characters who are also writers frequently appear. Famous writer detectives, for instance, include Ellery Queen and Lord Peter Wimsey's fiancée, Harriet Vane, a mystery writer who was undoubtedly creator Dorothy L. Sayers's alter ego and who leads Lord Peter to the solution of a case of her own in *Gaudy Night.* Aaron Marc Stein's George Bagby is a notable "Watson" for the cases of Inspector Schmidt. In nonseries books, Anthony Boucher's *The Case of the Baker Street Irregulars* (1940) deals with murder in that august Sherlockian society, while his *Rocket to the Morgue* (1942, as by H. H. Holmes) combines mayhem and the science-fiction writing community of the period. Bill Pronzini's *Hoodwink*

(1981) takes place at a pulp-magazine convention and reunion of a group of ex-pulp writers.

Novels about the untimely demise of writers are not uncommon. One dies rather unpleasantly on stage at the annual awards banquet of the Mystery Writers of America, in *The Shattered Raven* (1969) by Edward D. Hoch; another is disposed of on his country estate in England in Robert Barnard's *Death of a Mystery Writer* (1978). (The subject, unfortunately, holds no guarantee of quality, as evidenced by Eric Heath's classically bad 1953 novel, *Murder of a Mystery Writer.*)

The publishing industry has been the setting for a number of fictional intrigues. Isaac Asimov terrorized the American Booksellers' Association in his *Murder at the A.B.A.* (1976). William G. Bogart's *Hell on Friday* (1941) has a pulp-magazine publishing background. Rex Stout's *Plot It Yourself* (1959) deals with that sticky publishing problem, plagiarism. Editors and publishers are messily eliminated in a number of books, including *Hoodwink, Fatal Descent* (1939) by John Rhode and Carter Dickson, and in more than one Mr. and Mrs. North adventure by Frances and Richard Lockridge (Jerry North, of course, was a book publisher himself). And Hunt Collins's (Evan Hunter) 1953 novel *Cut Me In* concerns itself with that shadowy link between writer and publisher, the literary agent (a.k.a. the "ten-percenter").

Collecting and bibliophilia also figure prominently in crime fiction. Sherlock Holmes had a small but carefully selected library for the times when his copious memory failed him. Sayers's Lord Peter amassed a library of rare books when he wasn't engaged in solving murders. The same was true of Elizabeth Daly's Henry Gamadge, a bibliophile and rare-book consultant who appears in such bookish mysteries as *Unexpected Night* (1940) and *Murders in Volume 2* (1941); and of Frank Gruber's Simon Lash, a collector whose cases include *Simon Lash: Private Detective* (1941) and *Murder '97* (1948). On the modern scene, Bill Pronzini's "Nameless Detective" is an avid collector of pulp magazines. And nonseries bibliophilic mysteries include William Hallahan's superb 1973 tale of the forging of some Thomas Wise pamphlets, *The Ross Forgery;* and Robert J. Randisi's novel about a pulp collector, *The Steinway Collection* (1983).

Libraries, while they seem an unlikely setting for crime, are another favorite. W. Bolingbroke Johnson's *The Widening Stain* (1942), Charity Blackstock's *Dewey Death* (1956), Andrew Garve's *The Galloway Case* (1958), Julian Symons's *The Color of Murder* (1958), and Charles Goodrum's *Dewey Decimated* (1977) are just a few of the novels that disturb the peace of the stately halls of knowledge.

Nor have booksellers been forgotten. Roy Harley Lewis's Matthew Coll is an antiquarian book dealer who becomes entangled with murder in *A Cracking of Spines* (1981), *The Manuscript Murders* (1982), and *A Pension for Death* (1983). M. K. Wren's Conan Flagg, hero of such novels as *Seasons for Death* (1981), operates a bookshop in Oregon. Bookstores figure prominently in numerous other titles, including Ed McBain's *Lady, Lady I Did It!* (1961) and Raymond Chandler's *The Big Sleep* (1939), in which Philip Marlowe runs afoul of a rare-book dealer who is fronting for a pornographic lending library.

In these pages we have gathered together sixteen of the best short crime stories on the various bookish themes, by some of the finest suspense writers past and present. They are peopled by writers and editors, bibliophiles and booksellers and librarians. They involve rare books, common books, the Bible, pulp magazines, paperback hackwork Their settings range from public libraries to the Library of Congress, from publishing houses to the Bouchercon, from bookstores to the homes of private collectors.

We think you'll enjoy these stories. And we think, too, that you'll agree authors are at the top of their form when writing about what they know best—the wide world of books.

—MARCIA MULLER AND BILL PRONZINI
San Francisco, California
February 1984

One of the most literate detectives in modern suspense fiction is Lillian de la Torre's Dr. Samuel Johnson. The eighteenth-century lexicographer and his "Watson," James Boswell, appear in twenty-six stories, collected in Dr. Sam: Johnson, Detector *(1946) and* The Detections of Dr. Sam: Johnson *(1960). (These collections have recently been reprinted; two new collections,* The Return of Dr. Sam: Johnson, Detector *and* The Exploits of Dr. Sam: Johnson, Detector *are due to be published in 1986.) In these delightful pastiches, Ms. de la Torre depicts the world of Dr. Sam and Boswell with colorful historical accuracy, and the somewhat testy interplay between the two characters serves to entertain, as well as further the course of scholarly detection. In "The Missing Shakespeare Manuscript," Johnson and his sidekick visit Stratford-on-Avon for the 1769 Shakespeare Jubilee, where, as usual, they encounter a puzzling dilemma.*

THE MISSING SHAKESPEARE MANUSCRIPT

Lillian de la Torre

(as related by James Boswell after the Shakespeare Jubilee, Stratford, September 1769)

'Twas Dr. Sam: Johnson, in the end, who returned the missing Shakespeare manuscript at the Stratford Jubilee; though in the beginning he would not so much as look at it. He preferred to hug the fire at the Red Lion Inn.

"Do, Dr. Johnson," I urged, "give me your company to Mr. Ararat's though you come but to scoff."

"I shall not remain to pray, I promise you," rejoined the great *Cham* of literature intransigently.

"So much is unnecessary," I replied, "but indeed I have promised we would there meet with Dr. Percy and his young friend Malone, the Irish lawyer."

"This is very proper for Thomas Percy and his scavenging friends," remarked Dr. Johnson, lifting his coattails before the blaze, "for they are very methodists in the antiquarian *enthusiasm*. But truly this is ill for a scholar, to run with the vulgar after a parcel of old waste paper."

"Sir, sir," I protested, "the antiquarian zeal of Mr. Ararat has preserved to us a previously unknown tragedy of Shakespeare, 'Caractacus; or, the British Hero.' "

"Which little Davy Garrick is to represent in the great amphitheatre tomorrow night. Let him do so. Let us see him do so. Let us not meddle with the musty reliques of the writing desk."

"Musty!" I cried. "Let me tell you this is no musty old dog's-eared folio that has lost its wrappings for pyes or worse, like the ballad-writings Percy cherishes, but a manuscript as fair and unblemished, so Dr. Warton assures me, as the day it came from the bard's own hand. By singular good luck Mr. Ararat is of antiquarian mind, and the manuscript was preserved from a noisome fate in the out-house."

"That it was preserved for Garrick to play and Dodsley to publish, this is luck indeed; but now that the playhouse copies are taken off, it may end in the out-house for all of me," replied my learned friend. "No, sir; let a good play be well printed and well played; but to idolize mere paper and ink is rank superstition and idolatry."

"Why, sir, you need not adore it, nor look at it if you will not; but pray let us not disappoint Dr. Percy and his young friend."

Dr. Johnson's good nature was not proof against this appeal to friendship; he consented to walk along with me to Mr. Ararat's.

I made haste to don my hat and be off before anything could supervene. As we set off on foot from the yard of the Red Lion, my revered friend peered at me with puckered eyes.

"Pray, Mr. Boswell," he enquired in tones of forced forbearance, "what is the writing inserted in your hat?"

I doffed the article in question and gazed admiringly at the neatly inscribed legend which adorned it.

"CORSICA BOSWELL," read off my learned friend in

tones of disgust. "Corsica Boswell! Pray, what commodity are you touting, Mr. Boswell, that you advertize the world of your name in this manner?"

"A very precious commodity," I retorted with spirit, "liberty for down-trodden Corsica. Do but attend the great masquerade tonight, you shall see how I speak for Corsica."

"Well, sir, you may speak for whom you will, and advertize Stratford of your name as you please. For me, let me remain *incognito.* I should be loath to parade about Stratford as DICTIONARY JOHNSON."

"Say rather," I replied, "as SHAKESPEARE JOHNSON, for your late edition of the Bard must endear you to the town of his birth."

"I come to Stratford," remarked Dr. Johnson with finality, "to observe men and manners, and not to tout for my wares."

"Be it so," I replied, "here is material most proper for your observation."

As I spoke, we were crossing the public square, which teemed with bewildered Stratfordians and jostling strangers. The center of a milling crowd, a trumpeter was splitting the air with his blasts and loudly proclaiming:

"Ladies and gentlemen! The famous Sampson is just going to begin—just going to mount four horses at once with his feet upon two saddles—also the most wonderful surprizing feats of horsemanship by the most *notorious* Mrs. Sampson."

A stringy man and an Amazon of a woman seconded his efforts by giving away inky bills casting further light on their own notorious feats. As we strolled on, we met a man elbowing his way through the press beating a drum and shouting incessantly:

"The notified Porcupine Man, and all sorts of outlandish birds and other beasts to be seen without loss of time on the great meadow near the amphitheatre at so small a price as one shilling a piece. Alive, alive, alive, ho."

Behind him came a man leading a large bin, and a jostling crowd following. Dr. Johnson smiled.

"This foolish fellow will scarce make his fortune at the Jubilee," he remarked. "Who will pay a shilling to see strange animals in a house, when a man may see them for nothing going along the streets, alive, alive, ho?"

As we walked along, Dr. Johnson marvelled much at the elegant art of the decorations displayed about the town. The town hall was adorned with five transparencies on silk—in the center Shakespeare, flanked by Lear and Caliban, Falstaff, and Pistol. The humble cottage where Shakespeare was born, gave me those feelings which men of enthusiasm have on seeing remarkable places; and I had a solemn and serene satisfaction in contemplating the church in which his body lies.

Dr. Johnson, however, took a more lively interest in the untutored artistry of the townsfolk of Stratford, who had everywhere adorned their houses, according to their understanding and fantasy, in honour of their Bard. We read many a rude legend displayed to the glorification of Shakespeare and Warwickshire. We beheld many a crude portrait intended for the great playwright, and only a few less libels on the lineaments of David Garrick, as we strolled down to Mr. Ararat's.

"This is Garrick's misfortune that as steward of the Jubilee, he is man of the hour," remarked Dr. Johnson, "for the admiration of Warwickshire has done him no less wrong than the lampoons of London."

"In Shakespeare he has a notable fellow-sufferer," I replied.

JOHNSON "You say true, Bozzy. Alack, Bozzy, do my eyes inform me true as to the nature of the small building, set apart, which someone has seen fit to adorn with the honoured features of the Bard?"

BOSWELL "Your eyes inform you truly. We are approaching the stationer's shop of Mr. Ararat, whose zeal for

Shakespeare extends even to adorning the exterior of his out-house with the counterfeit presentment of the Bard."

JOHNSON "Better his face without than his works within."

BOSWELL "Sir, the antiquarian zeal of Mr. Ararat, 'tis said, extends even so far, for he provides for the convenience of his household a pile of old accounts of wonderful and hoary antiquity. The Stratfordians are long dead and gone who bought the paper for which the reckoning still awaits a last usefulness."

JOHNSON "Let Mr. Ararat keep Thomas Percy out of here. Last year he published the Earl of Northumberland's reckonings for bread and cheese from the year 1512; next year, unless he's watched, I'll be bound, he'll rush to the press with a parcel of stationer's accounts he's *borrowed* from Ararat's out-house."

BOSWELL "Sir, you wrong Thomas Percy. He's a notable antiquarian and his works are much sought after."

JOHNSON "He's a snapper-up of unconsidered trifles, and that young Irishman who's followed him hither is no better. Sir, be it a Shakespeare manuscript or a publican's reckoning, just so it be old, I'd watch it narrowly while Percy is about."

Speaking thus, we turned the corner, when the full complexity of Mr. Ararat's decorative scheme struck us at once. Limned by an unskillful hand, the characters of Shakespeare's plays crowded the ancient facade, dominated under the gabled roof by the lineaments of the Bard, for which the portrait on the necessary-house was clearly a preliminary study. Hamlet leaned a melancholy elbow on the steep gable of the window, Macbeth and Macduff fought with claymores over the front door, a giant warrior guarded the corner post, all endued with a weird kind of life in the gray glare of the sky, for a storm was threatening.

"Ha," said Dr. Johnson, "who is this painted chieftain? Can it be Cymbeline?"

"No, sir, this is Caractacus, hero of the new play just recovered."

JOHNSON "Why has he painted himself like an Onondaga?"

BOSWELL "Sir, he is an ancient Briton. He has painted himself with woad."

JOHNSON "Will little Davy Garrick paint himself blue?"

BOSWELL "I cannot say, sir, though 'tis known he means to present the character in ancient British dress."

JOHNSON "This is more of your *antiquarianism.* Let Davy Garrick but present a *man,* he may despise the fribbles of the tiring-room."

As we thus stood chatting before the stationer's shop, a strange creature insinuated himself before us. From his shoulder depended a tray full of oddments.

"Tooth-pick cases, needle cases, punch ladles, tobacco stoppers, inkstands, nutmeg graters, and all sorts of boxes, made out of the famous mulberry tree," he chanted.

"Pray, sir, shall we venture?"

"Nay, Bozzy, the words of the bard are the true metal, his mulberry tree is but dross. You seem determined to make a papistical idolator of me."

"Yet perhaps this box—" I indicated a wooden affair large enough for a writing-desk—"this box is sufficiently useful in itself—"

With a resentful scowl the man snatched it rudely from my hand.

"'Tis not for sale," he mumbled, and ran down the street with his boxes hopping.

"Are all the people mad?" quoted Dr. Johnson from the "Comedy of Errours"; and the shop bell tinkled to herald our entrance into the stationer's shop of Mr. Ararat.

Behind the counter in the dim little shop stood a solid-built man in a green baize apron. He had a sanguine face fringed with gingery whiskers and a sanguine bald top fringed with gingery hair. This was Mr. Ararat, stationer of Stratford, Shakespearean enthusiast, and owner of the precious manuscript of "Caractacus; or, the British Hero." He spelled out the sign on my hat and gave me a low bow.

"Welcome, Mr. Boswell, to you and your friend."

We greeted Mr. Ararat with suitable distinction. Being made known to Dr. Johnson, he greeted him with surprised effusion.

"This is indeed an unlooked-for honour, Dr. Johnson," cried Mr. Ararat.

"Percy is late," I observed to Dr. Johnson.

"Dr. Percy was here, and has but stepped out for a moment," Mr. Ararat informed us.

We whiled away the time of waiting by examining the honest stationer's stock, and Dr. Johnson purchased some of his laid paper, much to my surprise to good advantage. As the parcel was wrapping Thomas Percy put his long nose in at the door, and followed it by his neat person attired in clerical black. He laid his parcel on the counter and took Dr. Johnson by both his hands.

"We must count ourselves fortunate," he cried, "to have attracted Dr. Johnson hither. I had feared we could never lure you from Brighthelmstone, where the witty and fair conspired to keep you."

"Why, sir, the witty and fair, if by those terms you mean to describe Mrs. Thrale, took a whim that the sea air gave her a megrim, and back she must post to Streatham; and I took a whim not to wait upon her whims, so off I came for Stratford."

"We are the gainers," cried Percy.

Dr. Johnson's eye fell on the counter, where lay his package of paper and the exactly similar parcel Percy had laid down. He picked up the latter.

"Honest Mr. Ararat does well by us Londoners," he remarked, "to sell us fine paper so cheap."

"Yes, sir," replied Percy, possessing himself of his parcel

with more haste than was strictly mannerly, "you see I know how to prize new folios as well as old, ha ha."

He gripped his parcel, and during the whole of our exciting transactions in the house of Mr. Ararat it never left his hands again.

At that moment the shop-bell tinkled to admit a stranger. I saw a fresh-faced Irishman with large spiritual eyes the colour of brook water, a straight nose long at the tip, and a delicate smiling mouth. He was shabbily dressed in threadbare black. The new-comer nodded to Percy, and made a low bow to my venerable friend.

"Your servant, Dr. Johnson," he exclaimed in a soft mellifluous voice, "Permit me to recall myself—Edmond Malone, at your service. I had the honour to be made known to you some years since by my countryman Edmund Southwell."

"I remember it well," replied Dr. Johnson cordially, " 'Twas at the Grecian, in the Strand. I had a kindness for Southwell."

"He will be happy to hear it," replied Malone.

'Twas thus that I, James Boswell, the Scottish advocate, not quite twenty-nine, met Edmond Malone, the Irish lawyer, then in the twenty-eighth year of his age, who was destined to become—but I digress.

Our party being complete, we repaired into the inner room and were accommodated with comfortable chairs. Seated by the chimney-piece was a boy of about sixteen, a replica of old Mr. Ararat, with a rough red mop of hair and peaked red eyebrows. He looked at us without any expression on his round face.

" 'Tis Anthony," said his father with pride. "Anthony's a good boy."

"What do you read so diligently, my lad?" enquired Dr. Johnson kindly, peering at the book the boy held. "Johnson's *Shakespeare!* I am honoured!"

"Nay, sir, 'tis we who are honoured," said Malone fervently. "To inspect the Shakespeare manuscript in the company of him who knows the most in England of the literature of our country and the plays of the Bard, to read the literature of yesterday in the presence of Dictionary Johnson, who knows the age and lineage of every English word from the oldest to the word minted but yesterday, this is to savour the fine flower of scholarship."

The red-haired boy turned his eyes toward Dr. Johnson.

"Pray, sir," replied Dr. Johnson, "don't cant. In restoring a lost play this worthy boy has deserved as well as I of his fellow-Englishmen."

"Anthony's a good boy," said his father with pride. "He knows the plays of Shakespeare by heart, 'Caractacus' included."

I looked at Anthony, and doubted it.

"Shall you make him a stationer, like his fathers before him?" enquired Dr. Percy politely.

"No, sir," replied Ararat, "he's prenticed to old Mr Quiney the scrivener over the way. Here, Anthony, fetch my strong-box, we'll show the gentleman what they came to see."

Anthony nodded, and went quickly out of the room.

"This is a great good fortune," said Dr. Percy eagerly, "to see the very writing of Shakespeare himself. We are your debtors that it has been preserved."

" 'Tis nothing," but old Ararat began to swell like a turkey-cock. He launched into the story: "The first Anthony Ararat was a stationer in Stratford, like me, and Will Shakespeare was his neighbour. Anthony saved his life in the Avon, and in recompense he had of Will the manuscript of this very play, 'Caractacus; or, the British Hero,' to be his and his children's forever. Old Anthony knew how to value it, for he folded it in silk, and laid with it a writing of how he came by it, and laid it away with his accounts and private papers."

"Then how came it to be lost?" enquired Dr. Percy.

" 'Twas my grandmother, sir, who took the besom to all

the old papers together, and bundled one with another into the shed, and there they lay over the years with the lumber and the stationer's trash. I played in there when I was a boy, and so did Anthony after me. I remember, there was paper in there my father said his grandfather had made when he was prenticed in the paper-mills. But I never turned over the old accountings, nor paid them any heed. But to make a long story short, gentlemen, come Jubilee time I thought to turn an honest penny letting lodgings, so I bade Anthony turn out the lumber in the shed and make a place where the horses could stand. Anthony turned out a quantity of waste paper and lumber, and my mother's marriage lines that went missing in '28, and the manuscript of 'Caractacus,' wrapped in silk as the first Anthony had laid it by. He had the wit to bring it to me, and I took it over to old Mr. Quiney the engrosser, and between us we soon made out what we had. Warton of Trinity rode over from Oxford, and Mr. Garrick came down from London and begged to play it . . ."

The words died in his throat. I followed his gaze toward the inner door. There stood young Anthony, pale as death. Tears were streaming down his wet face. Angrily he dashed the drops from his shoulder. In his hand he held a brass-bound coffer, about the size of the mulberry-wood box the pedlar had snatched from us. Wordlessly, though his throat constricted, he held out the strong-box toward his father. It was empty. We saw the red silk lining, and the contorted metal where the lock had been forced.

The manuscript of "Caractacus" had vanished quite away.

Old Ararat was beside himself. Thomas Percy was racked between indignation and pure grief. Only Dr. Johnson maintained a philosophical calm.

"Pray, Mr. Ararat, compose yourself. Remember the playhouse copies are safely taken off. You have lost no more than a parcel of waste paper."

"But, sir," cried Malone, "the very hand of the Bard!"

"And a very crabbed hand too," rejoined Johnson, "old Quiney over the way will engross you a better for a crown."

"But, pray, Dr. Johnson," I enquired, "is not its value enormous?"

"Its value is nil. 'Tis so well-known, and so unique, that the thief can never sell it; he can only feed his fancy, that it is now his. Let him gloat. 'Caractacus' is ours. Tomorrow we shall see Garrick play the British hero; the day after tomorrow it will be given to the world in an elegant edition. The thief has gained, Mr. Ararat has lost, nothing but old paper."

But Percy and the Ararats thought otherwise. We deployed like an army through the domain of the good stationer, and left no corner unsearched. We had up the red satin lining of the coffer; we turned over the stationer's stock-in-trade and the old papers in the shed; we searched the house from top to bottom; all to no purpose. In the end we went away without finding anything, leaving young Anthony stupefied by the chimney-piece and old Ararat, red with rage and searching, blaming the whole thing on the Jubilee.

We were a dreary party as we walked back to the Red Lion in the rain. Percy and Malone stalked on in heartbroken silence. Having given his parcel into Percy's keeping, Dr. Johnson swayed along muttering to himself and touching the palings as we passed. Alone retaining my wonted spirits, I broached in vain half a dozen cheerful topicks, and at last fell silent like the rest.

Arrived in the court-yard of the Red Lion, Dr. Johnson took his parcel from Percy's hand and vanished without a word. I lingered long enough to take a dram for the prevention of the ague. Percy and Malone were sorry company, quaffing in silence by my side, and soon by mutual consent we parted to shift our wet raiment.

In the chamber I shared with Dr. Johnson (dubbed,

according to the fancy of Mr. Peyton the landlord, after one of Shakespeare's plays, "Much Ado about Nothing") I found my venerable friend, shifted to dry clothing, muffled in a counterpane and staring at the fire.

I ventured to enquire where in his opinion the sacred document had got to.

"Why, Bozzy," replied he, "some Shakespeare-maniac has got it, you may depend upon it, or as it might be, some old-paper maniac. Some scavenging antiquarian has laid hold of it and gloats over it in secret."

"I cry your pardon," said Dr. Percy, suddenly appearing at our door. He was white and uneasy still. In his hand he carried a parcel.

"Pray, Dr. Johnson, do you not have my parcel that I brought from Mr. Ararat's?"

"I, Dr. Percy? I have my own parcel." Dr. Johnson indicated it where it lay still wrapped on the table.

Percy seized it, and scrutinized the wrappings narrowly.

"You are deceived, Dr. Johnson. This parcel is mine. Here is yours, which I retained in errour for my own. I fear I have disarranged it in opening. Pray forgive me. I see you have opened mine more neatly."

" 'Tis as I had it of you," replied Dr. Johnson.

"You have not opened it!" cried Percy. "Well, Dr. Johnson, now we each have our own again, and no harm's done, eh? We lovers of good paper have done a shrewd day's bargaining, have we not, ha ha ha!"

"I will wager mine was the better bargain," said Dr. Johnson good-humouredly. "Come, open up, let us see."

"No, no, Dr. Johnson, I must be off," and Percy whipped through the door before either of us could say a word.

"Now," remarked Dr. Johnson, " 'tis seen that Peyton was well advised to name our chamber 'Much Ado about Nothing'."

* * *

The rain continued in a dreary stream, so that boards had to be laid over the kennel to transport the ladies dry-shod into the amphitheatre; but for all that, the great masquerade that night was surely the finest entertainment of the kind ever witnessed in Britain. I was sorry that Dr. Johnson elected to miss it. There were many rich, elegant, and curious dresses, many beautiful women, and some characters well supported. Three ladies personated Macbeth's three witches with devastating effect, while a person dressed as the devil gave inexpressible offence.

I own, however, that 'twas my own attire that excited the most remark. Appearing in the character of an armed Corsican chief, I wore a short, dark-coloured coat of coarse cloth, scarlet waistcoat and breeches, and black spatterdashes, and a cap of black cloth, bearing on its front, embroidered in gold letters, VIVA LA LIBERTA, and on its side a blue feather and cockade. I also wore a cartridge-pouch, into which was stuck a stiletto, and on my left side a pistol. A musket was slung across my shoulder, and my hair, unpowdered, hung plaited down my neck, ending in a knot of blue ribbons. In my right hand I carried a long vine staff, with a bird curiously carved at the long curving upper end, emblematical of the sweet bard of Avon. In this character of a Corsican chief I delivered a poetical address on the united subjects of Corsica and the Stratford Jubilee.

I cannot forbear to rehearse the affecting peroration:

"But let me plead for LIBERTY distrest,
And warm for her each sympathetick Breast:
Amongst the splendid Honours which you bear,
To save a Sister Island! be your Care:
With generous Ardour make US also FREE;
And give to CORSICA, a NOBLE JUBILEE."

As I came to an applauded close, I heard a resonant voice at my elbow.

"Pray, Bozzy," demanded Dr. Johnson, peering at me with disfavour, "what is the device on your coat? The head of a blackamoor upon a charger, garnished with watercress?"

"That, sir," I replied stiffly, "is the crest of Corsica, a Moor's head surrounded by branches of laurel. But what brings you from your bed, whither you were bound when I left you?"

"Sir," replied Dr. Johnson, "somebody in Stratford is in possession of the missing manuscript of Mr. Ararat. Here I have them all gathered under one roof, and all out of character, or into another character, which is just as revealing. I am here to observe. Let us retire into this corner and watch how they go on. To him who will see with his eyes, all secrets are open."

"Tooth-pick cases, needle cases, punch ladles, tobacco stoppers, inkstands, nutmeg graters, and all sorts of boxes, made out of the famous mulberry tree," chanted a musical voice behind us. We turned to behold the very figure of the man with the tray. His brilliant eyes twinkled behind his mask.

"Goods from the mulberry tree," he chanted, "made out of old chairs and stools and stained according, tooth-pick cases, needle cases, punch ladles—"

A blast from a trumpet cut him off. Beside him stood a second mask, garbed "like Rumour painted full of tongues," impersonating Fame with trumpet and scroll.

"Pray, sir," said Dr. Johnson, entering into the spirit of the occasion, "let us glimpse your scroll, whether our names be not inscribed thereon."

The mask withheld the scroll, and spoke in a husky voice:

"Nay, sir, my scroll is blank."

"Why, sir, then you are the prince of cynics. What, not one name? Not *Corsica* Boswell? Not Garrick? Not Shakespeare? Sir, were I to betray this to the Corporation, you should stand in the pillory."

"Therefore I shall not reveal myself—even to Dr. Johnson—" replied the mask in his husky voice. He would have slipped away, when one of those spasmodic movements which cause my venerable friend so much distress hurled to the ground both trumpet and scroll. In a contest of courtesy, Fame retrieved the trumpet and my venerable friend the scroll.

"You say true," remarked the last-named sadly, re-rolling the scroll, "on the roster of Fame, my name is not inscribed."

He restored the scroll with a bow, and Fame made off with the mulberry-wood vendor.

"I interest myself much in the strange personages of this assemblage," remarked my philosophical friend. "Alack, there's a greater guy than you, *Corsica* Boswell, for he's come out without his breeches."

I recognized with surprize the fiery mop and blank face of young Ararat, whom I had last seen that morning weeping for the lost manuscript. He was robed in white linen, and carried scrip and claymore. He wore no mask, but his face was daubed with blue.

" 'Tis Anthony," said I, "he personates Caractacus, the British hero. Sure he trusts in vain if he thinks to conceal his identity behind a little blue paint."

"To the man with eyes, the heaviest mask is no concealment," replied Dr. Johnson. "Sure you smoaked our friends with the scroll and the mulberry wood in spite of their valences."

"Not I, trust me. Fame's husky voice was no less strange to me than the wizened figure of the pedlar."

"The husky voice, the bent figure, were assumed for disguise," replied Dr. Johnson, "but Percy's long nose was plain for all to see, and Malone's mellifluous tones were no less apparent. They thought to quiz me, but I shall quiz them tomorrow."

I was watching young Ararat, with his father the center of a sycophantic group of masks who made *lions* of them.

Young Anthony was as impassive as ever, but his face was as red as his father's. Lady Macbeth plucked at his elbow; the three Graces fawned upon him; in the press about him I saw the trumpet of Fame and the tray of the mulberry pedlar.

"A springald Caractacus," remarked Dr. Johnson, following my gaze, "how long, think you, could he live in equal combat if his life depended on that dull-edged claymore?"

"Yet see," I commented severely, "how the ladies flatter him, whose only claim on their kindness amounts to this, that through no merit of his own he found a dusty bundle of papers in his father's shed."

"While those who can compose, ay and declaim, verses upon *liberty,*" supplied Dr. Johnson slyly, "stand neglected save by a musty old scholar."

"Nay, sir," I protested, but Dr. Johnson cut me off:

"Why, sir, we are all impostors here. Fame with an empty scroll, mulberry wood cut from old chairs and stools! Sir, I have canvassed the abilities of the company, and I find that but one sailor out of six can dance a horn-pipe, and but one more box his compass. Not one conjuror can inform me whether he could tell my fortune better by chiromancy or catoptromancy. None of four farmers knows how a score of runts sells now; and the harlequin is as stiff as a poker. So your Caractacus is an impostor among impostors, and we must not ask too much of him."

I looked at the press of masks around the finder and the owner of the missing manuscript, buzzing like bees with talk and laughter. There was a sudden silence, broken by a bellow from old Ararat. The buzzing began again on a higher note, and the whole swarm bore down on our corner, old Ararat in the lead. He brandished in his hand an open paper.

Worldlessly he extended the paper to my friend. Peering over his shoulder, I read with him:

"Sir,

The manuscript of Caractacus is safe, and I have a

mind to profit from it in spite of your teeth. Lay £100 in the font at the church, and you shall hear further.

Look to it; for if the value of the manuscript is nil, and profits me nothing, as God is my judge I will destroy it. I do not steal in sport.

I am,
Sir,
Your obliged humble servant,
Ignotus"

"The scoundrel!" cried old Ararat. "Where am I to find £100?"

"This is more of your antiquarianism," I remarked. "Like a knight of old, the miscreant holds his captive to *ransom.*"

Dr. Johnson turned the letter in his hands, and held it against the lights of the great chandelier. 'Twas writ in a fair hand on ordinary laid paper and sealed with yellow wax; but instead of using a seal, the unknown writer had set his thumb in the soft wax.

"Why," says he, "the thief has signed himself with *hand* and *seal* indeed. Now were there but some way to match this seal to the thumb that made it, we should lay the robber by the heels and have back the manuscript that Shakespeare wrote."

"Alack, sir," I replied, "there is no way."

"Nevertheless, let us try," said Dr. Johnson sturdily. "Pray, Mr. Malone, set your thumb in this seal."

"I?" said the mulberry-wood pedlar, drawing back.

"I will," said I, and set my thumb in the waxen matrix. It fitted perfectly. The eyes of the maskers turned to me, and I felt my ears burning. Dr. Johnson held out the seal to old Ararat, who with a stormy mutter of impatience tried to crowd his huge thumb into the impression. 'Twas far too broad.

Dr. Johnson tried in turn the thumb of each masker.

The ladies' thumbs were too slender, Malone's too long; but there were many in the group that fitted. Dr. Johnson shook his head.

"This is the fallacy of the undistributed middle term," said he. "Some other means must be found than gross measurement to fit a thumb to the print it makes. Pray, how came you by this letter?"

" 'Twas tossed at my feet by some mask in the press," replied old Ararat. "Come, Dr. Johnson, advise me how am I to come by £100 to buy back my lost manuscript?"

"A subscription!" cried Fame. "The price is moderate for so precious a prize. I myself will undertake to raise the sum for you."

So it was concerted. Dr. Johnson enjoined secrecy upon the maskers, and Fame with his visor off, revealed as Dr. Percy indeed, bustled off to open the subscription books.

We lay late the next day in the "Much Ado about Nothing" chamber. Dr. Johnson was given over to indolence and declined to say what he had learned at the masquerade, or whether he thought that the mysterious communication held out any hope that the missing manuscript might be recovered.

The rain continuing, the pageant was dispensed with. We whiled away the hours comfortably at the Red Lion, while Percy and Malone spent a damp day with their subscription books. Representing the collection merely as "for the Ararats," they found the sum of £100 not easy to be amassed. Toward evening, however, they returned to the Red Lion with £87 in silver and copper, and Garrick's promise to make up the sum when the play's takings should be counted.

Dr. Johnson spurned at the idea of buying back mere paper and faded ink. In his roaring voice he *tossed* and *gored* Dr. Percy for his magpie love of old documents, adverting especially to Percy's recent publication of "The Household Book of the Earls of Northumberland."

"Pray, sir," he demanded with scorn, "of what conceivable utility to mankind can the 'Household Book' be supposed to be? The world now knows that a dead-and-gone Percy had beef to the value of twelve pence on a Michaelmas in 1512. Trust me, 'twill set no beef on the table of any living Percy."

The young Irish lawyer came to the unfortunate clergyman's defense, and fared no better. Johnson was in high good spirits as we dined off a veal pye and a piece of good beef (which the living Percy relished well).

We then repaired to the amphitheatre, where Percy had concerted to meet the Ararats with Caractacus's ransom.

Old Ararat would have none of Dr. Johnson's advice, to ignore Ignotus's letter. He was hot to conclude the business, and would hear of no other plan, than to deposit the £100 in the font as soon as the play should be over and the takings counted.

"Then, sir," said Dr. Johnson in disgust, "at least let us entrap Ignotus, and make him Gnotus. Mr. Boswell and I will watch by the font and take him as he comes for his ill-gotten gains."

"We must stand watch and watch," cried Percy. "Malone and I will relieve you."

"Nay, let me," cried old Ararat.

"So be it," assented Dr. Johnson, and we repaired to our respective boxes to see the play.

We shared a box with Percy and Malone. Dr. Johnson grunted to himself when David Garrick made his first entrance on the battlements, wearing white linen kilts and bedaubed with blue paint. In spite of this antiquarianism, I found myself moved deeply by the noble eloquence, the aweful elevation of soul, with which Garrick spoke the words of this play so strangely preserved for our generation.

I was most affected by the solemn soliloquy which concluded the first act:

O sovereign death,
"Thou hast for thy domain this world immense:
Churchyards and charnel-houses are thy haunts,
And hospitals thy sumptuous palaces;
And when thou would'st be merry, thou dost chuse
The gaudy chamber of a dying King.
O! Then thou dost ope wide thy boney jaw
And with rude laughter and fantastick tricks,
Thou clapp'st thy rattling fingers to thy sides:
And when this solemn mockery is o'er,
With icy hand thou tak'st him by the feet,
And upward so, till thou dost reach the heart,
And wrap him in the cloak of lasting night."

As the act ended, from the stage box the Ararats, father and son, rose to share the plaudits of the huzzaing crowd.

"Davy Garrick," remarked Dr. Johnson in my ear, "has surpassed himself; and King is inimitable as the Fool."

The second act opened with another scene of King's.

"Alack," cries the lovelorn Concairn,
"Alack, I will write verses of my love,
They shall be hung on every tree . . ."

King turned a cart-wheel, ending with a resounding smack on the rump.

"Say rather," he cried, "they shall be used in every jakes, for by'r lakin, such fardels does thy prentice hand compose, they are as caviare to the mob. I can but compliment thee thus, they do go to the *bottom* of the matter."

The pit roared.

"Ha, what?" exclaimed Dr. Johnson. "Bozzy, Bozzy, where's my hat?"

"Your hat, sir? Why, the play is not half over."

Dr. Johnson fumbled around in the dark.

"No matter. Do you stay and see it through. Where's this hat of mine?"

"Here, sir." I handed it to him.

"Whither do you go, sir?" enquired Malone eagerly.

"To do what must be done. Fool that I was, not to see—but 'tis not yet too late." Dr. Johnson lumbered off as the pit began to cry for silence.

We were on pins and needles in our box, but we sat through till Davy Garrick had blessed the land of the Britons and died a noble death, and we joined in the plaudits that rewarded the great actor and the great playwright and the finders of the manuscript. The Ararats were the cynosure of all eyes. It was long till we brought them away from their admirers and down to the church. Percy carried the £100 in a knitted purse. The rain had ceased, and a pale round moon contended with the clouds.

The solemn silence oppressed me as we pushed back the creaking door and entered, and my heart leaped to my mouth when a shadowy figure moved in the silent church. 'Twas Dr. Johnson. He had wrapped himself in his greatcoat, and armed himself with a dark lanthorn. I could smell it, but it showed no gleam.

Without ceremony old Ararat dropped the heavy purse in the empty font, and carried young Anthony off for home, promising to return and relieve our watch. I envied Percy and Malone as they, too, departed, with the Red Lion's mulled ale in their minds. They promised to return in an hour's time. Dr. Johnson quenched the lanthorn, and we were left alone in the dark.

I own I liked it little, alone in the dark with the bones of dead men under our feet, and a desperate thief who knows how near? There was no sound. Dead Shakespeare lay under our feet, his effigy stared into the dark above our heads.

We sat in the shadow, back from the font. I fixed my eyes on its pale gleam, whereon the cloudy moon dropped a fitful light through the open door.

I will swear I saw nothing, no shadow on the font, no stealing figure by the open door; I heard nothing, I neither nodded nor closed my eyes. Dr. Johnson fought sleep by my side. The hour was gone, and he was beginning to snore, when the light of a link came toward us, and Percy and Malone came in with the Ararats. Johnson awoke with a snort.

"For this relief much thanks," he muttered. "What, all four of you?"

"Ay," returned Percy, extinguishing the link, "for the Ararats are as eager as we to stand the next watch."

"Let it be so," replied Dr. Johnson, approaching the font, "we will but verify it, that the money is here, and passes from our keeping into yours."

He bent over the font, and his voice changed.

"Pray, gentlemen, step over here."

We did so as he made a light and opened his dark lanthorn.

The money was gone. In its place lay a pile of yellowed papers, thick-writ in a fair court-hand.

Beholding with indescribable feelings this relique of the great English Bard, I fell on my knees and thanked heaven that I had lived to see this day.

"Get up, Bozzy," said Dr. Johnson, "and cease this flummery."

"Oh, sir," I exclaimed, "the very hand-writing of the great Bard of Stratford!"

" 'Tis not the handwriting of the great Bard of Stratford," retorted Dr. Johnson.

Old Ararat's jaw fell. The boy Anthony opened his mouth and closed it again. By the light of the lanthorn Dr. Percy peered at the topmost page.

"Yet the paper is old," he asserted.

"The paper may be old," replied Dr. Johnson, "yet the words are new."

"Nay, Dr. Johnson," cried old Mr. Ararat, "this is merely to affect singularity. Eminent men from London have certified that my manuscript is genuine, including David Garrick and Dr. Warton."

"Garrick and Warton are deceived," returned Dr. Johnson sternly. " 'Caractacus; or, the British Hero' is a modern forgery, and no ancient play."

"Pray, sir, how do you make that good?" enquired Malone.

"I knew it," replied Dr. Johnson, "when I heard King use a word Shakespeare never heard—'mob'—a word shortened from 'mobile' long after Shakespeare died. Nor would Shakespeare have understood the verb 'to compliment.' "

"Then," said I, "the thief has had his trouble for his pains, for he has stolen but waste paper indeed."

"Not so," replied Dr. Johnson, "the thief has come nigh to achieving his object, for the thief and the forger are one."

"Name him," cried Dr. Percy. All eyes turned to old Ararat. His face showed the beginnings of a dumb misery, but no guilt. Anthony's face might have been carved out of a pumpkin.

"If," said Dr. Johnson slowly, "if there were in Stratford a young man, apprenticed to a scrivener and adept with his pen; a young man who has the plays of Shakespeare by heart; and if that young man found as it might be a packet of old paper unused among the dead stationers' gear; is it unreasonable to suppose that that young man was tempted to try out his skill at writing like Shakespeare? And when his skill proved more than adequate, and the play 'Caractacus,' was composed and indited, and the Jubilee had raised interest in Shakespeare to fever pitch—what must have been the temptation to put forward the manuscript as genuine?"

"Yet why should he steal his own manuscript?"

"For fear of what has happened," replied Dr. Johnson,

"for fear that Dictionary Johnson, the editor of Shakespeare, with his special knowledge might scrutinize the manuscript and detect the imposture."

Old Ararat's face was purple.

"Pray, sir," said Dr. Johnson, "moderate your anger. The boy is a clever boy, and full of promise. Let him be honest from this time forward."

Old Ararat looked at his son, and his jaw worked.

"But, Dr. Johnson," cried Percy, "the hundred pounds!"

Anthony Ararat fell on his knees and raised his hand to Heaven.

"I swear before God," he cried vibrantly, "that I never touched the hundred pounds."

It was the first word I had heard out of Anthony. By the fitful light of the lanthorn I stared in amazement at the expressionless face. The boy spoke like a player.

"Believe me, Father," cried Anthony earnestly, still on his knees by the font, "I know nothing of the hundred pounds; nor do I know how the manuscript came to be exchanged for the money, for indeed I never meant to restore it until Dr. Johnson was once more far from Stratford."

"He speaks truth," said Dr. Johnson, "for here is the hundred pounds, and it was I who laid the manuscript in the font."

He drew the purse from his capacious pocket and handed it to Dr. Percy.

"How came you by the manuscript?" asked Percy, accepting of the purse.

"It was not far to seek. The forger was the thief. It was likely that the finder was the forger. If Malone's panegyric on my learning frightened him into sequestering the manuscript to prevent it from falling under my eye, then it must have been hid between the time young Anthony left the shop and the time he returned with the empty coffer. He was gone long enough for Mr. Ararat to spin us his long-winded tale. In that space of time he hid the manuscript—

surely no further afield than his father's out-buildings. When he came in to us his face and shoulders were wet with rain."

"Tears, surely?"

"Why, his eyes were full of tears. The boy is a comedian. But the drops on his shoulders never fell from his eyes; they were rain-drops."

"But, Dr. Johnson," put in Edmond Malone, "we searched the out-buildings thoroughly, and the manuscript was not to be found."

"The manuscript," replied Dr. Johnson, "lay in plain sight before your eyes, and you passed it by without seeing it."

"How could we?" cried Malone, "we turned over the old papers in the shed."

"Did you turn over the other old papers?"

"There were no other old papers."

"There were," said Dr. Percy suddenly, "for when I visited the—the necessary-house, I turned over a pile of old accounts of the greatest interest, put to this infamous use by the carelessness of the householder. I—ah—" his voice trailed off.

"The forged sheets of 'Caractacus' were hastily thrust among them," said Dr. Johnson. "I guessed so much when I heard the allusion to the jakes as the destination of bad poetry. This thought belongs to the present century, not the age of Elizabeth; and if the thought was in the mind of the writer of 'Caractacus,' what more likely hiding-place for a day or two, till Dr. Johnson be far from Stratford once more? In short, I left the play and hurried thither, and found the pages undisturbed where young Ararat had thrust them into the heart of the pile."

"Yet if you only meant to sequester the writings, boy," said Dr. Percy sternly, "how came you to offer to barter them for money?"

Anthony rose to his feet.

"Sir," he said respectfully, "I never meant to touch the

money. But Dr. Johnson saw clearly, and said so, that 'twas no theft for profit; and I feared that such thoughts might lead him to me. I saw a way by which a thief might profit, and I wrote the letter and dropped it at my father's feet that the deed might seem after all the work of a real thief. Consider my apprehension, sir," he turned to Dr. Johnson, "when you fitted my thumb into the impression it had made."

Dr. Johnson shook his head.

"Too many thumbs fitted it," he said. "Another way must be found to fit a thumb to its print. 'Twas so, too, with the paper. 'Twas clearly from your father's shop; but Percy and I and half Stratford were furnished with the same paper. Again the undistributed middle term."

"Pray, sir, how came you to spare me in your thoughts?" enquired old Ararat.

"I acquitted you," replied Dr. Johnson, "because after Malone's eulogy you never left my side; nor did your thumb fit the print in the wax."

"Pray, Dr. Johnson," added Malone, "coming down here from Mr. Ararat's necessary-house with the manuscript in your pocket, why did you play out the farce? Why not reveal all at once?"

"To amuse Mr. Boswell," replied my friend with a broad smile. "I thought an hour's watch by the bones of Shakespeare, and a dramatic discovery at its end, would give him a rich range of those sensations native to a man of sensibility, and enrich those notes he is constantly taking of my proceedings."

In the laugh that followed at my expense, the Ararats sullenly took themselves off, and we four repaired to the Red Lion.

"Sir," said young Malone, taking leave of us at the door of "Much Ado about Nothing," "this is a lesson in the detection of imposture which I will never forget."

"Sir," said Dr. Johnson, "you are most obliging. Be sure,

sir, that I shall stand by you in your every endeavour to make known the truth. Pray, Dr. Percy, accept of the forged manuscript as a memento of the pitfalls of *antiquarianism.*"

Dr. Percy accepted with a smile, and we parted on most cordial terms.

"I blush to confess it," I remarked as we prepared to retire, "but I made sure that Dr. Percy was carrying stolen documents about with him in yonder folio-sized packet he was so particular with."

"So he was," remarked Dr. Johnson. "Therefore I exchanged packets with him. I knew with certainty then that Thomas Percy had not stolen the Shakespeare manuscript, for all his antiquarian light fingers."

"How so?" I enquired.

"Because I knew what he *had* stolen."

"What?"

"A household reckoning of the first Anthony Ararat, showing that the good stationer's family consumed an unconscionable quantity of small beer during the year 1614. The magpie clergyman had filched it from old Ararat's necessary-house!"

Edgar Allan Poe was, of course, a master of the macabre story. Among contemporary writers, similar accolades have been bestowed on Robert Bloch, creator of Psycho *and numerous other novels and stories of mystery, horror, and suspense. What better writer than Bloch, then, to produce a story about the ultimate collector of Poe? One expects a few chills from any Bloch story, but "The Man Who Collected Poe" provides more than its fair share; you won't soon forget Mr. Launcelot Canning and his brooding Baltimore house that brims with first editions, letters, mementos, ephemera, and yes, far stranger items of "Poe-iana" . . .*

THE MAN WHO COLLECTED POE

Robert Bloch

During the whole of a dull, dark, and soundless day in the autumn of the year, when the clouds hung oppressively low in the heavens, I had been passing alone, by automobile, through a singularly dreary tract of country, and at length found myself, as the shades of the evening drew on, within view of my destination.

I looked upon the scene before me—upon the mere house, and the simple landscape features of the domain, upon the bleak walls, upon the vacant eye-like windows, upon a few rank sedges, and upon a few white trunks of decayed trees—with a feeling of utter confusion commingled with dismay. For it seemed to me as though I had visited this scene once before, or read of it, perhaps, in some frequently rescanned tale. And yet assuredly it could not be, for only three days had passed since I had made the acquaintance of Launcelot Canning and received an invitation to visit him at his Maryland residence.

The circumstances under which I met Canning were simple; I happened to attend a bibliophilic meeting in Washington and was introduced to him by a mutual friend. Casual conversation gave place to absorbed and interested discussion when he discovered my preoccupation with works of fantasy. Upon learning that I was traveling upon a vacation with no set itinerary, Canning urged me to become his guest for a day and to examine, at my leisure, his unusual display of memorabilia.

"I feel, from our conversation, that we have much in common," he told me. "For you see, sir, in my love of fantasy I bow to no man. It is a taste I have perhaps inherited from my father and from his father before him, together with their considerable acquisitions in the genre. No doubt you would be gratified with what I am prepared to show you, for in all due modesty, I beg to style myself the world's leading collector of the works of Edgar Allan Poe."

I confess that his invitation as such did not enthrall me, for I hold no brief for the literary hero-worshiper or the scholarly collector as a type. I own to a more than passing interest in the tales of Poe, but my interest does not extend to the point of ferreting out the exact date upon which Mr. Poe first decided to raise a moustache, nor would I be unduly intrigued by the opportunity to examine several hairs preserved from that hirsute appendage.

So it was rather the person and personality of Launcelot Canning himself which caused me to accept his proffered hospitality. For the man who proposed to become my host might have himself stepped from the pages of a Poe tale. His speech, as I have endeavored to indicate, was characterized by a courtly rodomontade so often exemplified in Poe's heroes—and beyond certainty, his appearance bore out the resemblance.

Launcelot Canning had the cadaverousness of complexion, the large, liquid, luminous eye, the thin, curved lips, the delicately modeled nose, finely molded chin, and dark, web-like hair of a typical Poe protagonist.

It was this phenomenon which prompted my acceptance and led me to journey to his Maryland estate, which, as I now perceived, in itself manifested a Poe-etic quality of its own, intrinsic in the images of the gray sedge, the ghastly tree stems, and the vacant and eye-like windows of the mansion of gloom. All that was lacking was a tarn and a moat—and as I prepared to enter the dwelling I half-expected to encounter therein the carved ceilings, the somber tapestries, the ebon floors and the phantasmagoric armorial trophies so vividly described by the author of *Tales of the Grotesque and Arabesque.*

Nor upon entering Launcelot Canning's home was I too greatly disappointed in my expectations. True to both the atmospheric quality of the decrepit mansion and to my own fanciful presentiments, the door was opened in response to my knock by a valet who conducted me, in silence, through dark and intricate passages to the study of his master.

The room in which I found myself was very large and lofty. The windows were long, narrow, and pointed, and at so vast a distance from the black oaken floor as to be altogether inaccessible from within. Feeble gleams of encrimsoned light made their way through the trellised panes, and served to render sufficiently distinct the more prominent objects around; the eye, however, struggled in vain to reach the remoter angles of the chamber or the recesses of the vaulted and fretted ceiling. Dark draperies hung upon the walls. The general furniture was profuse, comfortless, antique, and tattered. Many books and musical instruments lay scattered about, but failed to give any vitality to the scene.

Instead they rendered more distinct that peculiar quality of quasi-recollection; it was as though I found myself once again, after a protracted absence, in a familiar setting. I had read, I had imagined, I had dreamed, or I had actually beheld this setting before.

Upon my entrance, Launcelot Canning arose from a

sofa on which he had been lying at full length, and greeted me with a vivacious warmth which had much in it, I at first thought, of an overdone cordiality.

Yet his tone, as he spoke of the object of my visit, of his earnest desire to see me, and of the solace he expected me to afford him in a mutual discussion of our interests, soon alleviated my initial misapprehension.

Launcelot Canning welcomed me with the rapt enthusiasm of the born collector—and I came to realize that he was indeed just that. For the Poe collection he shortly proposed to unveil before me was actually his birthright.

Initially, he disclosed, the nucleus of the present accumulation had begun with his grandfather, Christopher Canning, a respected merchant of Baltimore. Almost eighty years ago he had been one of the leading patrons of the arts in his community and as such was partially instrumental in arranging for the removal of Poe's body to the southeastern corner of the Presbyterian Cemetery at Fayette and Green streets, where a suitable monument might be erected. This event occurred in the year 1875, and it was a few years prior to that time that Canning laid the foundation of the Poe collection.

"Thanks to his zeal," his grandson informed me, "I am today the fortunate possessor of a copy of virtually every existing specimen of Poe's published works. If you will step over here"—and he led me to a remote corner of the vaulted study, past the dark draperies, to a bookshelf which rose remotely to the shadowy ceiling—"I shall be pleased to corroborate that claim. Here is a copy of *Al Aaraaf, Tamerlane and other Poems* in the 1829 edition, and here is the still earlier *Tamerlane and other Poems* of 1827. The Boston edition, which, as you doubtless know, is valued today at fifteen thousand dollars. I can assure you that Grandfather Canning parted with no such sum in order to gain possession of this rarity."

He displayed the volumes with an air of commingled

pride and cupidity which is ofttimes characteristic of the collector and is by no means to be confused with either literary snobbery or ordinary greed. Realizing this, I remained patient as he exhibited further treasures—copies of the *Philadelphia Saturday Courier* containing early tales, bound volumes of *The Messenger* during the period of Poe's editorship, *Graham's Magazine,* editions of the *New York Sun* and the *New York Mirror* boasting, respectively, of "The Balloon Hoax" and "The Raven," and files of *The Gentleman's Magazine.* Ascending a short library ladder, he handed down to me the Lea and Blanchard edition of *Tales of the Grotesque and Arabesque,* the *Conchologist's First Book,* the Putnam *Eureka,* and, finally, the little paper booklet, published in 1843 and sold for twelve and a half cents, entitled *The Prose Romances of Edgar A. Poe;* an insignificant trifle containing two tales which is valued by present-day collectors at fifty thousand dollars.

Canning informed me of this last fact, and, indeed, kept up a running commentary upon each item he presented. There was no doubt but that he was a Poe scholar as well as a Poe collector, and his words informed tattered specimens of the *Broadway Journal* and *Godey's Lady's Book* with a singular fascination not necessarily inherent in the flimsy sheets or their contents.

"I owe a great debt to Grandfather Canning's obsession," he observed, descending the ladder and joining me before the bookshelves. "It is not altogether a breach of confidence to admit that his interest in Poe did reach the point of an obsession, and perhaps eventually of an absolute mania. The knowledge, alas, is public property, I fear.

"In the early seventies he built this house, and I am quite sure that you have been observant enough to note that it in itself is almost a replica of a typical Poe-esque mansion. This was his study, and it was here that he was wont to pore over the books, the letters, and the numerous mementos of Poe's life.

"What prompted a retired merchant to devote himself so fanatically to the pursuit of a hobby, I cannot say. Let it suffice that he virtually withdrew from the world and from all other normal interests. He conducted a voluminous and lengthy correspondence with aging men and women who had known Poe in their lifetime—made pilgrimages to Fordham, sent his agents to West Point, to England, and Scotland, to virtually every locale in which Poe had set foot during his lifetime. He acquired letters and souvenirs as gifts, he bought them, and—I fear—stole them, if no other means of acquisition proved feasible."

Launcelot Canning smiled and nodded. "Does all this sound strange to you? I confess that once I, too, found it almost incredible, a fragment of romance. Now, after years spent here, I have lost my own objectivity."

"Yes, it is strange," I replied. "But are you quite sure that there was not some obscure personal reason for your grandfather's interest? Had he met Poe as a boy, or been closely associated with one of his friends? Was there, perhaps, a distant, undisclosed relationship?"

At the mention of the last word, Canning started visibly, and a tremor of agitation overspread his countenance.

"Ah!" he exclaimed. "There you voice my own inmost conviction. A relationship—assuredly there must have been one—I am morally, instinctively certain that Grandfather Canning felt or knew himself to be linked to Edgar Poe by ties of blood. Nothing else could account for his strong initial interest, his continuing defense of Poe in the literary controversies of the day, and his final melancholy lapse into a world of delusion and illusion.

"Yet he never voiced a statement or put an allegation upon paper—and I have searched the collection of letters in vain for the slightest clue.

"It is curious that you so promptly divine a suspicion held not only by myself but by my father. He was only a child at the time of my Grandfather Canning's death, but the attendant circumstances left a profound impression upon his sensitive nature. Although he was immediately removed from this house to the home of his mother's people in Baltimore, he lost no time in returning upon assuming his inheritance in early manhood.

"Fortunately being in possession of a considerable income, he was able to devote his entire lifetime to further research. The name of Arthur Canning is still well known in the world of literary criticism, but for some reason he preferred to pursue his scholarly examination of Poe's career in privacy. I believe this preference was dictated by an inner sensibility; that he was endeavoring to unearth some information which would prove his father's, his, and for that matter, my own, kinship to Edgar Poe."

"You say your father was also a collector?" I prompted.

"A statement I am prepared to substantiate," replied my host, as he led me to yet another corner of the shadow-shrouded study. "But first, if you would accept a glass of wine?"

He filled, not glasses, but veritable beakers from a large carafe, and we toasted one another in silent appreciation. It is perhaps unnecessary for me to observe that the wine was a fine old amontillado.

"Now, then," said Launcelot Canning. "My father's special province in Poe research consisted of the accumulation and study of letters."

Opening a series of large trays or drawers beneath the bookshelves, he drew out file after file of glassined folios, and for the space of the next half-hour I examined Edgar Poe's correspondence—letters to Henry Herring, to Dr. Snodgrass, Sarah Shelton, James P. Moss, Elizabeth Poe; missives to Mrs. Rockwood, Helen Whitman, Anne Lynch, John Pendleton Kennedy; notes to Mrs. Richmond, to John Allan, to Annie, to his brother, Henry—a profusion of documents, a veritable epistolary cornucopia.

During the course of my perusal my host took occasion

to refill our beakers with wine, and the heady draught began to take effect—for we had not eaten, and I own I gave no thought to food, so absorbed was I in the yellowed pages illumining Poe's past.

Here was wit, erudition, literary criticism; here were the muddled, maudlin outpourings of a mind gone in drink and despair; here was the draft of a projected story, the fragments of a poem; here was a pitiful cry for deliverance and a paean to living beauty; here was a dignified response to a dunning letter and an editorial pronunciamento to an admirer; here was love, hate, pride, anger, celestial serenity, abject penitence, authority, wonder, resolution, indecision, joy, and soul-sickening melancholia.

Here was the gifted elocutionist, the stammering drunkard, the adoring husband, the frantic lover, the proud editor, the indigent pauper, the grandiose dreamer, the shabby realist, the scientific inquirer, the gullible metaphysician, the dependent stepson, the free and untrammeled spirit, the hack, the poet, the enigma that was Edgar Allan Poe.

Again the beakers were filled and emptied.

I drank deeply with my lips, and with my eyes more deeply still.

For the first time the true enthusiasm of Launcelot Canning was communicated to my own sensibilities—I divined the eternal fascination found in a consideration of Poe the writer and Poe the man; he who wrote Tragedy, lived Tragedy, was Tragedy; he who penned Mystery, lived and died in Mystery, and who today looms on the literary scene as Mystery incarnate.

And Mystery Poe remained, despite Arthur Canning's careful study of the letters. "My father learned nothing," my host confided, "even though he assembled, as you see here, a collection to delight the heart of a Mabbott or a Quinn. So his search ranged further. By this time I was old enough to share both his interest and his inquiries. Come," and he led me to an ornate chest which rested beneath the windows against the west wall of the study.

Kneeling, he unlocked the repository, and then drew forth, in rapid and marvelous succession, a series of objects each of which boasted of intimate connection with Poe's life.

There were souvenirs of his youth and his schooling abroad—a book he had used during his sojourn at West Point, mementos of his days as a theatrical critic in the form of playbills, a pen used during his editorial period, a fan once owned by his girl-wife, Virginia, a brooch of Mrs. Clemm's; a profusion of objects including such diverse articles as a cravat-stock and, curiously enough, Poe's battered and tarnished flute.

Again we drank, and I own the wine was potent. Canning's countenance remained cadaverously wan, but, moreover, there was a species of mad hilarity in his eye—an evident restrained hysteria in his whole demeanor. At length, from the scattered heap of curiosa, I happened to draw forth and examine a little box of no remarkable character, whereupon I was constrained to inquire its history and what part it had played in the life of Poe.

"In the *life* of Poe?" A visible tremor convulsed the features of my host, then rapidly passed in transformation to a grimace, a rictus of amusement. "This little box—and you will note how, by some fateful design or contrived coincidence it bears a resemblance to the box he himself conceived of and described in his tale "Berenice"—this little box is concerned with his death, rather than his life. It is, in fact, the selfsame box my grandfather Christopher Canning clutched to his bosom when they found him down there."

Again the tremor, again the grimace. "But stay, I have not yet told you of the details. Perhaps you would be interested in seeing the spot where Christopher Canning was stricken. I have already told you of his madness, but I did no more than hint at the character of his delusions. You have been patient with me, and more than patient. Your understanding shall be rewarded, for I perceive you can be fully entrusted with the facts."

What further revelations Canning was prepared to make I could not say, but his manner was such as to inspire a vague disquiet and trepidation in my breast.

Upon perceiving my unease he laughed shortly and laid a hand upon my shoulder. "Come, this should interest you as an *aficionado* of fantasy," he said. "But first, another drink to speed our journey."

He poured, we drank, and then he led the way from that vaulted chamber, down the silent halls, down the staircase, and into the lowest recesses of the building until we reached what resembled a donjon-keep, its floor and the interior of a long archway carefully sheathed in copper. We paused before a door of massive iron. Again I felt in the aspect of this scene an element evocative of recognition or recollection.

Canning's intoxication was such that he misinterpreted, or chose to misinterpret, my reaction.

"You need not be afraid," he assured me. "Nothing has happened down here since that day, almost seventy years ago, when his servants discovered him stretched out before this door, the little box clutched to his bosom; collapsed, and in a state of delirium from which he never emerged. For six months he lingered, a hopeless maniac—raving as wildly from the very moment of his discovery as at the moment he died, babbling his visions of the giant horse, the fissured house collapsing into the tarn, the black cat, the pit, the pendulum, the raven on the pallid bust, the beating heart, the pearly teeth, and the nearly liquid mass of loathsome—of detestable putridity from which a voice emanated.

"Nor was that all he babbled," Canning confided, and here his voice sank to a whisper that reverberated through the copper-sheathed hall and against the iron door. "He hinted other things far worse than fantasy; of a ghastly reality surpassing all of the phantasms of Poe.

"For the first time my father and the servants learned the purpose of the room he had built beyond this iron door, and learned too what Christopher Canning had done to establish his title as the world's foremost collector of Poe.

"For he babbled again of Poe's death, thirty years earlier, in 1849—of the burial in the Presbyterian cemetery, and of the removal of the coffin in 1874 to the corner where the monument was raised. As I told you, and as was known then, my grandfather had played a public part in instigating that removal. But now we learned of the private part—learned that there was a monument and a grave, but no coffin in the earth beneath Poe's alleged resting place. The coffin now rested in the secret room at the end of this passage. That is why the room, the house itself, had been built.

"I tell you, he had stolen the body of Edgar Allan Poe—and as he shrieked aloud in his final madness, did not this indeed make him the greatest collector of Poe?

"His ultimate intent was never divined, but my father made one significant discovery—the little box clutched to Christopher Canning's bosom contained a portion of the crumbled bones, the veritable dust that was all that remained of Poe's corpse."

My host shuddered and turned away. He led me back along that hall of horror, up the stairs, into the study. Silently, he filled our beakers and I drank as hastily, as deeply, as desperately as he.

"What could my father do? To own the truth was to create a public scandal. He chose instead to keep silence; to devote his own life to study in retirement.

"Naturally the shock affected him profoundly; to my knowledge he never entered the room beyond the iron door, and, indeed, I did not know of the room or its contents until the hour of his death—and it was not until some years later that I myself found the key among his effects.

"But find the key I did, and the story was immediately and completely corroborated. Today I am the greatest collector of Poe—for he lies in the keep below, my eternal trophy!"

This time I poured the wine. As I did so, I noted for the first time the imminence of a storm; the impetuous fury of its gusts shaking the casements, and the echoes of its thunder rolling and rumbling down the time-corroded corridors of the old house.

The wild, overstrained vivacity with which my host hearkened, or apparently hearkened, to these sounds did nothing to reassure me—for his recent revelation led me to suspect his sanity.

That the body of Edgar Allan Poe had been stolen; that this mansion had been built to house it; that it was indeed enshrined in a crypt below; that grandsire, son, and grandson had dwelt here alone, apart, enslaved to a sepulchral secret was beyond sane belief.

And yet, surrounded now by the night and the storm, in a setting torn from Poe's own frenzied fancies, I could not be sure. Here the past was still alive, the very spirit of Poe's tales breathed forth its corruption upon the scene.

As thunder boomed, Launcelot Canning took up Poe's flute, and, whether in defiance of the storm without or as a mocking accompaniment, he played; blowing upon it with drunken persistence, with eerie atonality, with nerve-shattering shrillness. To the shrieking of that infernal instrument the thunder added a braying counterpoint.

Uneasy, uncertain, and unnerved, I retreated into the shadows of the bookshelves at the farther end of the room, and idly scanned the titles of a row of ancient tomes. Here was the *Chiromancy* of Robert Flud, the *Directorium Inquisitorum,* a rare and curious book in quarto Gothic that was the manual of a forgotten church; and betwixt and between the volumes of pseudo-scientific inquiry, theological speculation, and sundry incunabula, I found titles that arrested and appalled me. *De Vermis Mysteriis* and the *Liber Eibon,* treatises on demonology, on witchcraft, on sorcery moldered in crumbling bindings. The books were old, but the books were not dusty. They had been read—

"Read them?" It was as though Canning divined my inmost thoughts. He had put aside his flute and now approached me, tittering as though in continued drunken defiance of the storm. Odd echoes and boomings now sounded through the long halls of the house, and curious grating sounds threatened to drown out his words and his laughter.

"Read them?" said Canning. "I study them. Yes, I have gone beyond grandfather and father, too. It was I who procured the books that held the key, and it was I who found the key. A key more difficult to discover, and more important, than the key to the vaults below. I often wonder if Poe himself had access to these selfsame tomes, knew the selfsame secrets. The secrets of the grave and what lies beyond, and what can be summoned forth if one but holds the key."

He stumbled away and returned with wine. "Drink," he said. "Drink to the night and the storm."

I brushed the proffered glass aside. "Enough," I said. "I must be on my way."

Was it fancy or did I find fear frozen on his features? Canning clutched my arm and cried, "No, stay with me! This is no night on which to be alone; I swear I cannot abide the thought of being alone, I can bear to be alone no more!"

His incoherent babble mingled with the thunder and the echoes; I drew back and confronted him. "Control yourself," I counseled. "Confess that this is a hoax, an elaborate imposture arranged to please your fancy."

"Hoax? Imposture? Stay, and I shall prove to you beyond all doubt"—and so saying, Launcelot Canning stooped and opened a small drawer set in the wall beneath and beside the bookshelves. "This should repay you for your interest in my story, and in Poe," he murmured. "Know that you are the first other person than myself to glimpse these treasures."

He handed me a sheaf of manuscripts on plain white

paper; documents written in ink curiously similar to that I had noted while perusing Poe's letters. Pages were clipped together in groups, and for a moment I scanned titles alone.

" 'The Worm of Midnight,' by Edgar Poe," I read, aloud. " 'The Crypt,' " I breathed. And here, " 'The Further Adventures of Arthur Gordon Pym' "—and in my agitation I came close to dropping the precious pages. "Are these what they appear to be—the unpublished tales of Poe?"

My host bowed.

"Unpublished, undiscovered, unknown, save to me—and to you."

"But this cannot be," I protested. "Surely there would have been a mention of them somewhere, in Poe's own letters or those of his contemporaries. There would have been a clue, an indication, somewhere, someplace, somehow."

Thunder mingled with my words, and thunder echoed in Canning's shouted reply.

"You dare to presume an imposture? Then compare!" He stooped again and brought out a glassined folio of letters. "Here—is this not the veritable script of Edgar Poe? Look at the calligraphy of the letter, then at the manuscripts. Can you say they are not penned by the selfsame hand?"

I looked at the handwriting, wondered at the possibilities of a monomaniac's forgery. Could Launcelot Canning, a victim of mental disorder, thus painstakingly simulate Poe's hand?

"Read, then!" Canning screamed through the thunder. "Read, and dare to say that these tales were written by any other than Edgar Poe, whose genius defies the corruption of Time and the Conqueror Worm!"

I read but a line or two, holding the topmost manuscript close to eyes that strained beneath wavering candlelight; but even in the flickering illumination I noted that which told me the only, the incontestable truth. For the paper, the curiously *unyellowed* paper, bore a visible watermark; the name of a firm of well-known modern stationers, and the date—1949.

Putting the sheaf aside, I endeavored to compose myself as I moved away from Launcelot Canning. For now I knew the truth; knew that one hundred years after Poe's death a semblance of his spirit still lived in the distorted and disordered soul of Canning. Incarnation, reincarnation, call it what you will; Canning was, in his own irrational mind, Edgar Allan Poe.

Stifled and dull echoes of thunder from a remote portion of the mansion now commingled with the soundless seething of my own inner turmoil, as I turned and rashly addressed my host.

"Confess!" I cried. "Is it not true that you have written these tales, fancying yourself the embodiment of Poe? Is it not true that you suffer from a singular delusion born of solitude and everlasting brooding upon the past; that you have reached a stage characterized by the conviction that Poe still lives on in your own person?"

A strong shudder came over him and a sickly smile quivered about his lips as he replied. "Fool! I say to you that I have spoken the truth. Can you doubt the evidence of your senses? This house is real, the Poe collection exists, and the stories exist—they exist, I swear, as truly as the body lying in the crypt below!"

I took up the little box from the table and removed the lid. "Not so," I answered. "You said your grandfather was found with this box clutched to his breast, before the door of the vault, and that it contained Poe's dust. Yet you cannot escape the fact that the box is empty." I faced him furiously. "Admit it, the story is a fabrication, a romance. Poe's body does not lie beneath this house, nor are these his unpublished works, written during his lifetime and concealed."

"True enough." Canning's smile was ghastly beyond belief. "The dust is gone because I took it and used it—because in the works of wizardry I found the formulae, the arcana whereby I could raise the flesh, re-create the body from the essential salts of the grave. Poe does not *lie* beneath this house—he *lives!* And the tales are *his posthumous works!*"

Accented by thunder, his words crashed against my consciousness.

"That was the end-all and the be-all of my planning, my studies, of my work, of my life! To raise, by sorcery, the veritable spirit of Edgar Poe from the grave—reclothed and animate in flesh—set him to dwell and dream and do his work again in the private chambers I built in the vaults below—and this I have done! To steal a corpse is but a ghoulish prank; mine is the achievement of true genius!"

The distinct, hollow, metallic, and clangorous yet apparently muffled reverberation accompanying his words caused him to turn in his seat and face the door of the study, so that I could not see the workings of his countenance—nor could he read my own reaction to his ravings.

His words came but faintly to my ears through the thunder that now shook the house in a relentless grip; the wind rattling the casements and flickering the candle flame from the great silver candelabra sent a soaring sighing in an anguished accompaniment to his speech.

"I would show him to you, but I dare not; for he hates me as he hates life. I have locked him in the vault, alone, for the resurrected have no need of food or drink. And he sits there, pen moving over paper, endlessly moving, endlessly pouring out the evil essence of all he guessed and hinted at in life and which he learned in death.

"Do you not see the tragic pity of my plight? I sought to raise his spirit from the dead, to give the world anew of his genius—and yet these tales, these works, are filled and fraught with a terror not to be endured. They cannot be shown to the world, he cannot be shown to the world; in bringing back the dead I have brought back the fruits of death!"

* * *

Echoes sounded anew as I moved toward the door—moved, I confess, to flee this accursed house and its accursed owner.

Canning clutched my hand, my arm, my shoulder. "You cannot go!" he shouted above the storm. "I spoke of his escaping, but did you not guess? Did you not hear it through the thunder—the grating of the door?"

I pushed him aside and he blundered backward, upsetting the candelabra, so that flames licked now across the carpeting.

"Wait!" he cried. "Have you not heard his footstep on the stair? *Madman, I tell you that he now stands without the door!*"

A rush of wind, a roar of flame, a shroud of smoke rose all about us. Throwing open the huge, antique panels to which Canning pointed, I staggered into the hall.

I speak of wind, of flame, of smoke—enough to obscure all vision. I speak of Canning's screams, and of thunder loud enough to drown all sound. I speak of terror born of loathing and of desperation enough to shatter all my sanity.

Despite these things, I can never erase from my consciousness that which I beheld as I fled past the doorway and down the hall.

There without the doors there *did* stand a lofty and enshrouded figure; a figure all too familiar, with pallid features, high, domed forehead, moustache set above a mouth. My glimpse lasted but an instant, an instant during which the man—the corpse, the apparition, the hallucination, call it what you will—moved forward into the chamber and clasped Canning to his breast in an unbreakable embrace. Together, the two figures tottered toward the flames, which now rose to blot out vision forevermore.

From that chamber, and from that mansion, I fled aghast. The storm was still abroad in all its wrath, and now fire came to claim the house of Canning for its own.

Suddenly there shot along the path before me a wild light, and I turned to see whence a gleam so unusual could have issued—but it was only the flames, rising in supernatural splendor to consume the mansion, and the secrets, of the man who collected Poe.

The pulps—those cheap jack-of-all-fiction magazines with the lurid covers that flourished between the two World Wars—provided a steady income for thousands of writers, many of them hacks but many more newcomers and talented professionals who eventually graduated to bigger and better literary endeavors. Cornell Woolrich (1903–68) was one of the talented professionals; during his pulp years he produced hundreds of penny-a-word stories, and knew the grind of pulp-writing as well as anyone. "The Penny-a-Worder" tells it the way it was back in the '30s and '40s—a tragicomic story with much deeper meaning than its simple plot elements of a pulpster working under deadline pressure at first indicate. In addition to his short fiction, the best of which appears in such outstanding collections as I Wouldn't Be in Your Shoes *(1943),* The Dancing Detective *(1946), and* Nightwebs *(1971), Woolrich—and his alter ego, William Irish—wrote some of the most harrowing suspense novels ever committed to paper, among them such classics as* The Bride Wore Black *(1940),* Black Alibi *(1942), and* Phantom Lady *(1942).*

THE PENNY-A-WORDER

Cornell Woolrich

The desk clerk received a call early that afternoon, asking if there was a "nice, quiet" room available for about six o'clock that evening. The call was evidently from a business office, for the caller was a young woman who, it developed, wished the intended reservation made in a man's name, whether her employer or one of the firm's clients she did not specify. Told there was a room available, she requested, "Well, will you please hold it for Mr. Edgar Danville Moody, for about six o'clock?" And twice more she reiterated her emphasis on the noiselessness. "It's got to be quiet, though. Make sure it's quiet. He mustn't be disturbed while he's in it."

The desk man assured her with a touch of dryness, "We run a quiet hotel altogether."

"Good," she said warmly, "because we don't want him

to be distracted. It's important that he have complete privacy."

"We can promise that," said the desk clerk.

"Thank you," said the young woman briskly.

"Thank you," answered the desk man.

The designated registrant arrived considerably after six, but not late enough for the reservation to have been voided. He was young—if not under thirty in actuality, still well under it in appearance. He had tried to camouflage his youthful appearance by coaxing a very slim, sandy mustache out along his upper lip. It failed completely in its desired effect. It was like a make-believe mustache ochred on a child's face.

He was a tall lean young man. His attire was eye-catching—it stopped just short of being theatrically flamboyant. Or, depending on the viewer's own taste, just crossed the line. The night being chilly for this early in the season, he was enveloped in a coat of fuzzy sand-colored texture, known generically as camel's-hair, with a belt gathered whiplash-tight around its middle. On the other hand, chilly or not, he had no hat whatever.

His necktie was patterned in regimental stripes, but they were perhaps the wrong regiments, selected from opposing armies. He carried a pipe clenched between his teeth, but with the bowl empty and turned down. A wide band of silver encircled the stem. His shoes were piebald affairs, with saddles of mahogany hue and the remainder almost yellow. They had no eyelets or laces, but were made like moccasins, to be thrust on the foot whole; a fringed leather tongue hung down on the outer side of each vamp.

He was liberally burdened with belongings, but none of these was a conventional, clothes-carrying piece of luggage. Under one arm he held tucked a large flat square, wrapped in brown paper, string-tied, and suggesting a picture canvas. In that same hand he carried a large wrapped parcel, also brown-paper-bound; in the other a cased portable typewriter. From one pocket of the coat protruded rakishly a long oblong, once again brown-paper-wrapped.

Although he was alone, and not unduly noisy either in his movements or his speech, his arrival had about it an aura of flurry and to-do, as if something of vast consequence were taking place. This, of course, might have derived from the unsubdued nature of his clothing. In later life he was not going to be the kind of man who is ever retiring or inconspicuous.

He disencumbered himself of all his paraphernalia by dropping some onto the floor and some onto the desk top, and inquired, "Is there a room waiting for Edgar Danville Moody?"

"Yes, sir, there certainly is," said the clerk cordially.

"Good and quiet, now?" he warned intently.

"You won't hear a pin drop," promised the clerk.

The guest signed the registration card with a flourish.

"Are you going to be with us long, Mr. Moody?" the clerk asked.

"It better not be too long," was the enigmatic answer, "or I'm in trouble."

"Take the gentleman up, Joe," hosted the clerk, motioning to a bellboy.

Joe began collecting the articles one by one.

"Wait a minute, not Gertie!" he was suddenly instructed.

Joe looked around, first on one side, then on the other. There was no one else standing there. "Gertie?" he said blankly.

Young Mr. Moody picked up the portable typewriter, patted the lid affectionately. "This is Gertie," he enlightened him. "I'm superstitious. I don't let anyone but me carry her when we're out on a job together."

They entered the elevator together, Moody carrying Gertie.

Joe held his peace for the first two floors, but beyond

that he was incapable of remaining silent. "I never heard of a typewriter called Gertie," he remarked mildly, turning his head from the controls.

"I've worn out six," Moody proclaimed proudly. "Gertie's my seventh." He gave the lid a little love-pat. "I call them alphabetically. My first was Alice."

Joe was vastly interested. "How could you wear out six, like that? Mr. Elliot's had the same one in his office for years now, ever since I first came to work here, and he hasn't wore his out yet."

"Who's he?" said Moody.

"The hotel accountant."

"Aw-w-w," said Moody with vast disdain. "No wonder. He just writes figures. I'm a *writer.*"

Joe was all but mesmerized. He'd liked the young fellow at sight, but now he was hypnotically fascinated. "Gee, are you a writer?" he said, almost breathlessly. "I always wanted to be a writer myself."

Moody was too interested in his own being a writer to acknowledge the other's wish to be one too.

"You write under your own name?" hinted Joe, unable to take his eyes off the new guest.

"Pretty much so." He enlarged on the reply. "Dan Moody. Ever read me?"

Joe was too innately naïve to prevaricate plausibly. He scratched the back of his head. "Let me see now," he said. "I'm trying to think."

Moody's face dropped, almost into a sulk. However in a moment it had cleared again. "I guess you don't get much time to read, anyway, on a job like this," he explained to the satisfaction of the two of them.

"No, I don't, but I'd sure like to read something of yours," said Joe fervently. "Especially now that I know you." He wrenched at the lever, and the car began to reverse. It had gone up three floors too high, so intense had been his absorption.

Joe showed him into Room 923 and disposed of his encumbrances. Then he lingered there, unable to tear himself away. Nor did this have anything to do with the delay in his receiving a tip; for once, and in complete sincerity, Joe had forgotten all about there being such a thing.

Moody shed his tent-like topcoat, cast it onto a chair with a billowing overhead fling like a person about to immerse in a bath. Then he began to burst open brown paper with explosive sounds all over the room.

From the flat square came an equally flat, equally square cardboard mat, blank on the reverse side, protected by tissues on the front. Moody peeled these off to reveal a startling composition in vivid oil paints. Its main factors were a plump-breasted girl in a disheveled, lavender-colored dress desperately fleeing from a pursuer, the look on whose face promised her additional dishevelment.

Joe became goggle-eyed, and remained so. Presently he took a step nearer, remaining transfixed. Moody stood the cardboard mat on the floor, against a chair.

"You do that?" Joe breathed in awe.

"No, the artist. It's next month's cover. I have to do a story to match up with it."

Joe said, puzzled, "I thought they did it the other way around. Wrote the story first, and then illustri-ated it."

"That's the usual procedure," Moody said, professionally glib. "They pick a feature story each month, and put that one on the cover. This time they had a little trouble. The fellow that was supposed to do the feature didn't come through on time, got sick or something. So the artist had to start off first, without waiting for him. Now there's no time left, so I have to rustle up a story to fit the cover."

"Gee," said Joe. "Going to be hard, isn't it?"

"Once you get started, it goes by itself. It's just getting started that's hard."

From the bulkier parcel had come, in the interim, two sizable slabs wrapped alike in dark-blue paper. He tore one open to extract a ream of white first sheets, the other to extract a ream of manila second sheets.

"I'm going to use this table here," he decided, and planted one stack on one corner of it, the second stack on the opposite corner. Between the two he placed Gertie the typewriter, in a sort of position of honor.

Also from the same parcel had come a pair of soft house slippers, crushed together toe-to-heel and heel-to-toe. He dropped them under the table. "I can't write with my shoes on," he explained to his new disciple. "Nor with the neck of my shirt buttoned," he added, parting that and flinging his tie onto a chair.

From the slender pocket-slanted oblong, last of the wrapped shapes, came a carton of cigarettes. The pipe, evidently reserved for non-occupational hours, he promptly discarded.

"Now, is there an ashtray?" he queried, like a commander surveying an intended field of action.

Joe darted in and out of several corners of the room. "Gee, no, the last people must have swiped it," he said. "Wait a minute, I'll go get—"

"Never mind, I'll use this instead," decided Moody, bringing over a metal wastebasket. "The amount of ashes I make when I'm working, a tray wouldn't be big enough to hold it all anyway."

The phone gave a very short ring, querulously interrogative. Moody picked it up, then relayed to Joe, "The man downstairs wants to know what's holding you, why you don't come down."

Joe gave a start, then came down to his everyday employment level from the rarefied heights of artistic creation he had been floating about in. He couldn't bear to turn his back, he started going backward to the door instead. "Is there anything else—?" he asked regretfully.

Moody passed a crumpled bill over to him. "Bring me back a—let's see, this is a cover story—you better make it an even dozen bottles of beer. It relaxes me when I'm working. Light, not dark."

"Right away, Mr. Moody," said Joe eagerly, beating a hasty retreat.

While he was gone, Moody made his penultimate preparations: sitting down to remove his shoes and put on the slippers, bringing within range and adjusting the focus of a shaded floor lamp, shifting the horrendous work of art back against the baseboard of the opposite wall so that it faced him squarely just over the table.

Then he went and asked for a number on the phone, without having to look it up.

A young woman answered, "Peerless, good evening."

He said, "Mr. Tartell please."

Another young woman said, "Mr. Tartell's office."

He said, "Hello, Cora. This is Dan Moody. I'm up here and I'm all set. Did Mr. Tartell go home yet?"

"He left half an hour ago," she said. "He left his home number with me, told me to give it to you; he wants you to call him in case you run into any difficulties, have any problems with it. But not later than eleven—they go to bed early out there in East Orange."

"I won't have any trouble," he said self-assuredly. "How long have I been doing this?"

"But this is a cover story. He's very worried. We have to go to the printer by nine tomorrow—we can't hold him up any longer."

"I'll make it, I'll make it," he said. "It'll be on his desk waiting for him at eight-thirty on the dot."

"Oh, and I have good news for you. He's not only giving you Bill Hammond's rate on this one—two cents a word—but he told me to tell you that if you do a good job, he'll see to it that you get that extra additional bonus over and above the word count itself that you were hinting about when he first called you today."

"Swell!" he exclaimed gratefully.

A note of maternal instruction crept into her voice. "Now get down to work and show him what you can do. He really thinks a lot of you, Dan. I'm not supposed to say this. And try to have it down here before he comes in tomorrow. I hate to see him worry so. When he worries, I'm miserable along with him. Good luck." And she hung up.

Joe came back with the beer, six bottles in each of two paper sacks.

"Put them on the floor alongside the table, where I can just reach down," instructed Moody.

"He bawled the heck out of me downstairs, but I don't care, it was worth it. Here's a bottle opener the delicatessen people gave me."

"That about kills what I gave you." Moody calculated, fishing into his pocket. "Here's—"

"No," protested Joe sincerely, with a dissuading gesture. "I don't want to take any tip from *you,* Mr. Moody. You're different from other people that come in here. You're a Writer, and I always wanted to be a writer myself. But if I could ever get to read a story of yours—" he added wistfully.

Moody promptly rummaged in the remnants of the brown paper, came up with a magazine which had been entombed there. "Here—here's last month's," he said. "I was taking it home with me, but I can get another at the office."

Its title was *Startling Stories!*—complete with exclamation point. Joe wiped his fingertips reverently against his uniform before touching it, as though afraid of defiling it.

Moody opened it for him, offered it to him that way. "Here I am, here," he said. "Second story. Next month I'm going to be the lead story, going to open the book on account of doing the cover story." He harked back to his humble beginnings for an indulgent moment. "When I first began, I used to be all the way in the back of the book. You know, where the muscle-building ads are."

" 'Killing Time, by Dan Moody,' " Joe mouthed softly, like someone pronouncing a litany.

"They always change your titles on them, I don't know why," Moody complained fretfully. "My own title for that one was 'Out of the Mouths of Guns.' Don't you think that's better?"

"Wouldje—?" Joe was fumbling with a pencil, half afraid to offer it.

Moody took the pencil from Joe's fingers, wrote on the margin alongside the story title: "The best of luck to you, Joe—Dan Moody," Joe the while supporting the magazine from underneath with the flaps of both hands, like an acolyte making an offering at some altar.

"Gee," Joe breathed, "I'm going to keep this forever. I'm going to paste transparent paper over it, so it won't get rubbed off, where you wrote."

"I would have done it in ink for you," Moody said benevolently, "only the pulp paper won't take it—it soaks it up like a blotter."

The phone gave another of its irritable, foreshortened blats.

Joe jumped guiltily, hastily backed toward the door. "I better get back on duty, or he'll be raising cain down there." He half closed the door, reopened it to add, "If there's anything you want, Mr. Moody, just call down for me. I'll drop anything I'm doing and beat it right up here."

"Thanks, I will, Joe," Moody promised, with the warm, comfortable smile of someone whose ego has just been talcumed and cuddled in cottonwool.

"And good luck to you on the story. I'll be rooting for you!"

"Thanks again, Joe."

Joe closed the door deferentially, holding the knob to the end, so that it should make a minimum of noise and not disturb the mystic creative process about to begin inside.

Before it did, however, Moody went to the phone and

asked for a nearby Long Island number. A soprano that sounded like a schoolgirl's got on.

"It's me, honeybunch," Moody said.

The voice had been breathless already, so it couldn't get any more breathless; what it did do was not get any less breathless. "What happened? Ooh, hurry up, tell me! I can't wait. Did you get the assignment on the cover story?"

"Yes, I got it! I'm in the hotel room right now, and they're paying all the charges. And listen to this: I'm getting double word-rate, two cents—"

A squeal of sheer joy answered him.

"And wait a minute, you didn't let me finish. If he likes the job, I'm even getting an extra additional bonus on top of all that. Now what do you have to say to that?"

The squeals became multiple this time—a series of them instead of just one. When they subsided, he heard her almost gasp: "Oh, I'm so proud of you!"

"Is Sonny-bun awake yet?"

"Yes. I knew you'd want to say good night to him, so I kept him up. Wait a minute, I'll go and get him."

The voice faded, then came back again. However, it seemed to be as unaccompanied as before. "Say something to Daddy. Daddy's right here. Daddy wants to hear you say something to him."

Silence.

"Hello, Sonny-bun. How's my little Snooky?" Moody coaxed.

More silence.

The soprano almost sang, "Daddy's going to do a big important job. Aren't you going to wish him luck?"

There was a suspenseful pause, then a startled cluck like that of a little barnyard fowl, "Lock!"

The squeals of delight this time came from both ends of the line, and in both timbres, soprano and tenor. "He wished me luck! Did you hear that? He wished me luck! That's a good omen. Now it's bound to be a lulu of a story!"

The soprano voice was too taken up distributing smothered kisses over what seemed to be a considerable surface area to be able to answer.

"Well," he said, "guess I better get down to business. I'll be home before noon—I'll take the ten forty-five, after I turn the story in at Tartell's office."

The parting became breathless, flurried, and tripartite.

"Do a bang-up job now"/"I'll make it a smasheroo"/ "Remember, Sonny-bun and I are rooting for you"/"Miss me"/"And you miss us, too"/*"Smack, smack"/"Smack, smack, smack"/"Gluck!"*

He hung up smiling, sighed deeply to express his utter satisfaction with his domestic lot. Then he turned away, lathered his hands briskly, and rolled up his shirt sleeves.

The preliminaries were out of the way, the creative process was about to begin. The creative process, that mystic life force, that splurge out of which has come the Venus de Milo, the Mona Lisa, the Fantaisie Impromptu, the Bayeux tapestries, *Romeo and Juliet,* the windows of Chartres Cathedral, *Paradise Lost*—and a pulp murder story by Dan Moody. The process is the same in all; if the results are a little uneven, that doesn't invalidate the basic similarity of origin.

He sat down before Gertie and, noting that the oval of light from the lamp fell on the machine, to the neglect of the polychrome cardboard mat which slanted in comparative shade against the wall, he adjusted the pliable lamp socket so that the luminous egg was cast almost completely on the drawing instead, with the typewriter now in the shadow. Actually he didn't need the light on his typewriter. He never looked at the keys when he wrote, nor at the sheet of paper in the machine. He was an expert typist, and if in the hectic pace of his fingering he sometimes struck the wrong letter, they took care of that down at the office. Tartell had special proofreaders for that. That wasn't Moody's job—he was the creator, he couldn't be bothered with picayune details like a few typographic errors. By the same token, he never went back over what he had written to reread it; he couldn't afford to, not at one cent a word (his regular rate) and at the pressure under which he worked. Besides, it was his experience that it always came out best the first time; if you went back and reread and fiddled around with it, you only spoiled it.

He palmed a sheet of white paper off the top of the stack and inserted it smoothly into the roller—an automatic movement to him. Ordinarily he made a sandwich of sheets—a white on top, a carbon in the middle, and a yellow at the bottom; that was in case the story should go astray in the mail, or be mislaid at the magazine office before the cashier had issued a check for it. But it was totally unnecessary in this case; he was delivering the story personally to Tartell's desk, it was a rush order, and it was to be sent to press immediately. Several extra moments would be wasted between manuscript pages if he took the time to make up "sandwiches," and besides, those yellow second sheets cost forty-five cents a ream at Goldsmith's (fifty-five elsewhere). You had to watch your costs in this line of work.

He lit a cigarette, the first of the many that were inevitably to follow, that always accompanied the writing of every story—the cigarette-to-begin-on. He blew a blue pinwheel of smoke, craned his neck slightly, and stared hard at the master plan before him, standing there against the wall. And now for the first line. That was always the gimmick in every one of his stories. Until he had it, he couldn't get into it; but once he had it, the story started to unravel by itself—it was easy going after that, clear sailing. It was like plucking the edge of the gauze up from an enormous crisscrossed bandage.

The first line, the first line—

He stared intently, almost hypnotically.

Better begin with the girl—she was very prominent on the cover, and then bring the hero in later. Let's see, she was wearing a violet evening dress—

The little lady in the violet evening dress came hurrying terrifiedly down the street, looking back in terror. Behind her—

His hands poised avariciously, then drew back again. No, wait a minute, she wouldn't be wearing an evening dress on the street, violet or any other color. Well, she'd have to change into it later in the story, that was all. In a 20,000-word novelette there would be plenty of room for her to change into an evening dress. Just a single line would do it, anywhere along.

She went home and changed her dress, and then came back again.

Now, let's try it again—

The beautiful redhead came hurrying down the street, looking back in terror. Behind her—

Again he got stuck. Yes, but who was after her, and what had she done for them to be after her for? That was the problem.

I started in too soon, he decided. I better go back to where she does something that gets somebody after her. Then the chase can come in after that.

The cigarette was at an end, without having ignited anything other than itself. He started another one.

Now, let's see. What would a beautiful, innocent, *good* girl do that would be likely to get somebody after her? She had to be good—Tartell was very strict about that. "I don't want any lady-bums in my stories. If you have to introduce a lady-bum into one of my stories, see that you kill her off as soon as you can. And whatever you do, don't let her get next to the hero too much. Keep her away from the hero. If he falls for her, he's a sap. And if he doesn't fall for her, he's too much of a goody-goody. Keep her in the background—just let her open the door in a négligée when the big-shot gangster drops in for a visit. And close the door again—fast!"

He swirled a hand around in his hair, in a massage-like motion, dropped it to the table, pummeled the edge of the table with it twice, the way a person does when he's trying to start a balky drawer open. Let's see, let's see . . . She could find out something that she's not supposed to, and then *they* find out that she has found out, and they start after her to shut her up—good enough, that's it! Now *how* did she find it out? She could go to a beauty parlor, and overhear in the next booth—no, beauty parlors were too feminine; Tartell wouldn't allow one of them in his stories. Besides, Moody had never been in one, wouldn't have known how to describe it on the inside. She could be in a phone booth and through the partition—No, he'd used that gambit in the July issue—in *Death Drops a Slug.*

A little lubrication was indicated here—something to help make the wheels go around, soften up the kinks. Absently, he picked up the bottle opener that Joe had left for him, reached down to the floor, brought up a bottle and uncapped it, still with that same one hand, using the edge of the table for leverage. He poured a very little into the tumbler, and did no more than chastely moisten his lips with it.

Now. She could get a package at her house, and it was meant for someone else, and—

He had that peculiar instinctive feeling that comes when someone is looking at you intently, steadfastly. He shook it off with a slight quirk of his head. It remained in abeyance for a moment or two, then slowly settled on him again.

The story thread suddenly dropped in a hopeless snarl, just as he was about to get it through the needle's eye of the first line.

He turned his head to dissipate the feeling by glancing in the direction from which it seemed to assail him. And then he saw it. A pigeon was standing utterly motionless on the ledge just outside the pane of the window. Its head was cocked inquiringly, it was turned profileward toward him, and it was staring in at him with just the one eye. But the eye was almost leaning over toward the glass, it was so intent—less than an inch or two away from it.

As he stared back, the eye solemnly blinked. Just once, otherwise giving no indication of life.

He ignored it and turned back to his task.

There's a ring at the bell, she goes to the door, and a man hands her a package—

His eyes crept uncontrollably over to their extreme outer corners, as if trying to take a peek without his knowledge. He brought them back with a reprimanding knitting of the brows. But almost at once they started over that way again. Just knowing the pigeon was standing out there seemed to attract his eyes almost magnetically.

He turned his head toward it again. This time he gave it a heavy baleful scowl. "Get off of there," he mouthed at it. "Go somewhere else." He spoke by lip motion alone because the glass between prevented hearing.

It blinked. More slowly than the first time, if a pigeon's blink can be measured. Scorn, contempt seemed to be expressed by the deliberateness of its blink.

Never slow to be affronted, he kindled at once. He swung his arm violently around toward it, in a complete half circle of riddance. Its wing feathers erupted a little, subsided again, as if the faintest of breezes had caressed them. Then with stately pomp it waddled around in a half circle, brought the other side of its head around toward the glass, and stared at him with the eye on that side.

Heatedly, he jumped from his chair, strode to the window, and flung it up. "I told you to get off of there!" he said threateningly. He gave the air immediately over the surface of the ledge a thrashing swipe with his arm.

It eluded the gesture with no more difficulty than a child jumping rope. Only, instead of coming down again as the rope passed underneath, it stayed up! It made a little looping journey with scarcely stirring wings, and as soon as his arm was drawn in again, it descended almost to the precise spot where it had stood before.

Once more they repeated this passage between them, with identical results. The pigeon expended far less energy coasting around at a safe height than he did flinging his arm hectically about, and he realized that a law of diminishing returns would soon set in on this point. Moreover, he overaimed the second time and crashed the back of his hand into the stone coping alongside the window, so that he had to suck at his knuckles and breathe on them to alleviate the sting.

He had never hated a bird so before. In fact, he had never hated a bird before.

He slammed the window down furiously. Thereupon, as though it realized it had that much more advance warning against possible armstrikes, the pigeon began to strut from one side to the other of the window ledge. Like a picket, enjoining him from working. Each time he made a turn, it cocked that beady eye at him.

He picked up the metal wastebasket and tested it in his hand for solidity. Then he put it down again, regretfully. He'd need it during the course of the story; he couldn't just drop the cigarette butts on the floor, he'd be kept too busy stamping them out to avoid starting a fire. And even if the basket knocked the damned bird off the ledge, it would probably go over with it.

He picked up the phone, demanded the desk clerk so that he could vent his indignation on something human.

"Do I have to have pigeons on my window sill?" he shouted accusingly. "Why didn't you tell me there were going to be pigeons on my window sill?"

The clerk was more than taken aback; he was stunned by the onslaught. "I—ah—ah—never had a complaint like this before," he finally managed to stammer.

"Well, you've got one now!" Moody let him know with firm disapproval.

"Yes, sir, but—but what's it doing?" the clerk floundered. "Is it making any noise?"

"It doesn't have to," Moody flared. "I just don't want it there!"

There was a momentary pause, during which it was to be surmised the clerk was baffled, scrubbing the side of his jaw, or perhaps his temple or forehead. Then he came back again, completely at a loss. "I'm sorry, sir—but I don't see what you expect *me* to do about it. You're up there with it, and I'm down here. Haven't—haven't you tried chasing it?"

"Haven't I tried?" choked Moody exasperatedly. "That's all I've been doing! It freewheels out and around and comes right back again!"

"Well, about the only thing I can suggest," the clerk said helplessly, "is to send up a boy with a mop or broom, and have him stand there by the window and—"

"I can't work with a bellboy in here doing sentinel duty with a mop or broom slung over his shoulder!" Moody exploded. "That'd be worse than the pigeon!"

The clerk breathed deeply, with bottomless patience. "Well, I'm sorry, sir, but—"

Moody got it out first. " 'I don't see what I can do about it.' 'I don't see what I can do about it'!" he mimicked ferociously. "Thanks! You've been a big help," he said with ponderous sarcasm. "I don't know what I would have done without you!" and hung up.

He looked around at it, a resigned expression in his eyes that those energetic, enthusiastic irises seldom showed.

The pigeon had its neck craned at an acute angle, almost down to the stone sill, but still looking in at him from that oblique perspective, as if to say, "Was that about me? Did it have to do with me?"

He went over and jerked the window up. That didn't even make it stir anymore.

He turned and went back to his writing chair. He addressed the pigeon coldly from there. Aloud, but coldly, and with the condescension of the superior forms of life toward the inferior ones. "Look. You want to come in? Is that what it's all about? You're dying to come in? You won't be happy till you do come in? Then for the love of Mike come in and get it over with, and let me get back to work! There's a nice comfortable chair, there's a nice plumpy sofa, there's a nice wide bed-rail for a perch. The whole room is yours. Come in and have yourself a ball!"

Its head came up, from that sneaky way of regarding him under-wing. It contemplated the invitation. Then its twig-like little vermilion legs dipped and it threw him a derogatory chuck of the head, as if to say "That for you and your room!"—and unexpectedly took off, this time in a straight, unerring line of final departure.

His feet detonated in such a burst of choleric anger that the chair went over. He snatched up the wastebasket, rushed to the window, and swung it violently—without any hope, of course, of overtaking his already vanished target.

"Dirty damn squab!" he railed bitterly. "Come back here and I'll—! Doing that to me, after I'm just about to get rolling! I hope you run into a high-tension wire headfirst. I hope you run into a hawk—"

His anger, however, settled as rapidly as a spent Seidlitz powder. He closed the window without violence. A smothered chuckle had already begun to sound in him on his way back to the chair, and he was grinning sheepishly as he reached it.

"Feuding with a pigeon yet," he murmured deprecatingly to himself. "I'd better get a grip on myself."

Another cigarette, two good hearty gulps of beer, and now, let's see—where was I? The opening line. He stared up at the ceiling.

His fingers spread, poised, and then suddenly began to splatter all over the dark keyboard like heavy drops of rain.

"For me?" the young woman said, staring unbelievably at the shifty-eyed man holding the package.

"You're . . .

One hand paused, then two of its fingers snapped, demanding inspiration. "Got to get a name for her," he muttered. He stared fruitlessly at the ceiling for a moment, then glanced over at the window. The hand resumed.

"You're Pearl Dove, ain't ya?"

"Why, yes, but I wasn't expecting anything."

("Not too much dialogue," Tartell always cautioned. "Get them moving, get them doing something. Dialogue leaves big blanks on the pages, and the reader doesn't get as much reading for his money.")

He thrust it at her, turned and disappeared as suddenly as he appeared . . .

Two "appeareds" in one line—too many. He triphammered the x-key eight times. *and disappeared as suddenly as he had showed up. She tried to call him back but he was no longer in sight. Somewhere out in the night the whine of an expensive car taking off came to her ears.*

He frowned, closed his eyes briefly, then began typing automatically again.

She looked at the package she had been left holding.

He never bothered to consult what he had written so far—such fussy niceties were for smooth-paper writers and poets. In stories like the one he was writing, it was almost impossible to break the thread of the action, anyway. Just so long as he kept going, that was all that mattered. If there was an occasional gap, Tartell's proofreaders would knit it together with a couple of words.

He drained the beer in the glass, refilled it, gazed dreamily at the ceiling. The wide, blank expanse of the ceiling gave his characters more room to move around in as his mind's eye conjured them up.

"She has a boy friend who's on the Homicide Squad," he murmured confidentially. "Not really a boy friend, just sort of a brotherly protector." ("Don't give 'em sweethearts," was Tartell's constant admonishment, "just give 'em pals. You might want to kill the girl off, and if she's already his sweetheart you can't very well do that, or he loses face with the readers.") "She calls him up to tell him she has received a mysterious package. He tells her not to open it, he'll be right over—" The rest was mechanical fingerwork. Fast and furious. The keys dipped and rose like a canopy of leaves shot through by an autumn wind.

The page jumped up out of the roller by itself, and he knew he'd struck off the last line there was room for. He pitched it aside to the floor without even glancing at it, slipped in a new sheet, all in one accustomed, fluid motion. Then, with the same almost unconscious ease, he reached down for a new bottle, uncapped it, and poured until a cream puff of a head burgeoned at the top of it.

They were at the business of opening the package now. He stalled for two lines, to give himself time to improvise what was going to be inside the package, which he hadn't had an opportunity to do until now—

He stared down at it. Then his eyes narrowed and he nodded grimly.

"What do you make of it?" she breathed, clutching her throat.

Then he was smack up against it, and the improvisation had to be here and now. The keys coasted to a reluctant but full stop. There was almost smoke coming from them by now, or else it was from his ever-present cigarette riding the edge of the table, drifting the long way around by way of the machine.

There were always certain staples that were good for the contents of mysterious packages. Opium pellets—but that meant bringing in a Chinese villain, and the menace on the cover drawing certainly wasn't Chinese.

He got up abruptly, swung his chair out away from the table, and shifted it farther over, directly under the phantom tableau on the ceiling that had come to a halt simultaneously with the keys—the way the figures on a motion picture screen freeze into immobility when something goes wrong with the projector.

He got up on the chair seat with both feet, craned his neck, peered intently and with complete sincerity. He was only about two feet away from the visualization on the ceiling. His little bit of fetishism, or idiosyncrasy, had worked for him before in similar stoppages, and it did now. He could *see* the inside of the package, he could see—

He jumped lithely down again, looped the chair back into place, speared avidly at the keys.

Uncut diamonds!

"Aren't they beautiful?" she said, clutching her pulsing throat.

(Well, if there were too many clutches in there, Tartell's hirelings could take one or two of them out. It was always hard to know what to have your female characters do with their hands. Clutching the throat and holding the heart were his own favorite standbys. The male characters could always be fingering a gun or swinging a punch at someone, but it wasn't refined for women to do that in *Startling Stories!*)

"Beautiful but hot," he growled.

Her eyes widened. "How do you know?"

"They're the Espinoza consignment; they've been missing for a week." He unlimbered his gun. "This spells trouble for someone."

That was enough dialogue for a few pages—he had to get into some fast, red-hot action.

There weren't any more hitches now. The story flowed like a torrent. The margin bell chimed almost staccato, the roller turned with almost piston-like continuity, the pages sprang up almost like blobs of batter from a pancake skillet. The beer kept rising in the glass and, contradictorily, steadily falling lower. The cigarettes gave up their ghosts, long thin gray ghosts, in a good cause; the mortality rate was terrible.

His train of thought, the story's lifeline, beer-lubricated but no whit impeded, flashed and sputtered and coursed ahead like lightning in a topaz mist, and the loose fingers and hiccuping keys followed as fast as they could. Only once more, just before the end, was there a near hitch, and that wasn't in the sense of a stoppage of thought, but rather of an error in memory—what he mistakenly took to be a duplication. The line:

Hands clutching her throat, Pearl tore down the street in her violet evening dress . . . streamed off the keys, and he came to a lumbering, uneasy halt.

Wait a minute, I had that in in the beginning. She can't keep running down the street all the time in a violet evening dress; the readers'll get fed up. How'd she get into a violet evening dress anyway? A minute ago the guy *tore her white blouse and revealed her quivering white shoulder.*

He half turned in the chair (and none too steadily), about to essay the almost hopeless task of winnowing through the blanket of white pages that lay all around him on the floor, and then recollection came to his aid in the nick of time.

I remember now! I moved the beginning around to the middle, and began with the package at the door instead. (It seemed like a long, long time ago, even to him, that the package had arrived at the door; weeks and weeks ago; another story ago.) This is the first time she's run down the street in a violet evening dress, she hasn't done it before. Okay, let her run.

However, logically enough, in order to get her into it in the first place, he x-ed out the line anyway, and put in for groundwork:

"If it hadn't been for your quick thinking, that guy would have got me sure. I'm taking you to dinner tonight, and that's an order."

"I'll run home and change. I've got a new dress I'm dying to break in."

And that took care of that.

Ten minutes later (according to story time, not his), due to the unfortunate contretemps of having arrived at the wrong café at the wrong time, the line reappeared, now legitimatized, and she was duly *tearing down the street, screaming, clutching her throat with her violet evening dress.* (The "with" he had intended for an "in.") The line had even gained something by waiting. This time she was screaming as well, which she hadn't been doing the first time.

And then finally, somewhere in the malt-drenched mists ahead, maybe an hour or maybe two hours, maybe a dozen cigarettes or maybe a pack and a half, maybe two bottles of beer or maybe four, a page popped up out of the roller onto which he had just ground the words *The End,* and the story was done.

He blew out a deep breath, a vacuum-cleaner-deep breath. He let his head go over and rest for a few moments against the edge of the table. Then he got up from the chair, very unsteadily, and wavered over toward the bed, treading on the litter of fallen pages. But he had his shoes off, so that didn't hurt them much.

He didn't hear the springs creak as he flattened out. His ears were already asleep . . .

Sometime in the early morning, the very early early morning (just like at home), that six-year-old of the neighbors started with that velocipede of his, racing it up and down in front of the house and trilling the bell incessantly. He stirred and mumbled disconsolately to his wife, "Can't you call out the window and make that brat stay in front of his own house with that damn contraption?"

Moody struggled up tormentedly on one elbow, and at that point the kid characteristically went back into the house for good, and the ringing stopped. But when Moody opened his blurred eyes, he wasn't sitting up at home at all; he was in a hotel room.

"Take your time," a voice said sarcastically. "I've got all day."

Moody swiveled his head, stunned, and Joe was holding the room door open to permit Tartell, his magazine editor, to glare in at him. Tartell was short, but impressive. He was of a great age, as Moody's measurements of time went, a redwood-tree age, around forty-five or forty-eight or somewhere up there. And right now Tartell wasn't in good humor.

"Twice the printers have called," he barked, "asking if they get that story today or not!"

Moody's body gave a convulsive jerk and his heels braked against the floor. "Gee, is it that late—?"

"No, not at all!" Tartell shouted. "The magazine can come out anytime! Don't let a little thing like that worry you! If Cora hadn't had the presence of mind to call me at my house before I left for the office, I wouldn't have stopped by here like this, and we'd all be waiting around another hour down at the office. Now where is it? Let me have it. I'll take it down with me."

Moody gestured helplessly toward the floor, which looked as though a political rally, with pamphlets, had taken place on it the night before.

"Very systematic," Tartell commented acridly. He surged forward into the room, doubling over into a sort of cushiony right-angle as he did so, and began to zigzag, picking up papers without let-up, like a diligent, near-sighted park attendant spearing leaves at close range. "This is fine right after a heavy breakfast," he added. "The best thing I could do!"

Joe looked pained, but on Moody's behalf, not Tartell's. "I'll help you, sir," he offered placatingly, and started bobbing in turn.

Tartell stopped suddenly, and without rising, seemed to be trying to read, from the unconventional position of looking straight down from up above. "They're blank," he accused. "Where does it begin?"

"Turn them over," Moody said, wearied with so much fussiness. "They must have fallen on their faces."

"They're that way on both sides, Mr. Moody," Joe faltered.

"What've you been doing?" Tartell demanded wrathfully. "Wait a minute—!" His head came up to full height, he swerved, went over to Gertie, and examined the unlidded machine closely.

Then he brought both fists up in the air, each still clutching pinwheels of the sterile pages, and pounded them down with maniacal fury on both ends of the writing table. The noise of the concussion was only less than the noise of his unbridled voice.

"You damn-fool idiot!" he roared insanely, looking up at the ceiling as if in quest of aid with which to curb his assault-tempted emotions. "You've been pounding thin air all night! You've been beating the hell out of blank paper! *You forgot to put a ribbon in your typewriter!*"

Joe, looking beyond Tartell, took a quick step forward, arms raised in support of somebody or something.

Tartell slashed his hand at him forbiddingly, keeping him where he was. "Don't catch him, let him land," he ordered, wormwood-bitter. "Maybe a good clunk against the floor will knock some sense into his stupid—talented—head."

A recurring theme in the work of James Gould Cozzens is that of the moral dilemmas that arise in various professions; in "Clerical Error," he explores a problem in the bookselling business—and one man's way of handling it. Born in 1903, Cozzens was one of our most distinguished American authors, producing such novels as Confusion *(1924),* S.S. San Pedro *(1931),* The Just and the Unjust *(1942), and* Ask Me Tomorrow *(1969). His 1957 classic,* By Love Possessed, *was perhaps his most popular work, and* Guard of Honor *(1948), a story of three days on an airbase during World War II, won the 1949 Pulitzer Prize.*

CLERICAL ERROR

James Gould Cozzens

There were three steps down from the street door. Then the store extended, narrow and low between the book-packed walls, sixty or seventy feet to a little cubbyhole of an office where a large sallow man worked under a shaded desk lamp. He had heard the street door open, and he looked that way a moment, peering intently through his spectacles. Seeing only a thin, stiffly erect gentleman with a small cropped white mustache, standing hesitant before the table with the sign *Any Book 50 Cents,* he returned to the folded copy of a religious weekly on the desk in front of him. He looked at the obituary column again, pulled a pad toward him, and made a note. When he had finished, he saw, on looking up again, that the gentleman with the white mustache had come all the way down the store.

"Yes, sir?" he said, pushing the papers aside. "What can I do for you?"

The gentleman with the white mustache stared at him keenly. "I am addressing the proprietor, Mr. Joreth?" he said.

"Yes, sir. You are."

"Quite so. My name is Ingalls—Colonel Ingalls."

"I'm glad to know you, Colonel. What can I—"

"I see that the name does not mean anything to you."

Mr. Joreth took off his spectacles, looked searchingly. "Why, no, sir. I am afraid not. Ingalls. No. I don't know anyone by that name."

Colonel Ingalls thrust his stick under his arm and drew an envelope from his inner pocket. He took a sheet of paper from it, unfolded the sheet, scowled at it a moment, and tossed it onto the desk. "Perhaps," he said, "this will refresh your memory."

Mr. Joreth pulled his nose a moment, looked harder at Colonel Ingalls, replaced his spectacles. "Oh," he said, "a bill. Yes. You must excuse me. I do much of my business by mail with people I've never met personally. 'The Reverend Doctor Godfrey Ingalls, Saint John's Rectory.' Ah, yes, yes—"

"The late Doctor Ingalls was my brother. This bill is obviously an error. He would never have ordered, received, or wished to read any of these works. Naturally, no such volumes were found among his effects."

"Hm," said Mr. Joreth. "Yes, I see." He read down the itemized list, coughed, as though in embarrassment. "I see. Now, let me check my records a moment." He dragged down a vast battered folio from the shelf before him. "G, H, I—" he muttered. "*Ingalls.* Ah, now—"

"There is no necessity for that," said Colonel Ingalls. "It is, of course, a mistake. A strange one, it seems to me. I advise you strongly to be more careful. If you choose to debase yourself by surreptitiously selling works of the sort, that is your business. But—"

Mr. Joreth nodded several times, leaned back. "Well, Colonel," he said, "you're entitled to your opinion. I don't sit in judgment on the tastes of my customers. Now, in this case, there seems unquestionably to have been an order for the books noted from the source indicated. On the fifteenth of last May I filled the order. Presumably they arrived. What became of them, then, is no affair of mine; but in view of your imputation I might point out that such literature is likely to be kept in a private place and read privately. For eight successive months I sent a statement. I have never received payment. Of course, I was unaware that the customer was, didn't you say, deceased. Hence my reference to legal action on this last. I'm very sorry to have—"

"You unmitigated scoundrel!" roared Colonel Ingalls. "Do you really mean definitely to maintain that Doctor Ingalls purchased such books? Let me tell you—"

Mr. Joreth said, "My dear sir, one moment, if you please! Are you in a position to be so positive? I imply nothing about the purchaser. I mean to maintain nothing, except that I furnished goods, for which I am entitled to payment. I am a poor man. When people do not pay me, what can I do but—"

"Why, you infamous—"

Mr. Joreth held up his hand. "Please, please!" he protested. "I think you are taking a most unjust and unjustified attitude, Colonel. This account has run a long while. I've taken no action. I am well aware of the unpleasantness which would be caused for many customers if a bill for books of this sort was made public. The circumstances aren't by any means unique, my dear sir; a list of my confidential customers would no doubt surprise you."

Colonel Ingalls said carefully, "Be good enough to show me my brother's original order."

"Ah," said Mr. Joreth. He pursed his lips. "That's unfair of you, Colonel. You are quite able to see that I wouldn't have it. It would be the utmost imprudence for me to keep on file anything which could cause so much trouble. I have the carbon of an invoice, which is legally sufficient, under the circumstances, I think. You see my position."

"Clearly," said Colonel Ingalls. "It is the position of a dirty knave and a blackguard, and I shall give myself the satisfaction of thrashing you."

He whipped the stick from under his arm. Mr. Joreth slid agilely from his seat, caught the telephone off the desk, kicking a chair into the Colonel's path.

"Operator," he said, "I want a policeman." Then he jerked open a drawer, plucked a revolver from it. "Now, my good sir," he said, his back against the wall, "we shall soon see. I have put up with a great deal of abuse from you, but there are limits. To a degree I understand your provocation, though it doesn't excuse your conduct. If you choose to take yourself out of here at once and send me a check for the amount due me, we will say no more."

Colonel Ingalls held the stick tight in his hand. "I think I will wait for the officer," he said with surprising composure. "I was too hasty. In view of your list of so-called customers, which you think would surprise me, there are doubtless other people to be considered—"

The stick in his hand leaped, sudden and slashing, catching Mr. Joreth over the wrist. The revolver flew free, clattered along the floor, and Colonel Ingalls kicked it behind him. "It isn't the sort of thing the relatives of a clergyman would like to have made public, is it? When you read of the death of one, what is to keep you from sending a bill? Very often they must pay and shut up. A most ingenious scheme, sir."

Mr. Joreth clasped his wrist, wincing. "I am at loss to understand this nonsense," he said. "How dare you—"

"Indeed?" said Colonel Ingalls. "Ordinarily, I might be at loss myself, sir; but in this case I think you put your foot in it, sir! I happen to be certain that my late brother ordered no books from you, that he did not keep them in private or read them in private. It was doubtless not mentioned in the obituary, but for fifteen years previous to his death Doctor Ingalls had the misfortune to be totally blind. . . . There, sir, is the policeman you sent for."

This novelette, first published in 1942, came about when a magazine editor asked Lawrence G. Blochman an irresistable question: "How would you like to commit murder in the public library—the New York Public Library, to be exact?" Blochman's literary response is baffling, exciting, and offers modern readers a nostalgic look at the inner workings of the vast New York Public Library forty years ago. (A minor note for historians: The story was filmed in 1943 as Quiet Please, Murder! *But with wholesale changes in plot and characters, unfortunately, so that about all that remains in the screen version is the library setting.) Lawrence G. Blochman (1900–75) was a popular writer of mysteries for close to forty years, many of which were set in India* (Bombay Mail, Bengal Fire) *where he worked as a newspaperman in the 1920s. His most famous and accomplished detective creation is Dr. Coffee, head of pathology at a large hospital—the forerunner of TV's Quincy. The first gathering of Dr. Coffee stories,* Diagnosis: Homicide, *was awarded the Mystery Writers of America Edgar as the outstanding collection of 1950.*

MURDER WALKS IN MARBLE HALLS

Lawrence G. Blochman

Long before the storm broke, Phil Manning had an uneasy feeling that something unpleasant was about to happen. He had been jumpy ever since reading in the morning papers that Feodor Klawitz, the erudite screwball, was out on bail after having been arrested on charges of criminal libel preferred by H. H. Dorwin, a trustee of the public library. When Dorwin himself telephoned to say he was on his way over to discuss a matter of great importance, Manning's jumpiness increased by at least six latent jumps. And when his phone rang a second time, he winced and hit a handful of wrong typewriter keys.

Phil Manning did not believe in the occult or in premonitions. And as he had neither a hangover nor a guilty conscience, he decided he was suffering from an attack of the Deep-blue Willies *(Melancholia bibliotecalis),* an occupational disease afflicting the staff of the Public Library on dark Winter days. Even on the sunniest mornings of Spring there was a certain sepulchral chill about the marble grandeur of the library, and when the weather went into somber mourning for the dying year, the building was a positive mausoleum.

The phone rang again. The shaggy young man with the Willies reached for it apprehensively.

"Press relations. Manning speaking," he said.

"Phil, I've got to see you—right away!" It was Betty Vale's voice, usually guaranteed to restore fallen spirits with its cosmic music. Not today, though. Today it was without a single grace note. Today it was a taut, low-keyed call for help.

"What's happened, Betty?" Manning tried to fight off the sense of impending disaster with a facetious phrase. "Did somebody park a fire hydrant near your car again?"

"Don't joke, Phil." There was anguish in the tone. "Can you cross the street? I'm phoning from the cigar store at the corner."

"Why don't you come over here?" Manning asked. "I've got to wait for one of the trustees. H. H. Dorwin just phoned—"

"Dorwin?" The word was like a cry of pain. "I don't want to see Hugh Dorwin now, Phil. I can't."

"I didn't know he was a friend of yours," Manning said. "How—"

"I can't tell you about it now, Phil. And I'm afraid to come to the library. I'll wait here. You'll come when you can, Phil? Please."

"Of course, darling. Right away—if I can make it."

Manning banged down the phone and glanced at his typewriter, which had been automatically composing a press release on the library's exhibit opening the following week: The History of the Dog in America as Told by Contemporary Prints and Publications. The release could wait.

Uncoiling his long legs from the legs of the chair, Manning rose to his full six-feet-one and smoothed the sedentary wrinkles from his tweeds.

Suddenly Manning sat down again. This was indeed his off day. Dave Benson was flowing through the doorway, his white teeth flashing in an aggressive smile.

Manning never thought of Benson as walking; he moved as though the next step would see his pointed shoes gliding into a tango. The gait matched his double-breasted elegance, with its corner of blue-plaid handkerchief poking from his pocket to harmonize with his blue-plaid tie.

"Hi!" said Benson, turning on all his dark, slick-haired, self-conscious charm. "Where's Betty?"

He would ask that, Manning thought. Benson haunted Betty Vale like an unemployed ghost. He was always in the library if there was a chance of Betty's being there.

"Betty's gone to Bermuda for the onion season," Manning said. "And I'm leaving on the next plane myself. Good-bye, old man."

"Betty told me she was coming to the library this afternoon," Benson insisted through his white grin. "So I was thinking—"

"Stop boasting, Benson. And leave the door open as you go out. Good-bye." Benson's built-in smile slowly faded.

"Have it your own way," he said, fixing Manning with a curious stare. "But don't think Betty's going to thank you for this." He made his exit in two-four time.

Manning listened to his footsteps retreating down the marble corridor. He waited several minutes to give Benson plenty of chance to get out of range. Then he rose again quickly.

He was buttoning his coat when he heard the shot.

It was not a very loud report—a sharp explosion that made hollow, singing echoes in the halls and galleries—and Manning did not recognize it immediately for what it was. After all, gun fire was not a usual sound in the public library.

When the report was followed, however, by a cry, a shout, and the tattoo of running feet, Manning bolted from his office.

Fifty feet down the corridor he saw H. H. Dorwin flattened against the wall. Bullet-chipped flakes of marble from the bust of Sophocles above him were dusted over his well-tailored shoulders. His usually ruddy face was the color of the sculptured poet.

Halfway between Dorwin and the monumental staircase, a small target pistol lay on the floor. It was probably not more than .22 caliber.

Pounding down the stairs was big, white-thatched Tim Cornish, library guard, in pursuit of a shabby little man who had already reached the vast vestibule and was running for the street doors.

"You hurt, Mr. Dorwin?" Manning hesitated between joining the chase and helping the shaken trustee.

"Of course not!" Dorwin barked. "Manning, go after that guard! Don't let him turn the man over to the police!"

"But, Mr. Dorwin—"

"No cops!" Dorwin ordered, walking quickly down the corridor to pick up the pistol. "Bring him back here. Bring them both back here, Manning. And hurry."

Manning hurried. He went down the steps three at a time.

Once outside, he broke into a brisk trot, seeking Cornish and the threadbare fugitive among the throngs of women hurrying along the avenue, round-shouldered with the cold despite their furs.

Manning caught sight of Cornish near the corner. The guard had collared the seedy-looking assailant, apparently without a struggle. When Manning motioned, Cornish started toward him, his captive meekly in tow.

The man who had shot at Dorwin wore no overcoat, and his teeth were chattering. He was an unprepossessing specimen, thin and gray-haired. At first glance he seemed typical of the cold-weather derelicts now deserting the icy streets for the library, the homeless bums whose damp clothing gave off animal odors when it began to steam in the warmth of the reading rooms. When he came closer, however, Manning revised his estimate. The shabby stranger was young, despite the two-day stubble of graying beard on his tragically lined face; and his eyes were keen and intelligent.

"Maybe I ought to carry him," said the guard. The threadbare captive looked very small beside Tim Cornish. Tim was a big man, almost as big as Manning, with a Mark Twain mustache, hair like silver, and feet like a copper. Tim had in fact been pretty much all copper for most of his twenty-five years as library guard. Only after twenty years had he become aware of the millions of volumes which surrounded him daily. Three years ago he had discovered Shakespeare.

"You don't look like a gunman," Manning said to the seedy man beside him. "Why did you want to shoot H. H. Dorwin?"

There was no reply. They went up the steps to the portico.

"It was just the flash and outbreak of a fiery mind," said Tim. "A savageness in unreclaimed blood. That's from *Macbeth,* Mr. Manning."

The silent little man spoke at last. "It's from *Hamlet,*" he said.

"I said *Hamlet,* didn't I?" Tim demanded. He tightened his grip on his captive and pushed him indignantly through the entrance stile. The metal bar came between them and stuck—only for a fraction of a second. In the brief instant the man who had shot at Dorwin wrested himself free and ran.

Tim Cornish ran after him, with Phil Manning one click of the turnstile behind.

They ran past the elevators and up the steep vaulted stairway of the North Wing. On the first landing they stopped to pant in consternation. The seedy little would-be assassin was gone.

The stairways in the North Wing were a complex system of superimposed and parallel X's, a maze of crisscrossing marble tunnels, like false passages to detour ghouls from a Pharaoh's sepulchre. From the landing Manning and Cornish could continue upward by alternate branches of the X, either to the Music Room office, or to the elevators on the second floor; they could go down again by another leg of the stairway to the main floor. There was no way of knowing which of the three the fugitive had taken.

"Look, Tim," Manning said. "You stay on the scent. I'll warn the guards at all the doors."

When he returned to his office, after giving the description of the missing derelict to the guards at all the doors, Manning nearly collided with a young woman who was coming out. She was a sinuous little thing, lusciously proportioned and suspiciously blonde. She was probably pretty, although at the moment her sensuous features were distorted by an expression of dismay—or perhaps it was embarrassment at the brusqueness of the unexpected encounter. Manning did not remember having seen her before, although she was hatless and evidently worked in the library. As she muttered a hasty "Sorry," he thought her lips were white along their cosmetic edges. He was watching her hurry down the corridor, when Dorwin's voice from inside the office called, "Well?"

H. H. Dorwin had recovered his composure—at least outwardly.

"Where's Underwood?" he asked.

"Who's that, sir?"

"Underwood. James Underwood, the man I told you to bring here."

"He's still loose somewhere in the library, Mr. Dorwin. He won't get out of the building, though. Hadn't we better get the police?"

"No," snapped Dorwin. "The poor devil probably's sorry already for what he did."

"I see," said Manning, although he didn't.

"He has a brilliant mind, that Underwood," Dorwin went on. "Used to work for me, in my private library, cataloguing my first editions and incunabula. Resigned about a year ago, for some strange reasons of his own. Had a hard time of it ever since. On W.P.A. for a while, and I don't know what else. Been hanging around my place the last week, but I've been too busy to see him. I suspected he wanted his job back, and sent word I didn't have anything for him. Hard luck went to his head, I guess."

Dorwin paused expectantly. Manning didn't know what comment was expected of him. He said: "That young woman who just left here—was she looking for me?"

"No," said Dorwin quickly. Then he added, "She's a catalogue girl—new here. Doesn't know her way around yet, apparently. By the way, Manning, what happened to your notice on those Russian manuscripts I gave the library? They've been catalogued since Autumn and I haven't seen a word about them anywhere."

"There's a notice in next month's Bulletin, Mr. Dorwin," Manning replied. "Is that what you wanted to see me about?"

"There was something else," said Dorwin. He hesitated, got up, and went to the window. For a minute he seemed intent on the first flakes of snow swirling through the gloom.

His silhouette was slim and clean-lined against the window, particularly for a man in his fifties—the lusty fifties. He was a snappy dresser, too, for a banker and patron of the arts. Or for a collector. Dorwin was very much a collector. He collected interlocking directorates and symphony orchestras, tax-exempt securities and first editions, old masters and young blondes.

An unpleasant thought squirmed through Manning's mind. Betty Vale was on the blonde side. Betty Vale had admitted out of a clear sky that she knew Hugh Dorwin and didn't want to see him. And Betty Vale was scared of something. . . .

"You know about my fuss with Feodor Klawitz?" Dorwin demanded suddenly without turning around.

"I know about it roughly," Manning said.

"How well do you know the man?"

"Well . . ." Manning hesitated. He knew Feodor Klawitz as a bald-headed, horse-faced eccentric who spent most of his waking hours in the library, except for three nights a week when he broadcast over a small local radio station. It was a strange program, part news, part personalities, all lugubriously learned and much of it violently scurrilous. Manning had always thought Klawitz a little mad, an opinion which had been strengthened the day he was arrested. The warrant had been served on Klawitz in the Map Room, and he had immediately gone berserk, throwing maps and charts about, pelting the librarian and the arresting officer with Persia, Baluchistan and Bokhara. . . .

"I know him to speak to; that's about all," Manning said. "And of course I know him by sight—if he happens to be wearing a familiar wig."

"Wig?" Dorwin echoed.

"I thought everybody knew Klawitz wears a different toupee to suit his mood," Manning explained. "He wears a dignified gray wig when he's feeling severe and scholarly, a sleek black one for moments of glamour and romance, a reddish thatch when he feels argument and eloquence coming on."

"The fool libeled me again on his broadcast last night," Dorwin said. "Hadn't been out of jail two hours before he was calling me a lecherous plutocrat. Then at midnight I got a special delivery letter—anonymous, of course—saying that Klawitz had barely started on me. Said he'd rip my character completely to shreds, unless I did this or that, libel charge or no libel charge."

Dorwin turned around at last. He turned quickly, savagely. His face had gone white again.

"Damn it, Manning," the trustee said, "Nobody can blackmail me!"

"Do you think he . . . Do you think Klawitz had anything to do with this man Underwood taking a shot at you today?" Manning asked.

"I wouldn't put it past him," Dorwin said. "Klawitz is capable of anything. But I just wanted you to know, Manning, that I'm not backing down. I'm not dropping the libel charges against Klawitz. I'm telling you this, because in trying to get at me again, Klawitz may hurt you, Manning."

Manning moistened his lips. "Betty Vale?" he asked.

"I won't mention names, Manning. I'm a little old-fashioned that way. Whatever my bachelor habits may be, I still observe the old niceties. I just want to tell you that . . . that no matter what Klawitz may say, you mustn't lose your faith in . . . in anyone."

The interview was interrupted by the sudden appearance of Tim Cornish. The guard was panting slightly as he announced: "We haven't found him yet, Mr. Dorwin. But we will. He's still in the library."

"Yes. Well, bring him to the Trustees' Room when you find him." Dorwin picked up a large portfolio which Manning had not noticed before. It was a deep-red portfolio fastened with blue tapes. "I'll be there in half an hour," he added. "There's a Trustees' meeting."

"Don't you think you'd better wait here, Mr. Dorwin?" Tim suggested. "Do you think it's a good idea to go wandering around while that guy—?"

"I'm not afraid, Tim." Dorwin looked at the red portfolio with a curious expression of alarm in his eyes. He started to say something, then changed his mind. He tucked the portfolio under his left arm—gingerly, as though it contained something highly explosive. "I'm not afraid of *him,*" he said, patting his right coat pocket. "I've got the man's gun."

He strode out. Tim watched him admiringly. "He's right," Tim said. "Cowards die many times before their death, Mr. Manning."

Manning smiled. "*Hamlet,* Tim?"

"*Julius Caesar,* Mr. Manning. By the way, I've got a note for you." He fished a folded piece of paper from his pocket.

Manning quickly unfolded the paper. On it, Betty Vale's handwriting said: "Come to the Oriental Room as soon as you can! Please!! I'll wait for you there."

Thrusting the note into his pocket, Manning hurried past the guard without a word. He heard Tim say, "We'll have that guy rounded up in no time, Mr. Manning. Don't worry."

Manning waved an acknowledgement, and strode down the marbled whiteness of the crypt-like corridor. He turned into the long, low hall that housed the Oriental catalogue, passed the doors of the Slavonic and Hebrew rooms. His heart beat faster as he approached the entrance to the Oriental library. Not only was he anxious about Betty Vale's mysterious difficulties, but the Oriental Room was a sentimental symbol to him. It was here that he had rediscovered Betty.

They had been college sweethearts once, before Betty left the co-educational school for a Vermont college where a girl could study not only Greek philosophy and English poetry, but the Dance with a capital D. After that a million dollars and the Atlantic Ocean had come between them. The million was Edward Vale's—Betty's father's—the result of a smart advertising campaign for Vale Headache Powders, while Manning was learning the newspaper business in New York. And a million dollars can change almost anyone's social outlook, particularly in regard to a $60-a-week reporter; at least it would seem so to the reporter. The Atlantic Ocean came in when Manning was awarded a scholarship at Louvain—a year of study cut short by the blitzkrieg which blasted him out of the Louvain Library into the driver's seat of an ambulance—a year in which he and Betty did not even correspond.

Even after he was chased home with a Nazi bullet in his thigh and had settled down to his new job at the public library, he made no effort to get in touch with her. He was afraid of that million dollars.

He thought he had forgotten her, until the day, several months ago, he had found her in the Oriental Room, poring over the words of Kalidasa. He was pleased and puzzled—puzzled that he should be so pleased to learn that she was not yet married, even more puzzled that a pretty blonde with a rich father should be concerned with a Sanskrit poet fifteen centuries dead.

The answer to the first puzzle was not hard to find. The second, however, was more difficult. Betty Vale could be charmingly secretive. She seemed genuinely glad to pick up their old comradeship where they had left off, but she liked to talk more about the past than about the present.

If there had been any doubt in Manning's mind that she was in trouble, it was disspelled when he saw her face.

"I was scared to death you wouldn't come," she said.

"You're scared to death, all right, but you can't blame it on me, darling." He smiled desperately into her frightened eyes. "What happened?"

"I don't know where to begin."

"An anonymous letter?"

The girl gasped. Her eyes were almost round above her broad, high cheek bones. They were long eyes, normally—almost Oriental, if they hadn't been so blue. "How did you know?" she asked.

"A guess." Manning shrugged. He was not quite sure why he had not told her about H. H. Dorwin's anonymous letter—or the shot that hit Sophocles instead of Dorwin. He said: "Tell me about it."

Betty Vale pushed one hand into her muff, drew out a

crumpled piece of paper. "It came in this afternoon's mail," she said.

Manning smoothed out the paper and read:

> "If you don't stop seeing Hugh Dorwin, someone will stop you—and by the most primitive and certain means."

The message was printed in crudely formed block letters that did not fit the precise phrasing.

"*Have* you been seeing Dorwin?" Manning asked.

"This past week, yes."

"Then I can give you some very simple advice: Don't see him any more."

"But I must see him this afternoon, Phil. I *must.*"

"And let him make passes at you?"

"It's . . . it's not that."

The girl moistened her lips. Her long lashes fanned her cheek. She said in a low voice: "I've got to see him, that's all."

"That's a quick switch," Manning said. "When you phoned me, you didn't want to see him at all. You said you were even afraid to come to the library."

"I *was* afraid. Of that man."

"Underwood?"

"I don't know his name. The shabby man who needed a shave—and an overcoat. I was on my way to the library when I saw him go in. So I phoned you instead. But when I saw the guard arrest him, I thought it would be safe to come."

"The guard didn't arrest him," Manning said. "If it's Underwood you're talking about, he's still loose—in the library."

"He's—?" The girl started to rise, but sank back limply in her chair. "Oh, Phil."

Manning reached for her hand. It was cold and trembling.

"Why are you afraid of Underwood?" he asked.

"I think he wrote that letter."

"You don't know his name, but you think he wrote you a threatening letter. Why?"

"I saw him several times loitering outside of Hugh Dorwin's house on Fifth Avenue," Betty said. "Day before yesterday, when I came out, he was standing there, shivering in his thin coat. I almost felt sorry for him—until he looked into my face. Phil, his eyes! They're desperate, terrible eyes! They're—I can't explain, but they frightened me."

"That's the only reason you have for thinking Underwood wrote you an anonymous letter—the expression in his eyes?"

"Who else could it have been, Phil? No one else knew about my going to Dorwin's. And this man waiting outside there . . ."

Manning pulled thoughtfully at the lobe of one ear. It all sounded very strange—yet there were plenty of strange things going on in the library today. Betty was certainly holding something back—perhaps because she was still scared.

"Look, darling," Manning said, squeezing the girl's hand reassuringly. "I'm not going to ask you any more questions until I'm sure your Mr. Underwood is somewhere else. Wait here until I take a quick turn around the plant. The guards have probably rounded him up by this time."

Betty returned the pressure of his hand, but said nothing. . . .

The guard outside the Trustees' Room said: "Tim just went upstairs, Mr. Manning. He heard that man he's looking for is on the third floor."

Manning set out in pursuit.

As he climbed the stairs he noted that the afternoon darkness was as thick as night, and that the snow was falling in earnest outside.

Manning was wondering whether Tim had turned north toward the Music Room or south toward the map room, when he caught sight of Tim's white hair at the far end of the catalogue room, straight ahead. He followed.

He strode through the two-storied hush of the vast nave where men and women moved among high tables, like a swarm of termites boring into the six million listing cards impaled on metal spindles in the long oak drawers. He lost track of Tim among the people digging out their references to Anaphylaxis, Brazilian Railroads, and Chaucer. When he reached the queue waiting to present call slips to the pneumatic-tube station at the central desk, he decided that Tim must have disappeared into the great transept of the two reading rooms beyond the catalogue. He would find out which one.

He first circled the North Room, skirting the tall cliffs of encyclopedias and reference books. He saw no trace of Tim—or of James Underwood.

He passed the delivery desk—a corral of carved oak separating the two reading rooms—with its red lights flashing the numbers of books just arrived from the stacks by tiny elevator. He sidled through a parked caravan of low hand trucks loaded with volumes returning to the stacks, each ticketed with pink or white slips to announce its destination. He stepped into the South Reading Room and was about to repeat his circular voyage of exploration when two arresting objects sprang simultaneously into his field of vision.

The first, the trim figure of a woman rushing excitedly toward him, he saw only vaguely. Even when she stopped beside him, seized his arm, and made a small, half-strangled sound in her throat, he did not really look at her. His eyes were focused in horrid fascination on the narrow gallery which ran along the entire side of the immense room, halfway up the precipice of books.

H. H. Dorwin was standing unsteadily on the gallery, the door of the spiral staircase open behind him.

Blood was streaming down Dorwin's left cheek, and his face was a ghastly mask. He took two disjointed steps, like a man walking in his sleep, tottered an instant, then collapsed. He toppled over the iron railing, struck the top of the jutting bookcases below, pitched across a dictionary stand, and crashed heavily on a reading table.

Three nuns and half a dozen students arose in shocked surprise, backed away from the sprawled figure on the table, and screamed in unison.

Pandemonium swept through the South Reading Room like a rising wind. The small noises of startled readers pushing back their chairs swelled to a roar. The shrieks of the terrified nuns struck human echoes from the far tables. The august silence shrouding the ornate gilded ceiling was ripped to shreds by a bedlam of voices raised above a murmur for the first time in nearly half a century. There was a movement of vicious curiosity toward the broken form on the reading table, a movement of terror away from it, a surge of panic toward the passage to the Catalogue Room.

Three library guards blocked the exit. One of them was Tim Cornish who had instantly sensed the situation and was lustily engaged in restoring order. His big voice droned through the din, calling: "Everyone be seated, please. Do not try to leave the room."

Tim's metallic monotone roused Phil Manning from his brief stupefaction. Turning his eyes from the man on the table, he realized that the woman who had gripped his arm was Betty Vale. She clutched her muff closely against her breast with tense white fingers, and the hand on his arm shook violently.

"You and your rendezvous," Manning said. "Why didn't you stay put?"

The girl stared at him wordlessly, her lips frozen in a small, scarlet, horrified O.

"Did you get to see Dorwin?" Phil asked.

"No. That is, not until he . . . Not until just now."

"How much of this did you see happen?"

"Just what you saw—and that was too much. I'm all cold and hot inside. I'm afraid I'm going to—"

"Sit down here, darling. No, here. Turn your back. Now listen hard and talk fast, because you'll probably have to be on your own for a while. You can tell me the whole story as soon as I can get you away from here. Meanwhile, tell me this: Why were you meeting Dorwin?"

"Well, Hugh said he wanted to explain about somebody trying to involve me in a scandal—some radio gossip."

"What scandal?"

"There isn't any, Phil. Not really. But I did go to Hugh Dorwin's alone—at night. And there was this awful man, this Underwood, watching me come out. Then there's that letter . . . Phil, I don't know what my father would do if I got mixed up in—"

"In a murder? You're already in it, from all the signs. And you're just afraid of your father?"

The girl shook her head. "Somebody killed Hugh Dorwin," she said. "Suppose it's the person who wrote me that letter? Suppose he thinks I *am* mixed up with Dorwin? Suppose he wants to kill me, too?"

Manning suddenly remembered the curious change in Dorwin's face as he picked up the big portfolio just as he left the office, not long ago. He asked: "Do you know anything about a portfolio—a large red portfolio tied with blue tapes?"

The girl made a queer, moaning sound.

Manning remembered that Dorwin had said: "Klawitz may hurt you. Klawitz may try to use a woman's name." Perhaps the portfolio contained old love letters. Or innocent letters that might be misconstrued. Dorwin had said: "You mustn't lose your faith in anyone." Well, he wouldn't. But he would have to find that red portfolio before the police did. If there was any incriminating evidence in it, anything that might link the girl to Dorwin, he would get rid of it. Meanwhile he would have to keep Betty out of the hands of the police. He wouldn't try to abet a guilty-looking escape, naturally, but he would like to delay the inevitable questioning as long as possible, to give him time to establish her innocence.

"Just remember one thing," he said. "Forget about Dorwin. If anybody asks you, you came here to meet me after work. We were going out for a drink together. Come on."

Manning glanced at the crowd around H. H. Dorwin. The rear ranks parted to let a man come through. The man had a professional air about him and was probably a doctor.

Tim still guarded the only exit from the reading room. He was thoroughly enjoying the exercise of authority, and his Mark Twain mustache seemed to have assumed a martial twist. It was more like a Marshal Foch mustache, as he gave orders to his constantly arriving reinforcements. Half a dozen of his fellow guards had taken up their posts at strategic points, and several special investigators whose normal duties were to watch for vandals and book thieves had come into the room.

Manning took Betty's arm and guided her toward Tim. Two uniformed policemen from a squad car came up behind the guard as Manning and the girl approached.

"Sorry, Mr. Manning." Tim continued to bar the way. "Nobody's allowed to leave. The police are here."

Another squad of bluecoats came through from the Catalogue Room in single file. Manning watched them out of the corner of his eye as he asked Cornish: "Is he here, Tim?"

"I'm not sure," the guard replied. "Berger thought he saw him come in."

"If he's not here, somebody else had the same idea," Manning said.

"I know," Tim Cornish stepped closer to whisper in Manning's ear: "There's Klawitz, Mr. Manning."

Manning started. "Where, Tim?"

"Over there, halfway across the room—reading just like nothing happened."

Manning looked in the direction indicated by Tim's nod. Eight tables away, apparently oblivious of the hubbub around him, Feodor Klawitz was serenely poring over a book. The burnished curve of his naked pate, gleaming in the light of the overhead fixtures, was the only spot of calm in the room. A beribboned monocle screwed disdainfully into one eye, his ivory jowls devoid of any show of emotion, Klawitz quietly turned a page.

"I think we can leave Mr. Klawitz to the police, Tim. By the way, who called the cops?"

"I did, Mr. Manning."

"I'll be with you in a minute, Tim—if you need me," he said. "Come on, Betty."

The girl came with him silently.

"Listen hard," Manning said, as they walked between the reading tables. "What you have to do now is this: Make yourself as inconspicuous as possible until I find out what happened to that red portfolio of yours. When I locate it, we can discuss future strategy. Yes?"

"Of course—if you say so."

"Then find yourself a seat down at the south end of the room. Slip into the American History Collection if you can do it neatly. Wait until I come for you—and stick to your story."

He gave the girl's arm an affectionate pinch and watched her walk away.

When he turned back to Tim Cornish, the police were arriving in force.

The uniformed detectives were already widely deployed about the reading room, dripping melted snow all over the erudite terrain. A platoon of specialists tramped in, unslinging cameras, tripods, and cases of clue-gathering apparatus. They were all obviously awaiting instructions from a small, inoffensive-looking man in mufti, who in turn was intently watching a husky, big-boned, bushy-haired medical examiner make a preliminary survey of the Dorwin corpse.

Manning skirted the center of police operations, hoping against hope that he could start his surreptitious search for the red portfolio without attracting attention. He was wrong.

"Hey, you!" The small man in mufti halted him with a slight side motion of his head. "Where do you think you're going?"

"I'm Philip Manning. I'm a member of the library staff. I don't think I got your name."

The small man grunted. "Kenneth Kilkenny, Homicide Squad." The detective did not look at Manning as he talked. The snow-filled crease of his slouch hat fed a rivulet that trickled off the brim to extinguish his cigarette, thus complying with library regulations. He continued to watch the medical examiner. "I don't think we need you, Manning," he said.

"I think you do," Manning contradicted. "I saw the whole show. You'll want me to go over the scene with you."

Kilkenny grunted again. "Wait till Doc Rosenkohl gets through here," he said.

"I'm through, Kenny—and you can turn your bloodhounds loose," the medical examiner said.

"What do I look for, Rosie—swords, pistols, or a blunt instrument?" the detective asked him.

"The man's been stabbed through the left eye," Dr. Rosenkohl replied. "But I can't tell you until after the autopsy if that's what killed him."

A pair of scissors could have done it, Manning thought; or some tool from the bindery downstairs.

"Whatever it was, we'll find it," Kilkenny declared. "How soon can you get into him, Rosie?"

"I'll ride down to Bellevue with him now, if you want," said the medical examiner.

"You'd better, Rosie. I can't keep a thousand bookworms here all week. I never saw so many suspects at one murder since Madcap Maisie Clark got shot on the stage of Bensky's Burlicue Theatre. What's the capacity here?"

"Nearly eight hundred seats in both North and South Reading Rooms," Manning replied. "There are probably about two hundred people in this room."

"Any way to get from one room to the other except through that passage at the end there?"

"A member of the staff could go through the delivery-desk enclosure, but nobody else could," Manning said. "I've been here from the moment Mr. Dorwin toppled off the balcony, and I know Tim Cornish has had the exit blocked from the first, so there's been no chance of anyone leaving the South Room."

"We'll let the folks in the North Room go as soon as I've talked to the staff," Kilkenny said.

"Here's something, Kenny," said Dr. Rosenkohl. He handed over the .22 caliber pistol the late H. H. Dorwin had picked up off the floor while Cornish was pursuing Underwood down the stairs. "Found it in his pocket," the medical examiner added.

Kilkenny sniffed the muzzle. Holding the butt through a handkerchief, he examined the gun. "One shot gone," he said.

"And here's something else." Dr. Rosenkohl made the announcement with the triumphant ring of a prospector pouncing on a nugget. He pried open the dead man's fingers. Dorwin's hand had been clasped upon a roughly triangular scrap of paper.

The ragged edge of the hypotenuse, which was about four inches long, indicated that the fragment might have been torn from the corner of a heavy sheet of white paper. On it was drawn in light-blue ink a series of curious signs and symbols: Shaded curves, strange curlicues, angles, lines, dots, and tiny circles, all in queer combinations. Manning looked at the paper anxiously over the detective's shoulder.

"Hieroglyphics!" Kilkenny declared. "Maybe I'd better start looking for Egyptians!"

"It could be Sanskrit," said Dr. Rosenkohl.

At the word Sanskrit something cold turned over very slowly inside Phil Manning. He peered more closely at the scrap of paper in the detective's hand. Below the cabalistic symbols something had been written in pencil and then rubbed out. It was a single word, something that might be "Dharini" or "Dhavini" or something equally without sense. Manning was pretty sure the strange characters were not Sanskrit, but the restless lump of cold continued to stir in his viscera. He lifted his gaze, seeking Betty Vale.

He saw her almost at once, and the sight of her gave him another unpleasant turn. She was standing at the far end of the room, where he had told her to go, but she was talking to a dark, slick-haired young man who was quite unessential to Manning's personal happiness: Dave Benson.

"Okay, Manning," said Detective Kilkenny, breaking in on Manning's thoughts, "I'm ready to hear your story of what happened."

Manning took a last look at Betty Vale, at her silken legs extending below her beaver coat. They were pretty legs, exciting legs—but there was no doubt that the muscles of the calves, however graceful, were exceedingly well developed. He wondered whether Kilkenny, after he had followed the inevitable course of his investigation, would recognize them as the legs of a dancer.

The tumult and the shouting in the South Reading Room had long since subsided to an uneasy murmur. The late H. H. Dorwin had departed on a stretcher. Another platoon of police had arrived, headed by several gold badges, and including policewomen for searching female suspects. The gold badges had already established headquarters at the table nearest the exit and had started their preliminary questioning of the bookish horde before passing them out.

"All right. Spill it," said Kilkenny. "Where were you standing and just what did you see?"

Manning led the detective to the spot from which he had witnessed Dorwin's plunge.

As he listened, Kilkenny seemed to be memorizing the geography of the South Reading Room. His eyes roved over the west wall, which was a mass of books for its entire length and to a height of about twenty feet, where the great arched windows began. There were twelve tiers of bookshelves—the upper six reached from the gallery which jutted out above the lower six. A staff desk and four equally-spaced doors were all that broke the straight sweep of the gallery, which was just wide enough to allow the doors to be swung inward. Under the gallery was a supplemental bank of shelves, a long three-tiered bookcase which stood well out from the wall and ran the entire length of the room like a counter as high as the top button of a man's vest. There was only one door behind this counter, the one which opened into the short spiral staircase leading to the gallery. The detective interrupted Manning to point to this door, which was about thirty feet south of the oak-barred grating that marked the end of the delivery enclosure.

"When Dorwin took his nose-dive, was that door open?" Kilkenny asked.

"It was ajar, as I remember," Manning replied. "It stood open only a foot or so—not enough for me to see into the stairway."

"You didn't see anybody come out?"

"No."

"What are those other doors up there on the gallery? Do they lead to other stairways?"

"No, they just open on little two-by-four balconies on the outside of the building. They're opened in summer for ventilation."

"The outside balconies are big enough for a man to hide on, aren't they?"

"Yes," said Manning, "but the bronze outside doors are kept locked."

"We'll check, anyhow. Is there any other way to reach the gallery except by that spiral staircase?"

"No . . . except for the catwalk along the top of that wooden colonnade in front of the delivery desk. It connects with the gallery on the other side of the room. But anyone using that would be in plain view, and I can swear that nobody else was in sight on the gallery or the catwalk when Dorwin toppled over the railing."

"Then how did the murderer get out of the spiral staircase, since nobody saw him?"

"I don't know," said Manning—but he did know. He had figured it out while he was talking to Kilkenny. It was the only way possible. The murderer, bent double, could come out of the half-open door without being seen, because he—or she—would have been hidden by the parapet of the outer line of bookcases. While all eyes were on the spectacle of Dorwin's plunge from the gallery, he could make his crouching way half the length of the room behind the protection of this low wall of books. When he straightened up, he would be merely someone looking for a book, far from the scene of excitement.

There was no use of giving this theory to Kilkenny now, however. Manning needed an excuse for getting around a bit, to look for that red portfolio.

"I'd better look around on the gallery," he said.

"And what do *you* expect to find on the gallery, Manning?"

"Brain prints." Manning was improvising. "I thought if we looked at the books on this section of the balcony, we might get a line on what sort of man Dorwin was meeting."

Kilkenny pondered briefly. "Can't hurt anything, I guess," he said. "I'll go up with you."

Manning took two steps and then stopped. Halfway across the room he saw the shabby, unshaven little man whom Dorwin had called James Underwood. Underwood looked furtively about him as he talked, scarcely moving his lips, to a young woman in blue—a sinuous, luscious-looking blonde whom Manning recognized with a start as the woman he had nearly bowled over at the door to his office.

"What did you see?" Kilkenny said.

"The murderer," Manning blurted.

"Where?"

Manning hesitated no longer. "Right over here." He wheeled, starting off with long strides.

"Point him out." Kilkenny walked rapidly beside Manning—until Manning stopped again.

"Funny," he said. "He was standing right there a few seconds ago. He's gone now."

"How do you know he's the murderer? Did you see him kill Dorwin?"

"No, but he took a shot at Dorwin this afternoon, so I assume—"

"You don't have to assume. I can call headquarters and get all the details."

"Headquarters won't have the details," Manning said. "The police weren't called."

"Dorwin got shot at, and he didn't call the police? Say, what are you—?"

"I don't know why," Manning said. "But that gun you found in Dorwin's pocket is the one this man shot at him with. I saw Dorwin pick it up."

"But the man who did it disappeared in thin air?"

"He must be here," Manning insisted. "I just saw him."

"You wouldn't be trying to pull a fast one, would you, Manning?"

"Of course not," Manning replied.

"Then come on," said the detective. "If there really is a guy who shot at Dorwin, he won't get out of the room. I'll have time for him later."

The marble steps that spiraled upward about the short twist of aluminum-painted frame were densely populated by police technicians. Two men were dusting powdered graphite on the walls, and two others were busy with oblique lighting and a long-nosed fingerprint camera. They stood aside to let Kilkenny and Manning past.

"Getting much?" Kilkenny asked.

"Nothing to speak of," said the man with the camera. "We dusted that bronze outside door on the landing, but it hasn't been opened."

"You didn't find anything that might have been dropped?" Manning asked. "No weapon, for instance?"

"Nope. Nothing."

And there was no place within the staircase that the red portfolio could have been secreted.

Manning and the detective stepped out on the gallery. Manning immediately turned his attention to the six tiers of bookshelves to the right of the door. Ostensibly he was examining the titles of the volumes so that he could tell the detective the sort of man Dorwin had been meeting. Actually he was looking to see if the red portfolio had been concealed among the books, or behind them. He was having no luck.

"Good lord! Indians!"

The exclamation came from Detective Kilkenny, who was on his knees, peering at the bottom row of books on the opposite side of the door.

"There's been a scalping," the detective added, taking a pair of tweezers from his pocket. He removed a handsome thatch of wavy red hair which was caught on the edge of the books and had been half hidden by the open door.

"Klawitz!" declared Manning.

"You mean the guy on the radio?"

"That's right. Klawitz, the Highbrow's Winchell. He has at least a dozen toupees he wears to match his moods. Apparently he's in a naked mood today. That's him down there in Seat 274."

Kilkenny looked over the railing at the polished scalp of

Feodor Klawitz, who was still engrossed in his reading.

"Was this baldy-locks a good friend of the deceased?" he asked.

"Friend? I should say not. Dorwin was trying to get Klawitz jugged for libel."

"He was, eh?" Kilkenny pursed his lips reflectively. "I think we better ask him how he came to forget his pretty auburn hair up here. Come along and prompt me, Manning."

Manning followed the detective down the winding stairs, stepping over and around the technicians. The portfolio probably wouldn't be on the gallery anyhow, because the murderer himself had not appeared there. Manning was convinced, however, that the murderer had wrested the portfolio from Dorwin's hands at the time the trustee was killed. There seemed no other explanation for the scrap of paper in the dead man's fingers—unless, of course, it had been placed there deliberately to misdirect suspicion.

The detective marched straight to Klawitz's table.

"You're Feodor Klawitz?" said Kilkenny.

Klawitz looked up haughtily. He adjusted his monocle as though to say: Naturally, everyone knows who I am.

"You act pretty damn cool and collected for a man about to be arrested for murder," Kilkenny continued.

"Murder?" Klawitz echoed coldly.

"Sure, murder, I guess you've been so deep in your books that you don't even know that H. H. Dorwin was just killed here."

"Oh, that!" The corners of Klawitz's mouth turned down in a sarcastic crescent. "Neither the life nor death of H. H. Dorwin is of any particular importance compared to the work I am now doing. I am preparing to deliver the message of Demosthenes to the American people."

Kilkenny turned to Manning. "Who's this guy Demosthenes?"

"A Greek gent who died about two thousand years before the American people were invented," Manning replied. "Mr. Klawitz probably got his message by direct wire from the Hereafter."

"Bosh!" said Klawitz, flipping over a few pages. "Listen to this: 'There is one safeguard known generally to the wise, which is an advantage and security to all, but especially to democracies as against despots. What is it? Distrust!' True, Demosthenes was trying to rouse the Athenians from their supine smugness, trying to warn them against that other treaty-breaker, Philip of Macedon. But his Philippics are just as applicable today to—"

"Hey, wait a minute," Kilkenny cut in. "Don't change the subject. The dead man I'm interested in ain't a Greek. He's H. H. Dorwin. You killed him, Klawitz."

"Bosh! I'm not given to physical violence."

"You were violent enough in the Map Room, Mr. Klawitz," Manning said.

"I'm sorry about that," said Klawitz, without changing his disdainful expression. "I lost my temper. The stupid librarian insisted—"

"Is this yours?" Kilkenny suddenly produced the auburn toupee.

Klawitz again adjusted his monocle. "Yes," he said, extending his hand to take the wig. "Thank you very much."

"Nothing doing." The detective withdrew the toupee. "Know where I found this, Klawitz?"

"No."

"On the gallery—where Dorwin was killed."

"Really?"

"How did it get there?"

"Dropped from my pocket, undoubtedly. It frequently happens when I bend over. I must find a better way of carrying it."

"So you admit you were on the gallery, do you?"

"Yes, of course. I went there to get a book early this afternoon."

"Klawitz, you went there to meet Dorwin."

"Bosh! I should go nowhere on earth to meet Dorwin. I—" He removed his monocle and smiled with great self-satisfaction. "Now I understand," he said. "You're from the police, of course, and you want to know who killed Dorwin. You've come to the right person. I can give you a strong hint: Look for a woman, preferably a blonde woman. Dorwin was death on women so it is poetic justice that the reverse should ultimately prove true."

"You got any particular blonde in mind?" To Kilkenny, Klawitz was at last beginning to talk sense. Blondes were more comprehensible than Demosthenes.

"Yes," said Klawitz. "There was a blonde young woman on the gallery this afternoon shortly before Dorwin's death. I remember seeing her cross on that walk above the delivery desk."

Kilkenny looked at Manning.

"Was she one of the library staff?" Manning asked, feeling distinctly uncomfortable.

"Possibly. I've noticed her about frequently these past few days. A rather pretty girl. . . ."

Manning began to perspire.

"She's small and somewhat plump."

Manning felt better.

"When you arrest her, I shall be glad to identify her," Klawitz said. "But now you really must pardon me. I have a broadcast to prepare."

He was again deep in his Philippics.

Kilkenny's jaw set at a threatening angle. Then he relaxed and wagged his thumb at Manning.

"I'll needle him again later," the detective said as he walked away. "And if he's lying about that blonde on the catwalk, he'll do his next broadcast from Centre Street."

Manning hoped Klawitz was not lying about the blonde. She might well be the sinuous, sensuous, scared little blonde —"a new catalogue girl," Dorwin had called her—who had nearly collided with him coming out of his office and whom he had seen talking to Underwood.

Inasmuch as Detective Kenneth Kilkenny did not insist on his further collaboration on the problem of the blonde on the catwalk, Manning returned anxiously to the book shelves at the foot of the spiral stairway. He glanced once toward the south end of the reading room, where he had last seen Betty Vale. She was nowhere in sight, now. There was no one at the south end; the last nervous remnants of the crowd had congregated near the tables where the gold badges were conducting their inquisition, letting the innocents go home. Betty was probably beyond the open doorway which led into the small adjoining room that housed the American History Collection. Just as probably Dave Benson was with her. Manning didn't relish the idea, yet there was still the matter of the red portfolio with the blue tapes. Reluctantly he returned to the Bibliography shelves, began feverishly pulling out books.

He was halfway through the rows of Whitaker's Circulative Book List when he heard a woman scream.

The scream came from the far southern end of the room. It was muffled. All character was wrung from the voice by shrill, dry-throated terror. Yet, though he had never heard Betty scream, Manning was sure it was the voice of Betty Vale.

A crowd began to surge back toward the southwest corner of the Reading Room, where a short, straight stairway led down to the stacks. Manning followed the sudden movement of people toward the corner. His knees were of flabby cardboard, yet he forced them to function. He was only a few steps behind the hurrying Cornish, far ahead of Detective Kilkenny.

A woman was sprawled on the steps, her blonde head near the locked metal-grid door at the bottom. She was lying in a position of final abandon. Her sheer-stockinged legs pointed toward Manning, one knee crooked slightly with tragic jauntiness. The hem of her skirt was lifted diagonally across her bare thighs to spread its blue pleats over the stairs like an open fan. One arm reached back and down, in the direction her ash-blonde hair seemed to flow in silent, motionless ripples; the other arm was bent, with the back of her hand pressed across her forehead as though to ward off a blow. Her sensuous features were frozen in a grimace of dismay—the same expression that Manning had seen on her face when he almost collided with her outside his office door.

Tim Cornish went down the steps and picked up the girl tenderly in his arms.

Manning backed out through the crowd just as he saw Kilkenny edging in from the other side.

Betty Vale, as he had suspected, was just around the corner of the American History Collection partition. She stood very straight and her face was white. Dave Benson had his arm around her.

"You didn't scream," Manning said to her.

"She screamed," Benson volunteered. "She screamed bloody murder."

"She didn't scream," Manning insisted. "Remember that, Betty. You didn't scream. That other girl screamed."

"The other girl couldn't scream," Betty said. "She was already . . . She was lying on the stairs when I saw her."

"Did you see her fall?"

"No. She was just lying there. I started out, looking for you or Dave, when I saw her. I was afraid to stay in here alone any longer. Who is she, Phil?"

"I don't know," Manning said. "Where was Benson? I thought he was with you?"

"I was looking for you, Master Mind," Benson said. "I thought it was time you used your influence to get the little girl out of this place—but you were busy with the boys in blue."

"I'll take care of the little girl," Manning replied.

"If you let the cops start on her, she'll be here all night," Benson said. "They'll find out she knew Dorwin."

"You know a lot about cops for a musician," Manning said.

"Look." Benson turned on his prop smile. "I played the fiddle for pennies when I was eight years old. I got run off of all the good street corners in Manhattan, and half the apartment house courtyards. By the time I was twelve I knew more cops than anybody in a library will ever know. I didn't learn music out of books. I—"

"Did you know the girl on the stairs?" Manning interrupted.

"Never saw her before—until just now with Betty."

Manning saw Tim Cornish motioning to him. He reached out to touch Betty Vale's cold cheek and said: "I'll be right back, darling. And remember—you didn't see anything and you didn't scream."

"Look, Manning, you'd better—"

"I'll take care of her," said Manning. He walked off to join the guard who was hovering at the fringe of the crowd around the figure of the blonde in the blue dress.

"The detective wants to talk to you," Cornish said.

Manning pushed through to Kilkenny who was looking at the body of the blonde in blue, stretched on a table.

Kilkenny summoned Manning with a wag of his thumb. "Broken neck," he said. "The guard here says she worked in the library. What's her name?"

"I don't know her name," Manning replied. "She's new here. I think she was a catalogue girl."

"Get her name for me," Kilkenny demanded. "Maybe when we know her name we'll know whether she fell down the stairs or got pushed down."

Kilkenny was walking toward the delivery enclosure, toward the tables where the gold badges were still questioning people. Manning walked beside him.

"She didn't fall down," Manning said.

"She wore damned high heels."

"Why don't you ask Klawitz if—"

"I'm ahead of you, Manning. Klawitz just looked at her. He says she was the blonde on the catwalk, all right."

"And you still think she fell down the stairs?"

"Why not? Klawitz thinks she killed Dorwin. She could have been trying to sneak out in a hurry."

"That door at the foot of the stairs is locked," Manning said.

"If she worked in the library, she'd have a key, wouldn't she?" Kilkenny asked.

"She might. Mind if I guess, too?"

"Go on and guess."

"I'll guess you ought to start looking for a thin, shabby-looking man in a shiny blue-serge suit," Manning said. "He's about five-feet-four. He's got prematurely gray hair that needs cutting, and a two-day stubble on his face. His eyes—"

"I was wondering if you were going to bring him up again, Manning." The detective stopped walking, turned on Manning with bland warning in his grin. "Why didn't you tell me his name was Underwood?"

"How did you know?"

"I get around," said Kilkenny.

"So you've arrested Underwood?"

"Why arrest him? He didn't kill anybody. He couldn't have. He wasn't in the reading room."

"I'm pretty sure I saw him."

"Must of been two other guys," said the detective. "Underwood offered to give himself up to one of our boys in the outside corridor—clear outside the Catalogue Room. Said he knew he'd be suspected eventually so he wanted to tell his story now. They brought him inside and I heard him talking to the lieutenant."

"Underwood is the man who took a shot at Dorwin this afternoon," Manning said, "with that gun you found in Dorwin's pocket."

"You see him shoot?"

"Well, no," Manning admitted. "But I heard the shot. I saw the gun on the floor, where Underwood dropped it, and I saw Underwood running away."

"That's what Underwood said you'd say," Kilkenny observed. "He claims he was coming in the library to get out of the cold, when he heard the shot. He saw Dorwin and he saw the gun on the floor—so he ran. He used to work for Dorwin about a year ago—had some sort of row with him, in fact—so his first impulse was to scram. When he got thinking about it, he came back to tell his story."

"And you let him go—just on his own story?" Manning was incredulous.

"We didn't let him go all the way. He's still in the library. The lieutenant didn't give him a pass for the street door."

"Good," said Manning. "Because that gun—"

"That gun's the reason the lieutenant believes him," Kilkenny broke in. "We're not amateurs, Manning. We traced the number. The gun belongs to a woman. It's covered by a pistol permit issued a year ago to a lady called Viola Smith, who lived with her papa and mama, Mr. and Mrs. H. R. Smith at 120 East 18th Street."

"That's funny," Manning said.

"In case you can't guess," Kilkenny continued, "I'll tell you that some of my boys are digging up the vital statistics on Miss Smith at this very moment. Now what about the blonde in blue?"

"Here's the man who can tell you about her," Manning replied. He indicated a round little man who was approaching with Tim Cornish. "This is Mr. Leonard of the cataloguing department."

Mr. Leonard was slightly green around the gills, and his bulging eyes announced that he had already seen the blonde in the blue dress. He stammered with excitement as he said to the detective:

"It—it's the girl who came to work last week. Mr. Dorwin recommended her. She—"

"What's her name?" snapped Kilkenny.

"W-why her name was Viola Smith," said Mr. Leonard.

Manning chuckled. "Still think Miss Smith fell down the stairs, Kilkenny?" he asked.

Kilkenny did not answer—perhaps because at that moment a plainclothesman handed him a leaf from a notebook.

As Kilkenny glanced at the sheet of paper, the plainclothesman said: "I just come from Dorwin's office, Kenny. I copied this dope off his desk pad. It's his engagements for today."

"Okay, thanks," said Kilkenny. He stuffed the paper into his pocket—but not before Manning, staring over his shoulder, had read the line: "Betty Vale—4:30 P.M., Library."

Manning moistened his lips. "You don't need me any more now, do you, Kilkenny?"

"You'll stay right with me now," Kilkenny declared. "You've got ideas on this whole business—too many. Come on."

The detective led Manning into the delivery enclosure. The thick, colored trays in which the books came up in the elevators from the stacks were piled on the tables, but the desk staff and the book-laden hand trucks had been cleared out. The police had evidently shut down the reference department for the night, and Kilkenny was using the delivery desk for his own research.

Three librarians were awaiting Kilkenny, and when Manning saw them, he knew what they had been doing. One of the men was Dr. Flack, whose full black beard was as much an ornament to the Library as his knowledge of Egyptology. The second was Dr. de Winnah, who had only a half portion of whiskers, but who was a well-known Orientalist. The third was Dr. Bellows, who had no beard and no neck, but had plenty of forehead and oversized eyes which looked even more tremendous through his thick spectacles. Dr. Bellows collected rare dialects of the Near East. Obviously the three experts had been studying the cryptic symbols on the scrap of paper found in the dead hand of H. H. Dorwin.

"Well, gents?" said Kilkenny. "What's the lowdown on the hieroglyphics?"

"They're not hieroglyphs—definitely." Dr. Flack stated.

"And obviously the characters are not cuneiform," added Dr. Bellows.

"There is a slight resemblance to Phoenician in this letter—and this," intoned Dr. de Winnah. "However, I imagine the similarity is purely accidental."

"In other words, you birds are stumped," said Detective Kilkenny. "What do you make of the hen tracks, Manning?"

"Just that," Manning replied. "Phone-booth etchings. Keep-on-ringing-them arabesques."

"I don't quite agree with you, Manning," said Dr. Flack. "There seems to be too much of a plan to allow for a subconscious explanation."

"I suggest the characters may be mathematical or scientific symbols of some sort," said Dr. de Winnah. "Engineering, perhaps."

"Why not try the technical librarians?" said Dr. Bellows.

"I'll try every expert you've got here and then send uptown to Columbia for more if you fellows can't crack it," Kilkenny said.

"I'll crack it," Manning volunteered. He held out his hand. "Let's have the puzzle."

"No soap," said Kilkenny.

"You don't think I can crack it?"

"Sure you can, Manning. But without the diagrams. You'll do it with mirrors."

"Do I get half an hour?"

"I'll give you an hour."

"And the right to circulate?"

"Inside the building. I don't want you to leave the building."

"I just want to get to my office on the second floor. Okay?"

Kilkenny chewed an imaginary toothpick for a few seconds. Then he took a card from his pocket, scribbled on it, and handed it to Manning without a word.

Manning instantly left the oaken corral of the delivery desk and headed south for Betty Vale. He had not taken twenty steps before his path crossed the suavely gliding course of Dave Benson.

"Hi!" said Benson, with a challenging smile. "Did you fix it for the little girl?"

"She's fixed, all right," Manning replied.

"Then she can leave now with me?"

"She'd better not."

"I expected something like that." Benson expanded his white smile by a full inch. "I'll go to bat for her myself."

"Lay off, will you, Benson?" Manning gripped the musician's arm. "Betty's in a spot. You know that. So don't even call attention to the fact that she's here."

"Betty's old man knows the District Attorney," Benson said. "I'm going out and start the wheels within wheels."

"The hell you're going out."

"Sure I am." Benson flourished a police pass. "I've just been through the works. All tests strictly negative. Goodbye, Manning."

Manning watched Benson's rhythmic exit. Then he resumed his quest for Betty Vale.

The south end of the Reading Room was deserted again. The mortal remains of Viola Smith, the blonde catalogue girl with a pistol permit, had been spirited away by the medical examiner's office. Two moulage men, with their plaster-dusted fingers and shellac sprayers, came out of the stairway to the stackrooms—apparently empty-handed. Manning waited until they sauntered off. Then he found Betty, still waiting anxiously just around the corner in the American History Collection.

She arose eagerly, but before she could speak, he said hurriedly: "Listen hard, because the police will be looking for you in about half a sec. I've got to know a lot of things before they monopolize you."

"But how—?"

"They've got Dorwin's desk pad. We'll go where we won't be disturbed until I'm good and ready."

"Where, Phil?"

"Take my arm and follow, darling."

Betty obediently hooked her slim fingers about his elbow. They walked to the head of the descending stairs to the stacks. Manning stopped.

"Turn around," he said. "And when I give the word, go down quickly but deliberately."

"Go down—*there?*" Betty's eyes widened. She stared as though she still saw the crumpled body of the blonde in blue sprawled on the steps.

Manning didn't reply at once. He carefully surveyed the room, watching until he thought no one at the other end of the room was looking in his direction. Then he said quietly, "Now."

Betty moved swiftly down the steps. Manning was right behind her, his keys already in his hand. He unlocked the metal-grid door, pushed the girl into the bookstacks ahead of him, closed the door.

He felt Betty recoil against him as though she were shying from the sudden vista of whiteness: the white corridor stretching far between the white end-panels of the steel bookcases, the low white ceiling with its long row of lights, the white marble floor.

"Now," he said. "I want the whole story."

"Of what, Phil?"

"Everything. Let's start with Dhavini."

Betty gasped. "You mean Dharini?"

"All right, Dharini. Who is she?"

"She's King Agnimitra's senior queen. You've been snooping."

"Do you know where I got the name Dharini—even if I got it wrong?"

"Certainly," the girl replied. "From Kalidasa's *Malavika and Agnimitra.*"

"No. From a scrap of paper that H. H. Dorwin held in his hand when he was killed. I recognized your writing—the *r* that looks like a *v*—and vice versa. There were hieroglyphics on the paper, too."

Betty paled. She thrust her hands deep into her muff and fixed Manning with round, frightened eyes.

"Did the scrap of paper come from that red portfolio Dorwin was carrying?" Manning continued.

"It—it might have. I guess it did."

"I don't know what happened to the portfolio or when and where it's going to turn up," Manning said. "But sooner or later Detective Kilkenny is going to find out that the hieroglyphics are ballet-dancer's shorthand. Then, when he runs down all the ramifications and finds out that one leads to you, he's going to ask a lot of questions. I want the answers now. Who—?"

"Phil, where in the world did you learn to read choreographic notation?"

"In the Louvain Library. I happened to have a job there re-cataloguing Feuillet, Magny, Guillemin, and the other old masters who invented ways of writing down dance steps with conventional symbols."

"You're wonderful, Phil."

"Save those lovely lapel drawings, darling. So the Kalidasa research was for a ballet?"

"An original oriental ballet—called *Malavika.* I'm going to dance the title role."

"You also did the choreography, apparently. Who did the music?"

The girl lowered her eyes. "Dave," she said.

"Benson!" Manning made an aspirin grimace. "And did Benson by any chance give Dorwin the score of *Malavika* this afternoon?"

"He did not. I did—day before yesterday." Betty looked Manning full in the eyes.

"Why?" Manning demanded.

"Because Hugh Dorwin was going to put up the money to produce the ballet," the girl said. "He was going to put up twenty thousand dollars."

Manning frowned. "That doesn't make sense," he said. "Your Old Man makes a million dollars out of other people's headaches, and still you go to Dorwin for a measly twenty grand. Why?"

"Father doesn't want any ballets in the family," Betty said. "He doesn't approve of careers for women. Not for me, anyhow. He thinks woman's place is on the society page. That's why I haven't even told him I was going to that ballet school in the Village. That's why I didn't even tell you."

"I thought it was because Dave Benson played piano down there," Manning said. "Was it Benson's idea to get Dorwin to angel the ballet?"

"Well, yes. Dave thought if the ballet could be produced and made a hit, Father wouldn't oppose my career any more."

"And might even accept Benson as a son-in-law?"

"Phil, you're being catty. Dave's been terribly sweet."

"All right, he's been terribly sweet," Manning said. "And he went to H. H. Dorwin for the sugar?"

"Yes. He knew Hugh Dorwin was a patron of the arts, but he didn't know he was an old friend of the Vale family. When Hugh heard my name, he immediately offered to put up the money—and I began to get scared. I hurried out to see Hugh, to explain that Father didn't know anything about *Malavika.* I asked Hugh to keep my secret until opening night."

"And H. H. Dorwin made passes at you," Manning suggested.

"Only with his eyes, Phil. But I was afraid of the gleam. I was afraid—well, that his interest wasn't entirely artistic. I told him so. I told him I wanted his help only on a basis of artistic merit. I insisted on bringing him the score, the choreography, the maquettes—in the red portfolio. He was going to give me a decision today. And then I got that anonymous letter. . . ."

She looked at Manning with eyes as big as sapphires in Cartier's window. They had been that way just a few seconds before Dorwin died.

"Did Benson know you were meeting Dorwin here today?" Manning asked.

"I don't think so. . . ." The girl spoke hesitantly. "Dave knew that Hugh was to put up the money today, but I don't think I told him where I was meeting Hugh, Phil! What do you mean?"

"Maybe Dorwin was going to change his mind. Maybe he didn't like Benson's score."

"That's no reason for murder, Phil. Dave and I have confidence in the ballet. We know it will get backing on its own. The music is really superb. Everyone who's heard it is crazy about it."

"Who, for instance?"

"Well, a man from Transcontinental Broadcasting heard Dave run over the score on the piano. You know, Dave won second prize with a quartet in the Transcontinental chamber music competition last week. He's got talent, Phil."

"He's got something, all right," said Manning glumly. "Does the name Viola Smith mean anything to you?"

"Nothing."

"All right. Now I have an idea. You wait for me here in the stacks," said Manning.

The girl looked about her uneasily. "Alone?" she asked.

"You won't be alone. You have all the wisdom of the ages to keep you company—sixty-seven miles of it."

Betty smiled nervously. She looked down through the narrow ventilating slits in the marble floor at the base of each stack—narrow glimpses of more stacks on the floor below in monotonous and diminishing repetition, like reflections in a double mirror.

"The catacombs of learning." She shuddered. "Will you be long?"

"I hope not. I just want you to stay out of sight for a little while longer—and still you can truthfully say you hadn't left the building. If you run into some member of the staff, refer them to me. And don't wander too far, because there are seven floors of these stacks, and I might not find you again for years."

"And what if you *don't* find me?"

"I'll find you, darling."

"Phil . . ." The girl lifted her face. Manning bent quickly and kissed her.

He walked away rapidly, the exciting fragrance of her kiss sweet on his lips, the desperation of her fear cold in his heart.

Manning left the stacks through the second-floor exit which led through the headquarters of the cataloguing staff, where hundreds of new listings were indexed and cross-indexed daily. Viola Smith had been working here, making new cards to be added to the millions already on file, but Manning did not tarry. His own office was just down the corridor.

His office was dark as he entered. Groping for the light switch, he could see the falling snow turn to flakes of whirling gold in the glow of the windows across the courtyard. He sat at his desk, lost in thought for a moment. Then he picked up the telephone and called a friend of his in the publicity department of Transcontinental Broadcasting.

"Hello, Joe. This is Phil Manning. Did a man named Dave Benson win a prize in your chamber music contest last week?"

"Benson's real enough," the voice replied. "He won the hundred bucks, all right. Only—What's the library want to know about him, Phil?"

"It's not the library. Just personal curiosity. What's wrong?"

"Nothing's wrong. As a matter of fact, I just got up a release on Benson this afternoon, but I don't know if the front office is ready to put it out yet. Can I call you back, Phil?"

"Do that," said Manning. Instead of waiting, however, he returned to the third floor.

Manning saw Kilkenny and half a dozen other men clustered about a scared, esthetic-looking youth with blue eyes and wavy blond hair.

The detective wagged an imperative thumb at Manning.

"I think we got something here," Kilkenny said. "It says its name is Dexter P. Dexter, Junior. It had a stiletto in its pocket."

"I explained all that," protested the blond young man, pursing his lips. "It's a 15th Century Italian stiletto. There's a coat-of-arms engraved on the hilt. I was doing some heraldic research on the coat-of-arms for a client of mine. I'm a genealogist."

"Mr. Dorwin was stabbed through the left eye with a weapon narrow enough to pierce the—" Kilkenny consulted the back of an envelope"—the sphenoidal fissure," he continued, "entering the brain to cause death by cerebral hemorrhage. I just got the autopsy report from Dr. Rosenkohl. Dorwin could have lived long enough to stagger up a few stairs and out to the balcony, Rosy says, but he couldn't have yelled, because the motor-speech centers were damaged. This Mr. Dexter with the stiletto knew Dorwin."

"I never saw the man in my life," objected Dexter P. Dexter, Junior in a thin treble.

"You had correspondence with him, Mr. Dexter. You tried to sell him a phoney family tree, complete with coat-of-arms."

"Well, yes," admitted Dexter, blushing. "I did offer to do some genealogical research for him. I thought I had traced his forebears."

"And Dorwin wrote back that he was a self-made man," said Kilkenny. "He said that most of his ancestors never had a decent coat, let alone a coat-of-arms—and that he was going to have you kicked out of the National Genealogical Society and maybe get you jugged for using the mails to defraud. We got copies of the correspondence."

Dexter P. Dexter, Junior lowered his long lashes and pressed his esthetic fingers nervously against his temples. "Evidently I was working on the wrong Dorwin family," he said. "We all make mistakes."

Kilkenny turned abruptly to Manning. "What about those hen-tracks you were going to translate for me?" he demanded.

"No luck yet," Manning replied.

"Then quit trying. I got the answer right here. Those funny marks are what ballet dancers use to write down their jumps and swan dives. It's like a code."

"No fooling!" said Manning.

"And that's one reason I'm sort of interested in Mr. Dexter, here. He looks like an adagio dancer to me."

"How did you find out about the code?"

"Your music librarian was up here just now and spotted it."

"Very smart of you to send for him," said Manning.

"Hell, I didn't send for him," the detective admitted. "He really came up to tell us that Dorwin was in the Music Library about five minutes before he was killed."

"What was he doing there?"

"He just walked in, picked up an envelope off the librarian's desk, and walked out again. He was alone, the librarian said, and he had a red portfolio under his arm."

"Where did the envelope come from?" Manning asked.

"Somebody left it on the desk while the librarian was busy somewhere else. He didn't see who it was. It was addressed to Dorwin, and the librarian was going to send it over to the Trustees' Room when Dorwin came in and got it. What was in the red portfolio, Manning?"

"Knowing Dorwin, I'd guess etchings," Manning said.

The telephone on the delivery desk rang. A policeman answered and motioned to Kilkenny.

The detective took the instrument, said "Hello, Brannigan," then, except for an occasional grunt, lapsed into scowling silence. When he came back to Manning his face was grim.

"Did you know Viola Smith was married?"

"No."

"Smith was her maiden name," said Kilkenny. "Legally she was Mrs. James Underwood."

"Good God."

"She and Underwood used to work for Dorwin in his private library up on Fifth Avenue. A year ago Dorwin thought up some cute extra assignments for Mrs. U. to do after hours, and Underwood resigned for both of 'em. Dorwin accepted Underwood's resignation, but kept his wife on the payroll. He just shifted her down here a week ago. I don't know why—yet. But the thing begins to make sense now. The old story: Irate Husband Kills Guilty Pair."

"Any more theories, Kilkenny?" Manning sat down.

"Yes." The detective looked at Manning narrowly. "Where's this Betty Vale?"

Manning made what he thought was a gesture of astonishment. "Why ask me?"

"Because she's a friend of yours. The Oriental expert with the goat whiskers said you were with her in the Oriental Library this afternoon."

"That was hours ago."

"She was supposed to meet Dorwin at four-thirty. Did she?"

"Not that I know of. Anyhow, why waste your time on Miss Vale, when you let James Underwood roam the library? Haven't you even tried—?"

Manning broke off suddenly. The lights winked out.

Somewhere in the darkness there was a flurry of sound—running feet, something overturned, an avalanche of books falling, an agonized series of gasps. The noises seemed to come from somewhere close by, perhaps the North Reading Room.

Manning sprang up, his scalp tingling. Through the blackness of the Catalogue Room he could see figures hurrying through the oblong of light that was the door to the third-floor atrium. Flashlight beams stabbed the darkness, swinging, darting forward, converging.

When the lights came on again, Detective Kilkenny was wrestling with a man with sleek black hair.

Even before the black hair slid off to reveal a shiny bald pate, Manning recognized Feodor Klawitz and one of his toupees.

"What," demanded the detective, forcing Klawitz into a chair, "do you think you're doing?"

"But I told you I must leave here."

"And I told you you couldn't," countered Kilkenny.

"But my broadcast—"

"Canceled," said the detective.

From the next room, Manning heard excited voices. He left Klawitz and the detective, rushed through the passageway at the end of the delivery-desk enclosure.

In a corner of the North Reading Room, men were bending over something near the Photostat Desk, their flashlights focused on the floor.

As Manning approached, someone switched on the heavy chandeliers overhead.

There, propped up against the Photostat Desk, his eyes

bulging, his uniform coat ripped open, his white hair disheveled, was Tim Cornish.

The motionless figure of the big guard was surrounded by a litter of papers. The Photostat Desk behind him was a picture of disorder. Drawers had been pulled out and obviously ransacked. Filing cards were strewn over the floor.

Kilkenny came in from the South Reading Room, accompanied by another plainclothesman.

"Nobody could of got out, Kenny," the other detective said. "Not even in the dark nobody could of got out. I was right in the doorway all the time."

"People could have gone back and forth between the North and South Rooms in the dark," Manning suggested. "People by the name of Klawitz, for instance."

"Shut up!" said Kilkenny. "Cornish is coming around."

Tim slowly raised his hand to his head. He blinked. Then he tried to get up.

Two uniformed policemen helped him to his feet. He leaned weakly against the desk, looked from one to the other, then grinned at Manning.

"The law hath not been dead, though it hath slept," Tim said, touching the ends of his white mustache.

"All's well that ends well, Tim," said Manning. He was genuinely relieved. He had thought Tim was the third corpse of the day.

"Wrong, Mr. Manning. *Measure for Measure.*"

"What happened, Tim?"

"Nothing," said the guard. "That is, I don't know exactly. I heard somebody in here—prowling around back of the Photostat Desk, I thought. When I started in to investigate, the lights went out. I felt somebody brush past me, and I grabbed him. Then something cracked me in the head, and I guess I was out for a minute. I think he hit me with a book."

"With a complete Shakespeare," Manning smiled.

"Whoever it was practically undressed you, Cornish," said Detective Kilkenny. "Did he steal anything?"

"Probably not." Cornish felt of his pockets. "Who steals my purse steals—Hey! My keys!"

Keys! Manning's glance swept to the northwest corner of the vast room where, within the glass-walled enclosure of the Theatre Collection, a short, straight stairway led steeply downward. Like the parallel staircase in the South Reading Room, these steps ended at a metal-grilled door to the stack-rooms. With Tim Cornish's keys, the killer could open this door—and Betty Vale was in the stacks!

Manning felt the cold perspiration beading his fore-head. He said: "Maybe you left the keys in your civvies, Tim."

"I don't think so, Mr. Manning."

"I'll run down and take a look. I'll get the super to open your locker for me." Manning turned questioning eyes to Kilkenny. "Or will it menace the public safety, Chief?"

"Okay. Go on." Kilkenny fixed Manning with a curious stare. "But make it snappy."

Manning hurried out through the Catalogue Room, his heart pounding. He did not go directly to the stacks by the stairs in the corner, because he did not want Kilkenny to know where he was going. It was foolish, perhaps, not to make Kilkenny an out-and-out ally. Now that the killer was probably in the stacks, keeping the police out might be exposing Betty Vale to needless danger. Yet Manning was determined to play his hand alone until he had found the red portfolio with the blue tapes—until he was certain that its discovery would not point a guilty finger at Betty Vale. And he knew now where the portfolio was.

It had to be there, he told himself, as he went down the marble stairs to the second floor. The portfolio had to be in the stacks. That was the only explanation of its disappear-ance—promptly and completely—from the South Reading Room.

Manning swore at himself for not having thought of it sooner. He was so used to seeing book-laden hand trucks in the delivery enclosure that he had not noted particularly that one of them had been standing against the oak-barred grating that separated the delivery desk from a corner of the South Reading Room. The grating was only a few steps from the door to the spiral stairway, so that the person who killed Dorwin could have reached it, hidden by the parapet of the outer bookshelves, to push the portfolio—and the weapon—through the oaken bars into one of the book trucks. And Kilkenny, considering the delivery enclosure not to be part of the South Reading Room, had allowed the trucks to be removed. They were in the stack rooms now.

And the murderer evidently considered the time had come to retrieve the evidence—or rather to make doubly sure that it would never be found. Why else would he have stolen a guard's keys? Yes, he was certainly in the stacks, although Manning could not see how he hoped to locate the particular truck, once it had left the delivery enclosure. Manning was not sure he himself could find the right truck in all the six floors and many miles of stacks. It would be a hopeless task. Unless—

Yes, Manning remembered seeing pink tickets on at least one book truck that stood near the delivery desk that afternoon. Books tagged with pink slips were duplicates, of which sufficient copies were already in the reference department. Books tagged with pink slips went directly to the Duplicate Cage in Stack Six, to await transfer to other libraries. Books tagged—

Manning broke into a run. Stack Six was where he had left Betty Vale!

His footsteps made rapid, hollow echoes, like frightened heartbeats, as he entered the stacks. He went directly to the Duplicate Cage, glanced through the metal grille, then passed on. He would come back later. First he hurried to the aisle in which he had left Betty.

She was not there.

The familiar whiteness of the stacks suddenly lost its neat impersonality. The row on row of bookcases were grim bastions behind which lurked unknown perils.

"Betty."

Manning called softly. There was no response, but the sound of his own voice steadied him. He walked slowly down the center aisle, stopped, and called again.

Again there was no answer—but this time Manning heard something that made his scalp crawl: a muted footstep.

It was the merest whisper of leather on marble, but it told a story of stealth. It was not the light, clicking, high-heeled step of a woman, but a broad, solid, full-soled tread. And the sound seemed to come from the stairs which led down to Stack Five on the floor below.

Quietly, quickly, Manning made for the stairway, and went down.

There was no one in Stack Five, either—no one in sight, although the rank after rank of bookcases were a maze that might conceal a battalion. He stood a moment looking about him, his spirits oppressed by the lowness of the white ceiling, the danger of ambush in the vast labyrinth of books. Then he heard the scrape of shoe leather again.

This time the sound seemed to come from directly below him. He dropped to his knees, peered through the ventilating slot. He saw a shadow pass—a dark flicker on the floor below that was gone before he could hope to identify it.

He hurried down to Stack Four.

He had never before noticed the peculiar silence of the stack rooms at night. It was a tomb-like hush, and yet it was alive.

Someone seized Manning's arm.

He whirled, his nerves taut, his fists clenched, his free arm drawn back to strike. Then he went limp.

"Betty!" he breathed.

The girl clung to him. "You're just in time," she said. "One more minute and I'd have gone crazy."

"Why didn't you stay in Stack Six where I left you?"

"I was scared, Phil. I heard somebody walking, and I thought it was you coming back. I started out to meet you—and then I discovered that instead of following someone, I was being followed. I couldn't see anyone, but I could hear him walk a little, then stop—walk again and stop. So naturally my only thought was to get away . . ."

"But everything's all right now?"

"Of course."

"Then let's go back upstairs to Six," said Manning. "I think I know what happened to your portfolio."

Betty held tightly to his arm all the way to the Duplicate Cage. Manning opened the metal door. The little room was packed with hand trucks. The pink dupe slips decorating the volumes gave a flag-bedecked gaiety to the musty place. Manning rolled out the two carts nearest him.

"There it is!" Betty started forward.

"Don't touch it!"

Manning, too, saw the red covers. He spread a handkerchief over his fingers before grasping the portfolio. As he lifted it from the truck, something fell to the floor with a metallic clang.

"I'll be damned!" he exclaimed. "So that's what stabbed Dorwin."

He bent over a long, slender brass rod with a milled knob at one end. The other end bore dark stains, which might be blood.

"What is it?" Betty asked.

"A spindle from a catalogue drawer," Manning replied. "Funny . . ." He frowned. "It's not from the Public Catalogue Room, either."

"How do you know, Phil?"

"The spindles in the main catalogue drawers aren't like

this one," Manning said. "They're smooth all the way up, and you can pull them out by pressing a catch at the end of the drawer. This one is threaded near the knob, so it has to be unscrewed to come out. I wonder—"

Manning interrupted himself to open the portfolio. The blue tapes were untied, so that the red halves fell apart readily—at a torn page of choreographic symbols.

"Dorwin must have just opened it here when he was stabbed," said Manning. Carefully touching only the edges, he flipped over pages of costume sketches, designs for scenery, page after page of cryptic choreographic notation, the ruled sheets of music manuscript . . .

Suddenly he stood up.

"Betty, darling," he said. "I want you to get out of here right away. Do you know where the library printshop is?"

"No."

"It's in the basement. Would you be afraid to go there?"

"Alone?"

"It will be safer than the stacks, unless I miss my guess. And unless the police have shut it up, it will be full of printers working on the next issue of the *Bulletin.*"

"All right. I'll go."

"Good. Just ask the foreman for the page proofs on the Dorwin article that I sent him a memo about. Tell him to give you all the pages, including the reproductions of the Russian manuscripts. And don't come back here. Bring them to my office. I'll be there by the time you get there."

He led the girl to the ornate bronze-barred door that led from Stack Six into the vaulted hall of the Oriental catalogue. He watched her walk off toward the arcade of the second floor balcony that looked out on the semi-circular arabesque of the great window of the vestibule.

Then he locked the door and hurried back to the red portfolio. He was looking through its loose pages again when something struck him a crashing blow at the base of his skull.

He pitched forward, sprawled face downward.

Detective Kenneth Kilkenny looked at the crumpled paper the Assistant Medical Examiner placed in front of him. He read the typewritten lines:

> "I received your message, but circumstances which I will explain when I see you make it impossible for me to come to the Music Room at the hour you mentioned. However, I will meet you on the West Balcony of the South Reading Room as soon as you can come."

The signature was a scrawl which Kilkenny could not decipher. Nobody, Kilkenny was convinced, could make anything of the scrawl except Dorwin, who knew the person he had asked to meet him. "Where'd you say this came from, Rosy?" the detective asked.

"Dorwin's trousers pocket," said Dr. Rosenkohl. "Don't know how I missed it the first time over, except it was wadded into a corner. I thought you'd want it, because the typewriter ought to be easy to trace. The second leg of the small *n* is badly nicked."

"I'll say it's going to be easy to trace," Kilkenny agreed. "I got the companion piece to it."

He produced an envelope addressed: "H. H. Dorwin, Esq. To be called for." The second leg of the small *n* in "Dorwin" was nicked.

"One of the boys just dug it out of a wastebasket in this guy Manning's office," Kilkenny added.

"Where's Manning?"

"He don't know it, but he's going to be with us very shortly," said the detective. "I just—well, well, well, well! Look who's here."

Tim Cornish marched up to the delivery desk, leading a shabby little man in a blue serge suit.

"Here's your James Underwood, Mr. Kilkenny," the guard said. "I caught him in the stacks."

Kilkenny stared at Underwood. The gray-haired derelict was trembling like a man with fever. The tragic lines of his face were etched deeper than ever, and his dark, intelligent eyes were blurred with misery.

"So that's where he was hiding," said Kilkenny.

"I knew he'd be in the stacks as soon as I found my keys were gone," Tim Cornish said. "I couldn't think of any other reason he'd want my keys. So I went clear down and started up from the bottom floor. In Stack Three I discover the king of shreds and patches, just as I'd figured."

"I didn't take your keys," said Underwood at last. "I told you three times that my wife let me into the stacks. I was waiting for her to come and get me."

"He claims he doesn't know his wife is dead," Cornish said.

"I don't believe it. You're telling me this to confuse me . . . to make me give her away. . . ."

"I think you'd better come with me to the morgue, Underwood," said Dr. Rosenkohl.

"Wait a minute, Rosy. I'm not through with him yet," Kilkenny objected. "Why did your wife let you into the stacks, Underwood?"

"I . . . I threatened her," said Underwood. "We were both in the reading room when Dorwin was killed, so I knew that after the shooting of this afternoon, I'd have to get out somehow."

"You told me you had nothing to do with the shooting," Kilkenny said.

"I lied," Underwood admitted. "But I'm not lying now. When Dorwin was killed I told Viola she'd have to get me out through the stacks or I'd—"

Underwood stopped.

"Or you'd tell the police that she was Dorwin's mistress?" Kilkenny prompted.

"Then you knew?"

"We know everything," said Kilkenny. "How long ago did Dorwin give her the brush-off? Two weeks?"

"He asked her to move out of his house about two weeks ago," Underwood replied. "He got her this job in the library. I swallowed my pride and asked her to come back to me, but she was still crazy about Dorwin. She wrote anonymous letters to some girl she thought was taking her place."

"Was the girl's name Vale?"

"I believe it was. Yes. Betty Vale. And Viola wrote threatening notes to Dorwin, saying she'd give their whole history to Feodor Klawitz, who would broadcast it on the radio. She was really beside herself. That was when I decided that the best thing would be to shoot Dorwin."

"And so when you missed, you stabbed him instead?" Kilkenny suggested.

"I swear I didn't! You can hang me for it, and I suppose I'd deserve it, since I did mean to kill him—but as soon as the gun went off I knew I could never take a man's life."

"What about a woman's? What about Viola Smith?" Tim Cornish demanded.

"Why would I kill Viola?" Underwood's voice was a wail. "I loved her."

"That's why," said Kilkenny. "You were jealous. So you killed her and her lover. How did you happen to have her gun?"

"I took it with me when we separated a year ago," Underwood said. "But I didn't kill her. I didn't kill anybody."

"Did she know you shot at Dorwin with her gun?"

"Yes, I told her. I—I threatened to say she was the one who shot at him—unless she let me through the stacks. I didn't want to be found inside the reading room."

"How'd you get back in the stacks?" Kilkenny interrupted.

"I left a door ajar."

"Sounds to me like the lie direct, or at least the lie with

circumstance," volunteered Tim Cornish. "Why would this Viola Smith help you out if she thought you killed the man she loved?"

"She knew I didn't kill Dorwin," said Underwood.

"How did she know that?"

"She saw the man who killed him."

"She —*what?*"

"Viola told me she was on the catwalk above the delivery desk just before Dorwin staggered out on that gallery. From her vantage point she could see down behind that outer row of book shelves—and she saw a man come out of the door to the circular staircase, crouching down so he wouldn't be seen from the floor. She—"

"Who was it?" Kilkenny demanded.

"She didn't know him. He looked up, and she thinks he saw her. But she didn't recognize him. She didn't think she'd ever seen him before."

"Why didn't she tell us all this?" the detective asked.

"She was going to tell you," Underwood said. "She was—God, she *is* dead! I believe it now! She's dead—and that's why."

"Don't let him put on an act for you, Mr. Kilkenny," Tim Cornish said. "I still think he's got plenty to tell about what he was doing in the stacks. Take him down those steps where Viola Smith got her neck broke. Take him down those steps to the stacks and see how he acts."

"That's an idea," Kilkenny agreed. "I got a good mind to take 'em all down there. Brannigan, herd your people over to the head of those stairs, in the corner there. Come on, Cornish."

Phil Manning was stunned as he fell. Even the painful impact of his face against the marble floor did not rouse him from his dazed moment of paralysis. He felt someone leap astride his back, but he could not summon his muscles to action. Before he could fight his way back to full consciousness, long, hard fingers closed about his throat in a tight, strangling grip.

He struggled, but feebly. He could feel his strength ebbing into the agony of darkness, the emptiness of death seeping into his tortured lungs. The claws tightened on his windpipe, digging into his throat.

With a last desperate effort he squirmed, twisted, jabbed back and upward with his elbow. A grunt told him he had struck home. The crushing pressure on his windpipe relaxed for an instant. Air rushed into his aching lungs.

He heard an echo—or was it an echo?—of his involuntary cry.

A sudden lightness on his back told him his assailant had fled.

He heard the confused tramp of many footsteps.

He breathed again and again, hungrily savoring the delicious air. He got painfully to his feet. When he turned around, he saw what seemed to him a crowd pouring out of the stairway from the South Reading Room.

He recognized Detective Kenneth Kilkenny with his gun drawn. He saw Feodor Klawitz, Dr. Rosenkohl, Dave Benson, Tim Cornish, Underwood, the genealogical Dexter P. Dexter, and half a dozen policemen in and out of uniform.

"I might have known it would be you, Manning," said Kilkenny. "You better have a good story."

"I've been catching up on my reading," said Manning.

"You've been catching hell," said Tim Cornish. "You hurt, Mr. Manning?"

"Ay, beyond all surgery, Tim. Would you mind running down to the print shop to see if Betty Vale is all right? I just sent her—"

"I want to talk to that Vale dame myself," Kilkenny interrupted. "I just found out she's a dancer."

"Forget about the girl, Kilkenny. I've dug up the evidence that's going to crack your case," Manning said. "Here's the weapon that killed Dorwin."

"What is it?"

"The spindle from a catalogue drawer."

"Looks sort of long for a dagger," Kilkenny said. "How about it, Rosie?"

"It could have done the trick, all right," said Dr. Rosenkohl, "particularly if the murderer held it short when he jabbed."

"And here's the rest of the page of hieroglyphics to match the torn handful Dorwin was grabbing when he was killed," Manning said.

Kilkenny squinted at the open portfolio on the floor.

"Maybe," he growled reluctantly. "But before I let you sidetrack me again, Manning, I—"

"I'll need only one word to explain this mess," Manning broke in.

"The next word out of you," said Kilkenny, "is going to be written on a typewriter. Bring 'em along, Brannigan. And you, Cornish, show me how to get out of this place. I want to go to Manning's office."

A few minutes later Manning was seated in front of his own typewriter, taking dictation from Detective Kilkenny.

"I received your message," he wrote, "but circumstances which I will explain when I see you—"

"Well, well, well, well!" crowed Kilkenny over his shoulder. "That's plenty. The letter *n* has a nick in the second leg. What were the circumstances?"

"There weren't any circumstances," Manning replied. "And there was no nick in the second leg. There was a sock in the head."

"The note that decoyed Dorwin to the gallery to be killed was written on your typewriter. Who wrote it?"

"The man who killed Dorwin, obviously."

"In other words, you admit you killed Dorwin," said Kilkenny.

"I admit nothing of the kind. I admit I dawdled somewhat over lunch today, so that someone might have come into my office and used the typewriter while my assistant and I were out."

"But that wouldn't explain why the envelope addressed to Dorwin was found in your wastebasket."

"Wouldn't it?" Manning frowned. He looked at the dozen people the detective had crowded into his little office. He studied the faces of Klawitz, Underwood, Dexter P. Dexter, Tim Cornish, as though seeking the answer to the question uppermost in his mind: What could be keeping Betty Vale?

The telephone rang. Manning reached for it automatically. Kilkenny immediately imprisoned his hand before he could lift the receiver.

The detective nodded to another instrument on the next desk.

"Same circuit?" he asked.

"Yes."

"Okay. Answer."

As Manning said "Hello," the detective took up the second phone.

"Hello, Phil. This is Joe Dollar at Transcontinental Broadcasting," said the voice on the wire. "I called to tell you we're putting out that story after all."

"What story?" Manning asked.

"The one I called you about, half an hour ago."

"You didn't call me, Joe."

"The hell I didn't. Are you swacked, Phil? I told you—"

"You didn't tell me, Joe. Somebody else must have answered my phone. Let's have a repeat."

"Say, now that I think of it, your voice did sound funny," Dollar said. "But after all, I had your number, and whoever answered not only gave a good imitation of your voice, but he seemed to know what I was talking about."

"What were you talking about, Joe?"

"That chamber music competition you asked about. I

phoned you that a music professor at some fresh-water college out in Iowa wrote in to say Benson's quartet was a cold steal from an obscure Bohemian composer named Fibich who died in 1900. The front office was going to keep mum about it, which was what I called to tell you. Then the legal department said we'd better confess we were fooled and make another award, otherwise the Iowa professor might raise a stink and then all the other contestants could sue us. So—hey, what's going on down there? An air raid?"

Manning did not reply. He dropped the phone and sprang up.

Once again the unfamiliar thunder of gunfire echoed through the marble halls of the library. There were two shots—not the sharp crack of a .22 this time, but the deep-throated roar of a .45, followed by the shrill whine of a ricochet.

Almost instantly Betty Vale ran unsteadily into the little office, white faced and round-eyed with terror. She dropped some papers in front of Manning, then collapsed in a chair, buried her face in her hands and sobbed.

Manning was beside her at once. "What happened?" he said.

"I—I stopped at a phone booth downstairs to call my father," the girl said through her fingers.

"And they shot at you, just because you tried to phone?"

"They—they didn't shoot at me. I was coming up the stairs when the shooting started."

At that moment the target of the police guns appeared in the doorway: Feodor Klawitz, flanked by two blue-coats, with Tim Cornish bringing up the rear.

"He was trying to run out on us," Tim announced. "We stopped him."

"It's an outrage!" declared Klawitz. His effort to look imperious was balked by the fact that his toupee was badly askew over one eye. "I was merely on my way to my broadcast," he said. "I told you that I have never missed a broadcast in my life."

"And I told you you were going to miss this one," said Detective Kilkenny. "Sit down there. You're lucky you didn't stop one of those slugs. And you, Manning, get away from that girl. I got things to ask her."

Manning did not move. He turned to Cornish and said: "Tim, I'm not speaking to Mr. Kilkenny since he wounded my feelings by suspecting me unjustly, so will you tell him I suggest he scurry right out and arrest Mr. David Benson for first-degree murder—if he can catch him."

"Benson, my eye!" said Kilkenny. "I may be dumb, but not that dumb. I don't see how you can fit this guy Benson into the picture."

"I'll draw the diagrams," Manning volunteered. "Open that red portfolio you picked up in the stacks. No, here—to the first page of the music. It's supposed to be an original score that Benson wrote for a ballet that Dorwin was going to finance—$20,000 worth. Now look at this proofsheet. It's a reproduction of the first page of an unpublished manuscript, a tone-poem by the late Russian composer Scriabin, called *Dance.* Except for the title, Benson's music is a note-for-note steal from Scriabin. Benson evidently found the manuscript in the Music Library and had it photostated; that would explain the raid on the photostat desk which Tim Cornish interrupted. Benson was out to destroy the records. He thought he could get away with stealing the music, since it had never been published. Unfortunately he didn't know that the Scriabin manuscript was part of a collection of Russian manuscripts which H. H. Dorwin himself had presented to the library. That fact had not yet been announced. But Dorwin, of course, recognized the music, and was about to expose Benson as a phony."

"You mean he'd kill a man just to save his reputation as a composer?" Kilkenny objected.

"There was the matter of twenty grand."

"Not with Dorwin dead, there wouldn't have been twenty grand," the detective said.

"With Dorwin dead, the ballet might still pass as a Benson original. He could find another sucker to put up the money."

"He'd already found the money," Betty Vale volunteered. "My father had already put up another twenty thousand. He just told me so on the phone. Dave sold him the idea that if the ballet were produced, it would be a flop—and that I would be cured of wanting a career in the ballet. It was a secret, of course—so that I wouldn't know my father was scheming to give me a lesson in failure, supposedly; actually, so that neither my father nor Hugh Dorwin would know that they were both being used. Dave must have planned to clear out with the whole forty thousand, once he got his hands on the money."

"Nice guy," said Kilkenny.

"Dorwin was to give his decision on the money to Miss Vale this afternoon," Manning continued. "He must also have planned to show up Benson as a transposer, rather than a composer. Evidently the rendezvous was in the Music Library, where Dorwin would confront Benson with the original Scriabin manuscript, and his identical copy. However, the choice of the rendezvous was the tip-off to Benson. He knew that if Dorwin exposed him, he would have no chance of getting away with the money he had already collected from Betty's father. Therefore he wrote that note on my typewriter, and left it on the desk of the music librarian to lure Dorwin into the spiral staircase of the South Reading Room where he could be murdered in privacy."

"Are you sure Dave planned all this in advance, Phil—in cold blood?" Betty Vale asked.

"He must have," Manning replied. "That catalogue spindle he used to stab Dorwin comes from the music catalogue. It's a different type from the spindles in the general catalogue. Therefore Benson must have unscrewed it at the time he delivered the note. He probably carried it under his coat to the spiral staircase, to wait for Dorwin.

"When Dorwin opened the portfolio that contained the plagiarized music—he must have opened it since the tapes were untied when I found it, and since a torn fragment of the portfolio's contents was in his hand when he died—Benson knew the game was up and stabbed Dorwin through the eye.

"Benson ran down the circular stairs, carried the portfolio and the metal spindle to the delivery enclosure, concealed, as he thought, by the outer row of book shelves, and shoved them through the oaken bars into a hand truck bound for the stacks. A moment later Dorwin staggered out on the gallery and fell dead.

"We know from Klawitz's story that Viola Smith crossed on the raised catwalk just before Dorwin tumbled off the gallery. We know from Underwood's story that Viola Smith, from her point of vantage, had seen the murderer come out of the staircase—and that he had looked up and seen her looking at him. He would naturally want to get rid of this only witness at the first opportunity, which was when Miss Smith—or Mrs. Underwood—started back up the steps on which she was killed, just after opening the stackroom door for her husband. Benson must have pushed her down the steps."

"That doesn't explain how the envelope addressed to Dorwin was found in your wastebasket, Manning," Detective Kilkenny said.

"I'll have to guess at that one," Manning said. "But it's a reasonable guess. After your people gave Benson a pass to leave the reading room, he must have gone back to the Music Library to make sure he had left no incriminating evidence. He had not been there since Dorwin picked up the note, remember. Suppose Dorwin had opened the note outside the Music Library and dropped the envelope. Probably he did—and probably Benson picked it up and brought it to this office to deposit in my wastebasket, in order to prompt your boys to match the typewriting with my machine. I'm pretty sure of this, because somebody was in this office within the last hour to intercept a call from my friend at Transcontinental Broadcasting."

"And what makes you think it was Benson who took the call?" Kilkenny demanded, chewing on his imaginary toothpick.

"Two things," said Manning. "First, up to that point, Benson had no reason to think he was suspected. But the call from Joe Dollar would let him know that I was not only on his trail, but also that I'd hit on something that would tie in with his motive for murder: Benson's penchant for stealing other men's music. Second, Benson had a police pass that let him go free of the library. Why would he come back, since the most incriminating piece of evidence seemed well hidden among more than two million books? It must have been that he learned that the evidence contained in the red portfolio was at least suspect. He would have learned by that phone call that I was digging in his garden of plagiarism.

"That's why he came back to ransack the Photostat Desk, to destroy the records of the fact that he had asked for copies of the Scriabin manuscript. That's why he knocked out Tim to steal his keys—to get into the stacks and try to find and obliterate the score for *Malavika.* And that's why, when he found me poring over the red portfolio, he set out to kill me, too. Which reminds me, Kilkenny, that, much as it hurts me, I must thank you for barging in when you did to scare him off. I was a goner. You saved my life."

"Think nothing of it," said Kilkenny. "I guess I'm indebted to you, too, for clearing up a few minor points. There's one more thing, though. Who put out the lights?"

"I did," volunteered Feodor Klawitz. "I wanted to get out for my broadcast. I—" He glanced at his watch. "Ten o'clock! I must get to the studio. Will you permit it, Inspector?"

"Inspector, my eye!" said Detective Kilkenny. "But go

ahead. I guess I can always put my hands on you if I need you. Beat it."

Klawitz tucked a book under his arm and left.

"You might even put your hands on Benson, if you hurry," Manning said. "He's probably still hiding in the stacks, after taking a crack at me—although he's had time to get out, thanks to that pass you gave him, Kilkenny."

"He's still in the building, Kenny," Brannigan said. "I just checked with the men on the exits. Nobody's gone out in the last half hour."

"Then he'll go out wearing bracelets," Kilkenny said. "Brannigan, run up and tell the lieutenant I need fifty more men to comb the building. Meanwhile we'll do a little preliminary combing ourselves. Get moving, men."

"Wait a minute, Kilkenny," Manning said.

"Now what do you want?"

"A pass," said Manning, "for Miss Vale and myself. There's a murderer at large in the library, and he might not like Miss Vale and me anymore. I'm taking her out of here."

"Okay," said the detective. He scribbled something on a piece of paper, handed it to Manning, and went out.

Betty Vale watched him go. She stood silent, as though stunned. There was an expression of deep hurt in her eyes. Manning put his arms around her gently.

"Phil, I feel as though Dave had murdered part of me, too," she said slowly. "Knowing that Dave could kill two people is ghastly, of course, but somehow the thing that hurts most is knowing that he could use my faith in him to . . . to . . . Oh, Phil, I feel—well, empty inside . . . !"

"You're probably hungry," Manning said. "Shall we eat?"

"How can you talk of food now, Phil?"

"We might try a little liquid nourishment. I'd like to drink to *Malavika.*"

"Poor Malavika. I'm afraid she won't marry King Agnimitra after all!"

"Why not? Personally I think the recasting will be a great improvement. Music by Alexander Scriabin. Choreography by Elizabeth Vale Manning. It will look fine on the program."

"Phil!"

"I'll get my hat and coat," said Manning.

He opened the door to the coat closet—and took a startled step backward.

Betty Vale gasped.

Dave Benson stood in the closet, his usual smile flashing ominously. His hands were pushed into the pockets of his coat. The right pocket, stiffly distended by something long and cylindrical, pointed at Manning.

"Raise your hands! Both of you!" Benson spoke quickly between his white teeth.

"Dave, you wouldn't dare—"

"Won't I?" said Benson. He stepped from the closet and moved between Manning and the door. Manning recognized his own hat and overcoat on Benson. "What can I lose?" Benson demanded.

"What can you gain, Dave?" The girl stared at him with hard-eyed, tight-lipped fury. Her voice was vibrant with cold, deep rage.

"Freedom," said Benson. "I'm going to get out of here. And you're coming with me, Betty." His left hand pulled the brim of Manning's hat lower over his eyes. "Where's that police pass Kilkenny just gave you, Manning?"

"Wouldn't you like to know," said Manning.

"I'm through talking," Benson said. "I'll count to three. It's your last chance. One!"

"Go to hell," said Manning.

Benson did not hear Feodor Klawitz come in behind him. Neither did he see what it was that Klawitz poked into the small of his back. He felt, however, the hard, sharp pressure. He went suddenly limp.

"Hands up, you plagiaristic swine!" Klawitz roared.

"You stealer of golden notes, you despoiler of the dead Scriabin's tomb—"

Benson's arms went up promptly. Klawitz lifted the book, the corner of which he had poked into Benson's back. The book crashed down on Benson's head.

"Grave robber!" said Klawitz.

Silently, neatly, like the cloth figure in a puppet show, Benson folded up. He bent first at the knees, then at the hips—rhythmically, elegantly, as became a Benson.

With a yell Manning sprang on the prostrate Benson. His hand dove into Benson's right pocket—and came out holding a large fountain pen.

"The four-flusher!" he said sheepishly.

The yell brought Kilkenny, Cornish, and three policemen piling into Manning's office. Handcuffs glittered about Benson's wrists almost before Manning had got to his feet again.

"What good angel brought you back, Klawitz?" Manning asked, as he gratefully pumped the hand of the horse-faced radio commentator.

"Angel!" snorted Klawitz. "A stupid policeman. He wouldn't let me out without a pass. He sent me back to get a pass from the Inspector."

"Give him a pass, Kilkenny," Manning said. "Quick—or he'll miss his broadcast."

Once outside the library, Phil Manning and Betty Vale hurried along the street, blinded by the big, wet, stinging snowflakes.

As they sank into curbside drifts and stumbled out again, a tall, familiar figure stalked up beside them.

"What a guy, this Benson, eh, Mr. Manning?" said Tim Cornish. "A man whose blood is very snow-broth; one who never feels the wanton stings and motions of the sense. Know what that's from?"

"No," said Manning. "But I've got one for you, Tim. 'A

little warmth, a little light of love's bestowing—' Know the next line, Tim?"

"Gosh, I don't seem to remember. Is that Shakespeare, Mr. Manning?"

"It's George Louis Palmella Busson Du Maurier, and it's from *Trilby,* Tim."

"And the next line, Mr. Manning?"

" 'And so, good night,' Tim."

In its opening pages, "Reflections on Murder" sounds like an essay on the mystery novel, but it quickly takes a less scholarly and more sinister turn as events begin to parallel those in the fiction under discussion. Although the narrator's name, occupation, and even sex are left to the imagination of the reader, the story is a poignant portrayal of two people who are the victims of their own self-imposed solitude. Throughout her fiction, Nedra Tyre has concerned herself with the plight of the old, helpless, and lonely. And the considerable variety with which she treats this theme may be seen in such novels as Death of an Intruder *(1953), which illustrates the perils of old people living alone;* Hall of Death *(1960), a mystery about young people at a Georgia reformatory; and* Mouse in Eternity *(1952), a murder story set in the social services milieu where Ms. Tyre once worked.*

REFLECTIONS ON MURDER

Nedra Tyre

Since you are reading this it is not unlikely that murder interests you. It fascinates me, I confess, and although I can no longer trace the origin of my predilection for death in print it may have begun when I first confronted *The Murder of Roger Ackroyd.* Do you remember the first time that detective fiction held you in thrall and that you realized forever after you would follow it down its labyrinthine ways?

How I wish we might sit facing each other, perhaps in front of a fire and over a glass of wine, and talk of murder as literature and figuratively smack our guilty lips over the classics of the genre and stop to disagree or even to spar over preferences.

All addicts of fanatical proportions—and I am one of them—have their heresies and I would parade mine and, even in this curious and arid predicament in which I find myself, welcome your ripostes however prejudiced I might secretly find them. Would this statement shake you? If you share most of the conventional opinions about detective fiction it may, so brace yourself. I have always found *Trent's Last Case* a bore. While I have no taste for Heard's *A Taste for Honey* I do not think that his *The Black Fox* has ever received its due; to me it is one of the unmistakable masterpieces. As for Josephine Tey, I consider her *The Daughter of Time* unsurpassed, but the rest of her work, except for *Miss Pym Disposes,* I find, in spite of critical raves, no better than the good average that is maintained by most mystery writers.

Are you one of the apostates who denigrate *The Moonstone* and say it is no detective story at all? Then may the briars and thorns of Sergeant Cuff 's roses prick and scratch you!

In recent years I have deplored the decline of the nice person murder and have grown concerned over the ascendancy of the private eye, but then you may agree with a reviewer with whose opinion I usually concur and always respect who says that the private eye of detective fiction has become the folk hero of our present-day culture. Puzzles have piqued my interest but have not ever satisfied it, so on the whole I do not care for this type of mystery. And instead of police procedure in its minutiae which now floods the field, I have wanted to read of the guilt that the murderer feels. It is his reactions I hunger after rather than his pursuit by detectives.

All of this is opinionated, I admit, and if only you were here to talk with me your exchange might help me to modify my ideas on murder, but I do not think that I would ever alter them to any considerable extent.

I have often wondered over the appeal of fiction dealing with death by violence. A certain school of analysts may be correct in its hypothesis that it is our guilt that is catered to and our sadistic tendencies that are fed and momentarily satiated. I think there may be other reasons. We are all threatened by disaster. Death may approach us at any time—a flight of steps, a street crossing, even the bath is filled with hazard. Illness or ruin may confront us at any moment. This sense of doom can haunt us. Detective fiction, on the other hand, gives us a feeling of peril which has form and shape to it; its peril has cause and effect, it is not the blind, idiotic, unnamed anxiety that stalks us in everyday living. Or something like that.

Yes, I wish someone with a passion like mine for this art form of the detective story could be with me to recite the names that are music and that I can scan as if they were meters of a poem: Collins, Iles, Christie, Sayers, Queen, Chandler, Innes, Crispin, Daly, Poe, Hammett, all these and dozens more.

And—like you, I'm sure—I've often thought after reading a mediocre piece of mystery fiction that I could write one just as good with one or both hands tied behind my back. So I began one, only to find that even the least of them required more than was apparent to the reading eye.

And of course in my unconscious as in everyone's there is down some unlit corridor in some dark and secret room the thought of actual murder; it is undoubtedly a remnant of our childhood, of the megalomania of the infantile mind in which lurks the wish of death for everyone that stands in its way. Perhaps it is a refinement of those early feral impulses that is in a calm contemplation of potential murder and of a dispassionate speculation on such a question as: what murder would create good? The death of what public figure would have the most felicitous result? Or since many of us are not of a political turn, this question can center on the death of which person of our acquaintance would be most fortunate—perhaps a nagging wife, but the more logical of us would counter that no one has to put up with a nagging wife, a man has chosen such a wife out of some valid need for her. Surely a fit object of murder would be a possessive mother who will not release her child to marriage, but a child in his torturous progress toward adulthood must have effected his own release or he could not use the freedom provided by a fortunate murder. What then? Who then? Perhaps a person hopelessly ill suffering the continuous torment of pain. Call it humane or inhumane, as your conscience prescribes, but I have found the thought untenable that a person doomed to invalidism and to constant pain should have an indeterminate stay on this earth.

All these random thoughts and more I jotted down in what I call my commonplace book on murder. It has been a pleasant exercise of the mind to consider and reconsider such reflections, to argue with myself, or to put aside the suspense or detective novel I had in my hand and parry the point of view presented, not that many writers choose the philosophical aspects of murder; with most of them it is simply a matter of crime and punishment or the tracking down of a criminal.

I would like to keep my reflections on murder general, but they must now become specific. I must present myself to you, but I should like to do so without reference to my name or my age or my profession. I may even try to keep my sex out of it, and if I am successful I might make a feeble joke about this being one of the rare modern instances where sex in murder is minimized. Well, to begin: I am, or I was, a reasonably satisfied person, and though I have neither talents nor gifts and very little competitive spirit, I have considerable application and conscientiousness and I have had a fair share of what is called success.

I should mention that my profession requires a great deal of traveling so that I am out of town much of the time. My work is such that I have had few friends. No one can count on me for a fourth at bridge because too often I have to go away unexpectedly, and I have left too many last-minute gaps in seating arrangements to be a welcome dinner guest. Almost two years ago my headquarters were moved to this city and I have not formed anything resembling a friendship, though I am glad to say that my job, which is one of responsibility, presupposes that I can establish immediate rapport with persons of all classes and positions.

The place where I live is for persons of fairly substantial means or at least for those who for one reason or another can afford rather steep rents. In my particular section of the building there are only two apartments, both of identical size, but for a while I knew nothing at all about my neighbor. I had not ever had even an accidental contact, such as being on the elevator at the same time, or happening to answer the door just when he or she entered or left.

This interpolation is necessary: A fondness for flowers is another passion with me, perhaps not so marked as my attachment for detective fiction, but keen and intense. I would like to have a garden but my life being what it is I cannot, and since I am away from my apartment so much of the time even pot flowers are beyond me. For a while I tried to keep them and entrusted their care in my long absences to the elevator boy and the janitor or the assistant superintendent, but I would return only to find the flowers drowned or parched, killed by too much or too little attention. Since I was in no position then to indulge my taste for flowers I was delighted with the remarkable arrangements on a long low table in the hall which I shared with the tenant about whom I had no knowledge. I had thought at first that the flowers were supplied by the management and were a recompense for the high rental we paid and I commented once on their beauty to the elevator operator; he shrugged and told me that she did it, and he pointed to the apartment across from mine.

Talent and care and thought invariably went into the arrangements; sometimes they were pot flowers, sometimes they were leaves, and very often they were cut flowers and these were not allowed to stay beyond their first beauty.

Shortly before Christmas there appeared an especially attractive display; this consisted of one of those interesting wooden figures, a primitive carving, Mexican I believe, some two feet high, painted in rich dark colors, and beside it there was a huge brass container filled with cedar boughs. My description is shamefully inadequate and does not in any way suggest the taste and artistry that went into the piece.

At Christmas time I count my blessings and my obligations, and I thought how during the four months I had so far lived in the apartment house the flowers had been a constant joy to me, and I did not know at all how to show my appreciation of them. I realized that it was not usual for people living on the same floor to make calls on a newcomer, or even necessarily to know when there was a newcomer, but I felt that if any advance were made it should issue from the person already there when a new tenant arrived. So it appeared obvious to me that whoever lived across the hall wanted to be left alone. Still I was most eager to show my gratitude. At last I thought that a gift of a bottle of wine at the door might be acceptable, but then I had misgivings that the tenant might be abstemious, in which case she would resent my offering. Then I decided on brandy instead of wine and that I would write a brief ambiguous greeting that the brandy might be used for cooking or fruit, so that my neighbor if a teetotaler would not think I was plying her with spirits. Somehow this idea confused me even more and I decided that I would do nothing, that however much I enjoyed the flowers they were of the tenant's doing and had no connection with me. But again I felt like an ingrate not to do something, especially just after I entered or left the hall and my eyes were delighted by the centerpiece; so my dilemma grew more painful.

Here I am reliving my uncertainty on that first Christmas, and it is well that I do because if I had done nothing I might not now have occasion to make some of these reflections on murder.

It was sherry that I settled on after all, an expensive cream sherry. Around the bottle's neck I attached a ribbon and a note. My note was not overly cordial and I purposely said nothing about wishing to thank personally the one who was so generous with her flowers. I remember the message as rather warm but on the whole formal.

On Christmas Eve I placed the wine at the door.

Days went by and there was no acknowledgement at all; not that I wanted or even expected one; I simply hoped the recipient understood my gratitude.

The winter days passed pleasantly, my job was demanding but most rewarding and at night I indulged myself in my usual delight of reading detective fiction. Occasionally I would stop reading and write an observation or so in my commonplace book on murder. I do not now remember the title of the book which I put aside for an instant to write: *The Murder of An Absolute Stranger. Would not the true connoisseur of murder take the most satisfaction in causing the death of someone he did not know, with whom he had no ties at all? No one could ever assign the murder to him, and because he was in no way connected with his victim he could not know great remorse. Is this perhaps what happens in war? Men who kill in war cannot feel guilt for the unknown persons who are their victims.*

So the months went on and I was satisfied; my job gave me pleasure and my reading of murder and speculations about the subject made as happy a life as one could ever expect when intimate personal relationships are impossible.

The exquisite flower arrangements continued.

There is only one flower to which I am allergic, or rather I should say which I dislike. The lily. It is beautiful but its odor is pervasive and obnoxious to me and I do not care for it. For that reason I was somehow dreading Easter and what might appear in the hall; but when Easter came there was one gigantic pot of white hyacinths in a white wrapping and around it clustered a number of small pots of white and pink and blue hyacinths. My sense of beauty was so satisfied and captivated that again I wanted to do something to show appreciation and once more, but this time with no note of any kind, I set a bottle of sherry at the door.

Again there was no acknowledgment and I wanted none; so spring left and summer came and went and fall blustered in with that suddenness that eternally confounds me.

It was the first of October and I remember being grateful that the heat had been turned on. I did not plan to read that night but intended to devote some time to my fall clothes—pulling them out of mothproof bags, deciding what was usable and what had to be discarded, for no matter how satisfactory clothes may look when they are put away they somehow acquire a shabbiness.

I had just ripped a dangling button from a jacket when I heard a frantic knock at the door. I was expecting no one and in my lonely existence I had few callers. I was somewhat disheveled from working with my clothes, but the knock was so doom-laden that I did not take the time to tidy myself.

A woman stood at my door. I knew at once that she was my neighbor. She was in a dressing gown, there was true elegance about her; the gown was black satin, her hair was white and beautifully kept, and her eyes were the only violet ones I have ever seen; her face wore a mask of concern and though it was distorted by worry and consternation I saw that age had only increased its beauty. Voices are apt to be affected by tension and when she spoke hers was, but even in that high, unnatural range her voice had a resonance of remarkable loveliness.

In my early days in statistics and research when I made door to door canvasses I was confronted by extraordinarily varied receptions, and I have found that however inwardly I may be concerned or even shocked I can maintain a certain external complacency. I was shocked by her appearance on my threshold and concerned by her obvious distress.

"Good evening," I said. "Won't you come in?"

There was a wariness about her, she took a step forward but stopped as if she could not pass beneath the lintel and I thought fleetingly of witches who cannot cross water or passages that have nails embedded in them.

She turned and went to her own door and then she said: "If you will, please come in here."

I followed her across the hall into a place of matchless taste. My eyes did not have time to particularize the furnishings, I only knew that I was in one of the most gracious series of rooms I had ever entered. She motioned to me to sit beside her on a small sofa upholstered in deep green velvet and I glanced at a Manet and a Berthe Marisot before I concentrated on the woman who was my hostess.

"I've a most unusual request to make of you," she said. "I've no one else to appeal to. You've been so understanding. I couldn't have asked for a more considerate neighbor."

This is what she wanted of me, and she instructed me in deadly earnest. At nine-fifteen I was to ring her doorbell, there would be guests with her, I was to act ill at ease as if I hadn't known she had company, she would insist that I come in and I would agree after some hesitation. I was to mention casually a few times that she had dined with me and refer to several games of bridge she had played with me and some other friends, and I was to leave with the reminder that she had promised to play cards in my apartment on the following Friday and she was not to disappoint me as I was inviting two dear friends who wanted most especially to meet her.

She made no explanation of her request and gave no reason for the need for such fabrications on my part. There was a shyness about her and an absolute goodness. I knew intuitively that my lies would be for an innocent purpose.

It was then eight-thirty. I had a brief rehearsal which

quite satisfied her and then I went back to my apartment. I sat down at my commonplace book and I wrote easily and without thought as if it were automatic writing: *Does the victim choose the killer even more than the killer chooses the victim?* I found my question so provocative that I thought of it until nine-fifteen.

When I rang her bell I heard her voice cry out to me to enter. Three persons were present beside herself. I could tell that a conversation of extreme urgency had been interrupted and it took very little acting on my part to offer apologies and try to withdraw, but she insisted that I join them. I was somehow flattered to see that the sherry I had given her was on the table in front of her though I would have thought with the lovely decanter on the sideboard she would have emptied the wine into it; no matter, I began my speech about the dinners and the hands of bridge; she had assigned names to some of the persons supposedly my guests and she said wasn't Charles wonderfully witty and that Frank was a superb bridge player; she thanked me for my kindness in sending her more of the sherry that I knew she liked so well and wouldn't I have a glass; I declined with some reference to claret being the only wine I enjoyed, and then I mentioned the forthcoming bridge game and made my adieux. I was so intent on our dialogue that I did not pay much attention to the other persons there, but it seemed to me that there was a resemblance, not necessarily of the nature of close relatives, but perhaps of cousins; she might even have been the aunt of the two younger men. Their interest in our brief conversation was what I can only term profound and intense.

Since we had been conspirators I thought that when her guests left she might sneak across the hall to smile over our performance and to explain the reason for it, but nothing of the sort happened. Anyway, I hoped the charade in which we acted out a history of social contact was convincing. I did not speculate to any extent as to its purpose. Long since I have taken as a tenet for my conduct this quotation from Henry James: *Remember that every life is a special problem which is not yours but another's, and content yourself with the terrible algebra of your own.* I had no intention whatever of probing or delving into the woman's affairs.

Again time passed and the flowers in their beauty and their variety continued to appear, but there was no word from the tenant across the hall.

Another spring had almost progressed into summer when there was another knock on my door. It was she; this time she wore a blue robe and this time there was nothing at all distressful about her appearance; the third time I saw her I realized that she had beauty of remarkable proportions and not even youth had been kinder to her looks than age was, not that I could judge her age, she might have been in her middle forties, she could even have been sixty, and though she smiled I sensed a sadness and a wistfulness about her.

"I didn't think it would work," she said, "but it has. All these months. My dear, I have no right to drag you into matters that don't concern you. Those people whom you saw are my relatives. I feel no real affection for them—nothing but the goodwill I try to feel toward all human beings. But they were trying to manipulate me. Their behavior was monstrous. I can't give you the details of my life—I've been fortunate in many ways and unfortunate in others. I came to mistrust people, to mistrust the world, and all I want is to be let alone, to stay by myself in quietness. But they insisted that I move out in the world. They even wanted me to come live with them. They said my withdrawal was a sign of a breakdown. I thought if they couldn't understand my point of view, then—well, our little hoax—if they could be made to think that I did go out occasionally and that I had friends. I can't thank you enough for what you did. I can't tell you how grateful I am. If I'm made to leave here for any reason, I'll die or I'll go into a madness that is worse than death."

Though I found her words melodramatic she spoke quietly. She made no further elaborations and I did not ask any questions; I only know that her thank you to me when she left my living room was the most genuine statement ever directed to me.

Then some weeks later there was the morning when the flowers looked rather wilted and that had not ever happened in our corridor; she did not allow the slightest taint of wilt to touch them, they were removed at the very peak of their beauty. The next day the crisp brownness of death had laid its blight on the flowers and withered petals were strewn on the table. That evening when I returned late from dinner the dead flowers were a desecration to the time of their loveliness and I removed them.

I was concerned over my neighbor but I did not venture to make an inquiry; I remembered her desperate need to be left alone, or I thought that perhaps the dead flowers had left their own message and she had finally been persuaded by her relatives to move in with them. The hall table remained bare and I grew nostalgic for its former beauty.

One night after a particularly trying day at the office I took too long over my after dinner coffee and I was startled to see that I had only moments to pack and to get a plane. I was frantically jerking clothes from the closet and out of drawers when someone knocked on my door.

A woman in a nurse's uniform stood there. I saw that beyond the frame of my door in which she stood the door across the hall had swung open. Even as the nurse spoke she was pulling on a coat. "I must go," she said. "My husband is downstairs waiting for me. The other nurse is late. My patient said perhaps you wouldn't mind coming in for a moment. She belongs in a hospital, and no matter how she objects they're going to put her in one tomorrow."

I did not protest my own lateness for the plane, but went at once to the apartment.

My neighbor looked small on the tremendous tester

bed; she was ravaged, it seemed to me, not so much by illness as by hopelessness, and beauty that had stayed with her so long was still faithful, it had not deserted her even in this nadir of despair. I looked at her as through bars of a cage, she was of a particular and rare loveliness and deserved nothing so little as the trap in which she obviously found herself, she could exist only in an atmosphere of her own choosing, she could not survive removal from this beautiful retreat. I have wished for many things in my life but I know they were idle wishes with no real intent behind them in comparison with the passionate desire I then had to do something to relieve her suffering and her predicament. We looked at each other and I do not know what there was in the stare that we exchanged, we had lived as neighbors for almost two years in that house and we had seen each other only three times before and those times were moments only, but in those moments she had revealed herself and she had fathomed my nature.

"In the living room, in the top drawer," she said to me in her exquisite voice. I went where her lovely, pathetic gesture indicated. Various objects were there in the secretary but I had not the slightest hesitation when I saw the box. There was no need for words. I knew what she wanted. I knew what she meant. I did not need to read the label or the dosage or the warning. Neither of us faltered as I helped her to a sitting position and handed her the box and a glass of water. Yes, I knew very well what I had done, what we had done together, and then she said: "Please go. I feel I can rest now. I am forever grateful to you."

I saw then that only four minutes had passed since the nurse had summoned me and if I hurried and if I were lucky I could still get my plane. I snatched my suitcase and buzzed continuously for the elevator and shouted down the shaft for service, something I had not ever done before, and I begged the operator to hurry when he made his casual appearance. He later testified as to my hysteria, my frantic and distressed air as I tried to escape from the terrible deed of murder.

We want to question you about the circumstances surrounding the death of so-and-so, and you should be warned that anything you say may be taken down as evidence against you. I had read those words a hundred times in detective fiction; I did not know their import until the police in the city where I had flown on the business trip told me that the authorities in the town where I lived wanted to question me in connection with the death of Miss Teresa Covington, and they did not believe me when I said I was not acquainted with any person by that name; you see we had not introduced ourselves, there was no nameplate at her door, and since there was a desk at which we received our mail I had not even seen her name on a box.

The police had found my commonplace book on murder before I returned, they were interested in my various observations, and when I protested that I had not known the dead woman long enough or intimately enough to kill her they produced my specualations about the perfect murder, the murder that could not be solved, that of a stranger. But my protestation that I did not know her well was contradicted by the relatives who testified against me; they had seen me in her apartment and we had exchanged conversation which confirmed many meetings. They described me as fawning, ingratiating. But even now I think that nothing would have come of it if Miss Covington had not left me a small fortune, at least it was a fortune in my estimation. It was not that she disinherited her relatives in my favor, they received handsome bequests, as did many charitable organizations, but a legacy of fifty thousand dollars was enough to convince the most lenient jury that I had motive and to spare for murder.

Yes, yes, yes, I *was* the instrument of her death. I admit it, as I later admitted in testimony. She selected me as her murderer and it was exactly as I had written: does the victim choose the killer even more than the killer chooses the victim? And the answer was yes.

I at last came to that awful, that fateful moment when sentence was pronounced and I almost forgot the despair in her eyes and their terrible pleading for death, and I wished then that she were alive and suffering; I was overcome by the profound intimation that every moment of being, under whatever conditions, is a prize and a premium.

Time that has so often stumbled and stood still is now galloping and my final night is almost gone. I must be detached about what will happen to me early tomorrow and I will turn even now for comfort to what has so often buoyed me. Not even this last predicament can altogether deaden it, though my taste for murder fiction did falter and leave me for a while when the feeling of numbness and puzzlement and bewilderment engulfed me. It is back now, almost as strong as ever, and in the few hours that remain I am wondering what I will ask for to sustain me. My mind has considered many choices; those possibilities have narrowed however; and at the moment I cannot decide between *The Hands of Mr. Ottermole* and *The Two Bottles of Relish.*

August Derleth (1909–71) was Wisconsin's foremost regional writer, having published dozens of novels, collections, and nonfiction works set in the Sac Prairie region of his home state. He was also a lifelong student and writer of macabre fiction, an interest which led him to found the Arkham House publishing imprint in 1939. He founded a second publishing imprint as well, Mycroft & Moran, for the book appearances of his Solar Pons detective stories—a series felt by many to be the best of all the pastiches of Sherlock Holmes. Some ten collections of Pons's adventures have appeared from Mycroft & Moran, among them "In Re: Sherlock Holmes" *(1945),* The Memoirs of Solar Pons *(1951),* The Return of Solar Pons *(1958), and* Mr. Fairlie's Final Journey *(1968). Pons solves his cases exactly as Holmes does, through a combination of keen observation, esoteric knowledge, and ratiocination; and each one is narrated by his "Watson," Dr. Parker, who is properly in awe of the master's genius. Here, Pons undertakes an investigation into the origin of a particular copy of one of the rarest of all American books, Poe's* Tamerlane and Other Poems.

THE ADVENTURE OF THE SPURIOUS TAMERLANE

August Derleth

"A summer idyl," was what my friend Solar Pons called the curious adventure which began one July afternoon with the appearance on the threshold of our quarters in Praed Street of a street gamin bearing a somewhat begrimed folded note. Under tousled blond hair, his blue eyes looked up at me out of a freckled face.

"Mr. Pons?" he asked. "Mr. Solar Pons?"

It was a rare occasion on which a visitor did not immediately identify Pons, who stood behind me in the living room, and I hesitated a moment before replying.

" 'E said as it was 7B," said the boy urgently.

"And it is, my lad," said Pons, coming up behind me and reaching for the paper clutched in our visitor's fingers, while with the other hand he tossed him a bob.

The boy caught his tip and was off like a flash, clattering

down the steps in marked contrast to the careful manner in which he had mounted to our floor.

Pons stepped over to the window, unfolding the note as he walked. He read it without expression, but his eyes were twinkling when he handed me the paper. It was rough to the touch, and had a torn edge characteristic of the valley of a book. Its message had been hastily scrawled with a pencil on the first piece of paper to come to hand.

"Mr. Pons, dear sir," it read, *"I would be obliged to you if you could step around to my barrow. I have something of a problem that may interest you. I am, sir, your respectful servant, Joshua Bryant."*

"What do you make of that, Parker?" asked Pons.

I was sure of my ground and answered confidently. "This note is written on the endpaper of a book—an old book, and no doubt second hand," I said. "Mr. Bryant is very probably a dealer in second-hand books."

Pons burst into approving laughter, clapped me heartily on the back and cried, "At any time now I can retire to Sussex and keep bees! Is it not remarkable what a little exposure to ordinary ratiocination will do for one!"

"You know him, then?"

"He has a book barrow in Farringdon Road. I have on occasion paused to look over his wares."

"You're going then?"

"I never scorn the possibility of a little adventure to vary the prosaic routine," he said. "Let us just step around and pay Mr. Bryant a call."

The Farrington Road Book Market consisted of a row of barrows—some on wheels, some on wooden supports which held only boards on which books were displayed—set along the curb. The wheeled barrows were supplied with canvas covering which could be rolled back on sunny days, and unrolled to cover books and browsers on days of rain and weather. The market was not far from the Farringdon Station in one direction and the Great Northern Railway Depot in the other, and the spire of St. Peter's rose on the horizon behind the row of barrows. A score of people browsed among the books at the curb, most of them men.

Joshua Bryant was a short, rotund man with a florid face which made a strong contrast to his thatch of white hair. His eyes were bright and alert, and bespoke more than ordinary intelligence. He acknowledged his introduction to me with a friendly nod, but his face told us nothing.

"I appreciate your coming, Mr. Pons," he said, without preamble. "Have a look at that."

So saying, he took from the side pocket of his jacket a slender, tea-colored, paperbound booklet and laid it before Pons, deftly turning back the cover to the title page, which could be read at a glance. "*Tamerlane and Other Poems.* By a Bostonian." A quotation from Cowper followed, though somewhat badly printed: "Young bards are giddy, and young hearts are warm,/ And make mistakes for manhood to reform." Then came the name of the publisher: "Boston: Calvin F. S. Thomas . . . Printer." and the date: "1827."

I glanced at Pons and saw his eyes lit with interest. He in turn looked inquiringly at Bryant.

"Mr. Pons," he said earnestly, "that book was not in my barrow when I came here this morning. It doesn't belong to me. I neither bought it nor took it in in trade. Yet I found it among the books about two hours ago." His eyes challenged Pons. "Do you know its value?"

"It is one of the rarest of American books," said Pons. "Worth perhaps five thousand pounds."

Bryant nodded. "It's worth more than I am," he said wryly. "I said to myself right away, there's a smell of fish about this! So I sent off that note to you."

Pons picked up the booklet. "May I borrow it?"

"Do, Mr. Pons."

"But first, a question or two. What of your clientele this morning?"

"Oh, the usual. I have the regulars, Mr. Pons, the same

as anyone else. Then there are those who come and go."

"Ah, but anyone unusual?"

Bryant looked thoughtful. "A lady," he said presently. "She bought a book of poems. Rupert Brooke."

"Describe her."

"Young, well-dressed, married. Not the sort I'd have expected to see here, but then, Mr. Pons, books draw from all walks of life."

"Dark or light?"

"Oh, on the dark side. Chestnut brown."

"The color of her eyes?"

"She wore tinted glasses."

"I see. Anyone else?"

"A young barrister, I took him to be. He bought a *Raffles.* Then there was the elderly gentleman in morning clothes. Got out of a Daimler, driven by a chauffeur. The barrister was perhaps thirty-five, the elderly gentleman certainly thirty years older. They lingered a bit, whereas the lady more or less drifted by."

"What did the elderly gentleman buy?"

"Nothing, Mr. Pons. I thought he'd take a book on chess he looked at for a while, but he put it back."

"Did any of these people go to any other barrow, if you noticed?"

"The barrister stopped at them all. The lady just walked away, and the elderly gentleman returned to his car and was driven off."

"Can you describe him?"

"Gray-haired, but not as white as I am, Mr. Pons. He wore a Masonic ring. His hands were well groomed. There was a moustache on his upper lip, but his chin was clean-shaven. He had blue eyes, and a squarish face."

"Anyone further?"

Bryant shook his head.

"Very well. You'll hear from me, Mr. Bryant."

Pons said not a word all the way back to 7B, and, once

there, he retired at once to the corner of the room by the window where he kept his scientific laboratory, such as it was. There I left him to attend to three calls I had to make.

When I returned to our quarters in time for dinner, I found Pons sitting deep in thought in his favorite chair, his eyes closed and his fingers tended before him. He had evidently only just finished a pipeful of the odoriferous shag he smoked, for our quarters reeked of it.

"I suppose you've solved the mystery of Mr. Bryant's valuable book," I ventured.

"No, no," he said almost irritably, "it is more of a mystery than ever. And the book is not valuable. It is spurious—a very clever copy, but a forgery."

He came to his feet and strode to the table where the *Tamerlane* lay.

"Look here, Parker. The date of publication is 1827. Less than a dozen copies of this book are known to exist, though a considerably larger edition was printed. Poe wrote that the book was 'suppressed for private reasons'—this accounts for its scarcity. But this copy could not have been printed in 1827, for an analysis of the paper on which it has been printed shows that the paper was made of chemically treated wood pulp. Chemical treatment for wood pulp was not, however, introduced in papermaking until after 1880. Further, the paper contains esparto grass, which was not used until 1861. And most obvious of all, the type has no kerns, and alphabets without kerns were not introduced anywhere in the world until the early 1880's. This book therefore has no value except as a literary curiosity."

"Then no one, after all, has lost or misplaced a valuable book," I said.

"Ah, that is the nub of the problem. I submit that the reason for being of this spurious *Tamerlane* is likely to be of more interest than its discovery in Bryant's barrow. One of his customers this morning left it there."

"But which?"

"I submit it was the lady. I detected lint from her white gloves on the book, but even so, it is quite the sort of thing a lady would be more likely to do than a man. The book is a skilled, professional job. How came it into being? Was it done with the intention of deceiving someone into buying it? If so, how came it into Bryant's barrow?"

"It was certainly done with the intention of deceiving someone," I said. "What other purpose would a spurious copy of anything have?"

"Elementary," agreed Pons. "But I submit that the precise purpose of the deception is not nearly so clear. Presumptive evidence suggests that the copy was not made to be sold."

"What then, was it made for?"

"That seems to be the problem. Had it been made to be sold, we could hardly expect to discover it 'lost' in a barrow on Farringdon Road. But its only other purpose must have been to deceive a collector for some reason."

"You infer then that it served its purpose?"

"Precisely."

"Then why not simply destory it?"

"A man would logically have done so. But women are not as logical. I put it to you that the lady could not bear to destroy something in the creation of which so much effort was expended."

"Where do you go from here, then?" I asked.

"I hoped you might be able to tell me," he said gently. "Does no course of action suggest itself to you?"

I threw up my hands. "To find a woman on so slight a description as that supplied by Bryant seems to me next to impossible. There must be a hundred thousand women who fit that description in greater London."

"More," agreed Pons.

"But perhaps there is a genuine *Tamerlane* in London."

"Capital!" cried Pons. "My dear fellow, I congratulate you. It so happens that there is such a book. It is in the possession of the well-known bibliophile, Lord Heltsham. My brother knows him reasonably well. While you were on your rounds I took the opportunity of sending around to Bancroft asking him to dispatch a note by messenger to His Lordship asking that I be permitted to examine his genuine *Tamerlane* for a few minutes directly after noon tomorrow."

"Heltsham is hardly likely to be home at that hour," I pointed out.

"Oh, it isn't His Lordship I wish to see. I count on seeing his wife. He would hardly be likely to trust a servant to show me such a treasure."

"Lady Heltsham!"

"I fancy Her Ladyship knows considerably more about the spurious *Tamerlane* than Lord Heltsham does. I am eager to add her knowledge to my own," said Pons with an enigmatic smile. "I chose tomorrow, because I saw in this morning's *Times* that His Lordship has a committee meeting in the Lords at noon."

Promptly at one o'clock next day we presented ourselves at the front door of Lord Heltsham's town house in Bedford Square. The butler admitted us, showed us into the drawing room, and retired. Presently Lady Heltsham swept into the room—a young, attractive, and vivacious woman, considerably her husband's junior. Her pleasant brown eyes looked from one to the other of us, and without hesitation fixed upon Pons.

"Mr. Pons? I have the pleasure of your brother's acquaintance."

"I presume upon it, Your Ladyship," said Pons, and introduced me.

"You are reclusive, sir," said Lady Heltsham. "While your brother moves about socially, I see nothing of you."

"Ah, Your Ladyship, we move in different circles. Bancroft would not be seen in mine, and I do not derive much profit in his."

"You are a collector of books?" she asked them.

"Say, rather, of circumstances, events, and curious happenings," said Pons. "My interest is in the human comedy."

A little nonplussed, Her Ladyship came to the point of our visit. "My husband tells me you wish to examine his copy of *Tamerlane.*"

"If I could impose upon you for a few minutes," said Pons.

"This way, please."

Lady Heltsham led the way into her husband's study, a room lined with books behind locked glass doors almost from floor to ceiling to such an extent that the room was unnaturally dark. Lady Heltsham moved directly to the mahogany table in the center of the room and turned on the strong light there.

"I will bring it to you, Mr. Pons," she said.

She crossed to one of the cases, unlocked it, and took from it a slender slipcase. This she brought to the table, and from it removed what seemed at first glance to be the duplicate of the book Joshua Bryant had laid before Pons the previous day.

Pons, however, was peering not at the *Tamerlane,* but at the wall behind Lady Heltsham. "Forgive me," he said, "but surely that is not a set of Dickens in first editions?"

She turned.

Instantly Pons exchanged for the genuine *Tamerlane* on the table the spurious copy he had carried along from our quarters.

"I believe it is, Mr. Pons," said Lady Heltsham, amused. "It hasn't the value, of course, of this little book—hardly more than a chapbook, as you see."

Pons turned back the cover with a reverent air.

"What could have been the 'private reasons' which caused Poe to suppress it?" he murmured.

"I suppose we will never know, Mr. Pons."

"That is surely a challenge for some biographer," Pons went on, turning to the first page of text.

He bent to peer closely at the page, then turned from this position to look strangely at Lady Heltsham.

"What is it, Mr. Pons?"

"Surely His Lordship is aware that this is not a genuine *Tamerlane?*" he asked quietly.

Lady Heltsham bent instantly at his side, her face quickening with alarm.

"The absence of kerns, you see," began Pons.

But he did not go on. Lady Heltsham's simultaneous reaction was so violent that Pons' words were stopped in his throat. She uttered a great cry of anguish, and without a moment's hesitation rushed headlong from the room.

Pons immediately exchanged books once more, returned the genuine *Tamerlane* to its slipcase, and the encased book to its place on the shelf. He turned the key in the lock and brought the little ring of keys to which it was attached to the table to leave it in place of the book.

The motor of a car roared into life somewhere outside the house.

"Her Ladyship is now on her way to Farringdon Road," said Pons.

"That was a cruel trick, Pons," I said hotly.

"Was it not!" he agreed. "I rather think, however, that Lady Heltsham would never have admitted to any part in the matter of the spurious *Tamerlane* if I had not tricked her so. I regret the shock to her."

Pons sat in silence in the cab on the way back to our quarters until I broke into his meditation.

"I fail to understand Lord Heltsham's role," I said.

"If I am not mistaken, the spurious *Tamerlane* was used to occupy the slipcase during the absence of the genuine one," said Pons.

"Then Lord Heltsham never saw it!"

"In all likelihood he did not. I submit that the forgery was intended to deceive him should he have occasion to glance into the slipcase, though a close examination would have revealed the deception. The forged copy having served its purpose, it was dropped into Bryant's barrow. The gambit I took was intended to make Lady Heltsham believe that, in spite of her certainty to the contrary, she had inadvertently dropped the real *Tamerlane* in Farringdon Road. She has gone there to see. Bryant, who has no reason to dissemble, will tell her what has happened to the copy she left there, and in all probability Her Ladyship will then arrive at the correct explanation of the little scene in which she played such an impetuous role. She will return to her husband's study and discover the real *Tamerlane* in its slipcase; she will then know that I deliberately tricked her."

"And she will call on you," I put in.

"I doubt it. Lady Heltsham will wait upon me to make the next move."

"Pons, you cannot go back to the house."

"At the moment I have no intention of doing so. If I read Her Ladyship aright, she will tell us nothing. I shall have to use other means to learn why she found it necessary to remove her husband's valuable *Tamerlane* for some time from its slipcase and substitute a spurious copy."

"Could it not have been used to make a potential buyer of the spurious copy believe he was buying the genuine *Tamerlane?*" I asked.

"If that were the explanation," said Pons a trifle impatiently, "surely I would not now be in possession of the forgery."

"Of course not," I agreed.

"You imply further that Lady Heltsham might have been guilty of such criminal deception. Far from it. I submit that the lady acted out of desperation."

"I find this matter more baffling every moment," I said.

"Tut, tut! If we accept the premise that the spurious copy was meant only for the casual deception I have postulated, an interesting use for the real *Tamerlane* then suggests itself. Indeed, at the moment, unlikely as it seems, it remains as the only tenable one. You will remember my credo—when all the impossible explanations have been eliminated, then whatever remains, improbable as it may be, must be the truth."

"And that?"

"Surely so valuable an object as the rare *Tamerlane* would make excellent collateral!"

"Of course."

"And if Her Ladyship needed money urgently and could not ask her husband for it, she might persuade herself to borrow the *Tamerlane.* I myself would lend her up to three thousand pounds on such security—providing I had it to lend. I submit that any bank in London would do the same."

"Then you need only apply to the banks."

"Ah, that is information no reputable bank would divulge. Yet, in the interests of Lady Heltsham, we shall have to examine into this matter from another quarter. Unless I am badly mistaken, she may yet have further need for the spurious *Tamerlane* she had made for her desperate purpose."

"I daresay you are hardly the person Lady Heltsham would care to see at this point."

"I do not doubt it," agreed Pons. "She will not see me."

"Lord Heltsham then?"

"The very last person to whom to make application." He shook his head. "No, Parker—these waters run a little deeper than you may think. We shall have to proceed with caution lest we precipitate the very tragedy Lady Heltsham seems to fear."

Thereafter he said no more, and we rode the rest of the way in silence, Pons leaning back with eyes closed so that the passing scene might not distract him from his train of thought.

Pons was up and away before I rose next morning, and without touching the breakfast Mrs. Johnson had brought up. I went out on my rounds soon after, pausing only briefly at our quarters in passing at mid-day, only to find Pons still absent. He did not return until the dinner hour, following me in by thirty minutes, and wearing a sober, preoccupied air.

"I have been inquiring into that little matter of the spurious *Tamerlane,*" he said as he took up a position at the mantel and began to fill his pipe with shag.

"Ah, you have solved it," I cried.

He shook his head impatiently. "Come, come, Parker, it is not a matter of solving, as you put it, but of knowing just where to take hold of it to bring about its resolution. How did Lady Heltsham strike you? A woman of character?"

"I thought so."

"And I."

"And under considerable stress."

"Elementary."

"But controlled—apart, that is, from exposure to sudden shocks prepared by Mr. Solar Pons."

Pons bowed his acknowledgement. "Would you not conclude, then, that if such a woman needed money, she would attempt to raise it through her own possessions before she borrowed her husband's?"

"I would, indeed."

"I have been making the rounds of the pawnshops for the better part of the day," said Pons then. "A description of the lady, with tinted glasses added and, no doubt, an assumed name, has led me to conclude that Lady Heltsham has borrowed money against all but her most essential jewels, two autographed books of some rarity belonging to her, some valuable furs—and, at last, the *Tamerlane,* which alone has been redeemed because Lady Heltsham was fortunate enough to come into a small inheritance from an uncle. Indeed, announcement of it appears only in the afternoon papers, though the inheritance was obviously paid some days ago—two thousand pounds, all of which, I venture to guess, went to redeem her husband's *Tamerlane.*"

"You've not confronted her with these facts?"

"Certainly not. I shall not. This need for money has been of comparatively short duration. Scarcely a year. Would it surprise you to learn that within that time Lady Heltsham has also begun to bet on horses and to invest in the stock market?"

"Ah, it is that vice!"

"Gently, gently, Parker. That is surely not a vice so rapidly acquired."

"But it is one in which she could hardly expect her husband to foot the bill," I put in.

"It does not strike you as curiously coincidental that Lady Heltsham who had previously shunned the races and the market, should suddenly begin to wager money and to invest it—somewhat incautiously?"

"Which came first?" I asked. "The pawning of her valuables or the wagering?"

"The pawning."

I shrugged. "And with that money she gambled!"

"You have a tidy mind, Parker, and you are always singularly direct. It does not seem to you unlikely that Lord Heltsham is too penurious to deny his wife a little money for a pleasure which has always commanded the allegiance of the upper classes?"

"I haven't the noble Lord's acquaintance, so I can hardly speak for him," I said, "but it is not improbable."

Pons added, his lips pursed, his eyes intent upon some point in space beyond the walls of our quarters. "There is one little aspect of the matter that puts an added light on it," said Pons then. "Her wagers and her investments have been far from matching the money she has borrowed—and I can say nothing of such securities as she may have taken to the banks."

"Did she in fact borrow against securities as well?" I asked.

"I think it highly likely that she did. There is everything

to show that in her need to raise considerable sums of money, she explored every avenue before turning to securities that were not her own."

"Like Lord Heltsham's *Tamerlane.*"

Pons nodded.

"But there is plenty of precedent for sudden changes in living patterns," I said. "Lady Heltsham is not the first woman who has suddenly altered her way of life; she will not be the last."

"In these matters I must defer to your judgment, Parker," said Pons dryly.

"What do you propose to do?" I asked. "After all, you've solved the matter as far as Bryant is concerned."

"True, true. But I have not satisfied myself. And at this point I have gone as far as I can go alone."

"If there is anything I can do," I began.

"I count on your loyalty always, Parker, but in this case, I need expert help. I have called upon Bancroft and commanded the power that is only the Foreign Office's. I have had to inform him in the strictest secrecy that I have reason to believe Lady Heltsham is the victim of a conspiracy that may involve espionage."

I studied his face to see whether he jested, but the grimness of his features gave me no alternative but to believe him. Nevertheless, I could not but express my amazement. "Surely not Lady Heltsham! Perhaps her husband."

"Lord Heltsham is on the Munitions Committee," said Pons significantly.

"But what can Bancroft do?"

"He has done what I asked, and discreetly. Lady Heltsham's mail will be opened and her telephone tapped. I need to know who communicates with her. Unless I am very much mistaken, she will receive a communication of some importance within twenty-four hours. I am prepared to act upon it.

"You astound me," I cried.

"It is surely not the first time," said Pons, his eyes twinkling.

Early the next evening, Pons received from his brother the first batch of copies of the mail delivered to Lady Heltsham during the day. He pounced upon it eagerly. There were nine letters in all; I could not see that Pons read most of them, only beginning each of them, and tossing it aside. But at last, when he came to the seventh one, he paused, read it at a glance, and smiled.

"I fancy this is what we want, Parker," he said, handing it to me.

It was but the briefest of notes.

"Dear Lady,
"I count on your joining me
tomorrow at two for a cocktail
at Sardi's.

"Victor."

I looked up. "You cannot know the sender?"

"I fancy I do. He is Victor Affandi, a man about town. He is hardly more than an international gigolo, but highly popular with the ladies. He is of Egyptian descent, and lives at The Larches in Laburnum Crescent."

"You think him guilty of espionage?"

"I should not be surprised if he were. He is an ingenious man, one who has managed to live conspicuously well without visible means of support other than a small allowance left him many years ago. If you are not averse to an adventure in larceny, we shall pay his quarters a visit tomorrow afternoon."

I looked at Pons askance. "As your friend Bryant puts it, 'There's a smell of fish about this,' " I said. "What can you hope to find at Affandi's place?"

Pons smiled. "We shall see."

However much I may have been inclined to hold back, I was at Pons' side next afternoon when his skeleton keys let him into the sumptuously furnished apartment occupied by Victor Affandi. Once the door was closed behind us, Pons stood quietly in the middle of the living room examining our surroundings. His keen eyes darted from one to another of the framed pictures on the walls—some patently original watercolors and oils—until he came to one only a trifle out of line. He strode across the room and lifted the picture enough to disclose a wall safe.

He stood for a moment contemplating it, then gently lowered the picture. "Affandi could hardly be so obvious," he murmured.

He resumed his scrutiny of the room. He contemplated the furniture, but discarded this, too. He went around the rug, raising it for any evidence of a receptacle in the floor. He passed on into the spare kitchen, the bathroom, and the bedroom, examining each in turn before he came back into the living room.

"We don't have much time," he said. "I dare say Affandi's cocktail engagement will be a cruelly short one."

Apart from the costliness of its appointments, the living room was simply furnished. Pons examined the furniture, but only desultorily; clearly he did not believe that what he sought was hidden in it any more than he believed the wall safe to be its place of concealment.

Finally, his eyes fixed upon a recessed shelf of books. He crossed to it, and I followed. The volumes Victor Affandi had collected were almost depressingly prosaic—a Forsyte novel by Galsworthy, a Proust novel in French, books by Dickens, George Meredith, Thomas Hardy, the poems of Byron, and, somewhat incongruously, two over-sized leather-bound volumes containing the Old and New Testament. It was this two-volume edition of the Bible which had caught Pons' attention. His eyes quickened as he drew one of them from the shelf and opened it.

"An uncommonly light book for one of its size," he said. "I fancy this is what we are looking for, Parker."

He turned back the pages until he came at last to a page that would not turn—and the rest of the pages were solid. The book was a dummy.

Pons sought and found the tiny lever that unlatched the cover of the dummy portion, and the lid flew back. There lay disclosed papers, documents, packets of letters, and newspaper clippings.

Without a moment's hesitation, Pons dipped into Affandi's treasure and proceeded methodically to stuff the contents of the book into his pockets.

"Pons, what are you doing?"

"Robbing Affandi of his treasures," said Pons blandly. "How many of his visitors would think of looking into a Bible!" he added, chuckling.

He locked the book, closed it, and returned it to its place on the shelf.

Then he took down the other book, also a dummy, and emptied this in similar fashion.

"Now, quickly, Parker, out of the place," he said.

In short order, we found ourselves back at our quarters. There Pons lost no time in sending a note to Lady Heltsham, inviting her to call at 7B at her convenience, and promising that she would learn something to her advantage. To all my questions, he turned a deaf ear, or worse, a scornful retort.

"It is as plain as a pikestaff, Parker. You disappoint me. You began so well in this matter, and you have been misled so easily."

He spent the next two hours, spurning supper, making an inventory of the contents of Victor Affandi's Bible. Some of the papers and letters he slipped into manila envelopes and addressed them for mailing; some he put aside for further examination.

Lady Heltsham presented herself promptly at eight o' clock. She entered our rooms with understandable reserve, and as she threw back the veil which covered her features it was patent that she was under tension not untouched by indignation.

"Ah, my dear Lady Heltsham," said Pons, "I owe you an apology for that little substitution I played upon you. Nevertheless, it has led to a result I am sure you will agree is a happy one for you. I believe these belong to you."

So saying, he handed her a packet of letters from Victor Affandi's collection.

For a few moments she gazed wide-eyed at the letters Pons held out to her. Then she seized hold of them with trembling hands, and her liquidly beautiful eyes stared uncomprehendingly at Pons.

"Pray make sure they are all there," urged Pons.

She untied them eagerly and went through the packet. She nodded as if she did not trust herself to speak.

Pons turned and indicated the fire on the hearth. "I assure Your Ladyship I have not read them, but surely their nature is such that it would be dangerous for you even to carry them home."

She crossed to the fire and threw the letters into the flames. Then she turned and fell back against the mantel with a great sobbing sigh of relief.

"Oh, Mr. Pons!" she cried. "I cannot thank you enough. I cannot pay you. I cannot tell you how much this has meant to me. If my husband had learned of them—as *he* threatened . . ."

"Pray say no more, Lady Heltsham. If I may retain that spurious *Tamerlane,* I shall feel amply repaid."

"Please do!" she said earnestly. "Thank you, sir. I am happy to learn there are still gentlemen left in England!"

She bade us good night and slipped away.

"A woman of rare discretion," said Pons. "You will note she asked no questions, but accepted gratefully what fate had been kind enough to offer her."

"So it was blackmail! Why then all this talk of espionage?"

"My brother would hardly have responded to anything other," said Pons. "You ought not to have responded to it at all. It was surely obvious that only the most pressing matter could have caused Lady Heltsham to pawn her valuables and then to take the extreme measure of borrowing money against His Lordship's genuine *Tamerlane.* Affandi must have taken a tidy sum from her. Men of his stamp never know an end to greed. I knew he could not resist the chance to make new demands upon her when he read the story of her inheritance, and I was certain his approach to her would be made very quickly, as it was."

"And the letters Affandi held?"

Pons shrugged. "I submit they were the customary letters of a woman in love unwise enough to put down in her own handwriting things which ought never to have been written at all. Affandi learned of their existence somehow, and probably bought them. Knowing that she could not afford to have her husband know of their existence, he proceeded with methodical cold-bloodedness to blackmail her." He picked up the spurious *Tamerlane,* his eyes dancing. "I am delighted to add this curious memento to my little collection of items associated with my adventures in deduction."

Writers are notoriously underpaid for their work; just ask any writer. James Trevathan, for instance. Editors, on the other hand, don't believe this for a minute—particularly magazine editors, of which Warren Jukes is an all-too-prime example. Trevathan was sick and tired of grinding out fiction for Jukes at the rate of five cents a word; what he wanted—and surely deserved—was quite a bit more. Say, one thousand dollars a word. . . . This little slice of wry is a quintessential writer's story and one of Lawrence Block's best, which makes it something special indeed. Block is also a first-rate novelist, one of the most accomplished working in the suspense field today, with an impressive credit list of straight suspense novels (Ariel, The Deadly Honeymoon) *and no less than three successful mystery series—the adventures of spy Evan Tanner* (Me Tanner, You Jane), *burglar Bernie Rhodenbarr* (The Burglar Who Quoted Kipling), *and tough private investigator Matt Scudder. Scudder's most recent case,* Eight Million Ways to Die, *was voted the Shamus award of the Private Eye Writers of America as the best novel about a private detective for the year 1982.*

ONE THOUSAND DOLLARS A WORD

Laurence Block

The editor's name was Warren Jukes. He was a lean sharp-featured man with slender long-fingered hands and a narrow line for a mouth. His black hair was going attractively gray on top and at the temples. As usual, he wore a stylish three-piece suit. As usual, Trevathan felt logy and unkempt in comparison, like a bear having trouble shaking off the torpor of hibernation.

"Sit down, Jim," Jukes said. "Always a pleasure. Don't tell me you're bringing in another manuscript already? It never ceases to amaze me the way you keep grinding them out. Where do you get your ideas, anyway? But I guess you're tired of that question after all these years."

He was indeed, and that was not the only thing of which James Trevathan was heartily tired. But all he said was, "No, Warren. I haven't written another story."

"Oh?"

"I wanted to talk with you about the last one."

"But we talked about it yesterday," Jukes said, puzzled. "Over the telephone. I said it was fine and I was happy to have it for the magazine. What's the title, anyway? It was a play on words, but I can't remember it offhand."

" 'A Stitch in Crime,' " Trevathan said.

"Right, that's it. Good title, good story, and all of it wrapped up in your solid professional prose. What's the problem?"

"Money," Trevathan said.

"A severe case of the shorts, huh?" The editor smiled. "Well, I'll be putting a voucher through this afternoon. You'll have the check early next week. I'm afraid that's the best I can do, Jimbo. The corporate machinery can only go so fast."

"It's not the time," Trevathan said. "It's the amount. What are you paying for the story, Warren?"

"Why, the usual. How long was it? Three thousand words, wasn't it?"

"Thirty-five hundred."

"So what does that come to? Thirty-five hundred at a nickel a word is what? One seventy-five, right?"

"That's right, yes."

"So you'll have a check in that amount early next week, as soon as possible, and if you want I'll ring you when I have it in hand and you can come over and pick it up. Save waiting a couple of days for the neither-rain-nor-snow people to get it from my desk to yours."

"It's not enough."

"Beg your pardon?"

"The price," Trevathan said. He was having trouble with this conversation. He'd written a script for it in his mind on the way to Jukes's office, and he'd been infinitely more articulate then than now. "I should get more money," he managed. "A nickel a word is . . . Warren, that's no money at all."

"It's what we pay, Jim. It's what we've always paid."

"Exactly."

"So?"

"Do you know how long I've been writing for you people, Warren?"

"Quite a few years."

"Twenty years, Warren."

"Really?"

"I sold a story called 'Hanging by a Thread' to you twenty years ago last month. It ran twenty-two hundred words and you paid me a hundred and ten bucks for it."

"Well, there you go," Jukes said.

"I've been working twenty years, Warren, and I'm getting the same money now that I got then. Everything's gone up except my income. When I wrote my first story for you I could take one of those nickels that a word of mine brought and buy a candy bar with it. Have you bought a candy bar recently, Warren?"

Jukes touched his belt buckle. "If I went and bought candy bars," he said, "my clothes wouldn't fit me."

"Candy bars are forty cents. Some of them cost thirty-five. And I still get a nickel a word. But let's forget candy bars."

"Fine with me, Jim."

"Let's talk about the magazine. When you bought 'Hanging by a Thread,' what did the magazine sell for on the stands?"

"Thirty-five cents, I guess."

"Wrong. Twenty-five. About six months later you went to thirty-five. Then you went to fifty, and after that sixty and then seventy-five. And what does the magazine sell for now?"

"A dollar a copy."

"And you still pay your authors a nickel a word. That's really wealth beyond the dreams of avarice, isn't it, Warren?"

Jukes sighed heavily, propped his elbows on his desk

top, tented his fingertips. "Jim," he said, dropping his voice in pitch, "there are things you're forgetting. The magazine's no more profitable than it was twenty years ago. In fact, we're working closer now than we did then. Do you know anything about the price of paper? It makes candy look pretty stable by comparison. I could talk for hours on the subject of the price of paper. Not to mention all the other printing costs, and shipping costs and more other costs than I want to mention or you want to hear about. You look at that buck-a-copy price and you think we're flying high, but it's not like that at all. We were doing better way back then. Every single cost of ours has gone through the roof."

"Except the basic one."

"How's that?"

"The price you pay for material. That's what your readers are buying from you, you know. Stories. Plots and characters. Prose and dialogue. Words. And you pay the same for them as you did twenty years ago. It's the only cost that's stayed the same."

Jukes took a pipe apart and began running a pipe cleaner through the stem. Trevathan started talking about his own costs—his rent, the price of food. When he paused for breath Warren Jukes said, "Supply and demand, Jim."

"What's that?"

"Supply and demand. Do you think it's hard for me to fill the magazine at a nickel a word? See that pile of scripts over there? That's what this morning's mail brought. Nine out of ten of those stories are from new writers who'd write for nothing if it got them into print. The other ten percent is from pros who are damned glad when they see that nickel-a-word check instead of getting their stories mailed back to them. You know, I buy just about everything you write for us, Jim. One reason is I like your work, but that's not the only reason. You've been with us for twenty years and we like to do business with our old friends. But you evidently want me to raise your word rate, and we don't pay more than five cents a word to anybody, because in the first place we haven't got any surplus in the budget and in the second place we damn well don't *have* to pay more than that. So before I raise your rate, old friend, I'll give your stories back to you. Because I don't have any choice."

Trevathan sat and digested this for a few moments. He thought of some things to say but left them unsaid. He might have asked Jukes how the editor's own salary had fluctuated over the years, but what was the point of that? He could write for a nickel a word or he could not write for them at all. That was the final word on the subject.

"Jim? Shall I put through a voucher or do you want 'A Stitch in Crime' back?"

"What would I do with it? No, I'll take the nickel a word, Warren."

"If there was a way I could make it more—"

"I understand."

"You guys should have got yourselves a union years ago. Give you a little collective muscle. Or you could try writing something else. We're in a squeeze, you know, and if we were forced to pay more for material we'd probably have to fold the magazine altogether. But there are other fields where the pay is better."

"I've been doing this for twenty years, Warren. It's all I know. My God, I've got a reputation in the field, I've got an established name—"

"Sure. That's why I'm always happy to have you in the magazine. As long as I do the editing, Jimbo, and as long as you grind out the copy, I'll be glad to buy your yarns."

"At a nickel a word."

"Well—"

"Nothing personal, Warren. I'm just a little bitter. That's all."

"Hey, think nothing of it." Jukes got to his feet, came around from behind his desk. "So you got something off your chest, and we cleared the air a little. Now you know where you stand. Now you can go on home and knock off something sensational and get it to me, and if it's up to your usual professional standard you'll have another check coming your way. That's the way to double the old income, you know. Just double the old production."

"Good idea," Trevathan said.

"Of course it is. And maybe you can try something for another market while you're at it. It's not too late to branch out, Jim. God knows I don't want to lose you, but if you're having trouble getting by on what we can pay you, well—"

"It's a thought," Trevathan said.

Five cents a word.

Trevathan sat at his battered Underwood and stared at a blank sheet of paper. The paper had gone up a dollar a ream in the past year, and he could swear they'd cheapened the quality in the process. Everything cost more, he thought, except his own well-chosen words. They were still trading steadily at a nickel apiece.

Not too late to branch out, Jukes had told him. But that was a sight easier to say than to do. He'd tried writing for other kinds of markets, but detective stories were the only kind he'd ever had any luck with. His mind didn't seem to produce viable fictional ideas in other areas. When he'd tried writing longer works, novels, he'd always gotten hopelessly bogged down. He was a short-story writer, recognized and frequently anthologized, and he was prolific enough to keep himself alive that way, but—

But he was sick of living marginally, sick of grinding out story after story. And heartily sick of going through life on a nickel a word.

What would a decent word rate be?

Well, if they paid him twenty-five cents a word, then he'd at least be keeping pace with the price of a candy bar. Of course after twenty years you wanted to do a little better than stay even. Say they paid him a dollar a word. There were writers who earned that much. Hell, there were writers who earned a good deal more than that, writers whose books wound up on best-seller lists, writers who got six-figure prices for screenplays, writers who wrote themselves rich.

One thousand dollars a word.

The phrase popped into his mind, stunning in its simplicity, and before he was aware of it his fingers had typed the words on the page before him. He sat and looked at it, then worked the carriage return lever and typed the phrase again.

One thousand dollars a word.

He studied what he had typed, his mind racing on ahead, playing with ideas, shaking itself loose from its usual stereotyped thought patterns. Well, why not? Why shouldn't he earn a thousand dollars a word? Why not branch out into a new field?

Why not?

He took the sheet from the typewriter, crumpled it into a ball, pegged it in the general direction of the wastebasket. He rolled a new sheet in its place and sat looking at its blankness, waiting, thinking. Finally, word by halting word, he began to type.

Trevathan rarely rewrote his short stories. At a nickel a word he could not afford to. Furthermore, he had acquired a facility over the years which enabled him to turn out acceptable copy in first draft. Now, however, he was trying something altogether new and different, and so he felt the need to take his time getting it precisely right. Time and again he yanked false starts from the typewriter, crumpled them, hurled them at the wastebasket.

Until finally he had something he liked.

He read it through for the fourth or fifth time, then took it from the typewriter and read it again. It did the job, he decided. It was concise and clear and very much to the point.

He reached for the phone. When he'd gotten through to Jukes he said, "Warren? I've decided to take your advice."

"Wrote another story for us? Glad to hear it."

"No," he said, "another piece of advice you gave me. I'm branching out in a new direction."

"Well, I think that's terrific," Jukes said. "I really mean it. Getting to work on something big? A novel?"

"No, a short piece."

"But in a more remunerative area?"

"Definitely. I'm expecting to net a thousand dollars a word for what I'm doing this afternoon."

"A thousand—" Warren Jukes let out a laugh, making a sound similar to the yelp of a startled terrier. "Well, I don't know what you're up to, Jim, but let me wish you the best of luck with it. I'll tell you one thing. I'm damned glad you haven't lost your sense of humor."

Trevathan looked again at what he'd written. *"I've got a gun. Please fill this paper sack with thirty thousand dollars in used tens and twenties and fifties or I'll be forced to blow your stupid head off."*

"Oh, I've still got my sense of humor," he said. "Know what I'm going to do, Warren? I'm going to laugh all the way to the bank."

Nick Noble, the dipsomaniac ex-cop who is constantly pestered by an imaginary fly, appears in nine short stories published between 1942 and 1954. All are exercises in classic detection, and none is better than this one set in a branch of the Los Angeles Public Library and involving the murder of a cataloguer and a dying message in which "QL 696. C9" is the key component. William A. P. White (1911–68) wrote many other criminous short stories under the pseudonym of Anthony Boucher, some of which feature a second prominent series detective, Fergus O'Breen, and the best of which can be found in the recent collection from Southern Illinois University Press, Exeunt Murderers; *and several excellent novels, including* The Case of the Seven of Calvary *(1937),* The Case of the Baker Street Irregulars *(1940), and* Rocket to the Morgue *(1942, as by H. H. Holmes). But he was much more than just a writer of detective fiction; indeed, he was a modern Renaissance Man. Among his other achievements are stories of fantasy and science fiction, the most incisive series of book reviews either the mystery or sf field has yet known, the editorship of many fine anthologies, and passions for opera, poker, foreign languages, and several scholarly subjects. He was also the co-founder (in 1949) and editor of* The Magazine of Fantasy and Science Fiction, *a periodical which is still being published today.*

QL 696.C9

Anthony Boucher

The librarian's body had been removed from the swivel chair, but Detective Lieutenant Donald MacDonald stood beside the desk. This was only his second murder case, and he was not yet hardened enough to use the seat freshly vacated by a corpse. He stood and faced the four individuals, one of whom was a murderer.

"Our routine has been completed," he said, "and I've taken a statement from each of you. But before I hand in my report, I want to go over those statements in the presence of all of you. If anything doesn't jibe, I want you to say so."

The librarian's office of the Serafin Pelayo branch of the Los Angeles Public Library was a small room. The three witnesses and the murderer (but which was which?) sat crowded together. The girl in the gray dress—Stella Swift, junior librarian—shifted restlessly. "It was all so . . . so confusing and so awful," she said.

MacDonald nodded sympathetically. "I know." It was this girl who had found the body. Her eyes were dry now, but her nerves were still tense. "I'm sorry to insist on this, but . . ." His glance surveyed the other three: Mrs. Cora Jarvis, children's librarian, a fluffy kitten; James Stickney, library patron, a youngish man with no tie and wild hair; Norbert Utter, high-school teacher, a lean, almost ascetic-looking man of forty-odd. One of these . . .

"Immediately before the murder," MacDonald began, "the branch librarian Miss Benson was alone in this office typing. Apparently" (he gestured at the sheet of paper in the typewriter) "a draft for a list of needed replacements. This office can be reached only through those stacks, which can in turn be reached only by passing the main desk. Mrs. Jarvis, you were then on duty at that desk, and according to you only these three people were then in the stacks. None of them, separated as they were in the stacks, could see each other or the door of this office." He paused.

The thin teacher spoke up. "But this is ridiculous, officer. Simply because I was browsing in the stacks to find some fresh ideas for outside reading . . ."

The fuzzy-haired Stickney answered him. "The Loot's right. Put our stories together, and it's got to be one of us. Take your medicine, comrade."

"Thank you, Mr. Stickney. That's the sensible attitude. Now Miss Benson was shot, to judge by position and angle, from that doorway. The weapon was dropped on the spot. All four of you claim to have heard that shot from your respective locations and hurried toward it. It was Miss Swift who opened the door and discovered the body. Understandably enough, she fainted. Mrs. Jarvis looked after her while Mr. Stickney had presence of mind enough to phone the police. All of you watched each other, and no one entered this room until our arrival. Is all that correct?"

Little Mrs. Jarvis nodded. "My, Lieutenant, you put it all so neatly! You should have been a cataloguer like Miss Benson."

"A cataloguer? But she was head of the branch, wasn't she?"

"She had the soul of a cataloguer," said Mrs. Jarvis darkly.

"Now this list that she was typing when she was killed." MacDonald took the paper from the typewriter. "I want you each to look at that and tell me if the last item means anything to you."

The end of her list read:

Davies: MISSION TO MOSCOW (2 cop)
Kernan: DEFENSE WILL NOT WIN THE WAR
FIC MacInnes: ABOVE SUSP
QL 696. C9

The paper went from hand to hand. It evoked nothing but frowns and puzzled headshakings.

"All right." MacDonald picked up the telephone pad from the desk. "Now can any of you tell me why a librarian should have jotted down the phone number of the F.B.I.?"

This question fetched a definite reaction from Stickney, a sort of wry exasperation; but it was Miss Swift who answered, and oddly enough with a laugh. "Dear Miss Benson . . ." she said. "Of course she'd have the F.B.I.'s number. Professional necessity."

"I'm afraid I don't follow that."

"Some librarians have been advancing the theory, you see, that a librarian can best help defense work by watching what people use which books. For instance, if somebody keeps borrowing every work you have on high explosives, you know he's a dangerous saboteur planning to blow up the aqueduct and you turn him over to the G-men."

"Seriously? It sounds like nonsense."

"I don't know, Lieutenant. Aside from card catalogues and bird study, there was one thing Miss Benson loved. And that was America. She didn't think it was nonsense."

"I see . . . And none of you has anything further to add to this story?"

"I," Mr. Utter announced, "have fifty themes to correct this evening and . . ."

Lieutenant MacDonald shrugged. "O.K. Go ahead. All of you. And remember you're apt to be called back for further questioning at any moment."

"And the library?" Miss Jarvis asked. "I suppose I'm ranking senior in charge now and I . . ."

"I spoke to the head of the Branches Department on the phone. She agrees with me that it's best to keep the branch closed until our investigation is over. But I'll ask you and Miss Swift to report as usual tomorrow; the head of Branches will be here then too, and we can confer further on any matters touching the library itself."

"And tomorrow I was supposed to have a story hour. Well at least," the children's librarian sighed, "I shan't have to learn a new story tonight."

Alone, Lieutenant MacDonald turned back to the desk. He set the pad down by the telephone and dialed the number which had caught his attention. It took time to reach the proper authority and establish his credentials, but he finally secured the promise of a full file on all information which Miss Alice Benson had turned over to the F.B.I.

"Do you think that's it?" a voice asked eagerly.

He turned. It was the junior librarian, the girl with the gray dress and the gold-brown hair. "Miss Swift!"

"I hated to sneak in on you, but I want to know. Miss Benson was an old dear and I . . . I found her and . . . Do you think that's it? That she really did find out something for the F.B.I. and because she did . . . ?"

"It seems likely," he said slowly. "According to all the evidence, she was on the best of terms with her staff. She had no money to speak of, and she was old for a crime-of-passion set-up. Utter and Stickney apparently knew her only casually as regular patrons of this branch. What have we left for a motive, unless it's this F.B.I. business?"

"We thought it was so funny. We used to rib her about being a G-woman. And now . . . Lieutenant, you've got to find out who killed her." The girl's lips set firmly and her eyes glowed.

MacDonald reached a decision. "Come on."

"Come? Where to?"

"I'm going to drive you home. But first we're going to stop off and see a man, and you're going to help me give him all the facts of this screwball case."

"Who? Your superior?"

MacDonald hesitated. "Yes," he said at last. "My superior."

He explained about Nick Noble as they drove. How Lieutenant Noble, a dozen years ago, had been the smartest problem-cracker in the department. How his captain had got into a sordid scandal and squeezed out, leaving the innocent Noble to take the rap. How his wife had needed a vital operation just then, and hadn't got it. How the widowed and disgraced man had sunk until . . .

"Nobody knows where he lives or what he lives on. All we know is that we can find him at a little joint on North Main, drinking cheap sherry by the water glass. Sherry's all that life has left him—that, and the ability to make the toughest problem come crystal clear. Somewhere in the back of that wino's mind is a precision machine that sorts the screwiest facts into the one inevitable pattern. He's the court of last appeal on a case that's nuts, and God knows this one is. QL 696. C9 . . . Screwball Division, L.A.P.D., the boys call him."

The girl shuddered a little as they entered the Chula Negra Café. It was not a choice spot for the élite. Not that it was a dive, either. No juke, no B-girls; just a counter and booths for the whole-hearted eating and drinking of the Los Angeles Mexicans.

MacDonald remembered which booth was Nick Noble's sanctum. The little man sat there, staring into a half-empty glass of sherry, as though he hadn't moved since MacDonald last saw him after the case of the stopped timepieces. His skin was dead white and his features sharp and thin. His eyes were of a blue so pale that the irises were almost invisible.

"Hi!" said MacDonald. "Remember me?"

One thin blue-veined hand swatted at the sharp nose. The pale eyes rested on the couple. "MacDonald . . ." Nick Noble smiled faintly. "Glad. Sit down." He glanced at Stella Swift. "Yours?"

MacDonald coughed. "No. Miss Swift, Mr. Noble. Miss Swift and I have a story to tell you."

Nick Noble's eyes gleamed dimly. "Trouble?"

"Trouble. Want to hear it?"

Nick Noble swatted at his nose again. "Fly," he explained to the girl. "Stays there." There was no fly. He drained his glass of sherry. "Give."

MacDonald gave, much of the same précis that he had given to the group in the office. When he had finished, Nick Noble sat silent for so long that Stella Swift looked apprehensively at his glass. Then he stirred slightly, beckoned to a waitress, pointed to his empty glass, and said to the girl, "This woman. Benson. What was she like?"

"She was nice," said Stella. "But of course she *was* a cataloguer."

"Cataloguer?"

"You're not a librarian. You wouldn't understand what that means. But I gather that when people go to library school—I never did, I'm just a junior—most of them suffer through cataloguing, but a few turn out to be born cataloguers. Those are a race apart. They know a little of everything, all the systems of classification, Dewey, Library of Congress, down to the last number, and just how many spaces you indent each item on a typed card, and all about bibliography, and they shudder in their souls if the least little thing is wrong. They have eyes like eagles and memories like elephants."

"With that equipment," said MacDonald, "she might really have spotted something for the F.B.I."

"Might," said Nick Noble. Then to the girl, "Hobbies?"

"Miss Benson's? Before the war she used to be a devoted bird-watcher, and of course being what she was she had a positively Kieranesque knowledge of birds. But lately she's been all wrapped up in trying to spot saboteurs instead."

"I'm pretty convinced," MacDonald contributed, "that that's our angle, screwy as it sounds. The F.B.I. lead may point out our man, and there's still hope from the lab reports on prints and the paraffin test."

"Tests," Nick Noble snorted. "All you do is teach criminals what not to do."

"But if those fail us, we've got a message from Miss Benson herself telling us who killed her. And that's what I want you to figure out." He handed over the paper from the typewriter. "It's pretty clear what happened. She was typing, looked up, and saw her murderer with a gun. If she wrote down his name, he might see it and destroy the paper. So she left this cryptic indication. It can't possibly be part of the list she was typing; Mrs. Jarvis and Miss Swift don't recognize it as library routine. And the word above breaks off in the middle. Those letters and figures are her dying words. Can you read them?"

Nick Noble's pallid lips moved faintly. "Q L six nine six point C nine." He leaned back in the booth and his eyes glazed over. "Names," he said.

"Names?"

"Names of four."

"Oh. Norbert Utter, the teacher; James Stickney, the

nondescript; Mrs. Cora Jarvis, the children's librarian; and Miss Stella Swift here."

"So." Nick Noble's eyes came to life again. "Thanks, MacDonald. Nice problem. Give you proof tonight."

Stella Swift gasped. "Does that mean that he . . . ?"

MacDonald grinned. "You're grandstanding for the lady, Mr. Noble. You can't mean that you've solved that damned QL business like that?"

"Pencil," Nick Noble said.

Wonderingly, Lieutenant MacDonald handed one over. Nick Noble took a paper napkin, scrawled two words, folded it, and handed it to Stella. "Not now," he warned. "Keep it. Show to him later. Grandstanding . . . ! Need more proof first. Get it soon. Let me know about test. F.B.I."

MacDonald rose frowning. "I'll let you know. But how you can . . ."

"Good-bye, Mr. Noble. It's been so nice meeting you."

But Nick Noble appeared not to hear Stella's farewell. He was staring into his glass and not liking what he saw there.

Lieutenant MacDonald drew up before the girl's rooming house. "I may need a lot of help on the technique of librarianship in this case," he said. "I'll be seeing you soon."

"Thanks for the ride. And for taking me to that strange man. I'll never forget how . . . It seems—I don't know—uncanny, doesn't it?" A little tremor ran through her lithe body.

"You know, you aren't exactly what I'd expect a librarian to be. I've run into the wrong ones. I think of them as something with flat shirtwaists and glasses and a bun. Of course Mrs. Jarvis isn't either, but you . . ."

"I do wear glasses when I work," Stella confessed. "And you aren't exactly what I'd expected a policeman to be, or I shouldn't have kept them off all this time." She touched her free flowing hair and punned, "And you should see me with a bun on."

"That's a date. We'll start with dinner and—"

"Dinner!" she exclaimed. "Napkin!" She rummaged in her handbag. "I won't tell you what he said, that isn't fair, but just to check on—" She unfolded the paper napkin.

She did not say another word, despite all MacDonald's urging. She waved good-bye in pantomime, and her eyes, as she watched him drive off, were wide with awe and terror.

Lieutenant MacDonald glared at the reports on the paraffin tests of his four suspects. All four negative. No sign that any one of them had recently used a firearm. Nick Noble was right; all you do is teach criminals what not to do. They learn about nitrite specks in the skin, so a handkerchief wrapped over the hand . . . The phone rang.

"Lafferty speaking. Los Angeles Field Office, F.B.I. You wanted the dope on this Alice Benson's reports?"

"Please."

"O.K. She did turn over to us a lot of stuff on a man who'd been reading nothing but codes and ciphers and sabotage methods and explosives and God knows what all. Sounded like a correspondence course for the complete Fifth Columnist. We check up on him, and he's a poor devil of a pulp writer. Sure he wanted to know how to be a spy and a saboteur; but just so's he could write about 'em. We gave him a thorough going over, he's in the clear."

"Name?"

"James Stickney."

"I know him," said MacDonald dryly. "And is that all?"

"We'll send you the file, but that's the gist of it. I gather the Benson woman had something else she wasn't ready to spill, but if it's as much help as that was . . . Keep an eye on that library though. There's something going on."

"How so?"

"Three times in the past two months we've trailed suspects into that Serafin Pelayo branch, and not bookworms either. They didn't do anything there or contact anybody, but that's pretty high for coincidence in one small branch.

Keep an eye open. And if you hit on anything, maybe we can work together."

"Thanks. I'll let you know." MacDonald hung up. So Stickney had been grilled by the F.B.I. on Miss Benson's information. Revenge for the indignity? Damned petty motive. And still . . . The phone rang again.

"Lieutenant MacDonald? This is Mrs. Jarvis. Remember me?"

"Yes indeed. You've thought of something more about—?"

"I certainly have. I think I've figured out what the QL thing means. At least I think I've figured how we can find out what it means. You see . . ." There was a heavy sound, a single harsh thud. Mrs. Jarvis groaned.

"Mrs. Jarvis! What's the matter? Has anything—"

"Elsie . . ." MacDonald heard her say faintly. Then the line was dead.

"Concussion," the police surgeon said. "She'll live. Not much doubt of that. But she won't talk for several days, and there's no telling how much she'll remember then."

"Elsie," said Lieutenant MacDonald. It sounded like an oath.

"We'll let you know as soon as she can see you. O.K., boys. Get along." Stella Swift trembled as the stretcher bearers moved off. "Poor Cora . . . When her husband comes home from Lockheed and finds . . . I was supposed to have dinner with them tonight and I come here and find you . . ."

Lieutenant MacDonald looked down grimly at the metal statue. "The poor devil's track trophy, and they use it to brain his wife. . . . And what the hell brings you here?" he demanded as the lean figure of Norbert Utter appeared in the doorway.

"I live across the street, Lieutenant," the teacher explained. "When I saw the cars here and the ambulance, why naturally I . . . Don't tell me there's been another . . . ?"

"Not quite. So you live across the street? Miss Swift, do you mind staying here to break the news to Mr. Jarvis? It'd come easier from you than from me. I want to step over to Mr. Utter's for a word with him."

Utter forced a smile. "Delighted to have you, Lieutenant."

The teacher's single apartment was comfortably undistinguished. His own books, MacDonald noticed, were chosen with unerring taste; the library volumes on a table seemed incongruous.

"Make yourself at home, Lieutenant, as I have no doubt you will. Now what is it you wanted to talk to me about?"

"First might I use your phone?"

"Certainly. I'll get you a drink meanwhile. Brandy?"

MacDonald nodded as he dialed the Chula Negra. Utter left the room. A Mexican voice answered, and MacDonald sent its owner to fetch Nick Noble. As he waited, he idly picked up one of those incongruous library books. He picked it up carelessly and it fell open. A slip of paper, a bookmark perhaps, dropped from the fluttering pages. MacDonald noticed typed letters:

430945q57w7qo0oqd3 . . .

"Noble here."

"Good." His attention snapped away from the paper. "Listen." And he told the results of the tests and the information from the F.B.I. and ended with the attack on Mrs. Jarvis. Utter came to the door once, looked at MacDonald, at the book, and at the paper. "And so," MacDonald concluded, "we've got a last message again. 'Elsie. . . .' "

" 'Elsie . . .' " Nick Noble's voice repeated thoughtfully.

"Any questions?"

"No. Phone me tomorrow morning. Later tonight maybe. Tell you then."

MacDonald hung up frowning. That paper . . . Suddenly

he had it. The good old typewriter code, so easy to write and to decipher. For each letter use the key above it. He'd run onto such a cipher in a case recently; he should be able to work it in his head. He visualized a keyboard. The letters and figures shifted into

reportatusualplace . . .

Mr. Utter came back with a tray and two glasses of brandy. His lean face essayed a host's smile. "Refreshments, Lieutenant."

"Thank you."

"And now we can—or should you care for a cheese cracker?"

"Don't bother."

"No bother." He left the room. Lieutenant MacDonald looked at the cipher, then at the glasses. Deftly he switched them. Then he heard the slightest sound outside the door, a sigh of expectation confirmed and faint footsteps moving off. MacDonald smiled and switched the glasses back again.

Mr. Utter returned with a bowl of cheese wafers and the decanter. "To the success of your investigations, Lieutenant." They raised their glasses. Mr. Utter took a cautious sip, then coolly emptied his glass out the window. "You outsmarted me, Lieutenant," he announced. "I had not expected you to be up to the double gambit. I underrated you and apologize." He filled his own glass afresh from the decanter, and they drank. It was good brandy, unusually good for a teacher's salary.

"So we're dropping any pretense?" said MacDonald.

Mr. Utter shrugged. "You saw that paper. I was unpardonably careless. You are armed and I am not. Pretense would be foolish when you can so readily examine the rest of those books."

Lieutenant MacDonald's hand stayed near his shoulder

holster. "It was a good enough scheme. Certain prearranged books were your vehicles. Any accidental patron finding the messages, or even the average librarian, would pay little attention. Anything winds up as a marker in a library book. A few would be lost, but the safety made up for that. You prepared the messages here at home, returned them in the books so that you weren't seen inserting them in public..."

"You reconstruct admirably, Lieutenant."

"And who collected them?"

"Frankly, I do not know. The plan was largely arranged so that no man could inform on another."

"But Miss Benson discovered it, and Miss Benson had to be removed."

Mr. Utter shook his head. "I do not expect you to believe me, Lieutenant. But I have no more knowledge of Miss Benson's death than you have."

"Come now, Utter. Surely your admitted activities are a catamount to a confession of—"

"Is *catamount* quite the word you want, Lieutenant?"

"I don't know. My tongue's fuzzy. So's my mind. I don't know what's wrong. . . ."

Mr. Utter smiled, slowly and with great pleasure. "Of course, Lieutenant. Did you really think I had underrated you? Naturally I drugged both glasses. Then whatever gambit you chose, I had merely to refill my own."

Lieutenant MacDonald ordered his hand to move toward the holster. His hand was not interested.

"Is there anything else," Mr. Utter asked gently, "which you should care to hear—while you can still hear anything?"

The room began a persistent circular joggling.

Nick Noble wiped his pale lips, thrust the flask of sherry back into his pocket, and walked into the Main library. At the information desk in the rotunda he handed a slip of paper to the girl in charge. On it was penciled

QL 696. C9

The girl looked up puzzled. "I'm sorry, but—"

"Elsie," said Nick Noble hesitantly.

The girl's face cleared. "Oh. Of course. Well, you see, in this library we . . ."

The crash of the door helped to clear Lieutenant MacDonald's brain. The shot set up thundering waves that ripped through the drugwebs in his skull. The cold water on his head and later the hot coffee inside finished the job.

At last he lit a cigaret and felt approximately human. The big man with the moon face, he gathered, was Lafferty, F.B.I. The girl, he had known in the first instant, was Stella Swift.

". . . just winged him when he tried to get out of the window," Lafferty was saying. "The doc'll probably want us to lay off the grilling till tomorrow. Then you'll have your murderer, Mac, grilled and on toast."

MacDonald put up a hand to keep the top of his head on. "There's two things puzzle me. A, how you got here?"

Lafferty nodded at the girl.

"I began remembering things," she said, "after you went off with Mr. Utter. Especially I remembered Miss Benson saying just yesterday how she had some more evidence for the F.B.I. and how amazed she was that some people could show such an utter lack of patriotism. Then she laughed and I wondered why and only just now I realized it was because she'd made an accidental pun. There were other things too, and so I—"

"We had a note from Miss Benson today," Lafferty added. "It hadn't reached me yet when I phoned you. It was vaguely promising, no names, but it tied in well enough with what Miss Swift told us to make us check. When we found the door locked and knew you were here . . ."

"Swell. And God knows I'm grateful to you both. But

my other puzzle: Just now, when Utter confessed the details of the message scheme thinking I'd never live to tell them, he still denied any knowledge of the murder. I can't help wondering . . ."

When MacDonald got back to his office, he found a memo:

> *The Public Library says do you want a book from the Main sent out to the Serafin Pelayo branch tomorrow morning? A man named Noble made the request, gave you as authority. Please confirm.*

MacDonald's head was dizzier than ever as he confirmed, wondering what the hell he was confirming.

The Serafin Pelayo branch was not open to the public the next morning, but it was well occupied. Outside in the reading room there waited the bandaged Mr. Utter, with Moon Lafferty on guard; the tousle-haired James Stickney, with a sergeant from Homicide; Hank Jarvis, eyes bleared from a sleepless night at his wife's bedside; and Miss Trumpeter, head of the Branches Department, impatiently awaiting the end of this interruption of her well-oiled branch routine.

Here in the office were Lieutenant MacDonald, Stella Swift, and Nick Noble. Today the girl wore a bright red dress, with a zipper which tantalizingly emphasized the fullness of her bosom. Lieutenant MacDonald held the book which had been sent out from the Main. Nick Noble held a flask.

"Easy," he was saying. "Elsie. Not a name. Letters L. C. Miss Swift mentioned systems of classification. Library of Congress."

"Of course," Stella agreed. "We don't use it in the Los Angeles Library; it's too detailed for a public system. But you have to study it in library school; so naturally I didn't know it, being a junior, but Mrs. Jarvis spotted it and Miss

Benson, poor dear, must have known it almost by heart.

MacDonald read the lettering on the spine of the book. "U.S. Library of Congress Classification. Q: Science."

Stella Swift sighed. "Thank Heavens. I was afraid it might be English literature."

MacDonald smiled. "I wonder if your parents knew nothing of literary history or a great deal, to name you Stella Swift."

Nick Noble drank and grunted. "Go on."

MacDonald opened the book and thumbed through pages. "QL, Zoölogy. QL 600, Vertebrates. QL 696, Birds, systematic list (subdivisions, A–Z)."

"Birds?" Stella wondered. "It was her hobby of course, but . . ."

MacDonald's eyes went on down the page:

e.g., .A2, Accipitriformes (Eagles, hawks, etc.)
.A3, Alciformes (Auks, puffins)
Alectorides, *see* Gruiformes

"Wonderful names," he said. "If only we had a suspect named Gruiformes . . . Point C seven," he went on, "Coraciiformes, see also . . . here we are: Point C nine, Cypseli. . . ."

The book slipped from his hands. Stella Swift jerked down her zipper and produced the tiny pistol which had contributed to the fullness of her bosom. Nick Noble's fleshless white hand lashed out, knocking over the flask, and seized her wrist. The pistol stopped halfway to her mouth, twisted down, and discharged at the floor. The bullet went through the volume of L. C. classification, just over the line reading

.C9, Cypseli (Swifts)

A sober and embittered Lieutenant MacDonald unfolded the paper napkin taken from the prisoner's handbag and read, in sprawling letters:

STELLA SWIFT

"Her confession's clear enough," he said. "A German mother, family in the Fatherland, pressure brought to bear. . . . She was the inventor of this library-message system and running it unknown even to those using it, like Utter. After her false guess with Stickney, Miss Benson hit the truth with St . . . the Swift woman. She had to be disposed of. Then that meant more, attacking Mrs. Jarvis when she guessed too much, and sacrificing Utter, an insignificant subordinate, as a scapegoat to account for Miss Benson's further hints to the F.B.I. But how the hell did you spot it, and right at the beginning of the case?"

"Pattern," said Nick Noble. "Had to fit." His sharp nose twitched, and he brushed the nonexistent fly off it. "Miss Benson was cataloguer. QL business had to be book number. Not system used here or recognized at once, but some system. Look at names: Cora Jarvis, James Stickney, Norbert Utter, Stella Swift. Swift only name could possibly have classifying number."

"But weren't you taking a terrible risk giving her that napkin? What happened to Mrs. Jarvis?"

Noble shook his head. "She was only one knew you'd consulted me. Attack me, show her hand. Too smart for that. Besides, used to taking risks, when I . . ." He left unfinished the reference to the days when he had been the best damned detective lieutenant in Los Angeles.

"We've caught a murderer," said Lieutenant MacDonald, "and we've broken up a spy ring." He looked at the spot where Stella Swift had been standing when she jerked her zipper. The sun from the window had glinted through her hair. "But I'm damned if I thank you."

"Understand," said Nick Noble flatly. He picked up the spilled flask and silently thanked God that there was one good slug of sherry left.

After Anthony Boucher's death in 1968, a group of mystery fans banded together to arrange a small convention in his honor. Since that first Bouchercon was held in 1970, the convention has grown into a major annual event attended each year by hundreds of writers, editors, filmmakers, and aficionados of mystery and detective fiction. It is perhaps fitting that someone should have written a short story of "Murder at the Bouchercon," a story (and a happening) that would have pleased Tony Boucher immensely; and fitting, too, that the story's author should be Edward D. Hoch, the most prolific and acclaimed modern writer of short crime fiction. Hoch has published more than six hundred stories during his twenty-five-year career, many of which involve his four main series characters: Simon Ark, a mystical detective; Rand, a retired spy; Nick Velvet, a thief who steals unusual items; and Captain Leopold, a policeman whose investigation called "The Oblong Room" won the Mystery Writers of America Edgar for best short story of 1967. Also to Hoch's credit are four novels, one of which, The Shattered Raven *(1969), deals with murder at the annual Mystery Writers of America awards dinner—and not coincidentally stars the same mystery-writer detective as "Murder at the Bouchercon," the aptly named Barney Hamet.*

MURDER AT THE BOUCHERCON

Edward D. Hoch

Barney Hamet arrived early at the Parkview Arms on Central Park South. The modern highrise hotel was busy on this Friday morning in October, though he doubted that much of the activity was directly connected with the Bouchercon scheduled to open at the hotel that evening. October was a good time to visit New York City, and a great many people were doing just that.

"Ah, Barney Hamet—I was hoping you'd be here!" a familiar voice greeted him as he signed the room registration and accepted his key.

"Sid Coleman! How've you been?"

Sid was a writer in his mid-fifties who had been active in Mystery Writers of America during the years when Barney was on the Board of Directors of the organization. He'd hit the skids when his long-time publishers discontinued their unprofitable mystery line, and his only recent sales had been to a small paperback house on the West Coast. "I can't complain," Sid said, though the grin that split his bony face was only a shadow of the one Barney remembered from the old days. "I'm living in San Diego now."

"Somebody told me that. I've missed seeing you around. I live upstate now, but I come to the city when I can."

"Yeah. Well, I thought I'd fly in for the Bouchercon and look the old town over—catch up on old friends. I keep reading about you, Barney. Doing a book a year now and most of them making the best-seller lists! You're a big name now. How's Susan?"

"Great! She has an article in *The New Yorker* this week." Barney never tired of applauding his wife, who pursued a vigorous writing career of her own. "She's researching a new book, but she promised to come down for the closing luncheon on Sunday." He knew he'd be answering the same question all weekend as writers and mystery fans asked him about her.

Sid smiled sadly. "You're a lucky man, Barney. You've got everything."

"In the writing business it comes and goes, Sid."

"Don't I know it. My wife went about the same time as my publishers."

The bellman was waiting to carry his bags to his room.

"I'll see you tonight, Sid," Barney said. "We'll have a drink together."

"Let's do that," Sid agreed.

The Bouchercon had originated in Los Angeles in May of 1970 as an annual weekend gathering of mystery fans and writers. It was named in honor of the late Anthony Boucher, who died in 1968 after a long and distinguished career as a writer, editor, and critic in the mystery and science-fiction fields. In the second year of its existence, Bouchercon shifted to an October event, where it had remained most years, gradually falling into a pattern of moving from the West Coast to the East and then the Midwest before repeating the cycle. Although Barney Hamet had attended only a few of the thirteen previous Bouchercons, he knew they had been held in cities like Los Angeles, San Francisco, Boston, Chicago, New York, Washington, D.C., and Milwaukee.

Though they did not attract the thousands of people who flocked to science-fiction conventions, the Bouchercons had gradually built attendance from less than a hundred in the early years to a figure that generally approached five hundred these days. Many of the local fans who helped organize them were otherwise involved in the field, operating mystery bookshops or publishing critical studies of the genre.

This year's Bouchercon, organized by columnist and film critic Chris Steinbrunner and bookseller-publisher Otto Penzler, was the second they'd presented in New York. The two were authors of the highly regarded *Encyclopedia of Mystery & Detection.*

Barney had been in his room less than half an hour when he received a phone call from Otto, checking to make sure he'd arrived. His next call was from Mike Manners, a fan from Florida who corresponded with Barney and had published an annotated bibliography of his works.

"Barney," he said, "how are you? Are you free? A bunch of us are in my room with a jug of wine. Come join us."

"Well—" Barney hesitated. There were some errands he wanted to do.

"There's someone here who's been digging into Kazer's background. You should talk to him."

Part of Bouchercon XIV was going to be a retrospective tribute to Conrad Kazer, a midwestern mystery writer who had lived practically as a recluse until his death in a fire five years earlier. Barney was to take part in a panel discussion of Kazer's writing the following afternoon and planned to speak about him at Sunday's concluding luncheon as well. It couldn't do any harm to chat with this man about him and maybe pick up some fresh insight. And Barney knew his presence would please Manners, even if it was only for a half hour.

"Sure, Mike," he said. "What room are you in?"

"Five forty-three. Turn left when you get off the elevator."

"I'll be right down."

Barney combed his hair and slipped into his sport coat, leaving the tie on the bureau. The weekend's festivities were beginning, and he wished Susan was with him. . . .

Room 543 was already crowded when he arrived, and Mike introduced him to the few people he didn't know. Mike was a genial middle-aged man with a short beard and a paunch that had grown since the last time Barney had seen him. "Here, Barney—I want you to meet Rain Wilson."

She was a pretty girl in her twenties, with long blond hair worn straight to her shoulders. Barney shook her hand, noticed the nervously applied nailpolish, and said, "A character in my first novel was named Rain. It's an unusual name."

Her face lit up. "I know. I got it from your novel. It isn't the name I was born with."

"I'm flattered."

"I've read everything you've written, Mr. Hamet. I think I'm your biggest fan—even bigger than Mike here."

"Call me Barney. It will make me feel less old."

"All right. But I like older men."

Mike Manners tapped him on the shoulder.

"Barney, this is the fellow I mentioned on the phone. Dave Glass—Barney Hamet."

"Nice to meet you," Barney answered automatically. Glass was a thin young man with black hair and a prominent Adam's apple. The fans were getting younger every year.

"Kazer," the young man said at once, as if to grab Barney's attention before there were further interruptions. "What do you know about him?"

Barney shrugged. "A great mystery writer, something of a recluse in his last years—published a dozen novels and fifty or so short stories. He had a very cinematic style, which made his stuff great for movies and TV, but he was a hard man to deal with. Harder since he burned himself up in his Indiana farmhouse five years ago, leaving no heirs and only a small-town bank out there as literary executor of his estate. Nothing of his has been reprinted or filmed since his death because the bank's got it all tied up, and they're hell to deal with from what I hear."

Dave Glass nodded. "Those are the basic facts, but there's more. Did you know, for instance, that Kazer lived for a time in San Francisco, and was actually married for a few years?"

"Interesting," Barney admitted. "Maybe you can publish an article on him in one of the fan magazines."

"He was supposed to be fifty-seven when he died, but I think he was a year older than that."

Barney wondered if anyone but a few loyal Kazer fans would really care. It was the man's writings that were important, after all. "I can see you've done a great deal of research," he said politely.

"Not only that, but I've got a great idea for the future. Every year science-fiction fans hold dozens of weekend conventions here in the U.S. and even overseas. For the mystery fan there's only the Bouchercon. I've been thinking of organizing a Kazercon, in memory of Conrad Kazer."

"Well, good luck," Barney told David Glass. "These things take a great deal of planning."

"Oh, I know that, I've been talking with Otto and Chris about all the work involved. But I think I could do it. I'm wondering about next spring, maybe in Chicago. That's where I'm from."

"Kazercon," Barney repeated. "Well, I don't know—"

Rain Wilson reappeared at his elbow and Barney went off with her to a corner of the crowded room. She handed him a fresh glass of wine and said, "You really shouldn't spend too much time with some of these people. They'll talk your ears off if they get a chance."

"Thanks for rescuing me."

Mike Manners came over to join them. "What do you think of Dave's idea?"

"A Kazercon? Do we really need one?"

"I know—but he's a smart kid. He just might pull it off. Did you hear that Kazer's bank has sold the rights to all his books and stories?"

"Really? That's a surprise."

Manners nodded. "A guy named Howard Pryor. He sent out letters to publishers and film studios last week, with a copy of a letter from the bank confirming that he now owns the rights. Otto and Chris urged him to attend the Bouchercon tribute to Kazer and he said he'd be here tomorrow."

"I hear movie and TV companies have been trying to get those rights for years, to say nothing of paperback publishers. I wonder if Monica's heard about it." Monica Drews had been Kazer's editor before he died, but the books had gone out of print and her firm had relinquished all rights to them before the Kazer revival got under way.

"Is she coming?"

"I imagine so." Barney glanced at his watch. "Registration will be starting soon. I want to change and get down there."

"Chris asked me to introduce you at the opening session tonight. O.K.?"

"Fine! I always like to have a *friend* introduce me."

An hour later Barney was at the registration desk, smiling gamely as a pretty redhead pinned his nametag on his lapel and a photographer snapped a picture. Because the Bouchercon was a three-day event with admissions available on a daily basis, his tag had a little gold star indicating he had paid for all three days. Other symbols would be used for those who arrived on Saturday or Sunday.

"Good to see you, Barney," Monica Drews said, coming up to him with a drink in her hand.

"Monica!" Barney said, giving her a quick hug. "How've you been?"

"I'm feeling a little old, Barney. Maybe I need a man." Though past fifty, Monica was still one of the most striking women on the Manhattan literary scene—tall and handsome, with piercing blue eyes and a razor-sharp mind that went to the heart of any problem. She'd known Conrad Kazer perhaps better than anyone in New York.

Barney glanced around the registration area and said, "Sid Coleman is here."

"That pest. He's after me to buy his new novel. The man's a has-been, Barney."

"He was a good writer once."

"That's right, he was."

Barney looked at her glass. "Can I get you another drink?"

Monica shook her head. "I'd better stay sober for the first session at least. Are you going to speak?"

"Just briefly. I hear someone has bought the rights to Kazer's things."

"I heard it, too. Damn, I wish I could have gotten to that bank first! Now I'll have to deal with this fellow Pryor, whoever he is."

"Does Heathway want to reissue Kazer's novels?"

She nodded. "We're starting a line of trade paperback mysteries from our backlist, and I'd like Kazer on it. We were crazy to let him get away. Pryor's talking about movie sales and that could really spark a Kazer revival."

By the time the opening session began early that evening, the place was full of familiar faces. Barney was chatting with Don Westlake and Mary Higgins Clark when Carolyn Penzler, Otto's wife, urged everyone to be seated so the program could begin.

Finally Chris and Otto took the stage to introduce Phyllis White, Anthony Boucher's widow and a regular guest at the Bouchercons honoring her husband—a charming woman. Then it was Mike Manners's turn.

"There's a fine program ahead of us this weekend," he began, speaking from a page of notes. "I know Chris has a fine selection of films for us, and I'm personally looking forward to the Sherlock Holmes panel tomorrow afternoon. And as you know, we'll also have a panel on the life and work of that master of the macabre mystery, Conrad Kazer.

"But right now I have the privilege of introducing the best-selling author of fifteen novels and numerous short stories. He and his wife live upstate now, but he's with us in Manhattan tonight and it's my great pleasure to introduce him—Barney Hamet!"

Barney rose, acknowledging the applause, and stepped to the microphone to offer the usual thanks. The audience seemed to want him to speak more, but with two other appearances on the weekend schedule he didn't want to wear out his welcome.

Half an hour later, skipping the film program, he found himself in the bar with Sid Coleman and Rain Wilson. After a time Sid excused himself and he was alone with Rain. "Dave Glass keeps cornering Monica Drews," she told him.

"Probably telling her his plans for the Kazercon."

"What do you think of it?"

Barney shrugged.

"Tell me about your wife."

"She's Susan Veldt. She's a well-known writer."

"So are you," Rain Wilson reminded him.

Barney stayed drinking with Rain until well after midnight. When he finally went back to his room, he saw the telephone-message light blinking an angry red, and his first thought was that Susan had tried to reach him. He called the message desk to discover Monica Drews had phoned him about five minutes earlier. Monica lived alone up in Stamford and had taken a room for the weekend to avoid the extra train travel. She had left a message for Barney to call her in Room 712 whenever he got in.

He tried 712 but there was no answer. It was only one floor below and he took the stairs down, thinking she might be at a party in a room down the hall. But the seventh floor was quiet.

He knocked at her door and there was no answer. On an impulse, he tried the doorknob and it opened. A small piece of tape had been placed over the latch bolt to keep it from locking when the door was closed.

Monica was slumped over the writing desk near her bed. An ugly-looking hunting knife protruded from the center of her back.

Barney took a deep breath and steadied himself against the wall. Who in the world would want to murder Monica Drews? He looked closer and saw a hotel pen in her right hand. She'd written something on the little memo pad by the phone. *Barney 806*—his room number—and then in a shaky scrawl he could barely read: *Kazer con.*

He left the room, careful not to touch anything, and went downstairs to report his discovery to hotel security.

Following an hour of police questioning and a 2:00 A.M. meeting with Chris and Otto, it was decided that the Bouchercon should continue on schedule, with a morning tribute to Monica. The police seemed convinced a hotel thief was responsible for the killing, tending to rule out participants at the Bouchercon as suspects. Still, there was the matter of her dying message—they weren't overlooking that.

Barney phoned Susan to tell her what had happened before she read it in the morning papers.

"Are you involved?" she asked.

"Of course not!"

"Then stay out of it, Barney," she pleaded. "I'll be down Sunday morning."

"Good. See you then."

"Barney?"

"Yes?"

"I love you."

"Me, too," he said.

He managed about four hours of restless sleep before he awakened and sat on the edge of the bed. The hotel maintained a running track on the roof for guests who didn't like the idea of jogging through Central Park, especially in the early morning. He went up before breakfast and did a few laps. As he was about to go back down to his room, Dave Glass appeared from the stairwell, wearing running shorts.

"Morning, Mr. Hamet," he said with a wave.

"Barney."

"Sure. Barney. A terrible thing about Monica Drews."

"Terrible," Barney agreed.

"Do they know who did it?"

"The police think it was a sneak thief." He stopped at the door. "I saw you talking with Monica in the bar last night."

"Yes. I wanted to see what she thought of my idea for a Kazercon."

Barney was remembering the scrawled message the dying woman had left. So Monica had known about the Kazercon plans. Had her message been an attempt to implicate Dave Glass? Somehow he couldn't imagine this young man sneaking up behind anyone with a knife. "She was a fine editor," Barney said. "She'll be missed by a great many people."

As he turned toward the stairwell, Glass asked, "She was never married, was she?"

"Monica? No, I guess not. Not that I know of."

On the way downstairs, Barney wondered about the question.

After a quick breakfast, Barney found he was just in time for the opening nine o'clock session. A panel of collectors were discussing their personal libraries and the value of some out-of-print first editions. Barney knew his own first novel was often listed in catalogues for more than a hundred dollars, though that was nothing compared with some of the figures being discussed.

He drifted out when the session broke. Even at this early hour, the dealers' room was in full operation, and he headed in that direction.

More than a score of book dealers had tables, exhibiting a staggering variety of mystery and suspense fiction. There were musty volumes of Sax Rohmer and sleek dust-jacketed best sellers by Robert Ludlum and John D. MacDonald. One table specialized in British imports, with the latest Dick Francis novel next to those of Ruth Rendell and P. D. James. There were exhibits from small publishers who specialized in Sherlockiana and pulp reprints, and a university press that put out a line of popular culture books. At one end of the room was a blown-up photograph of Conrad Kazer. At the other end, Barney was horrified to note, was an equally large picture of himself.

As he was leaving the dealers' room, a slender man with gray hair and a blotched face stopped and gazed at his name tag. "You're Barney Hamet?"

"That's right," Barney admitted, reaching for his pen. By now he was used to encountering autograph seekers at these gatherings. But then he noticed the name beside the star on the man's own tag. "Howard Pryor. You're the one who bought the rights to Kazer's books!"

The slim man nodded. "Is there someplace we can talk?"

Barney led him to one of the conference rooms that was

not in use and they went inside and sat down. "I suppose you've heard we had a killing here last night."

Pryor nodded. "Monica Drews. I'd planned to meet with her today regarding the Kazer books. Her firm wished to make an offer. I thought you might know who I should see now."

"Her assistant, I suppose. I can find out the name for you."

"I just arrived this morning, and I only have a few days in New York. I've contacted other publishers, of course, but I feel Kazer would have wanted me to give Heathway first chance at the books."

"I understand you've offered the film and television rights as well."

Another nod. "I already have a tentative agreement with an independent producer. He's willing to take an option on all the available properties for a significant sum of money."

"How did you manage to purchase it all from the bank?"

"By the terms of Kazer's will, all profits from his literary estate were to go to a college in Ohio. The bank changed officers and the new man decided the easiest way to fulfill the terms was to sell everything to a single buyer and be rid of it. I happened to make an offer at the right time and I was accepted. It was a very generous offer, I might add. I've been a fan of Kazer for years. And of your books, too."

"Thank you."

Writer Ed Hunsburger stuck his head in the doorway to tell Barney the police wanted to question him some more. Barney said he'd be right there and got to his feet. "Are there any leads?" Pryor asked, following him to the door.

"Nothing much. They think it was a robbery."

"If I can be of service—"

"Thanks—I'll tell them you're here. Since you had an appointment with her today, they might want to talk to you."

* * *

Sergeant Ambrose, a detective he'd met last night, was waiting with a police stenographer. "We need a statement about your finding the body, Mr. Hamet. I brought the stenographer along to save you a trip down to the station."

Barney told him about the arrival of Howard Pryor and also about Dave Glass's plans for a Kazercon. "You'll remember I mentioned her dying message last night, Sergeant."

Ambrose was only mildly impressed. "The only dying message that means very much, Mr. Hamet, is when the victim lives long enough to point a finger at the accused and say, 'You killed me.' And some courts have been known to toss even that out."

"You're still stuck on your robbery motive, is that it?"

"Until you can give me a better one."

Barney felt the urge to play detective in spite of himself. "You saw the way that door was gimmicked with a piece of tape. The killer had to be in the room to do it. Hotel-room doors open in. If he'd merely knocked at her door with a question, Monica would have had the edge of the door, with its latch bolt, toward herself. A stranger couldn't have taped it like that. And a hotel employee would have no need to. But if the killer was an acquaintance visiting her room, who wanted to return later, he or she could have fixed the lock on the way out."

"No one admits being in her room last night."

"That's not surprising. But she tried to call me about something just before she was killed. I checked with the message desk and she phoned not five minutes before I returned to my room. At about the time I was trying to call her, the killer must have just finished the job. Someone was there. Someone alarmed her, or threatened her, and told her something that scared her. He or she returned to the room, overheard her trying to reach me, and stabbed her. It's the only thing that makes sense. She wasn't robbed, was she?"

"We still don't know. There was a little money in her

wallet, but more might have been taken. Or some jewelry. We can't know for a while."

"Monica wasn't big on jewelry."

Sergeant Ambrose sighed. "I'm keeping an open mind, Mr. Hamet. That's why I wanted to get your statement. I plan to question a great many other people, too."

Barney calmed down and quickly described the previous night's events once more. After a few more questions, Ambrose said he could go. Meeting Stanley Ellin in the hallway, Barney talked with him about the killing. The news had attracted more than the usual number of reporters and television crews, anxious to get some new angle on this murder among mystery fans and writers. Because he had found Monica, Barney was a special target of their attention, and so he spent the rest of the morning in his room just to be away from them.

The afternoon sessions went well and afterward Barney had dinner with Mike Manners and Rain Wilson at a surprisingly cozy restaurant only a block from the hotel.

"Did you meet Howard Pryor?" Manners asked Barney as the waitress served their drinks.

Barney nodded. "He saw a chance to buy up Kazer's works at a good price and now he's trying to make a bundle. I only wish the bankers had consulted with the Mystery Writers."

"Kazer never belonged to the Mystery Writers of America, did he?"

"I guess not. That was part of the problem—his reclusive life style."

"You know what Dave Glass told me?" Rain said. "He was talking about Kazer being married once and he said maybe his ex-wife was Monica Drews."

"That kid should know better than to dream up something like that," Barney said angrily. "Monica was Kazer's editor, period."

"I told him that. He backed down—said he was only kidding."

"Some joke."

"But you said she left a message about the Kazercon," Mike pointed out. "That could implicate Glass."

"The police don't think so," Barney told him.

After dinner, back at the hotel, Chris was running a film program of some rarely screened Hitchcock masterpieces. But the high point of the evening was an original one-act musical mystery, staged in the hotel's own theater. Barney enjoyed it immensely, and for a time he almost forgot about Monica's death. Afterward Sid Coleman suggested a drink and Barney found himself down in the bar once more. "They're having a big turnout for tomorrow's closing luncheon," Sid said. "What are you going to speak about?"

"Kazer." Barney was beginning to feel very tired.

"Are you going to talk about how eccentric he was?"

"No, I think I'll limit myself to what a great mystery writer he was. We're all eccentric in our own way, Sid, and maybe writers are bound to be eccentric. I guess no one will ever know about Kazer's messed-up life, but it seems he wanted it that way."

"The fire that killed him was never fully explained. Do you think it was murder?"

"By the same person who killed Monica?" Barney smiled. "Now you're talking like a mystery writer. But five years between crimes is a long time for there to be a connection. He lived in an old farmhouse with a wood-burning stove. He probably smoked. Anything could have caused the fire."

"He's buried out there, isn't he?"

"So I hear. With just a plain headstone."

Sid sighed. "I could have used a chance to talk with Monica before she died." He ordered another drink. "I need a break, Barney. I need one badly."

"Don't we all."

"Hell, you're doing all right."

"Most years Susan brings in as much income as I do just writing articles."

"You're not a has-been like me."

Barney got to his feet. The conversation was getting maudlin. "I'm going upstairs. I want to take in one of those Hitchcock films."

"Yeah."

Barney felt sorry for the man, but the tides of popularity were strange indeed. Perhaps Sid Coleman's day really had passed. Or maybe he'd have to wait until he was five years in his grave, like Conrad Kazer, to be rediscovered.

In the morning Barney woke up early. He lay in bed for a long time, staring at the gradually brightening ceiling as daylight seeped in around the drapes. Finally he called the desk and asked to be connected with one of the other rooms in the hotel. There was no answer and he decided maybe it was just as well. He didn't know exactly what he intended to say to the person he thought had killed Monica Drews.

He took the elevator to the roof once more and started his morning jogging. He'd been twice around the track, breathing in the fresh morning air of the quiet Sunday, when the stairwell door opened. He thought it would be Dave Glass again but it wasn't.

Howard Pryor closed the door and walked over to him. Barney broke his stride and said, "Good morning. Are you a runner?"

"Hardly," Pryor replied. "I was down in the lobby and the clerk told me you had just tried to phone my room. That young bore—Glass—was there and told me you run up here, so I thought I'd come up."

Barney gazed out toward Central Park, weighing his options. "I'm glad you did," he said. "I wanted to ask you something."

"What was that?"

"Why you killed Monica Drews."

Pryor laughed. "You must be joking."

"No."

"Why would I kill her?"

"That's what I asked you—but I think I can supply the answer. Your supposed purchase of the Kazer literary estate is a giant hoax, isn't it? The letter from the bank is a fraud. You made up the whole thing, hoping you could skim off several thousand dollars in book advances and film options, and be gone with the money before the truth was discovered. Monica somehow found out the truth, probably by phoning whoever she had dealt with at that bank. You were afraid she'd reveal the truth after she accused you, so when you left her room you taped the latch so you could reenter. When you heard her immediately pick up the phone and try to call me, you stabbed her to keep her quiet. But she lived long enough to scrawl out a dying message—not the single word *Kazercon* but two words, *Kazer con.* She was trying to tell us that the Kazer deal was a con game."

"You're guessing now."

"No. A dying woman wouldn't lift her pen from the paper accidentally. She made a space between the words because she meant it to be read as two words."

Howard Pryor moved a step closer. "I only arrived yesterday. I wasn't even here Friday night."

"That's what you told everyone, but your name tag has a star on it, and that star shows you registered Friday night for the full weekend. You probably arrived late or while most of us were attending one of the sessions, and so hardly anyone saw you. After the murder you decided it was best to say you got in Saturday morning."

Pryor moved fast, and Barney saw the knife in his hand. "If you went off this roof, you'd land all the way over in the park," he said quietly.

Barney was hemmed in, backed against the waist-high

parapet that ran around the roof. He felt foolishly at the mercy of this man twenty years older than himself. Pryor was crouched slightly, like an experienced knife fighter moving in for the kill.

"I'm going to tell you something before you die, Hamet. That money belongs to me. I wasn't conning anyone, whatever she thought. I think maybe she knew it, too. I think she recognized me at the end, and that's what her dying message really meant. It was the most basic sort of dying message. She was naming her killer."

Barney felt a chill pass through him. For the first time he was really frightened. "You can't mean—"

A grin spread across the blotched face. "Can't I? Those books are mine because I wrote them. I'm Conrad Kazer."

"You're insane. The fire—"

"The fire killed a homeless drifter who was visiting me. The police never knew about him so they assumed the body was mine. My face was burned a bit, but I got away and hid in the woods. Later I had plastic surgery to fix it, to give me a whole new appearance. But I need the money from my books. I came here to get it."

"I don't believe you," Barney said, but his mouth was dry.

Then there was a noise across the roof as Dave Glass opened the door. Howard Pryor waited no longer. He hurled himself forward. Barney dodged and Pryor went over the low wall.

He didn't make it as far as the park. He landed in the middle of the wide street below, between a cruising taxi and a horse-drawn carriage with three sightseers just turning to enter the park.

Susan was downstairs with Sergeant Ambrose. "Barney, a man just fell off the roof!"

He told them about Howard Pryor, but not about Conrad Kazer—maybe because he didn't want to believe it was true. Pryor was simply a madman who imagined himself to be Kazer.

That was the only explanation.

Wasn't it?

"I'm glad you're in time for my talk at lunch," he told Susan.

A few hours later she was with him and guest of honor John D. MacDonald at the head table when Barney rose to his feet. He waited for the applause to die and then gripped the microphone and began to speak.

"Today I want to talk about one of the great writers of our time," he said. "I want to tell you about Conrad Kazer. . . ."

The "crime" in this story about a bookseller and two of his prospective customers is a subtle one. And its title is fitting for an author whose suspense fiction often produces a feeling of ambiguity: The reader has the powerful sense that something is about to go very wrong, but is unsure as to what, how, or why this is. Shirley Jackson (1919–65) weaves this spell by the use of menace, which is sometimes subtle and psychological (as in "Seven Types of Ambiguity") or, as in her prize-winning story "The Lottery," overt and physically violent. Jackson was a prolific writer who drew heavily on the Gothic tradition, producing novels such as Hangsaman *(1951),* The Sundial *(1958),* The Haunting of Hill House *(1960), and* We Have Always Lived in the Castle *(1963); as well as short stories, a play, children's fiction, and various nonfiction works.*

SEVEN TYPES OF AMBIGUITY

Shirley Jackson

The basement room of the bookstore seemed to be enormous; it stretched in long rows of books off into dimness at either end, with books lined in tall bookcases along the walls, and books standing in piles on the floor. At the foot of the spiral staircase winding down from the neat small store upstairs, Mr. Harris, owner and sales clerk of the bookstore, had a small desk, cluttered with catalogues, lighted by one dirty overhead lamp. The same lamp served to light the shelves which crowded heavily around Mr. Harris' desk; farther away, along the lines of book tables, there were other dirty overhead lamps, to be lighted by pulling a string and turned off by the customer when he was ready to grope his way back to Mr. Harris' desk, pay for his purchases, and have them wrapped. Mr. Harris, who knew the position of any author or any title in all the heavy shelves, had one customer at the moment, a boy of about eighteen, who was standing far down the long room directly under one of the lamps, leafing through a book he had selected from the shelves. It was cold in the big basement room; both Mr. Harris and the boy had their coats on. Occasionally Mr. Harris got up from his desk to put a meagre shovelful of coal on a small iron stove which stood in the curve of the staircase. Except when Mr. Harris got up, or the boy turned to put a book back into the shelves and take out another, the room was quiet, the books standing silent in the dim light.

Then the silence was broken by the sound of the door opening in the little upstairs bookshop where Mr. Harris kept his best sellers and art books on display. There was the sound of voices, while both Mr. Harris and the boy listened, and then the girl who took care of the upstairs bookshop said, "Right on down the stairs. Mr. Harris will help you."

Mr. Harris got up and walked around to the foot of the stairs, turning on another of the overhead lamps so that his new customer would be able to see his way down. The boy put his book back in the shelves and stood with his hand on the back of it, still listening.

When Mr. Harris saw that it was a woman coming down the stairs he stood back politely and said, "Watch the bottom step. There's one more than people think." The woman stepped carefully down and stood looking around. While she stood there a man came carefully around the turn in the staircase, ducking his head so his hat would clear the low ceiling. "Watch the bottom step," the woman said in a soft clear voice. The man came down beside her and raised his head to look around as she had.

"Quite a lot of books you have here," he said.

Mr. Harris smiled his professional smile. "Can I help you?"

The woman looked at the man, and he hesitated a minute and then said, "We want to get some books. Quite a few of them." He waved his hand inclusively. "Sets of books."

"Well, if it's books you want," Mr. Harris said, and smiled again. "Maybe the lady would like to come over and sit down?" He led the way around to his desk, the woman following him and the man walking uneasily between the tables of books, his hands close to his sides as though he were afraid of breaking something. Mr. Harris gave the lady his desk chair and then sat down on the edge of his desk, shoving aside a pile of catalogues.

"This is a very interesting place," the lady said, in the same soft voice she had used when she spoke before. She was middle-aged and nicely dressed; all her clothes were fairly new, but quiet and well planned for her age and air of shyness. The man was big and hearty looking, his face reddened by the cold air and his big hands holding a pair of wool gloves uneasily.

"We'd like to buy some of your books," the man said. "Some good books."

"Anything in particular?" Mr. Harris asked.

The man laughed loudly, but with embarrassment. "Tell the truth," he said, "I sound sort of foolish, now. But I don't know much about these things, like books." In the large quiet store his voice seemed to echo, after his wife's soft voice and Mr. Harris'. "We were sort of hoping you'd be able to tell *us*," he said. "None of this trash they turn out nowadays." He cleared his throat. "Something like Dickens," he said.

"Dickens," Mr. Harris said.

"I used to read Dickens when I was a kid," the man said. "Books like that, now, good books." He looked up as the boy who had been standing off among the books came over to them. "I'd like to read Dickens again," the big man said.

"Mr. Harris," the boy asked quietly.

Mr. Harris looked up. "Yes, Mr. Clark?" he said.

The boy came closer to the desk, as though unwilling to interrupt Mr. Harris with his customers. "I'd like to take another look at the Empson," he said.

Mr. Harris turned to the glass-doored bookcase immediately behind his desk and selected a book. "Here it is," he said, "you'll have it read through before you buy it at this rate." He smiled at the big man and his wife. "Some day he's going to come in and buy that book," he said, "and I'm going to go out of business from shock."

The boy turned away, holding the book, and the big man leaned forward to Mr. Harris. "I figure I'd like two good sets, big, like Dickens," he said, "and then a couple of smaller sets."

"And a copy of *Jane Eyre,*" his wife said, in her soft voice. "I used to love that book," she said to Mr. Harris.

"I can let you have a very nice set of the Brontës," Mr. Harris said. "Beautiful binding."

"I want them to look nice," the man said, "but solid, for reading. I'm going to read through all of Dickens again."

The boy came back to the desk, holding the book out to Mr. Harris. "It still looks good," he said.

"It's right here when you want it," Mr. Harris said, turning back to the bookcase with the book. "It's pretty scarce, that book."

"I guess it'll be here a while longer," the boy said.

"What's the name of this book?" the big man asked curiously.

"*Seven Types of Ambiguity,*" the boy said. "It's quite a good book."

"There's a fine name for a book," the big man said to Mr. Harris. "Pretty smart fellow, reading books with names like that."

"It's a good book," the boy repeated.

"I'm trying to buy some books myself," the big man said to the boy. "I want to catch up on a few I've missed. Dickens, I've always liked his books."

"Meredith is good," the boy said. "You ever try reading Meredith?"

"Meredith," the big man said. "Let's see a few of your

books," he said to Mr. Harris. "I'd sort of like to pick out a few I want."

"Can I take the gentleman down there?" the boy said to Mr. Harris. "I've got to go back anyway to get my hat."

"I'll go with the young man and look at the books, Mother," the big man said to his wife. "You stay here and keep warm."

"Fine," Mr. Harris said. "He knows where the books are as well as I do," he said to the big man.

The boy started off down the aisle between the book tables, and the big man followed, still walking carefully, trying not to touch anything. They went down past the lamp still burning where the boy had left his hat and gloves, and the boy turned on another lamp farther down. "Mr. Harris keeps most of his sets around here," the boy said. "Let's see what we can find." He squatted down in front of the bookcases, touching the backs of the rows of books lightly with his fingers. "How do you feel about the prices?" he asked.

"I'm willing to pay a reasonable amount for the books I have in mind," the big man said. He touched the book in front of him experimentally, with one finger. "A hundred and fifty, two hundred dollars altogether."

The boy looked up at him and laughed. "That ought to get you some nice books," he said.

"Never saw so many books in my life," the big man said. "I never thought I'd see the day when I'd just walk into a bookstore and buy up all the books I always wanted to read."

"It's a good feeling."

"I never got a chance to read much," the man said. "Went right into the machine shop where my father worked when I was much younger than you, and worked ever since. Now all of a sudden I find I have a little more money than I used to, and Mother and I decided we'd like to get ourselves a few things we always wanted."

"Your wife was interested in the Brontës," the boy said. "Here's a very good set."

The man leaned down to look at the books the boy pointed out. "I don't know much about these things," he said. "They look nice, all alike. What's the next set?"

"Carlyle," the boy said. "You can skip him. He's not quite what you're looking for. Meredith is good. And Thackeray. I think you'd want Thackeray; he's a great writer."

The man took one of the books the boy handed him and opened it carefully, using only two fingers from each of his big hands. "This looks fine," he said.

"I'll write them down," the boy said. He took a pencil and a pocket memorandum from his coat pocket. "Brontës," he said, "Dickens, Meredith, Thackeray." He ran his hand along each of the sets as he read them off.

The big man narrowed his eyes. "I ought to take one more," he said. "These won't quite fill up the bookcase I got for them."

"Jane Austen," the boy said. "Your wife would be pleased with that."

"You read all these books?" the man asked.

"Most of them," the boy said.

The man was quiet for a minute and then he went on, "I never got much of a chance to read anything, going to work so early. I've got a lot to catch up on."

"You're going to have a fine time," the boy said.

"That book you had a while back," the man said. "What was that book?"

"It's aesthetics," the boy said. "About literature. It's very scarce. I've been trying to buy it for quite a while and haven't had the money."

"You go to college?" the man asked.

"Yes."

"Here's one I ought to read again," the man said. "Mark Twain. I read a couple of his books when I was a kid. But I guess I have enough to start on." He stood up.

The boy rose too, smiling. "You're going to have to do a lot of reading."

"I like to read," the man said. "I really like to read."

He started back down the aisles, going straight for Mr. Harris' desk. The boy turned off the lamps and followed, stopping to get his hat and gloves. When the big man reached Mr. Harris' desk he said to his wife, "That's sure a smart kid. He knows those books right and left."

"Did you pick out what you want?" his wife asked.

"The kid has a fine list for me." He turned to Mr. Harris and went on, "It's quite an experience seeing a kid like that liking books the way he does. When I was his age I was working for four or five years."

The boy came up with the slip of paper in his hand. "These ought to hold him for a while," he said to Mr. Harris.

Mr. Harris glanced at the list and nodded. "That Thackeray's a nice set of books," he said.

The boy had put his hat on and was standing at the foot of the stairs. "Hope you enjoy them," he said. "I'll be back for another look at that Empson, Mr. Harris."

"I'll try to keep it around for you," Mr. Harris said. "I can't promise to hold it, you know."

"I'll just count on its being here," the boy said.

"Thanks, son," the big man called out as the boy started up the stairs. "Appreciate your helping me."

"That's all right," the boy said.

"He's sure a smart kid," the man said to Mr. Harris. "He's got a great chance, with an education like that."

"He's a nice young fellow," Mr. Harris said, "and he sure wants that book."

"You think he'll ever buy it?" the big man asked.

"I doubt it," Mr. Harris said. "If you'll just write down your name and address, I'll add these prices."

Mr. Harris began to note down the prices of the books, copying from the boy's neat list. After the big man had written his name and address, he stood for a minute drumming his fingers on the desk, and then he said, "Can I have another look at that book?"

"The Empson?" Mr. Harris said, looking up.

"The one the boy was so interested in." Mr. Harris reached around to the bookcase in back of him and took out the book. The big man held it delicately, as he had held the others, and he frowned as he turned the pages. Then he put the book down on Mr. Harris' desk.

"If he isn't going to buy it, will it be all right if I put this in with the rest?" he asked.

Mr. Harris looked up from his figures for a minute, and then he made the entry on his list. He added quickly, wrote down the total, and then pushed the paper across the desk to the big man. While the man checked over the figures Mr. Harris turned to the woman and said, "Your husband has bought a lot of very pleasant reading."

"I'm glad to hear it," she said. "We've been looking forward to it for a long time."

The big man counted out the money carefully, handing the bills to Mr. Harris. Mr. Harris put the money in the top drawer of his desk and said, "We can have these delivered to you by the end of the week, if that will be all right."

"Fine," the big man said. "Ready, Mother?"

The woman rose, and the big man stood back to let her go ahead of him. Mr. Harris followed, stopping near the stairs to say to the woman, "Watch the bottom step."

They started up the stairs and Mr. Harris stood watching them until they got to the turn. Then he switched off the dirty overhead lamp and went back to his desk.

Dorothy L. Sayers's series character, Lord Peter Wimsey, was a noted bibliophile, and the mystery in this story, which revolves around book collecting, is a natural for the ever-inquisitive aristocrat. A bookish mystery is also a natural for its creator. While not a book collector herself, Ms. Sayers (1893–1957) was one of the first women to receive her degree from Somerville College, Oxford, in 1915, and during her distinguished career wrote not only the famous Wimsey novels and stories, but also works on philosophy, religion, and medieval literature. She drew heavily on her scholarly and intellectual pursuits in creating her major characters, and when she finally married Wimsey off (Busman's Honeymoon, *1937), she chose for him none other than a mystery writer with the same intellectual bent as herself.*

THE DRAGON'S HEAD

Dorothy L. Sayers

"UNCLE PETER!"

"Half a jiff, Gherkins. No, I don't think I'll take the Catullus, Mr. Ffolliott. After all, thirteen guineas is a bit steep without either the title or the last folio, what? But you might send me round the Vitruvius and the Satyricon when they come in; I'd like to have a look at them, anyhow. Well, old man, what is it?"

"Do come and look at these pictures, Uncle Peter. I'm sure it's an awfully old book."

Lord Peter Wimsey sighed as he picked his way out of Mr. Ffolliott's dark back shop, strewn with the flotsam and jetsam of many libraries. An unexpected outbreak of measles at Mr. Bultridge's excellent preparatory school, coinciding with the absence of the Duke and Duchess of Denver on the Continent, had saddled his lordship with his ten-year-old nephew, Viscount St. George, more commonly known as Young Jerry, Jerrykins, or Pickled Gherkins. Lord Peter was not one of those born uncles who delight old nurses by their fascinating "way with" children. He succeeded, however, in earning tolerance on honourable terms by treating the young with the same scrupulous politeness which he extended to their elders. He therefore prepared to receive Gherkins' discovery with respect, though a child's taste was not to be trusted, and the book might quite well be some horror of woolly mezzotints or an inferior modern reprint adorned with leprous electros. Nothing much better was really to be expected from the "cheap shelf" exposed to the dust of the street.

"Uncle! There's such a funny man here, with a great long nose and ears and a tail and dogs' heads all over his body. *Monstrum hoc Cracoviæ*—that's a monster, isn't it? I should jolly well think it was. What's *Cracoviæ,* Uncle Peter?"

"Oh," said Lord Peter, greatly relieved, "the Cracow monster?" A portrait of that distressing infant certainly argued a respectable antiquity. "Let's have a look. Quite right, it's a very old book—Münster's *Cosmographia universalis.* I'm glad you know good stuff when you see it, Gherkins. What's the *Cosmographia* doing out here, Mr. Ffolliott, at five bob?"

"Well, my lord," said the bookseller, who had followed his customers to the door, "it's in a very bad state, you see; covers loose and nearly all the double-page maps missing. It came in a few weeks ago—dumped in with a collection we bought from a gentleman in Norfolk—you'll find his name in it—Dr. Conyers of Yelsall Manor. Of course, we might keep it and try to make up a complete copy when we get another example. But it's rather out of our line, as you know, classical authors being our speciality. So we just put it out to go for what it would fetch in the *status quo,* as you might say."

"Oh, look!" broke in Gherkins. "Here's a picture of a man being chopped up in little bits. What does it say about it?"

"I thought you could read Latin."

"Well, but it's all full of sort of pothooks. What do they mean?"

"They're just contractions," said Lord Peter patiently. " '*Solent quoque hujus insulæ cultores*'—It is the custom of the dwellers in this island, when they see their parents stricken in years and of no further use, to take them down into the market-place and sell them to the cannibals, who kill them and eat them for food. This they do also with younger persons when they fall into any desperate sickness."

"Ha, ha!" said Mr. Ffolliott. "Rather sharp practice on the poor cannibals. They never got anything but tough old joints or diseased meat, eh?"

"The inhabitants seem to have had thoroughly advanced notions of business," agreed his lordship.

The viscount was enthralled.

"I *do* like this book," he said; "could I buy it out of my pocket-money, please?"

"Another problem for uncles," thought Lord Peter, rapidly ransacking his recollections of the *Cosmographia* to determine whether any of its illustrations were indelicate; for he knew the duchess to be strait-laced. On consideration, he could only remember one that was dubious, and there was a sporting chance that the duchess might fail to light upon it.

"Well," he said judicially, "in your place, Gherkins, I should be inclined to buy it. It's in a bad state, as Mr. Ffolliott has honourably told you—otherwise, of course, it would be exceedingly valuable; but, apart from the lost pages, it's a very nice clean copy, and certainly worth five shillings to you, if you think of starting a collection."

Till that moment, the viscount had obviously been more

impressed by the cannibals than by the state of the margins, but the idea of figuring next term at Mr. Bultridge's as a collector of rare editions had undeniable charm.

"None of the other fellows collect books," he said; "they collect stamps, mostly. I think stamps are rather ordinary, don't you, Uncle Peter? I was rather thinking of giving up stamps. Mr. Porter, who takes us for history, has got a lot of books like yours, and he is a splendid man at footer."

Rightly interpreting this reference to Mr. Porter, Lord Peter gave it as his opinion that book collecting could be a perfectly manly pursuit. Girls, he said, practically never took it up, because it meant so much learning about dates and type faces and other technicalities which called for a masculine brain.

"Besides," he added, "it's a very interesting book in itself, you know. Well worth dipping into."

"I'll take it, please," said the viscount, blushing a little at transacting so important and expensive a piece of business; for the duchess did not encourage lavish spending by little boys, and was strict in the matter of allowances.

Mr. Ffolliott bowed, and took the *Cosmographia* away to wrap it up.

"Are you all right for cash?" enquired Lord Peter discreetly. "Or can I be of temporary assistance?"

"No, thank you, Uncle; I've got Aunt Mary's half-crown and four shillings of my pocket-money, because, you see, with the measles happening, we didn't have our dormitory spread, and I was saving up for that."

The business being settled in this gentlemanly manner, and the budding bibliophile taking personal and immediate charge of the stout, square volume, a taxi was chartered which, in due course of traffic delays, brought the *Cosmographia* to 110A Piccadilly.

"And who, Bunter, is Mr. Wilberforce Pope?"

"I do not think we know the gentleman, my lord. He is

asking to see your lordship for a few minutes on business."

"He probably wants me to find a lost dog for his maiden aunt. What it is to have acquired a reputation as a sleuth! Show him in. Gherkins, if this good gentleman's business turns out to be private, you'd better retire into the dining-room."

"Yes, Uncle Peter," said the viscount dutifully. He was extended on his stomach on the library hearthrug, laboriously picking his way through the more exciting-looking bits of the *Cosmographia,* with the aid of Messrs. Lewis & Short, whose monumental compilation he had hitherto looked upon as a barbarous invention for the annoyance of upper forms.

Mr. Wilberforce Pope turned out to be a rather plump, fair gentleman in the late thirties, with a prematurely bald forehead, horn-rimmed spectacles, and an engaging manner.

"You will excuse my intrusion, won't you?" he began. "I'm sure you must think me a terrible nuisance. But I wormed your name and address out of Mr. Ffolliott. Not his fault, really. You won't blame him, will you? I positively badgered the poor man. Sat down on his doorstep and refused to go, though the boy was putting up the shutters. I'm afraid you will think me very silly when you know what it's all about. But you really mustn't hold poor Mr. Ffolliott responsible, now, will you?"

"Not at all," said his lordship. "I mean, I'm charmed and all that sort of thing. Something I can do for you about books? You're a collector, perhaps? Will you have a drink or anything?"

"Well, no," said Mr. Pope, with a faint giggle. "No, not exactly a collector. Thank you very much, just a spot—no, no, literally a spot. Thank you; no"—he glanced round the bookshelves, with their rows of rich old leather bindings—"certainly not a collector. But I happen to be—er, interested—sentimentally interested—in a purchase you made yesterday. Really, such a very small matter. You will think it foolish. But I am told you are the present owner of a copy of Münster's *Cosmographia,* which used to belong to my uncle, Dr. Conyers."

Gherkins looked up suddenly, seeing that the conversation had a personal interest for him.

"Well, that's not quite correct," said Wimsey. "I was there at the time, but the actual purchaser is my nephew. Gerald, Mr. Pope is interested in your *Cosmographia.* My nephew, Lord St. George."

"How do you do, young man," said Mr. Pope affably. "I see that the collecting spirit runs in the family. A great Latin scholar, too, I expect, eh? Ready to decline *jusjurandum* with the best of us? Ha, ha! And what are you going to do when you grow up? Be Lord Chancellor, eh? Now, I bet you think you'd rather be an engine-driver, what, what?"

"No, thank you," said the viscount, with aloofness.

"What, not an engine-driver? Well, now, I want you to be a real business man this time. Put through a book deal, you know. Your uncle will see I offer you a fair price, what? Ha, ha! Now, you see, that picture-book of yours has a great value for me that it wouldn't have for anybody else. When *I* was a little boy of your age it was one of my very greatest joys. I used to have it to look at on Sundays. Ah, dear! the happy hours I used to spend with those quaint old engravings, and the funny old maps with the ships and salamanders and *'Hic dracones'*—you know what *that* means, I dare say. What does it mean?"

"Here are dragons," said the viscount, unwillingly but still politely.

"Quite right. I *knew* you were a scholar."

"It's a very attractive book," said Lord Peter. "My nephew was quite entranced by the famous Cracow monster."

"Ah yes—a glorious monster, isn't it?" agreed Mr. Pope, with enthusiasm. "Many's the time I've fancied myself as Sir

Lancelot or somebody on a white war horse, charging that monster, lance in rest, with the captive princess cheering me on. Ah! Childhood! You're living the happiest days of your life, young man. You won't believe me, but you are."

"Now what is it exactly you want my nephew to do?" enquired Lord Peter a little sharply.

"Quite right, quite right. Well now, you know, my uncle, Dr. Conyers, sold his library a few months ago. I was abroad at the time, and it was only yesterday, when I went down to Yelsall on a visit, that I learnt the dear old book had gone with the rest. I can't tell you how distressed I was. I know it's not valuable—a great many pages missing and all that—but I can't bear to think of its being gone. So, purely from sentimental reasons, as I said, I hurried off to Ffolliott's to see if I could get it back. I was quite upset to find I was too late, and gave poor Mr. Ffolliott no peace till he told me the name of the purchaser. Now, you see, Lord St. George, I'm here to make you an offer for the book. Come, now, double what you gave for it. That's a good offer, isn't it, Lord Peter? Ha, ha! And you will be doing me a very great kindness as well."

Viscount St. George looked rather distressed, and turned appealingly to his uncle.

"Well, Gerald," said Lord Peter, "it's your affair, you know. What do you say?"

The viscount stood first on one leg and then on the other. The career of a book collector evidently had its problems, like other careers.

"If you please, Uncle Peter," he said, with embarrassment, "may I whisper?"

"It's not usually considered the thing to whisper, Gherkins, but you could ask Mr. Pope for time to consider his offer. Or you could say you would prefer to consult me first. That would be quite in order."

"Then, if you don't mind, Mr. Pope, I should like to consult my uncle first."

"Certainly, certainly; ha, ha!" said Mr. Pope. "Very prudent to consult a collector of greater experience, what? Ah! The younger generation, eh, Lord Peter? Regular little business men already."

"Excuse us, then, for one moment," said Lord Peter, and drew his nephew into the dining-room.

"I say, Uncle Peter," said the collector breathlessly, when the door was shut, "*need* I give him my book? I don't think he's a very nice man. I *hate* people who ask you to decline nouns for them."

"Certainly you needn't, Gherkins, if you don't want to. The book is yours, and you've a right to it."

"What would *you* do, Uncle?"

Before replying, Lord Peter, in the most surprising manner, tiptoed gently to the door which communicated with the library and flung it suddenly open, in time to catch Mr. Pope kneeling on the hearthrug intently turning over the pages of the coveted volume, which lay as the owner had left it. He started to his feet in a flurried manner as the door opened.

"Do help yourself, Mr. Pope, won't you?" cried Lord Peter hospitably, and closed the door again.

"What is it, Uncle Peter?"

"If you want my advice, Gherkins, I should be rather careful how you had any dealings with Mr. Pope. I don't think he's telling the truth. He called those woodcuts engravings—though, of course, that may be just his ignorance. But I can't believe that he spent all his childhood's Sunday afternoons studying those maps and picking out the dragons in them, because, as you may have noticed for yourself, old Münster put very few dragons into his maps. They're mostly just plain maps—a bit queer to our ideas of geography, but perfectly straightforward. That was why I brought in the Cracow monster, and, you see, he thought it was some sort of dragon."

"Oh, I say, Uncle! So you said that on purpose!"

"If Mr. Pope wants the *Cosmographia,* it's for some

reason he doesn't want to tell us about. And, that being so, I wouldn't be in too big a hurry to sell, if the book were mine. See?"

"Do you mean there's something frightfully valuable about the book, which we don't know?"

"Possibly."

"How exciting! It's just like a story in the *Boys' Friend Library.* What am I to say to him, Uncle?"

"Well, in your place I wouldn't be dramatic or anything. I'd just say you've considered the matter, and you've taken a fancy to the book and have decided not to sell. You thank him for his offer, of course."

"Yes—er, won't you say it for me, Uncle?"

"I think it would look better if you did it yourself."

"Yes, perhaps it would. Will he be very cross?"

"Possibly," said Lord Peter, "but if he is, he won't let on. Ready?"

The consulting committee accordingly returned to the library. Mr. Pope had prudently retired from the hearthrug and was examining a distant bookcase.

"Thank you very much for your offer, Mr. Pope," said the viscount, striding stoutly up to him, "but I have considered it, and I have taken a—a—a fancy for the book and decided not to sell."

"Sorry and all that," put in Lord Peter, "but my nephew's adamant about it. No, it isn't the price; he wants the book. Wish I could oblige you, but it isn't in my hands. Won't you take something else before you go? Really? Ring the bell, Gherkins. My man will see you to the lift. *Good* evening."

When the visitor had gone, Lord Peter returned and thoughtfully picked up the book.

"We were awful idiots to leave him with it, Gherkins, even for a moment. Luckily, there's no harm done."

"You don't think he found out anything while we were away, do you, Uncle?" gasped Gherkins, open-eyed.

"I'm sure he didn't."

"Why?"

"He offered me fifty pounds for it on the way to the door. Gave the game away. H'm! Bunter."

"My lord?"

"Put this book in the safe and bring me back the keys. And you'd better set all the burglar alarms when you lock up."

"Oo—er!" said Viscount St. George.

On the third morning after the visit of Mr. Wilberforce Pope, the viscount was seated at a very late breakfast in his uncle's flat, after the most glorious and soul-satisfying night that ever boy experienced. He was almost too excited to eat the kidneys and bacon placed before him by Bunter, whose usual impeccable manner was not in the least impaired by a rapidly swelling and blackening eye.

It was about two in the morning that Gherkins—who had not slept very well, owing to too lavish and grown-up a dinner and theatre the evening before—became aware of a stealthy sound somewhere in the direction of the fire-escape. He had got out of bed and crept very softly into Lord Peter's room and woken him up. He had said: "Uncle Peter, I'm sure there's burglars on the fire-escape." And Uncle Peter, instead of saying, "Nonsense, Gherkins, hurry up and get back to bed," had sat up and listened and said: "By Jove, Gherkins, I believe you're right." And had sent Gherkins to call Bunter. And on his return, Gherkins, who had always regarded his uncle as a very top-hatted sort of person, actually saw him take from his handkerchief drawer an undeniable automatic pistol.

It was at this point that Lord Peter was apotheosed from the state of Quite Decent Uncle to that of Glorified Uncle. He said:

"Look here, Gherkins, we don't know how many of these blighters there'll be, so you must be jolly smart and do anything I say sharp, on the word of command—even if I have to say 'Scoot.' Promise?"

Gherkins promised, with his heart thumping, and they sat waiting in the dark, till suddenly a little electric bell rang sharply just over the head of Lord Peter's bed and a green light shone out.

"The library window," said his lordship, promptly silencing the bell by turning a switch. "If they heard, they may think better of it. We'll give them a few minutes."

They gave them five minutes, and then crept very quietly down the passage.

"Go round by the dining-room, Bunter," said his lordship. "They may bolt that way."

With infinite precaution, he unlocked and opened the library door, and Gherkins noticed how silently the locks moved.

A circle of light from an electric torch was moving slowly along the bookshelves. The burglars had obviously heard nothing of the counter attack. Indeed, they seemed to have troubles enough of their own to keep their attention occupied. As his eyes grew accustomed to the dim light, Gherkins made out that one man was standing holding the torch, while the other took down and examined the books. It was fascinating to watch his apparently disembodied hands move along the shelves in the torch-light.

The men muttered discontentedly. Obviously the job was proving a harder one than they had bargained for. The habit of ancient authors of abbreviating the titles on the backs of their volumes, or leaving them completely untitled, made things extremely awkward. From time to time the man with the torch extended his hand into the light. It held a piece of paper, which they anxiously compared with the title-page of a book. Then the volume was replaced and the tedious search went on.

Suddenly some slight noise—Gherkins was sure *he* did not make it; it may have been Bunter in the dining-room—seemed to catch the ear of the kneeling man.

"Wot's that?" he gasped, and his startled face swung round into view.

"Hands up!" said Lord Peter, and switched the light on.

The second man made one leap for the dining-room door, where a smash and an oath proclaimed that he had encountered Bunter. The kneeling man shot his hands up like a marionette.

"Gherkins," said Lord Peter, "do you think you can go across to that gentleman by the bookcase and relieve him of the article which is so inelegantly distending the right-hand pocket of his coat? Wait a minute. Don't on any account get between him and my pistol, and mind you take the thing out *very* carefully. There's no hurry. That's splendid. Just point it at the floor while you bring it across, would you? Thanks. Bunter has managed for himself, I see. Now run into my bedroom, and in the bottom of my wardrobe you will find a bundle of stout cord. Oh! I beg your pardon; yes, put your hands down by all means. It must be very tiring exercise."

The arms of the intruders being secured behind their backs with a neatness which Gherkins felt to be worthy of the best traditions of Sexton Blake, Lord Peter motioned his captives to sit down and despatched Bunter for whiskey-and-soda.

"Before we send for the police," said Lord Peter, "you would do me a great personal favour by telling me what you were looking for, and who sent you. Ah! thanks, Bunter. As our guests are not at liberty to use their hands, perhaps you would be kind enough to assist them to a drink. Now then, say when."

"Well, you're a gentleman, guv'nor," said the First Burglar, wiping his mouth politely on his shoulder, the back of his hand not being available. "If we'd a known wot a job this wos goin' ter be, blow me if we'd a touched it. The bloke said, ses 'e, 'It's takin' candy from a baby,' 'e ses. 'The gentleman's a reg'lar softie,' 'e ses, 'one o' these 'ere sersiety toffs wiv a maggot fer old books,' that's wot 'e ses, 'an' ef yer can find this 'ere old book fer me,' 'e ses, 'there's a pony fer yer.' Well! Sech a job! 'E didn't mention as 'ow there'd be five 'undred fousand bleedin' ole books all as alike as a regiment o' bleedin' dragoons. Nor as 'ow yer kept a nice little machine-gun like that 'andy by the bedside, *nor* yet as 'ow yer was so bleedin' good at tyin' knots in a bit o' string. No—'e didn't think ter mention them things."

"Deuced unsporting of him," said his lordship. "Do you happen to know the gentleman's name?"

"No—that was another o' them things wot 'e didn't mention. 'E's a stout, fair party, wiv 'orn rims to 'is goggles and a bald 'ead. One o' these 'ere philanthropists, I reckon. A friend o' mine, wot got inter trouble onct, got work froo 'im, and the gentleman comes round and ses to 'im, 'e ses, 'Could yer find me a couple o' lads ter do a little job?' 'e ses, an' my friend, finkin' no 'arm, you see, guv'nor, but wot it might be a bit of a joke like, 'e gets 'old of my pal an' me, an' we meets the gentleman in a pub dahn Whitechapel way. W'ich we was ter meet 'im there again Friday night, us 'avin' allowed that time fer ter git 'old of the book."

"The book being, if I may hazard a guess, the *Cosmographia universalis?*"

"Sumfink like that, guv'nor. I got its jaw-breakin' name wrote down on a bit o' paper, wot my pal 'ad in 'is 'and. Wot did yer do wiv that 'ere bit o' paper, Bill?"

"Well, look here," said Lord Peter, "I'm afraid I must send for the police, but I think it likely, if you give us your assistance to get hold of your gentleman, whose name I strongly suspect to be Wilberforce Pope, that you will get off pretty easily. Telephone the police, Bunter, and then go and put something on that eye of yours. Gherkins, we'll give these gentlemen another drink, and then I think perhaps you'd better hop back to bed; the fun's over. No? Well, put a good thick coat on, there's a good fellow, because what your mother will say to me if you catch a cold I don't like to think."

So the police had come and taken the burglars away, and now Detective-Inspector Parker, of Scotland Yard, a great personal friend of Lord Peter's, sat toying with a cup of coffee and listening to the story.

"But what's the matter with the jolly old book, anyhow, to make it so popular?" he demanded.

"I don't know," replied Wimsey, "but after Mr. Pope's little visit the other day I got kind of intrigued about it and had a look through it. I've got a hunch it may turn out rather valuable, after all. Unsuspected beauties and all that sort of thing. If only Mr. Pope had been a trifle more accurate in his facts, he might have got away with something to which I feel pretty sure he isn't entitled. Anyway, when I'd seen—what I saw, I wrote off to Dr. Conyers of Yelsall Manor, the late owner—"

"Conyers, the cancer man?"

"Yes. He's done some pretty important research in his time, I fancy. Getting on now, though; about seventy-eight, I fancy. I hope he's more honest than his nephew, with one foot in the grave like that. Anyway, I wrote (with Gherkins' permission, naturally) to say we had the book and had been specially interested by something we found there, and would he be so obliging as to tell us something of its history. I also—"

"But what did you find in it?"

"I don't think we'll tell him yet, Gherkins, shall we? I like to keep policemen guessing. As I was saying, when you so rudely interrupted me, I also asked him whether he knew anything about his good nephew's offer to buy it back. His answer has just arrived. He says he knows of nothing specially interesting about the book. It has been in the library untold years, and the tearing out of the maps must have been done a long time ago by some family vandal. He can't think why his nephew should be so keen on it, as he certainly never pored over it as a boy. In fact, the old man declares the engaging Wilberforce has never even set foot in Yelsall Manor to his knowledge. So much for the fire-breathing monsters and the pleasant Sunday afternoons."

"Naughty Wilberforce!"

"M'm. Yes. So, after last night's little dust-up, I wired the old boy we were tooling down to Yelsall to have a heart-to-heart talk with him about his picture-book and his nephew."

"Are you taking the book down with you?" asked Parker. "I can give you a police escort for it if you like."

"That's not a bad idea," said Wimsey. "We don't know where the insinuating Mr. Pope may be hanging out, and I wouldn't put it past him to make another attempt."

"Better be on the safe side," said Parker. "I can't come myself, but I'll send down a couple of men with you."

"Good egg," said Lord Peter. "Call up your myrmidons. We'll get a car round at once. You're coming, Gherkins, I suppose? God knows what your mother would say. Don't ever be an uncle, Charles; it's frightfully difficult to be fair to all parties."

Yelsall Manor was one of those large, decaying country mansions which speak eloquently of times more spacious than our own. The original late Tudor construction had been masked by the addition of a wide frontage in the Italian manner, with a kind of classical portico surmounted by a pediment and approached by a semicircular flight of steps. The grounds had originally been laid out in that formal manner in which grove nods to grove and each half duly reflects the other. A late owner, however, had burst out into the more eccentric sort of landscape gardening which is associated with the name of Capability Brown. A Chinese pagoda, somewhat resembling Sir William Chambers' erection in Kew Gardens, but smaller, rose out of a grove of laurustinus towards the eastern extremity of the house, while at the rear appeared a large artificial lake, dotted with numerous islands, on which odd little temples, grottos, tea-houses, and bridges peeped out from among clumps of shrubs, once ornamental, but now sadly overgrown. A boat-house, with wide eaves like the designs on a willow-pattern plate, stood at one corner, its landing-stage fallen into decay and wreathed with melancholy weeds.

"My disreputable old ancestor, Cuthbert Conyers, settled down here when he retired from the sea in 1732," said Dr. Conyers, smiling faintly. "His elder brother died childless, so the black sheep returned to the fold with the determination to become respectable and found a family. I fear he did not succeed altogether. There were very queer tales as to where his money came from. He is said to have been a pirate, and to have sailed with the notorious Captain Blackbeard. In the village, to this day, he is remembered and spoken of as 'Cut-throat Conyers.' It used to make the old man very angry, and there is an unpleasant story of his slicing the ears off a groom who had been heard to call him 'Old Cut-throat.' He was not an uncultivated person, though. It was he who did the landscape-gardening round at the back, and he built the pagoda for his telescope. He was reputed to study the Black Art, and there were certainly a number of astrological works in the library with his name on the fly-leaf, but probably the telescope was only a remembrance of his seafaring days.

"Anyhow, towards the end of his life he became more and more odd and morose. He quarrelled with his family, and turned his younger son out of doors with his wife and children. An unpleasant old fellow.

"On his deathbed he was attended by the parson—a good, earnest, God-fearing sort of man, who must have put up with a deal of insult in carrying out what he firmly believed to be the sacred duty of reconciling the old man to this shamefully treated son. Eventually, 'Old Cut-throat' relented so far as to make a will, leaving to the younger son 'My treasure which I have buried in Munster.' The parson represented to him that it was useless to bequeath a treasure unless he also bequeathed the information where to find it, but the horrid old pirate only chuckled spitefully, and said that, as he had been at the pains to collect the treasure, his son might well be at the pains of looking for it. Further than that he would not go, and so he died, and I dare say went to a very bad place.

"Since then the family has died out, and I am the sole representative of the Conyerses, and heir to the treasure, whatever and wherever it is, for it was never discovered. I do not suppose it was very honestly come by, but, since it would be useless now to try and find the original owners, I imagine I have a better right to it than anybody living.

"You may think it very unseemly, Lord Peter, that an old, lonely man like myself should be greedy for a hoard of pirate's gold. But my whole life has been devoted to studying the disease of cancer, and I believe myself to be very close to a solution of one part at least of the terrible problem. Research costs money, and my limited means are very nearly exhausted. The property is mortgaged up to the hilt, and I do most urgently desire to complete my experiments before I die, and to leave a sufficient sum to found a clinic where the work can be carried on.

"During the last year I have made very great efforts to solve the mystery of 'Old Cut-throat's' treasure. I have been able to leave much of my experimental work in the most capable hands of my assistant, Dr. Forbes, while I pursued my researches with the very slender clue I had to go upon. It was the more expensive and difficult that Cuthbert had left no indication in his will whether Münster in Germany or Munster in Ireland was the hiding-place of the treasure. My journeys and my search in both places cost money and brought me no further on my quest. I returned, disheartened, in August, and found myself obliged to sell my library, in order to defray my expenses and obtain a little money with which to struggle on with my sadly delayed experiments."

"Ah!" said Lord Peter. "I begin to see light."

The old physician looked at him enquiringly. They had

finished tea, and were seated around the great fireplace in the study. Lord Peter's interested questions about the beautiful, dilapidated old house and estate had led the conversation naturally to Dr. Conyers' family, shelving for the time the problem of the *Cosmographia*, which lay on a table beside them.

"Everything you say fits into the puzzle," went on Wimsey, "and I think there's not the smallest doubt what Mr. Wilberforce Pope was after, though how he knew that you had the *Cosmographia* here I couldn't say."

"When I disposed of the library, I sent him a catalogue," said Dr. Conyers. "As a relative, I thought he ought to have the right to buy anything he fancied. I can't think why he didn't secure the book then, instead of behaving in this most shocking fashion."

Lord Peter hooted with laughter.

"Why, because he never tumbled to it till afterwards," he said. "And oh, dear, how wild he must have been! I forgive him everything. Although," he added, "I don't want to raise your hopes too high, sir, for, even when we've solved old Cuthbert's riddle, I don't know that we're very much nearer to the treasure."

"To the *treasure?*"

"Well, now, sir. I want you first to look at this page, where there's a name scrawled in the margin. Our ancestors had an untidy way of signing their possessions higgledy-piggledy in margins instead of in a decent, Christian way in the fly-leaf. This is a handwriting of somewhere about Charles I's reign: *Jac: Coniers.* I take it that goes to prove that the book was in the possession of your family at any rate as early as the first half of the seventeenth century, and has remained there ever since. Right. Now we turn to page 1099, where we find a description of the discoveries of Christopher Columbus. It's headed, you see, by a kind of map, with some of Mr. Pope's monsters swimming about in it, and apparently representing the Canaries, or, as they used to be called, the Fortunate Isles. It doesn't look much more accurate than old maps usually are, but I take it the big island on the right is meant for Lanzarote, and the two nearest to it may be Teneriffe and Gran Canaria."

"But what's that writing in the middle?"

"That's just the point. The writing is later than *Jac: Coniers'* signature; I should put it about 1700—but, of course, it may have been written a good deal later still. I mean, a man who was elderly in 1730 would still use the style of writing he adopted as a young man, especially if, like your ancestor the pirate, he had spent the early part of his life in outdoor pursuits and hadn't done much writing."

"Do you mean to say, Uncle Peter," broke in the viscount excitedly, "that that's 'Old Cut-throat's' writing?"

"I'd be ready to lay a sporting bet it is. Look here, sir, you've been scouring round Münster in Germany and Munster in Ireland—but how about good old Sebastian Münster here in the library at home?"

"God bless my soul! Is it possible?"

"It's pretty nearly certain, sir. Here's what he says, written, you see, round the head of that sort of sea-dragon:

Hic in capite draconis ardet perpetuo Sol.
(Here the sun shines perpetually upon the Dragon's head.)

Rather doggy Latin—sea-dog Latin, you might say, in fact."

"I'm afraid," said Dr. Conyers, "I must be very stupid, but I can't see where that leads us."

"No; 'Old Cut-throat' was rather clever. No doubt he thought that, if anybody read it, they'd think it was just an allusion to where it says, further down, that 'the islands were called *Fortunatæ* because of the wonderful temperature of the air and the clemency of the skies.' But the cunning old astrologer up in his pagoda had a meaning of his own. Here's a little book published in 1678—Middleton's *Practical As-*

trology—just the sort of popular handbook an amateur like 'Old Cut-throat' would use. Here you are: 'If in your figure you find Jupiter or Venus or *Dragon's head*, you may be confident there is Treasure in the place supposed. . . . If you find *Sol* to be the Significator of the hidden Treasure, you may conclude there is Gold, or some jewels.' You know, sir, I think we may conclude it."

"Dear me!" said Dr. Conyers. "I believe, indeed, you must be right. And I am ashamed to think that if anybody had suggested to me that it could ever be profitable to me to learn the terms of astrology, I should have replied in my vanity that my time was too valuable to waste on such foolishness. I am deeply indebted to you."

"Yes," said Gherkins, "but where *is* the treasure, Uncle?"

"That's just it," said Lord Peter. "The map is very vague; there is no latitude or longitude given; and the directions, such as they are, seem not even to refer to any spot on the islands, but to some place in the middle of the sea. Besides, it is nearly two hundred years since the treasure was hidden, and it may already have been found by somebody or other."

Dr. Conyers stood up.

"I am an old man," he said, "but I still have some strength. If I can by any means get together the money for an expedition, I will not rest till I have made every possible effort to find the treasure and to endow my clinic."

"Then, sir, I hope you'll let me give a hand to the good work," said Lord Peter.

Dr. Conyers had invited his guests to stay the night, and, after the excited viscount had been packed off to bed, Wimsey and the old man sat late, consulting maps and diligently reading Münster's chapter *"De Novis Insulis,"* in the hope of discovering some further clue. At length, however, they separated, and Lord Peter went upstairs, the book under his arm. He was restless, however, and, instead of going to bed, sat for a long time at his window, which looked out upon the lake. The moon, a few days past the full, was riding high among small, windy clouds, and picked out the sharp eaves of the Chinese tea-houses and the straggling tops of the unpruned shrubs. "Old Cut-throat" and his landscape-gardening! Wimsey could have fancied that the old pirate was sitting now beside his telescope in the preposterous pagoda, chuckling over his riddling testament and counting the craters of the moon. "If *Luna,* there is silver." The water of the lake was silver enough; there was a great smooth path across it, broken by the sinister wedge of the boat-house, the black shadows of the islands, and, almost in the middle of the lake, a decayed fountain, a writhing celestial dragon-shape, spiny-backed and ridiculous.

Wimsey rubbed his eyes. There was something strangely familiar about the lake; from moment to moment it assumed the queer unreality of a place which one recognizes without having ever known it. It was like one's first sight of the Leaning Tower of Pisa—too like its picture to be quite believable. Surely, thought Wimsey, he knew that elongated island on the right, shaped rather like a winged monster, with its two little clumps of buildings. And the island to the left of it, like the British Isles, but warped out of shape. And the third island, between the others, and nearer. The three formed a triangle, with the Chinese fountain in the centre, the moon shining steadily upon its dragon head. *"Hic in capite draconis ardet perpetuo—"*

Lord Peter sprang up with a loud exclamation, and flung open the door into the dressing-room. A small figure wrapped in an eiderdown hurriedly uncoiled itself from the window-seat.

"I'm sorry, Uncle Peter," said Gherkins. "I was so *dreadfully* wide awake, it wasn't any good staying in bed."

"Come here," said Lord Peter, "and tell me if I'm mad or dreaming. Look out of the window and compare it with the map—'Old Cut-throat's' 'New Islands.' He made 'em, Gherkins; he put 'em here. Aren't they laid out just like the Canaries? Those three islands in a triangle, and the fourth down here in the corner? And the boat-house where the big ship is in the picture? And the dragon fountain where the dragon's head is? Well, my son, that's where your hidden treasure's gone to. Get your things on, Gherkins, and damn the time when all good little boys should be in bed! We're going for a row on the lake, if there's a tub in that boat-house that'll float."

"Oh, Uncle Peter! This is a *real* adventure!"

"All right," said Wimsey. "Fifteen men on the dead man's chest, and all that! Yo-ho-ho, and a bottle of Johnny Walker! Pirate expedition fitted out in dead of night to seek hidden treasure and explore the Fortunate Isles! Come on, crew!"

Lord Peter hitched the leaky dinghy to the dragon's knobbly tail and climbed out carefully, for the base of the fountain was green and weedy.

"I'm afraid it's your job to sit there and bail, Gherkins," he said. "All the best captains bag the really interesting jobs for themselves. We'd better start with the head. If the old blighter said head, he probably meant it." He passed an arm affectionately round the creature's neck for support, while he methodically pressed and pulled the various knobs and bumps of its anatomy. "It seems beastly solid, but I'm sure there's a spring somewhere. You won't forget to bail, will you? I'd simply hate to turn round and find the boat gone. Pirate chief marooned on island and all that. Well, it isn't its back hair, anyhow. We'll try its eyes. I say, Gherkins, I'm sure I felt something move, only it's frightfully stiff. We might have thought to bring some oil. Never mind; it's dogged as does it. It's coming. It's coming. Booh! Pah!"

A fierce effort thrust the rusted knob inwards, releasing a huge spout of water into his face from the dragon's gaping throat. The fountain, dry for many years, soared rejoicingly heavenwards, drenching the treasure-hunters, and making rainbows in the moonlight.

"I suppose this is 'Old Cut-throat's' idea of humour," grumbled Wimsey, retreating cautiously round the dragon's neck. "And now I can't turn it off again. Well, dash it all, let's try the other eye."

He pressed for a few moments in vain. Then, with a grinding clang, the bronze wings of the monster clapped down to its sides, revealing a deep square hole, and the fountain ceased to play.

"Gherkins!" said Lord Peter. "We've done it. (But don't neglect bailing on that account!) There's a box here. And it's beastly heavy. No; all right, I can manage. Gimme the boat-hook. Now I do hope the old sinner really did have a treasure. What a bore if it's only one of his little jokes. Never mind—hold the boat steady. There. Always remember, Gherkins, that you can make quite an effective crane with a boat-hook and a stout pair of braces. Got it? That's right. Now for home and beauty. . . . Hullo! What's all that?"

As he paddled the boat round, it was evident that something was happening down by the boat-house. Lights were moving about, and a sound of voices came across the lake.

"They think we're burglars, Gherkins. Always misunderstood. Give way, my hearties—

"A-roving, a-roving, since roving's been my ru-i-in,
I'll go no more a-roving with you, fair maid."

"Is that you, my lord?" said a man's voice as they drew in to the boat-house.

"Why, it's our faithful sleuths!" cried his lordship. "What's the excitement?"

"We found this fellow sneaking round the boat-house," said the man from Scotland Yard. "He says he's the old gentleman's nephew. Do you know him, my lord?"

"I rather fancy I do," said Wimsey. "Mr. Pope, I think.

Good evening. Were you looking for anything? Not a treasure, by any chance? Because we've just found one. Oh! Don't say that. *Maxima reverentia,* you know. Lord St. George is of tender years. And, by the way, thank you so much for sending your delightful friends to call on me last night. Oh, yes, Thompson, I'll charge him all right. You there, Doctor? Splendid. Now, if anybody's got a spanner or anything handy, we'll have a look at Great-grandpapa Cuthbert. And if he turns out to be old iron, Mr. Pope, you'll have had an uncommonly good joke for your money."

An iron bar was produced from the boat-house and thrust under the hasp of the chest. It creaked and burst. Dr. Conyers knelt down tremulously and threw open the lid.

There was a little pause.

"The drinks are on you, Mr. Pope," said Lord Peter. "I think, Doctor, it ought to be a jolly good hospital when it's finished."

"R. L. Stevens" is one of several pseudonyms used by Edward D. Hoch, the dean of modern writers of short mystery fiction. As in his other story included in these pages, Hoch puts his extensive knowledge of writers and the publishing industry to excellent use in "The Great American Novel"—the tale of an editor's unusual discovery among the "slush pile" manuscripts, with a dandy ironic twist on its final page.

THE GREAT AMERICAN NOVEL

R. L. Stevens

She was curled on the bed like a tired question mark awaiting the answer of his body.

I read it over a second time but it didn't change. I flipped the pages till I reached the next chapter, but it was just as bad. "Lunchtime, Pete," someone called as he passed my cubicle. I nodded agreement and tossed the manuscript back on my desk. I needed some lunch to revive me.

We weren't top-echelon editors authorized to entertain authors on expense accounts, so we usually gravitated to the formica-countered coffee shops that lined the side streets off Fifth Avenue. They were good places for lunch—inexpensive, fast, and convenient. And they gave me a chance to meet and mingle with the slush readers from some of the other big publishing houses.

In fact, that was how I met Gilda—the only girl I ever

knew who was named after a Rita Hayworth movie. Gilda was a slush reader at Associated Publishers, though she sported a classier title than that when signing rejection letters. She was just two years out of college and still had something of the cheerleader about her.

"Hi, Pete," she said as she slid onto the stool next to me. "How goes the slush at Ryder & Ryder?"

"Same old stuff. I keep hoping for another *Ulysses,* but at this point I'd settle for another *Carpetbaggers.* Anything!"

She ordered a sandwich and Coke. "Is Brady still riding you?"

Sam Brady was a thirty-five-year-old managing editor trying hard to be the top man at Ryder & Ryder. Sometimes, when he couldn't take out his frustrations on executive editor Carlos Winter, he settled for me instead. "He's been in Washington at the ABA convention," I said. "But he's due back this afternoon."

"All you need is to find one good manuscript, Pete, and you'll have Brady's job."

"It's not quite that easy. I wish it were."

Gilda took a bite of her sandwich and thought about it. "I wish I could write. I'd write you the biggest, sexiest bestseller you ever saw! And you'd get credit for it!"

"I'm afraid Ryder & Ryder doesn't go for sexy best sellers," I told her. "They're more interested in quotes literature unquote."

"That's Carlos Winter's influence."

I had to agree. Winter was the grand old man of New York editorial circles. He'd been at Scribner's in the early days of Hemingway and worked with Pascal Covici when Steinbeck was first beginning to write. Though well past normal retirement age, he showed no sign of surrendering the editorial reins of Ryder & Ryder.

"Winter has certainly been nice to me," I said. "Even when he's loading me down with slush manuscripts, he always has time for a kind word."

Gilda finished her sandwich and Coke, and we strolled for a few minutes down Fifth Avenue until it was time to get back to work. In the elevator I ran into Winter himself, coming back early for a meeting. "How are you, Pete? Read any good manuscripts?"

"Not a thing, Mr. Winter. I keep hoping, though."

"That's the way." He nodded his white mane philosophically.

Back at my desk I found another batch of manuscripts from Carlos Winter's secretary. They'd come in the morning mail, addressed to him personally, and I was to read and report on them. Her note told me to spread them around if I couldn't handle them all, but with Winter's slush I always made an effort to get through it myself. A writer who knew the name of Carlos Winter had at least that much going for him.

The first couple of manuscripts I glanced at seemed to be more of the same—a novel about a young man's awakening and an intensely written book about the Arab-Israeli conflict. I tossed them both aside for later consideration. The third one was different. It even looked different. Its 300-odd typewritten pages were spiral-bound—something I'd never seen on a manuscript—and it had a stiff brown cover with the title and author's name neatly labeled: *Years of Earth* by Sumner Doud Chapin. I liked the title and I liked the author's name. Somehow they both had a literary ring about them.

The book itself was a novel set in the mid-twenties, which perked my interest right away. Sam Brady had told us only a few days earlier to be on the lookout for nostalgia items. It was well written for an unknown, and the earthy atmosphere of struggling farmers came through well. I settled down for a satisfying afternoon's reading.

"Is Pete Traven around?" Brady's voice interrupted my concentration after the first hour. I'd shifted to an empty cubicle to escape the phone.

"In here, Mr. Brady," I called out.

He poked his head in. "You hiding, Traven?"

"No, Mr. Brady. Just reading slush for Mr. Winter."

He glanced down at the manuscript. "I see. I wanted you to run an errand for me, but I'll get someone else." Running errands for Sam Brady was nothing unusual. He treated us all like office boys.

"I'll be glad to do it," I said.

"No, no, go on with your work." He turned to leave and then asked, "Is it any good?"

"I'll tell you—it's the best manuscript I've read in a year."

"Good! You looked as if you were enjoying it."

"It might fit your nostalgia angle. It's about a farm family back in the twenties. The sons that were supposed to carry on the farm all went off to war and didn't return. They got a taste of the city and liked it. The guy's quite a writer. A bit slow in spots, but good, real good."

Brady nodded. "Maybe we've got something. Take it in to Carlos as soon as you finish."

It was after five when I finished the last page of *Years of Earth,* but I stayed on to write my report while the manuscript was still fresh in my mind. *Sumner Doud Chapin is a writer of the twenties,* I wrote glowingly. *One might almost call him a rural Fitzgerald.*

My report ran three pages. I left it with the manuscript on the desk of Winter's secretary, where she'd find it first thing in the morning. Then I went home, satisfied with my job for the first time in a long while.

It was a week before Carlos Winter summoned me to his office. That was something of a treat in itself, since I hadn't been there long enough to be invited to attend the weekly editorial meetings. In fact, the last time I'd sat opposite the cluttered oak desk with its ship model and lighthouse lamp was the day I was hired.

"I read *Years of Earth* last night," he began, busily tamping the tobacco into his pipe. "Your recommendation of it was sound. It's a fine book."

"Then we'll publish it?"

My voice must have betrayed my excitement because he smiled as he answered. "Now, now, we don't rush into these things! The novel is publishable, certainly—but it needs work. Parts of it are terribly dull going, and I think it could use a bit more of the flavor of the period. Tell you what—this Chapin lives right here in Greenwich Village. His phone number's on the manuscript. Ring him up and arrange a meeting here. I'll sit in on it, but I want you to do most of the work with him."

"I've never done any real editing."

"Then it's time you got started, isn't it?"

I left his office walking on a cloud. Maybe I'd make it to being an editor after all! I sat down in my cubicle and dialed the number on Sumner Chapin's manuscript.

"Hello?" a feminine voice answered after the fourth ring.

"Is this the residence of Sumner Doud Chapin?"

She hesitated, then answered, "Yes."

"Could I speak to him, please?"

"Well—he's not here now."

"When do you expect him?"

"He works during the day."

"Is there any place I could reach him?" I asked, and then added, "I'm calling from Ryder & Ryder, about a manuscript he submitted."

"Oh! Could I have him call you back? Or could you call here this evening?"

"I'll call," I said. "After dinner."

I hung up the phone, a bit disappointed at not having made immediate contact with Chapin. I should have figured he'd be working. Unpublished authors have to live on something. I picked up his covering letter and read through its bare sentences again. He didn't say where he worked—only that this was the first story he'd ever tried to publish.

I phoned again from my apartment, a little before eight. The same girl answered the phone, but this time she put Chapin on at once. "My name's Pete Traven," I said. "I'm in the editorial department at Ryder & Ryder."

"Yes." The voice was a low monotone, devoid of expression.

"We like your novel, *Years of Earth,* very much. If you'd consent to a few minor changes we'd like to publish it."

"No changes," the voice said.

"No changes? I don't think you understand, Mr. Chapin—"

"You wish to publish, send me contract."

"Would it be possible for you to come to our office, Mr. Chapin? We're right up on Fifth Avenue—"

"Impossible. I work every day."

"On your lunch hour, perhaps?"

"No."

"You don't seem to understand, Mr. Chapin. We want to publish your novel."

"Send me contract," he repeated. I thought I caught a trace of an accent, but I couldn't be certain..

"Our executive editor, Carlos Winter, would like to meet you personally," I said, playing my last card.

"I cannot meet. Send contract."

"I'll have to get back to you, Mr. Chapin," I decided. I hung up and sat staring at the telephone, not knowing exactly what to do next. I hated to report failure to Carlos Winter on the first assignment he'd ever given me.

But by morning there seemed no alternative. I repeated the telephone conversation in Winter's office, with Sam Brady and the rest of the editorial board sitting in. It was just before their weekly meeting, at which they planned to discuss Chapin's manuscript.

"The hell with him!" was Brady's immediate response. "He needs us more than we need him!"

"Now, now," Winter cautioned. "Perhaps we have another Salinger or Pynchon here—a writer who craves anonymity. It might even be a pleasant change from those fellows who show up here once a month to be taken out to lunch!"

"You going to go crawling to him?" Brady grumbled.

"There's no crawling involved. After all, we work with most writers by mail. I only suggested a personal meeting because the man lives here in New York."

"Then what do you suggest?"

Winter turned toward me. "Pete, could you go down to Chapin's apartment with the contract? Explain to him that the changes would be minimal. Most of them could be done right here in the office and submitted for his approval."

"Sure," I agreed, anxious for a chance to redeem myself in Winter's eyes. "I could do that."

"Good! It's settled, then. We'll have the contract drawn up today."

When I called Chapin's number the following morning, the girl answered again. I announced that I would be coming down that evening if it was convenient. She said it would be. Sumner Doud Chapin would be in.

I took the subway downtown after a quick sandwich at a coffee shop that evening. Alighting at the West Fourth Street Station, I found myself only a few blocks from Chapin's address. The evening was warm and the summer sun had not yet set. A few children were in the streets. Near the corner of Eighth Street an artist was setting up his paintings against the wire fence of a parking lot, waiting for the tourists who would surely come.

I found the building I sought without any trouble and climbed to the third-floor apartment. The name *Chapin* was on a card thumbtacked to the door. Beneath it another card read: *Rose.* I knocked on the door.

A dark-haired girl in jeans and a sleeveless shirt answered the door. I knew at once it had been her voice on the phone. "Miss Rose? I'm Pete Traven from Ryder & Ryder."

"Come in." She tried a smile but it seemed forced. "Sumner will be with you in a minute."

The apartment was starkly furnished in approved Village style, with a half-finished abstract painting on an easel near the windows. "Is that yours?" I asked. "It's very good."

"Thank you."

Before I could say more, the bedroom door opened and a large bearded man came out. "You the guy from the publisher?" he asked in a deep angry voice. "Let's get on with it. I'm busy."

"You're Sumner Doud Chapin?"

"That's right."

"The author of *Years of Earth?*"

"Sure. Did you bring the contract?"

"How about some beer, Sumner?" the girl asked.

"Nah, not now. How about you?"

"No, thanks." I drew the manuscript and contract from my attaché case. "Now there are just a few points we'd like you to think about changing."

"You handle all that. Just gimme the contract." He took the document and scanned it quickly. "Only $1,500 advance?"

"At Ryder & Ryder that's customary for first novels."

"Okay." He flipped through the rest of the pages with what seemed like mild interest. Finally he signed each copy and Miss Rose signed as a witness. I glanced at her signature and saw that her first name was Helen.

"We'll send you an edited copy of the manuscript," I said, "so you can approve the changes we make."

"Sure, sure." He turned to the girl. "I'll have that beer now, Helen."

After a few more minutes of conversation I left the apartment and hurried downstairs. I was at my wits' end, not knowing what to do. Of one thing I was certain—the man who'd signed the contract was not Sumner Doud Chapin. He was not the author of the manuscript in my attaché case. And his was not the voice I'd spoken to on the telephone.

I went no farther than the corner, where I crossed over to the other side and took up a position in the doorway of a record shop. From there I had a good view of the building I'd just left. If I was correct, the man I'd met would not be staying there long. I couldn't imagine Helen Rose calling him Sumner any longer than was necessary.

I didn't have long to wait. About fifteen minutes later the bearded man came down the front steps and headed west, toward Eighth Avenue. Though I had no immediate plan, I followed him.

He walked about a block before disappearing into a dimly lit bar in the basement of an old brick building. I paused a moment, thought about it, and followed him inside. There were only men along the bar, mostly young, and every one of them turned to watch my entrance. I walked past them and joined the bearded man at a table toward the rear.

"Hey! Whatcha doin' here?"

"I should ask you the same thing. Your girl won't approve, will she?"

He waved away the words with his hand. "She's not my girl."

"And you're not Sumner Doud Chapin. Right?"

He stared into his beer and didn't answer.

I slipped a bill from my wallet and slid it across the table. "Right?"

The gesture seemed to embarrass him but he took the money. "Ah, she gave me twenty bucks to say I was Chapin and sign those papers. I don't even know her."

"Where's the real Chapin?"

"Who the hell knows? Who cares?"

I shook my head and left, climbing back up to the twilight street. Well, I'd certainly made a mess of things. I had a contract with a forged signature, and the real Sumner Doud Chapin was as much a mystery as ever.

And the only way to find the real Chapin was through the girl, Helen Rose.

She opened the door, saw my face, and immediately tried to close the door. But I had my foot in, and I pushed hard. "What in hell do you want?" she yelled at me.

"The real Sumner Chapin. Ryder & Ryder isn't paying out fifteen hundred bucks just because you hire some bearded guy to sign Chapin's name. Where is he?"

"Away."

Away where? In prison?"

"Just away."

"I spoke to him on the phone, didn't I?"

"Yes."

"Then he can't be very far away."

Her eyes darted to the clock, then back to my face. She seemed frightened of something but I didn't know what. It was an old banjo clock that hung on the wall near the door, and its hands were just one minute away from nine.

"Are you expecting—?" I began, and my question was answered for me by the sound of a key in the lock.

I was on my feet, starting for the door, when she screamed behind me, "Sumner! Run! He's here!"

I yanked open the door in time to catch a glimpse of someone on the stairs. "Come back, damn it!" I shouted, and started after him.

The stairs were in darkness, and I could see nothing below me. He was running, though, and the sound of his footsteps reached me clearly. When I got to the first floor he was nowhere in sight, but I realized the front door hadn't opened. He had to be hiding somewhere close by.

"Chapin," I said. "I know you're here. I just want to talk with you."

I stepped around the back of the staircase and heard a movement in the dark. Then there was a flash of pain as something struck me across the head and I went down hard.

"What happened to you?" Sam Brady asked the next morning as he surveyed the bandage on my head.

"Walked into a door," I mumbled. I was anxious to see Carlos Winter and didn't want to be sidetracked.

Winter listened to my story in sympathetic silence. When I'd finished he said, "I certainly didn't imagine for a moment I was getting you into anything like that. The man is obviously deranged."

"It would seem so," I agreed, placing a gentle hand to the bump on my head.

"Did you try to see the girl again when you regained consciousness?"

"No. I guess I was a little afraid at that point."

"The contract? The manuscript?"

"Both safe in my case. He took nothing."

"Odd," Carlos Winter murmured. "The entire business is extremely odd."

"It sure is! What do we do now?"

Winter shrugged. "Return the manuscript, I suppose. We can't publish it without a valid contract."

I went back to my desk deep in gloom. It had been my first real discovery, and now it had simply melted away, like the morning snow that turns to slush in the streets of Manhattan.

At lunch that day I met Gilda and told her what had happened. "There'll be other manuscripts, Pete. I'm more concerned about your head! Did you report it to the police?"

"No. Nothing was stolen, and my story wouldn't have

made much sense. They'd have listed it as an attempted mugging."

"But why should this Chapin attack you? It doesn't seem like the best way to get his novel published."

"There's something strange about the whole business. And it's a heck of a lot more than just a shy author."

I went back to the office in a state of depression. The pile of slush manuscripts from the day's mail held no promise for me any longer. The chances of finding another novel as good as *Years of Earth* seemed remote in the extreme.

When my telephone rang I answered it automatically. For a second I thought it was Sam Brady, complaining that I'd taken too long for lunch. But then the voice identified itself.

"This is Sumner Doud Chapin."

"Oh?" I couldn't think of anything else to say.

"I'm sorry about last night."

For some reason that angered me. "You sure as hell should be sorry! My head still hurts!"

"I think I could discuss the book now, with Carlos Winter."

"You do, huh? Well, let me tell you something, Mr. Chapin, I doubt very much whether Ryder & Ryder still wants to publish your book!"

"Could I speak to Mr. Winter about it? I can explain my odd behavior."

I had to admit the voice sounded more friendly and rational than the first time we'd talked. There was still an odd muffled accent about it, but the tone was more relaxed. "Winter is out right now. I can speak to him and call you back."

"I'm phoning from work. I'd better call you. In an hour?"

I said that was agreeable and hung up. Was it possible that Chapin was some sort of split personality—a genius of a writer who turned into a madman periodically?

When Carlos Winter returned, I asked to see him. I relayed the telephone message and waited for his reaction. When it came it surprised me. "All right, I suppose I can talk to him. There's no harm in that."

Back at my desk, while I waited for the call, I had a thought. I got out the Manhattan phone book and looked up Chapin's name. He wasn't listed. Then I looked up Helen Rose. She was listed, with the phone number I'd called that first time. As I'd suspected, the apartment was hers. Chapin might well be living there, or he might be living somewhere else.

Exactly on the hour my telephone rang. But this time it wasn't Chapin. It was Helen Rose. "He couldn't call back," she explained. "He asked me to call for him."

I went into Winter's office and told him. "Put her on," he said, and took the call, motioning me to remain in the office.

I could tell from his end of the conversation that she was arranging a meeting between Winter and Chapin. He tried to schedule it for the office during working hours, but obviously she was resisting. Finally he agreed to come to the apartment that evening. When he hung up he said to me, "I want you along, Pete. For protection, as much as anything."

I touched my bandaged head. "I'm afraid I'm not very good at that."

"You'll be good enough."

I had a sudden sense of danger, of walking into something I didn't fully understand. But with Carlos Winter I was willing to risk it.

A soft rain had started to fall by the time we reached the Village that evening. It made the narrow streets dimmer, the sidewalks almost deserted, the buildings somehow forbidding. "This is it," I said as the cab dropped us at the corner. "The second doorway."

We climbed the stairs as I had done twice the previous

night and knocked at Helen Rose's door. But one thing was different about the door tonight. The two name cards had been removed. The door was bare. "No answer," Winter said, and knocked again.

"Try the door," I suggested.

It swung open at his touch and we entered the apartment.

It was empty.

The banjo clock, the few chairs, the sparse furnishings—all were gone.

"Strange," I said.

"Perhaps not so strange." Though the apartment seemed surely empty, Carlos Winter raised his voice. "We're here. You can come out now, Mr. Chapin."

I saw the bathroom door start to move and a chill ran down my spine. I felt a touch of fear—the fear of the unknown. Then the door swung wide and I saw that it wasn't Sumner Doud Chapin at all. It was Sam Brady from the office.

But he was pointing a gun at us.

I glanced at Carlos Winter, but there was no surprise on his face. He nodded slightly, as if the presence of Sam Brady with a gun only confirmed what he'd been thinking all along.

"So it's finally come out in the open, has it, Sam?"

"It's out in the open, Carlos. You knew all along, didn't you? That's why you didn't come here alone."

Winter gestured toward me. "I felt this young man should be present. After all, he's the one who disrupted your scheme in the first place."

"Scheme?" I repeated, uncomprehending. "But where is Chapin?"

"Standing right here in front of us," Winter said. "And looking more like a thug than an author or editor."

"What about *Years of Earth*?" I wanted to know. "Did

he write it? Mr. Winter, that book could win the Pulitzer Prize!"

"It already did," Carlos Winter answered dryly. "In fact, it won the Pulitzer under its real title more than forty years ago."

"So I wasn't able to fool you," Sam Brady said. He was still pointing the gun at us, though neither of us had raised our hands. "I thought I could."

"I'm sure." Winter carefully shifted position, but did not try to get any closer to the weapon. "There must be half a dozen Pulitzer novels from the twenties and early thirties that are unknown today. Books like *The Able McLaughlins* and *Years of Grace* and *Lamb in His Bosom* are unread and unreprinted. Their authors are all but forgotten. By plagiarizing one of those books—having your girl friend type it up as a new work—you hoped to trick Ryder & Ryder into publishing it."

"Wait a minute," I argued. "That doesn't make any sense, Mr. Winter. A first novelist never gets much of an advance and surely once the book was published someone would remember it! What could he hope to gain by stealing a novel that had won the Pulitzer Prize?"

Carlos Winter drew a deep breath. "Embarrassment," he answered. "Embarrassment so great it would force my retirement from the company. It would be the greatest literary hoax since the Clifford Irving affair, and I would be the goat because I bought and published the book." There was a faint smile on his lips as he spoke those words. "You wanted my job that badly, did you, Sam?"

"But where did I come in?" I asked.

"Brady knew you'd read the book first when it came in with the slush. He carefully prepared you by saying we were anxious to publish some nostalgia. Isn't that right?"

"Yes, and he checked on me while I was reading it. But you mean it was Mr. Brady's voice on the telephone?" Even as I spoke I remembered my first impression that the voice was Brady's.

"It was his voice," Winter confirmed. "If we'd sent the contract by mail, his scheme might even have worked. But when we wanted to meet him in person, they had to ring in a substitute. You didn't fall for that, Pete, and you confronted the Rose woman with the truth. You even chased Sam down the stairs and got hit on the head. Of course I never would have countersigned the contract anyway—I just wanted to bring them into the open. With your help, I did it."

"But why this meeting?" I asked. "And why an empty apartment?"

"Sam can't get me out through a hoax, so he's going to try murder. Right, Sam? Isn't that why your girl friend cleared out with all her possessions?"

Sam Brady didn't answer.

"But now you'll have to kill two of us. Is my job worth that much, Sam? Is it?"

"I can't turn back now," Brady said, but his voice betrayed him. He was close to breaking.

"I left an envelope with my secretary, Sam. The whole story's in it."

That was when he broke. The gun suddenly lowered till it pointed at the floor. "All right, Carlos. You've won. Get yourself a new managing editor." He turned and walked out of the empty apartment.

For a full minute I stood frozen to the spot. "Was he really going to kill us?"

"I don't think so," Carlos Winter said. "Not really. When it came right down to it he didn't have the guts."

I went to the window and looked down at the street. The rain had stopped and the evening's tourists were beginning to arrive. I could see Sam Brady crossing the street and mingling with them. "How did you know about the manuscript?" I asked. "You couldn't have remembered the book from over forty years ago!"

Carlos Winter smiled. "I've been in publishing a long time, Pete. I started out reading slush, just like you. I read that very book when it was first submitted to my company, all those years ago. I read it and sent it back. Believe me, when you've rejected a Pulitzer Prize winner, you always remember it."

The collaborative team of Frederic Dannay (1905–82) and Manfred B. Lee (1905–71) is better known to the world as Ellery Queen, and the detective who stars in all but two of the Queen novels also bears the name of his pseudonymous creator. Ellery Queen's career began when the Brooklyn-born cousins submitted The Roman Hat Mystery *to a contest sponsored by* McClure's *magazine in 1928. Due to a bankruptcy and subsequent takeover of the publication, the prize that was originally awarded to Queen went to another writer, but the novel was later published and became an immediate success. Since 1928, Queen has appeared in such novels as* The French Powder Mystery *(1930),* The Dutch Shoe Mystery *(1931), and* The Chinese Orange Mystery *(1934); as well as in numerous short stories, films, radio plays, and a television series. A characteristic of all the Queen puzzles is "playing fair" with the reader—giving him a chance at solving the crime by making him privy to all the clues and knowledge possessed by the detective. In "Mystery at the Library of Congress," Queen challenges his reader to solve an intricate literary mystery taking place at one of our most revered institutions.*

MYSTERY AT THE LIBRARY OF CONGRESS

Ellery Queen

Ellery responded to Inspector Terence Fineberg's invitation with pleasure. Fineberg, in charge of the Central Office, was one of Inspector Queen's ancient beat buddies, and he used to slip Ellery candy bars. He detested amateur detectives, so the old mink must be desperate.

"Park it," Inspector Fineberg said, blowing hot and cold. "You know Inspector Pete Santoria of the Narcotics Squad?"

Ellery nodded to the stone-jawed Narcotics man.

"We'll skip the protocol, Ellery," Fineberg went on, gnashing his dentures. "Calling you in wasn't our idea. The big brass thought this case could use your screwb—your God-given talents."

"I'm ever at the beck of the law enforcement arm," Ellery said kindly, "especially when it's grasping at straws. You may fire when ready, Finey."

"The buck," Fineberg shouted to Inspector Santoria, "is yours."

Santoria said in tooth-sucking tones, "We got a line on a new dope ring, Queen. The junk is coming in, we think, from France, and in kilo lots. New York is the distribution depot. None of the lower echelons knows any of the others except the few in immediate contact. We want the big boy on the New York end. That this gang aren't regulars is about all we know for sure."

"Of course they're no regulars," the Central Office head grumbled. "Who ever heard of a regular dope-running crumbum who could read?"

"Read?" Ellery came to a point like a bird dog. "Read what, Finey?"

"Books, for gossakes!"

"Don't tell me we authors are now being blamed for the narcotics traffic, too," Ellery said coldly. "How do books come into this?"

"Using 'em as a code!" Terence Fineberg implored the ceiling to witness. "An information-passing operation is going on down in Washington that's an intermediate step between shipment and delivery. The Federal Bureau of Narcotics got on the trail of the D.C. members of the ring—two of 'em, anyway—and they're both being watched."

"One of the two," Inspector Santoria took it up, "is a colorless little shnook named Balcom who works for a Washington travel agency. He used to be a high school English teacher. The other—a girl named Norma Shuffing—is employed at the Library of Congress."

"The Library's being used as the contact rendezvous?"

"Yes. Balcom's job is to pass along the information as to when, where, and how a new shipment is coming into New York. The contact to whom he has to pass the information is identified for Balcom by the Shuffing girl. They play it cool—a different contact is used every time."

Ellery shrugged. "All you have to do is spot one as the Shuffing girl points him out to Balcom—"

"Yes, sir, Mr. Queen," the Narcotics chief said, sounding like the Witch in *Hansel and Gretel.* "Want a go at it?"

"Just what takes place?" Ellery asked intently.

Inspector Fineberg's glance quelled Santoria. "Balcom visits the Library only when the girl is on duty—she works out of the main desk filling call slips and bringing the books onto the floor. Balcom takes either Desk One Forty-seven or, if that's occupied, the nearest one that's vacant. When Shuffing spies him she brings him some books conforming to slips filled out by her in advance. It's the titles of the books that tip him off—she never communicates with him in any other way."

"Titles," Ellery said, nuzzling the word. "What does Balcom do?"

"He looks the books over, then takes an easy gander around his immediate neighborhood. And that's all. After that he just sits there reading, doesn't take his eyes off his books, till closing time, when he gets up and goes home."

"The Library bit is just so Balcom can identify the messenger," Inspector Santoria said. "The actual passage of the information is made at a different meeting."

"But if Balcom's being watched—"

"He works for a travel agency, I told you! Any idea how many people he comes in contact with daily?"

"We figure it works like this, Ellery," the Central Office head explained. "After a session at the Library—the next morning, say—the messenger that this Norma Shuffing identified for Balcom through the book titles shows up at the travel agency as a customer. Balcom recognizes him and passes him a legitimate ticket envelope, only it contains not just plane or railroad tickets, but the dope shipment info, too."

"And if you could spot one of these contacts—"

"We could track Balcom's message to its destination. That would be Big Stuff himself, who's sure as hell covered behind a smart front here in New York."

A contact and shipment, Ellery learned, occurred about

once every ten days. The Federals had set up their first stakeout a month before, and at that time Miss Shuffing had brought three books to Balcom's desk.

"What were they?"

Inspector Santoria fished a report from a folder. "Steve Allen's *The Funny Men,* Count Leo Tolstoy's *War and Peace,* and Sigmund Freud's *Interpretation of Dreams.*"

"Lovely!" Ellery murmured. "Allen, Tolstoy, Freud . . . Well." He seemed disappointed. "It's simple enough. A kindergarten acrostic—"

"Sure," Terence Fineberg retorted. "F for Freud, A for Allen, T for Tolstoy. F-A-T. There was a three-hundred-pound character sitting near Balcom."

"The trouble was," Santoria said, "the Feds and we weren't on to the system that first time, and by the time we'd figured it out the fat guy had already got his info from Balcom and taken off."

"What about the second contact?"

"Three books again. Chekhov's *The Cherry Orchard,* George R. Stewart's *Fire,* and Ben Hecht's *Actor's Blood.*"

"C-S-H. No acrostic there. Changed the system . . ." Ellery frowned. "Must be in the titles—something in common. . . . Was there an American Indian sitting near Balcom on that visit? Or someone with red hair?"

"Quick, isn't he, Pete?" Inspector Fineberg asked sourly. "Yeah, we saw that—cherries, fire, blood are all red. It was an old dame with dyed red hair sitting a couple seats from Balcom. Only again we doped it out too late to cover the actual contact. The third time we missed clean."

"Ah, couldn't find the common denominator."

"What common denominator?" Santoria asked angrily. "You got to have at least two items for that!"

"There was only *one* book the third time?"

"Right! I still say the doll got suspicious and never brought the other books. But do you think the brass would listen to me? No, they got to call in a screwb—an expert!"

"The thing is, Ellery," Inspector Fineberg said, "we do have evidence that a third shipment was picked up, which means a contact *was* made after that one-book deal."

"They did it some other way, Terence!" Santoria snapped.

"Sure, Pete, sure," Fineberg said soothingly. "I go along with you. Only the brass don't. They want Brains working on this. Who are we to reason why?"

"What was the book?" Ellery asked.

"Rudyard Kipling's *The Light That Failed.*"

Santoria growled. "We waited around the whole damn afternoon while people came and went—what a turnover they get down there—and our boy Balcom sits there at Desk One Forty-seven reading the Kipling book from cover to cover like he was enjoying it!"

"*The Light That Failed* was about a man who went blind. Was there someone in the vicinity wearing dark glasses, or immersed in a volume of Braille?"

"No blind people, no cheaters, no Braille, no nothing."

Ellery mused. "Do you have a written report of that visit?"

Santoria dug out another folder. Ellery glanced through it. It was a detailed account of the third Balcom-Shuffing contact, complete with descriptions of suspects, unclassified incidents, and so on. Ellery emerged from this rubble bearing a nugget.

"Of course," he said gently. "The one book by Kipling was all Balcom needed that day. A saintly-looking old gent wearing a clerical collar was consulting a card catalogue within view of Balcom and absently filled his pipe. He was flipping the wheel of his pocket lighter—flipped it unsuccessfully several times, it says here, boys—when a guard walked over and stopped him. The old fellow apologized for his absent-mindedness, put the lighter and pipe away, and went on consulting the index cards. *The Light That Failed.*"

"Lemme see that!" Fineberg snatched the folder, red in

the face. "Pete," he howled, "how the devil did we miss that?"

"We thought sure there'd be more books, Terence," Inspector Santoria stammered. "And the old guy was a preacher—"

"The old guy was a phony! Look, Ellery, maybe you can help us at that. We've been slow on the uptake—books yet! If on the next meet you could be sitting near Balcom and spot the contact man right away—how about it?"

"You couldn't keep me out of this with a court order, Finey," Ellery assured him. "What's more, it won't cost the City of New York a plugged subway token—I'll pay my own expenses to Washington. Can you arrange it with the Feds?"

Inspector Fineberg arranged it with the Feds, and on Monday of the following week Ellery was snugged down one desk behind and to the right of Desk 147 in the main reading room of the venerable gray Renaissance building east of the Capitol in downtown Washington. One of his fellow stakeout men, a balding Federal Narcotics agent named Hauck, who looked like a senior accountant in a wholesale drygoods firm, was parked in the outermost concentric circle of desks, near the entrance; they could signal each other by a half turn of the head. Another Federal agent and Inspector Santoria lounged around outside making like camera bugs.

Ellery's desk was loaded with reference books, for he was being an Author in Search of Material, a role he had often played at the Library of Congress in earnest.

He had filed his slips at the main desk with Norma Shuffing, whose photo—along with Balcom's—he had studied at the Federal Bureau. When she brought the books to his desk he was able to get a close look. Tense and sad-looking, she was a pretty, dark-eyed girl who had been at some pains to camouflage her prettiness. Ellery wondered how she had come to be mixed up in an international dope operation; she could not have been more than twenty years old.

The little travel agent, Balcom, did not appear that day. Ellery had not expected him to, for the Federal men had said that Balcom visited the Library only on his days off, which were unpredictable. Today he was reported swamped at the office by a tidal wave of travel orders.

"But it's got to be soon, Queen," Inspector Santoria said Monday night in Ellery's room at the Hotel Mayflower. "Tomorrow's the eleventh day since the last meet, and they've never gone this long before."

"Balcom may not be able to get away from his office."

"He'll manage it," Agent Hauck said grimly.

Early the next morning Ellery's phone rang. It was Santoria. "I just got the word from Hauck. It's today."

"How's Balcom managing it?"

"He's reported out sick. Better get on over to the Library."

Norma Shuffing was bringing Ellery an armful of books when a little man with mousy eyes and mousy hair, dressed in a mousy business suit, pat-patted past Ellery's desk and slipped into the seat of Desk 147. Ellery did not need Hauck's pencil-to-nose signal to identify the newcomer. It was Balcom.

The Shuffing girl passed Desk 147 without a glance. She placed Ellery's books softly before him and returned to her station. Ellery began to turn pages.

It was fascinating to watch them. Balcom and the girl might have inhabited different planets. Balcom stared at the encircling walls, the very picture of a man waiting. Not once did he look toward the main desk. There, her back to him, the pretty girl was quietly busy.

The reading room began to fill.

Ellery continued to study the two of them from above his book. Balcom had his dainty hands clasped on his desk now; he seemed to be dozing. Norma Shuffing was fetching books, working on the floor dozens of feet away.

A quarter of an hour passed.

Ellery sneaked an inventory of the readers in the vicinity. To Balcom's left sat a buxom woman in a smart strawberry silk suit; she wore bifocals and was raptly reading a volume of industrial reports.

To Balcom's right a very large man with wrestler's shoulders and no hair was absorbed in a three-volume set on African lovebirds.

Beyond the bird-lover a sloppily dressed Latin who looked like Fidel Castro's double was making secretive notes from some ancient *National Geographics*.

Near the Cuban-looking man sat a thin elongated lady with a lavender-rinse hairdo who reminded Ellery of Miss Hildegarde Withers; she was intent on the *Congressional Record.*

Also in the neighborhood were a scowling young priest who was leafing through a book on demonology; a Man of Distinction with a gray crewcut and an egg-spattered necktie who was frankly dozing; and a young lady with hearing-aid, eyeglasses, and some blue ink on one nostril who was copying something from a book on naval ordnance as if her life depended on it.

Suddenly the Shuffing girl started up the aisle. She was carrying a thick, oversized book.

Ellery turned a page. Was this it?

It was!

Miss Shuffing paused at Desk 147, placed the book deftly before Balcom, and walked away.

Balcom unclasped his little hands and opened the book to the title page.

The Complete Shakespeare.

The Complete Shakespeare?

Balcom began to idle through the volume. He made no attempt to survey his fellow readers.

Shakespeare . . . Some relevant quotation? Not likely, with thousands to cull.

Ellery concentrated.

Plays? A playwright? An actor? Nothing about anyone in the vicinity suggested the theater. Moreover, Balcom seemed obviously to be waiting.

Ten minutes later Miss Shuffing silently laid another book on Desk 147 and as silently took herself off.

This time Balcom reached for the book with something like eagerness. Ellery craned.

Shaw . . . Shaw's *Man and Superman.*

A playwright again! But how could you make an instant identification of a playwright—or an actor, for that matter? Ellery glanced about under the pretext of stretching. No one within eyeshot was even reading a play.

Shakespeare—Shaw. Initials? S, S. SS! An ex-Nazi Storm Trooper? The big bald wrestlerish character who was interested in African lovebirds? Possibly, but how could anyone be sure? It had to be something Balcom could interpret with certainty at a glance. Besides, the fellow didn't look Teutonic, but Slavic.

Shakespeare, Shaw . . . English literature. An Englishman? No one Ellery could see looked English, although any of them might be. Besides, Shaw was really Irish.

Man and Superman? Somehow that didn't fit in with Shakespeare.

Ellery shook his head. What the deuce was the girl trying to convey to Balcom?

Balcom was now reading Shaw with concentration. But then he had to keep doing something. Was he waiting for another volume? Or would he soon look around and spot the contact?

If he does, Ellery thought with exasperation, he's a better man than I am!

But Balcom did not look up from the Shaw book. He was showing no curiosity about his neighbors, so Ellery decided that he was expecting another book. . . .

Yes, a third book was coming!

The Shuffing girl placed it on Desk 147. Ellery could barely contain himself.

He read the title almost simultaneously with Balcom, blessing his sharp eyesight.

Personal Memoirs of U. S. Grant.

Blam went his theories! Shakespeare and Shaw, playwrights; Grant, a military man. S, S, now G. One Englishman, one Irishman, one American.

What did it all add up to?

Ellery couldn't think of a thing. He could feel Agent Hauck's eyes boring critical holes in his back.

And the minutes went bucketing by.

He now studied Balcom with ferocity. Did the three books mean anything to *him*? Not yet. Balcom was in trouble, too, as he pretended to glance through the Grant autobiography. Puzzlement showed in every slightest movement.

Shakespeare . . . Shaw . . . General Grant . . .

Balcom had it!

He was now looking around casually, his gaze never lingering, as if one glimpse was all he needed.

Ellery struggled with panic. Any moment Balcom's contact might get up and leave, knowing Balcom had spotted him. People were constantly coming and going; it would be impossible to identify the right one without the clue conveyed by the books. Ellery could already hear Inspector Santoria's horse laugh. . . .

And then—O blessed!—he had it, too!

Ellery rose. He plucked his hat from the desk, strolled up the aisle past Agent Hauck, who had chewed his pencil eraser to crumbs, and went out into the Washington sunshine. Inspector Santoria and the other Federal man were seated in an unmarked car now, and Ellery slipped into the rear seat.

"Well?" the Federal man demanded. The Feds had been polite, but skeptical, over the New York brass's inspiration.

"Wait for Hauck."

Agent Hauck came out two minutes later., He paused near the car to light a cigarette, and Ellery said, "Get set for the tail. The contact is sitting two seats over to Balcom's right in the same row. He's the sloppy little Cuban type."

"Afternoon, Finey," Ellery said on Friday of that week. "Don't tell me. You're stumped again."

"No, no, haha, sit down, my boy," Inspector Terence Fineberg said cordially. "You're ace-high around here! Thought you'd like to know Pete Santoria collared Big Stuff two hours ago in the act of taking possession of a shipment of H. The Feds are out right now picking up Balcom and the girl. By the way, that little Havana number who led us to him was never closer to Cuba than an El Stinko cigar. He's a poolroom punk name of Harry Hummelmayer from the Red Hook section of Brooklyn."

Ellery nodded unenthusiastically. The spirit of the chase had long since left him. "Well, Finey, congratulations and all that. Was there something else? I have a date with four walls and an empty typewriter."

"Wait, Ellery, for gossakes! I've been going Nutsville trying to figure out a connection between Shakespeare, Shaw, and old man Grant. Even knowing the contact was Hummelmayer, I can't see what the three have in common."

"With Hummelmayer looking like Fidel Castro?" Ellery reached over the desk and, gripping Inspector Fineberg's knotty chin firmly, waggled it. "Beards, Finey, beards."

This is a story about a man who craves originality—by a man who has no lack of that quality. Bill Pronzini is the author of thirty-three novels, a dozen of them in the popular Nameless Detective series, and some 275 short stories. In these, his fine characterization combines with a talent for keeping the reader off guard and guessing to the very last line. A fifteen-year veteran of the profession, Pronzini knows publishing and writers as only an insider can. "A Craving for Originality" is, in this editor's opinion, an exceptional and wryly humorous portrait of that garden-variety working writer—the professional hack. (M.M.)

A CRAVING FOR ORIGINALITY

Bill Pronzini

Charlie Hackman was a professional writer. He wrote popular fiction, any kind from sexless Westerns to sexy Gothics to oversexed historical romances, whatever the current trends happened to be. He could be counted on to deliver an acceptable manuscript to order in two weeks. He had published nine million words in a fifteen-year career, under a variety of different names (Allison St. Cyr being the most prominent), and he couldn't tell you the plot of any book he'd written more than six months ago. He was what is euphemistically known in the trade as "a dependable wordsmith," or "a versatile pro," or "a steady producer of commercial commodities."

In other words, he was well named: Hackman was a hack.

The reason he was a hack was not because he was fast

and prolific, or because he contrived popular fiction on demand, or because he wrote for money. It was because he was and did all these things with no ambition and no sense of commitment. It was because he wrote without originality of any kind.

Of course, Hackman had not started out to be a hack; no writer does. But he had discovered early on, after his first two novels were rejected with printed slips by thirty-seven publishers each, that (a) he was not very good, and (b) what talent he did possess was in the form of imitations. When he tried to do imaginative, ironic, meaningful work of his own he failed miserably; but when he imitated the ideas and visions of others, the blurred carbon copies he produced were just literate enough to be publishable.

Truth to tell, this didn't bother him very much. The one thing he had always wanted to be was a professional writer; he had dreamed of nothing else since his discovery of the Hardy Boys and Tarzan books in his preteens. So from the time of his first sale he accepted what he was, shrugged, and told himself not to worry about it. What was wrong with being a hack, anyway? The writing business was full of them—and hacks, no less than nonhacks, offered a desirable form of escapist entertainment to the masses; the only difference was, his readership had nondiscriminating tastes. Was his product, after all, any less honorable than what television offered? Was he hurting anybody, corrupting anybody? No. Absolutely not. So what was wrong with being a hack?

For one and a half decades, operating under this cheerful set of rationalizations, Hackman was a complacent man. He wrote from ten to fifteen novels per year, all for minor and exploitative paperback houses, and earned an average annual sum of twenty-five thousand dollars. He married an ungraceful woman named Grace and moved into a suburban house on Long Island. He went bowling once a week, played poker once a week, argued conjugal matters with his wife once a week, and took the train into Manhattan to see his agent and editors once a week. Every June he and Grace spent fourteen pleasant days at Lake George in the Adirondacks. Every Christmas Grace's mother came from Pennsylvania and spent fourteen miserable days with them.

He drank a little too much sometimes and worried about lung cancer because he smoked three packs of cigarettes a day. He cheated moderately on his income tax. He coveted one of his neighbors' wives. He read all the current paperback best sellers, dissected them in his mind, and then reassembled them into similar plots for his own novels. When new acquaintances asked him what he did for a living he said, "I'm a writer," and seldom failed to feel a small glow of pride.

That was the way it was for fifteen years—right up until the morning of his fortieth birthday.

Hackman woke up on that morning, looked at Grace lying beside him, and realized she had put on at least forty pounds since their marriage. He listened to himself wheeze as he lighted his first cigarette of the day. He got dressed and walked downstairs to his office, where he read the half page of manuscript still in his typewriter (an occult pirate novel, the latest craze). He went outside and stood on the lawn and looked at his house. Then he sat down on the porch steps and looked at himself.

I'm not just a writer of hack stories, he thought sadly, I'm a liver of a hack life.

Fifteen years of cohabiting with trite fictional characters in hackneyed fictional situations. Fifteen years of cohabiting with an unimaginative wife in a trite suburb in a hackneyed life-style in a conventional world. Hackman the hack, doing the same things over and over again; Hackman the hack, grinding out books and days one by one. No uniqueness in any of it, from the typewriter to the bedroom to the Adirondacks.

No originality.

He sat there for a long while, thinking about this. No

originality. Funny. It was like waking up to the fact that, after forty years, you've never tasted pineapple, that pineapple was missing from your life. All of a sudden you craved pineapple; you wanted it more than you'd ever wanted anything before. Pineapple or originality—it was the same principle.

Grace came out eventually and asked him what he was doing. "Thinking that I crave originality," he said, and she said, "Will you settle for eggs and bacon?" Trite dialogue, Hackman thought. Hackneyed humor. He told her he didn't want any breakfast and went into his office.

Originality. Well, even a hack ought to be able to create something fresh and imaginative if he applied himself; even a hack learned a few tricks in fifteen years. How about a short story? Good. He had never written a short story; he would be working in new territory already. Now how about a plot?

He sat at his typewriter. He paced the office. He lay down on the couch. He sat at the typewriter again. Finally the germ of an idea came to him and he nurtured it until it began to develop. Then he began to type.

It took him all day to write the story, which was some five thousand words long. That was about his average wordage per day on a novel, but on a novel he never revised so much as a comma. After supper he went back into the office and made pen-and-ink corrections until eleven o'clock. Then he went to bed, declined Grace's reluctant offer of "a birthday present," and dreamed about the story until 6 A.M. At which time he got up, retyped the pages, made some more revisions in ink, and retyped the story a third time before he was satisfied. He mailed it that night to his agent.

Three days later the agent called about a new book contract. Hackman asked him, "Did you have a chance to read the short story I sent you?"

"I read it, all right. And sent it straight back to you."

"Sent it back? What's wrong with it?"

"It's old hat," the agent said. "The idea's been done to death."

Hackman went out into the backyard and lay down in the hammock. All right, so maybe he was doomed to hackdom as a writer; maybe he just wasn't capable of *writing* anything original. But that didn't mean he couldn't *do* something original, did it? He had a quick mind, a good grasp of what was going on in the world. He ought to be able to come up with at least one original idea, maybe even an idea that would not only satisfy his craving for originality but change his life, get him out of the stale rut he was in.

He closed his eyes.

He concentrated.

He thought about jogging backward from Long Island to Miami Beach and then applying for an entry in the Guinness Book of World Records.

Imitative.

He thought about marching naked through Times Square at high noon, waving a standard paperback contract and using a bullhorn to protest man's literary inhumanity to man.

Trite.

He thought about adopting a red-white-and-blue disguise and robbing a bank in each one of the original thirteen states.

Derivative.

He thought about changing his name to Holmes, finding a partner named Watson, and opening a private inquiry agency that specialized in solving the unsolved and insoluble.

Parrotry.

He thought about doing other things legal and illegal, clever and foolish, dangerous, and harmless.

Unoriginal. Unoriginal. Unoriginal.

That day passed and several more just like it. Hackman became obsessed with originality—so much so that he found himself unable to write, the first serious block he had had as a professional. It was maddening, but every time he thought of a sentence and started to type it out, something would click in his mind and make him analyze it as original or banal. The verdict was always banal.

He thought about buying a small printing press, manufacturing bogus German Deutsche marks in his basement, and then flying to Munich and passing them at the Oktoberfest.

Counterfeit.

Hackman took to drinking a good deal more than his usual allotment of alcohol in the evenings. His consumption of cigarettes rose to four packs a day and climbing. His originality quotient remained at zero.

He thought about having a treasure map tattooed on his chest, claiming to be the sole survivor of a gang of armored car thieves, and conning all sorts of greedy people out of their life savings.

Trite.

The passing days turned into passing weeks. Hackman still wasn't able to write; he wasn't able to do much of anything except vainly overwork his brain cells. He knew he couldn't function again as a writer or a human being until he did something, *anything* original.

He thought about building a distillery in his garage and becoming Long Island's largest manufacturer and distributor of bootleg whiskey.

Hackneyed.

Grace had begun a daily and voluble series of complaints. Why was he moping around, drinking and smoking so much? Why didn't he go into his office and write his latest piece of trash? What were they going to do for money if he didn't fulfill his contracts? How would they pay the mortgage and the rest of their bills? What was the *matter* with him, anyway? Was he going through some kind of midlife crisis or what?

Hackman thought about strangling her, burying her body under the acacia tree in the backyard—committing the perfect crime.

Stale. Bewhiskered.

Another week disappeared. Hackman was six weeks overdue now on an occult pirate novel and two weeks overdue on a male-action novel; his publishers were upset, his agent was upset; where the hell were the manuscripts? Hackman said he was just polishing up the first one. "Sure you are," the agent said over the phone. "Well, you'd better have it with you when you come in on Friday. I mean that, Charlie. You'd better deliver."

Hackman thought about kidnapping the star of Broadway's top musical extravaganza and holding her for a ransom of one million dollars plus a role in her next production.

Old stuff.

He decided that things couldn't go on this way. Unless he came up with an original idea pretty soon, he might just as well shuffle off this mortal coil.

He thought about buying some rat poison and mixing himself an arsenic cocktail.

More old stuff.

Or climbing a utility pole and grabbing hold of a high-tension wire.

Prosaic. Corny.

Or hiring a private plane to fly him over the New Jersey swamps and then jumping out at two thousand feet.

Ho-hum.

Damn! He couldn't seem to go on, he couldn't seem *not* to go on. So what was he going to do?

He thought about driving over to Pennsylvania, planting certain carefully faked documents inside Grace's mother's house, and turning the old bat in to the FBI as a foreign spy.

Commonplace.

On Friday morning he took his cigarettes (the second of

the five packs a day he was now consuming) and his latest hangover down to the train station. There he boarded the express for Manhattan and took a seat in the club car.

He thought about hijacking the train and extorting twenty million dollars from the state of New York.

Imitative.

When the train arrived at Penn Station he trudged the six blocks to his agent's office. In the elevator on the way up an attractive young blonde gave him a friendly smile and said it was a nice day, wasn't it?

Hackman thought about making her his mistress, having a torrid affair, and then running off to Acapulco with her and living in sin in a villa high above the harbor and weaving Mexican *serapes* by day and drinking tequila by night.

Hackneyed.

The first thing his agent said to him was, "Where's the manuscript, Charlie?" Hackman said it wasn't ready yet, he was having a few personal problems. The agent said, "You think you got problems? What about *my* problems? You think I can afford to have hack writers missing deadlines and making editors unhappy? That kind of stuff reflects back on me, ruins my reputation. I'm not in this business for my health, so maybe you'd better just find yourself another agent."

Hackman thought about bashing him over the head with a paperweight, disposing of the body, and assuming his identity after first gaining sixty pounds and going through extensive plastic surgery.

Motheaten. Threadbare.

Out on the street again, he decided he needed a drink and turned into the first bar he came to. He ordered a triple vodka and sat brooding over it. I've come to the end of my rope, he thought. If there's one original idea in this world, I can't even imagine what it is. For that matter, I can't even imagine a partly original idea, which I'd settle for right now because maybe there *isn't* anything completely original any more.

"What am I going to do?" he asked the bartender.

"Who cares?" the bartender said. "Stay, go, drink, don't drink—it's all the same to me."

Hackman sighed and got off his stool and swayed out onto East Fifty-second Street. He turned west and began to walk back toward Grand Central, jostling his way through the midafternoon crowds. Overhead, the sun glared down at him between the buildings like a malevolent eye.

He was nearing Madison Avenue, muttering clichés to himself, when the idea struck him.

It came out of nowhere, full-born in an instant, the way most great ideas (or so he had heard) always do. He came to an abrupt standstill. Then he began to smile. Then he began to laugh. Passersby gave him odd looks and detoured around him, but Hackman didn't care. The idea was all that mattered.

It was inspired.

It was imaginative.

It was meaningful.

It was original.

Oh, not one-hundred-percent original—but that was all right. He had already decided that finding total originality was an impossible goal. This idea was close, though. It was close and it was wonderful and he was going to do it. Of course he was going to do it; after all these weeks of search and frustration, how could he *not* do it?

Hackman set out walking again. His stride was almost jaunty and he was whistling to himself. Two blocks south he entered a sporting goods store and found what he wanted. The salesman who waited on him asked if he was going camping. "Nope," Hackman said, and winked. "Something *much* more original than that."

He left the store and hurried down to Madison to a bookshop that specialized in mass-market paperbacks. Inside were several long rows of shelving, each shelf containing different categories of fiction and nonfiction, alphabetically arranged. Hackman stepped into the fiction section, stopped in front of the shelf marked HISTORICAL ROMANCES, and squinted at the titles until he located one of his own pseudonymous works. Then he unwrapped his parcel.

And took out the woodsman's hatchet.

And got a comfortable grip on its handle.

And raised it high over his head.

And—

Whack! Eleven copies of *Love's Tender Fury* by Allison St. Cyr were drawn and quartered.

A male customer yelped; a female customer shrieked. Hackman took no notice. He moved on to the shelf marked OCCULT PIRATE ADVENTURE, raised the hatchet again, and—

Whack! Nine copies of *The Devil Daughter of Jean Lafitte* by Adam Caine were exorcised and scuttled.

On to ADULT WESTERNS. And—

Whack! Four copies of *Ryder Rides the Outlaw Trail* by Galen McGee bit the dust.

Behind the front counter a chubby little man was jumping up and down, waving his arms. "What are you doing?" he kept shouting at Hackman. "What are you doing?"

"Hackwork!" Hackman shouted back. "I'm a hack writer doing hackwork!"

He stepped smartly to GOTHIC SUSPENSE. And—

Whack! Five copies of *Mansion of Dread* by Melissa Ann Farnsworth were reduced to rubble.

On to MALE ACTION SERIES, and—

Whack! Ten copies of Max Ruffe's *The Grenade Launcher #23: Blowup at City Hall* exploded into fragments

Hackman paused to survey the carnage. Then he nodded in satisfaction and turned toward the front door. The bookshop was empty now, but the chubby little man was visible on the sidewalk outside, jumping up and down and semaphoring his arms amid a gathering crowd. Hackman crossed to the door in purposeful strides and threw it open.

People scattered every which way when they saw him come out with the hatchet aloft. But they needn't have feared; he had no interest in people, except as bit players in this little drama. After all, what hack worth the name ever cared a hoot about his audience?

He began to run up Forty-eighth Street toward Fifth Avenue, brandishing the hatchet. Nobody tried to stop him, not even when he lopped off the umbrella shading a frankfurter vendor's cart.

"I'm a hack!" he shouted.

And shattered the display window of an exclusive boutique.

"I'm Hackman the hack!" he yelled.

And halved the product and profits of a pretzel vendor.

"I'm Hackman the hack and I'm hacking my way to glory!" he bellowed.

And sliced the antenna off an illegally parked Cadillac limousine.

He was almost to Fifth Avenue by this time. Ahead of him he could see a red signal light holding up crosstown traffic; this block of Forty-eighth Street was momentarily empty. Behind him he could hear angry shouts and what sounded like a police whistle. He looked back over his shoulder. Several people were giving pursuit, including the chubby little man from the bookshop; the leader of the pack, a blue uniform with a red face atop it, was less than fifty yards distant.

But the game was not up yet, Hackman thought. There were more bookstores along Fifth; with any luck he could hack his way through two or three before they got him. He decided south was the direction he wanted to go, pulled his head around, and started to sprint across the empty expanse of Forty-eighth.

Only the street wasn't empty any longer; the signal on Fifth had changed to green for the eastbound traffic.

He ran right out in front of an oncoming car.

He saw it too late to jump clear, and the driver saw him too late to brake or swerve. But before he and the machine joined forces, Hackman had just enough time to realize the full scope of what was happening—and to feel a sudden elation. In fact, he wished with his last wish that he'd thought of this himself. It was the crowning touch, the final fillip, the *coup de grâce;* it lent the death of Hackman, unlike the life of Hackman, a genuine originality.

Because the car which did him in was not just a car; it was a New York City taxicab.

Otherwise known as a hack.

The book featured in "Chapter and Verse" is a family Bible, and the chapter and verse are clues to long-ago murders. Dame Ngaio Marsh (1899–1982) wrote over thirty novels and a number of short stories featuring the sophisticated Superintendent Roderick Alleyn of Scotland Yard and his artist wife, Troy. The two make an effective and attractive pair of sleuths, each from time to time assuming the larger part in the investigation—or sharing, as in this story, where Troy spots the crime and Alleyn detects after the fact. In Dame Ngaio's work several biographical elements figure prominently. Her background in the fine arts (she originally hoped to become a painter) is incorporated into Troy Alleyn's character. She makes excellent use of her passion for the theater—which led her to direct, write and produce plays throughout her life. And she effectively uses detail about her native New Zealand, often in the form of important clues.

CHAPTER AND VERSE

Ngaio Marsh

When the telephone rang, Troy came in, sun-dazzled, from the cottage garden to answer it, hoping it would be a call from London.

"Oh," said a strange voice uncertainly. "May I speak to Superintendent Alleyn, if you please?"

"I'm sorry. He's away."

"Oh, dear!" said the voice, crestfallen. "Er—would that be—am I speaking to Mrs. Alleyn?"

"Yes."

"Oh. Yes. Well, it's Timothy Bates here, Mrs. Alleyn. You don't know me," the voice confessed wistfully, "but I had the pleasure several years ago of meeting your husband. In New Zealand. And he did say that if I ever came home I was to get in touch, and when I heard quite by accident that you were here—well, I *was* excited. But, alas, no good after all."

"I *am* sorry," Troy said. "He'll be back, I hope, on Sunday night. Perhaps—"

"Will he! Come, *that's* something! Because here I am at the Star and Garter, you see, and so—" The voice trailed away again.

"Yes, indeed. He'll be delighted," Troy said, hoping that he would.

"I'm a bookman," the voice confided. "Old books, you know. He used to come into my shop. It was always such a pleasure."

"But, of course!" Troy exclaimed. "I remember perfectly now. He's often talked about it."

"*Has* he? Has he, really! Well, you see, Mrs. Alleyn, I'm here on business. Not to *sell* anything, please don't think that, but on a voyage of discovery; almost, one might say, of detection, and I think it might amuse him. He has such an eye for the curious. Not," the voice hurriedly amended, "in the trade sense. I mean curious in the sense of mysterious and unusual. But I mustn't bore you."

Troy assured him that he was not boring her and indeed it was true. The voice was so much colored by odd little overtones that she found herself quite drawn to its owner. "I know where you are," he was saying. "Your house was pointed out to me."

After that there was nothing to do but ask him to visit. He seemed to cheer up prodigiously. "May I? May I, really? Now?"

"Why not?" Troy said. "You'll be here in five minutes."

She heard a little crow of delight before he hung up the receiver.

He turned out to be exactly like his voice—a short, middle-aged, bespectacled man, rather untidily dressed. As he came up the path she saw that with both arms he clutched to his stomach an enormous Bible. He was thrown into a fever over the difficulty of removing his cap.

"How ridiculous!" he exclaimed. "Forgive me! One moment."

He laid his burden tenderly on a garden seat. "There!" he cried. "Now! How do you do!"

Troy took him indoors and gave him a drink. He chose sherry and sat in the window seat with his Bible beside him. "You'll wonder," he said, "why I've appeared with this unusual piece of baggage. I *do* trust it arouses your curiosity."

He went into a long excitable explanation. It appeared that the Bible was an old and rare one that he had picked up in a job lot of books in New Zealand. All this time he kept it under his square little hands as if it might open of its own accord and spoil his story.

"Because," he said, "the *really* exciting thing to me is *not* its undoubted authenticity but—" He made a conspiratorial face at Troy and suddenly opened the Bible. "Look!" he invited.

He displayed the flyleaf. Troy saw that it was almost filled with entries in a minute, faded copperplate handwriting.

"The top," Mr. Bates cried. "Top left-hand. Look at *that.*"

Troy read: *"Crabtree Farm at Little Copplestone in the County of Kent.* Why, it comes from our village!"

"Ah, ha! So it does. Now, the entries, my dear Mrs. Alleyn. The entries."

They were the recorded births and deaths of a family named Wagstaff, beginning in 1705 and ending in 1870 with the birth of William James Wagstaff. Here they broke off but were followed by three further entries, close together.

Stewart Shakespeare Hadet. Died: Tuesday, 5th April, 1779. 2nd Samuel 1.10.

Naomi Balbus Hadet. Died: Saturday, 13th August, 1779. Jeremiah 50.24.

Peter Rook Hadet. Died: Monday, 12th September, 1779. Ezekiel 7.6.

Troy looked up to find Mr. Bates's gaze fixed on her. "And what," Mr. Bates asked, "my dear Mrs. Alleyn, do you make of *that?*"

"Well," she said cautiously, "I know about Crabtree Farm. There's the farm itself, owned by Mr. De'ath, and there's Crabtree House, belonging to Miss Hart, and—yes, I fancy I've heard they both belonged originally to a family named Wagstaff."

"You are perfectly right. Now! What about the Hadets? What about *them?*"

"I've never heard of a family named Hadet in Little Copplestone. But—"

"Of course you haven't. For the very good reason that there never have been any Hadets in Little Copplestone."

"Perhaps in New Zealand, then?"

"The dates, my dear Mrs. Alleyn, the dates! New Zealand was not colonized in 1779. Look closer. Do you see the sequence of double dots—ditto marks—under the address? Meaning, of course, 'also of Crabtree Farm at Little Copplestone in the County of Kent.' "

"I suppose so."

"Of course you do. And how right you are. Now! You have noticed that throughout there are biblical references. For the Wagstaffs they are the usual pious offerings. You need not trouble yourself with them. But consult the text awarded to the three Hadets. Just you look *them* up! I've put markers."

He threw himself back with an air of triumph and sipped his sherry. Troy turned over the heavy bulk of pages to the first marker. "Second of Samuel, one, ten," Mr. Bates prompted, closing his eyes.

The verse had been faintly underlined.

"So I stood upon him," Troy read, *"and slew him."*

"That's Stewart Shakespeare Hadet's valedictory," said Mr. Bates. "Next!"

The next was at the 50th chapter of Jeremiah, verse 24: *"I have laid a snare for thee and thou are taken."*

Troy looked at Mr. Bates. His eyes were still closed and he was smiling faintly.

"That was Naomi Balbus Hadet," he said. "Now for Peter Rook Hadet. Ezekiel, seven, six."

The pages flopped back to the last marker.

"An end is come, the end is come: it watcheth for thee; behold it is come."

Troy shut the Bible.

"How very unpleasant," she said.

"And how very intriguing, don't you think?" And when she didn't answer, "Quite up your husband's street, it seemed to me."

"I'm afraid," Troy said, "that even Rory's investigations don't go back to 1779."

"What a pity!" Mr. Bates cried gaily.

"Do I gather that you conclude from all this that there was dirty work among the Hadets in 1779?"

"I don't know, but I'm dying to find out. *Dying* to. Thank you, I should enjoy another glass. Delicious!"

He had settled down so cosily and seemed to be enjoying himself so much that Troy was constrained to ask him to stay to lunch.

"Miss Hart's coming," she said. "She's the one who bought Crabtree House from the Wagstaffs. If there's any gossip to be picked up in Copplestone, Miss Hart's the one for it. She's coming about a painting she wants me to donate to the Harvest Festival raffle."

Mr. Bates was greatly excited. "Who knows!" he cried. "A Wagstaff in the hand may be worth two Hadets in the bush. I am your slave forever, my dear Mrs. Alleyn!"

Miss Hart was a lady of perhaps sixty-seven years. On meeting Mr. Bates she seemed to imply that some explanation should be advanced for Troy receiving a gentleman caller in her husband's absence. When the Bible was produced, she immediately accepted it in this light, glanced with professional expertise at the inscriptions and fastened on the Wagstaffs.

"No doubt," said Miss Hart, "it was their family Bible and much good it did them. A most eccentric lot they were. Very unsound. Very unsound, indeed. Especially Old Jimmy."

"Who," Mr. Bates asked greedily, "was Old Jimmy?"

Miss Hart jabbed her forefinger at the last of the Wagstaff entries. "William James Wagstaff. Born 1870. And died, although it doesn't say so, in April, 1921. Nobody was left to complete the entry, of course. Unless you count the niece, which I don't. Baggage, if ever I saw one."

"The niece?"

"Fanny Wagstaff. Orphan. Old Jimmy brought her up. Dragged would be the better word. Drunken old reprobate he was and he came to a drunkard's end. They said he beat her *and* I daresay she needed it." Miss Hart lowered her voice to a whisper and confided in Troy. "Not a *nice* girl. You know what I mean."

Troy, feeling it was expected of her, nodded portentously.

"A drunken end, did you say?" prompted Mr. Bates.

"Certainly. On a Saturday night after Market. Fell through the top-landing stair rail in his nightshirt and split his skull on the flagstoned hall."

"And your father bought it, then, after Old Jimmy died?" Troy ventured.

"Bought the house and garden. Richard De'ath took the farm. He'd been after it for years—wanted it to round off his own place. He and Old Jimmy were at daggers-drawn over *that* business. And, of course, Richard being an atheist, over the Seven Seals."

"I beg your pardon?" Mr. Bates asked.

"Blasphemous!" Miss Hart shouted. "That's what it was, rank blasphemy. It was a sect that Wagstaff founded. If the rector had known his business he'd have had him excommunicated for it."

Miss Hart was prevented from elaborating this theory

by the appearance at the window of an enormous woman, stuffily encased in black, with a face like a full moon.

"Anybody at home?" the newcomer playfully chanted. "Telegram for a lucky girl! Come and get it!"

It was Mrs. Simpson, the village postmistress. Miss Hart said, "Well, *really!*" and gave an acid laugh.

"Sorry, I'm sure," said Mrs. Simpson, staring at the Bible which lay under her nose on the window seat. "I didn't realize there was company. Thought I'd pop it in as I was passing."

Troy read the telegram while Mrs. Simpson, panting, sank heavily on the window ledge and eyed Mr. Bates, who had drawn back in confusion. "I'm no good in the heat," she told him. "Slays me."

"Thank you so much, Mrs. Simpson," Troy said. "No answer."

"Righty-ho. Cheerie-bye," said Mrs. Simpson, and with another stare at Mr. Bates and the Bible and a derisive grin at Miss Hart, she waddled away.

"It's from Rory," Troy said. "He'll be home on Sunday evening."

"*As* that woman will no doubt inform the village," Miss Hart pronounced. "A busybody of the first water and ought to be taught her place. Did you ever!"

She fulminated throughout luncheon and it was with difficulty that Troy and Mr. Bates persuaded her to finish her story of the last of the Wagstaffs. It appeared that Old Jimmy had died intestate, his niece succeeding. She had at once announced her intention of selling everything and had left the district to pursue, Miss Hart suggested, a life of freedom, no doubt in London or even in Paris. Miss Hart wouldn't, and didn't want to, know. On the subject of the Hadets, however, she was uninformed and showed no inclination to look up the marked Bible references attached to them.

After luncheon Troy showed Miss Hart three of her paintings, any one of which would have commanded a high price at an exhibition of contemporary art, and Miss Hart chose the one that, in her own phrase, really did look like something. She insisted that Troy and Mr. Bates accompany her to the parish hall where Mr. Bates would meet the rector, an authority on village folklore. Troy in person must hand over her painting to be raffled.

Troy would have declined this honor if Mr. Bates had not retired behind Miss Hart and made a series of beseeching gestures and grimaces. They set out therefore in Miss Hart's car which was crammed with vegetables for the Harvest Festival decorations.

"And if the woman Simpson thinks she's going to hog the lectern with *her* pumpkins," said Miss Hart, "she's in for a shock. Hah!"

St. Cuthbert's was an ancient parish church around whose flanks the tiny village nestled. Its tower, an immensely high one, was said to be unique. Nearby was the parish hall where Miss Hart pulled up with a masterful jerk.

Troy and Mr. Bates helped her unload some of her lesser marrows to be offered for sale within. They were observed by a truculent-looking man in tweeds who grinned at Miss Hart. "Burnt offerings," he jeered, "for the tribal gods, I perceive." It was Mr. Richard De'ath, the atheist. Miss Hart cut him dead and led the way into the hall.

Here they found the rector, with a crimson-faced elderly man and a clutch of ladies engaged in preparing for the morrow's sale.

The rector was a thin gentle person, obviously frightened of Miss Hart and timidly delighted by Troy. On being shown the Bible he became excited and dived at once into the story of Old Jimmy Wagstaff.

"Intemperate, I'm afraid, in everything," sighed the rector. "Indeed, it would not be too much to say that he both preached and drank hellfire. He *did* preach, on Saturday nights at the crossroads outside the Star and Garter.

Drunken, blasphemous nonsense it was and although he used to talk about his followers, the only one he could claim was his niece, Fanny, who was probably too much under his thumb to refuse him."

"Edward Pilbrow," Miss Hart announced, jerking her head at the elderly man who had come quite close to them. "Drowned him with his bell. They had a fight over it. Deaf as a post," she added, catching sight of Mr. Bates's startled expression. "He's the verger now. *And* the town crier."

"What!" Mr. Bates exclaimed.

"Oh, yes," the rector explained. "The village is endowed with a town crier." He went over to Mr. Pilbrow, who at once cupped his hand round his ear. The rector yelled into it.

"When did you start crying, Edward?"

"Twenty-ninth September, 'twenty-one," Mr. Pilbrow roared back.

"I thought so."

There was something in their manner that made it difficult to remember, Troy thought, that they were talking about events that were almost fifty years back in the past. Even the year 1779 evidently seemed to them to be not so long ago, but, alas, none of them knew of any Hadets.

"By all means," the rector invited Mr. Bates, "consult the church records, but I can assure you—no Hadets. Never any Hadets."

Troy saw an expression of extreme obstinacy settle round Mr. Bates's mouth.

The rector invited him to look at the church and as they both seemed to expect Troy to tag along, she did so. In the lane they once more encountered Mr. Richard De'ath out of whose pocket protruded a paper-wrapped bottle. He touched his cap to Troy and glared at the rector, who turned pink and said, "Afternoon, De'ath," and hurried on.

Mr. Bates whispered imploringly to Troy, "*Would* you mind? I *do* so want to have a word—" and she was obliged to introduce him. It was not a successful encounter. Mr. Bates no sooner broached the topic of his Bible, which he still carried, than Mr. De'ath burst into an alcoholic diatribe against superstition, and on the mention of Old Jimmy Wagstaff, worked himself up into such a state of reminiscent fury that Mr. Bates was glad to hurry away with Troy.

They overtook the rector in the churchyard, now bathed in the golden opulence of an already westering sun.

"There they all lie," the rector said, waving a fatherly hand at the company of headstones. "All your Wagstaffs, right back to the sixteenth century. But no Hadets, Mr. Bates, I assure you."

They stood looking up at the spire. Pigeons flew in and out of a balcony far above their heads. At their feet was a little flagged area edged by a low coping. Mr. Bates stepped forward and the rector laid a hand on his arm.

"Not there," he said. "Do you mind?"

"Don't!" bellowed Mr. Pilbrow from the rear. "Don't you set foot on them bloody stones, mister."

Mr. Bates backed away.

"Edward's not swearing," the rector mildly explained. "He is to be taken, alas, literally. A sad and dreadful story, Mr. Bates."

"Indeed?" Mr. Bates asked eagerly.

"Indeed, yes. Some time ago, in the very year we have been discussing—1921, you know—one of our girls, a very beautiful girl she was, named Ruth Wall, fell from the balcony of the tower and was, of course, killed. She used to go up there to feed the pigeons, and it was thought that in leaning over the low balustrade she overbalanced."

"Ah!" Mr. Pilbrow roared with considerable relish, evidently guessing the purport of the rector's speech. "Terrible, terrible! And 'er sweetheart after 'er, too. Terrible!"

"Oh, no!" Troy protested.

The rector made a dabbing gesture to subdue Mr. Pilbrow. "I wish he wouldn't," he said. "Yes. It was a few days later. A lad called Simon Castle. They were to be married. People said it must be suicide but—it may have been wrong of me—I couldn't bring myself—in short, he lies beside her over there. If you would care to look."

For a minute or two they stood before the headstones.

"Ruth Wall. Spinster of this Parish. 1903–1921. *I will extend peace to her like a river.*"

"Simon Castle. Bachelor of this Parish. 1900–1921. *And God shall wipe away all tears from their eyes.*"

The afternoon having by now worn on, and the others having excused themselves, Mr. Bates remained alone in the churchyard, clutching his Bible and staring at the headstones. The light of the hunter's zeal still gleamed in his eyes.

Troy didn't see Mr. Bates again until Sunday night service when, on her way up the aisle, she passed him, sitting in the rearmost pew. She was amused to observe that his gigantic Bible was under the seat.

"We plow the fields," sang the choir, *"and scatter—"* Mrs. Simpson roared away on the organ, the smell of assorted greengrocery rising like some humble incense. Everybody in Little Copplestone except Mr. Richard De'ath was there for the Harvest Festival. At last the rector stepped over Miss Hart's biggest pumpkin and ascended the pulpit, Edward Pilbrow switched off all the lights except one and they settled down for the sermon.

"A sower went forth to sow," announced the rector. He spoke simply and well but somehow Troy's attention wandered. She found herself wondering where, through the centuries, the succeeding generations of Wagstaffs had sat until Old Jimmy took to his freakish practices; and whether Ruth Wall and Simon Castle, poor things, had shared the same hymnbook and held hands during the sermon; and whether, after all, Stewart Shakespeare Hadet and Peter Rook Hadet had not, in 1779, occupied some dark corner of the church and been unaccountably forgotten.

Here we are, Troy thought drowsily, and there, outside in the churchyard, are all the others going back and back—

She saw a girl, bright in the evening sunlight, reach from a balcony toward a multitude of wings. She was falling—dreadfully—into nothingness. Troy woke with a sickening jerk.

"—on stony ground," the rector was saying. Troy listened guiltily to the rest of the sermon.

Mr. Bates emerged on the balcony. He laid his Bible on the coping and looked at the moonlit tree tops and the churchyard so dreadfully far below. He heard someone coming up the stairway. Torchlight danced on the door jamb.

"You were quick," said the visitor.

"I am all eagerness and, I confess, puzzlement."

"It had to be here, on the spot. If you *really* want to find out—"

"But I do, I do!"

"We haven't much time. You've brought the Bible?"

"You particularly asked—"

"If you'd open it at Ezekiel, chapter twelve. I'll shine my torch."

Mr. Bates opened the Bible.

"The thirteenth verse. There!"

Mr. Bates leaned forward. The Bible tipped and moved.

"Look out!" the voice urged.

Mr. Bates was scarcely aware of the thrust. He felt the page tear as the book sank under his hands. The last thing he heard was the beating of a multitude of wings.

"—and forevermore," said the rector in a changed voice, facing east. The congregation got to its feet. He announced the last hymn. Mrs. Simpson made a preliminary rumble and Troy groped in her pocket for the collection plate. Presently they all filed out into the autumnal moonlight.

It was coldish in the churchyard. People stood about in

groups. One or two had already moved through the lych-gate. Troy heard a voice, which she recognized as that of Mr. De'ath. "I suppose," it jeered, "you all know you've been assisting at a fertility rite."

"Drunk as usual, Dick De'ath," somebody returned without rancor. There was a general laugh.

They had all begun to move away when, from the shadows at the base of the church tower, there arose a great cry. They stood, transfixed, turned toward the voice.

Out of the shadows came the rector in his cassock. When Troy saw his face she thought he must be ill and went to him.

"No, no!" he said. "Not a woman! Edward! Where's Edward Pilbrow?"

Behind him, at the foot of the tower, was a pool of darkness; but Troy, having come closer, could see within it a figure, broken like a puppet on the flagstones. An eddy of night air stole round the church and fluttered a page of the giant Bible that lay pinned beneath the head.

It was nine o'clock when Troy heard the car pull up outside the cottage. She saw her husband coming up the path and ran to meet him, as if they had been parted for months.

He said, "This is mighty gratifying!" And then, "Hullo, my love. What's the matter?"

As she tumbled out her story, filled with relief at telling him, a large man with uncommonly bright eyes came up behind them.

"Listen to this, Fox," Roderick Alleyn said. "We're in demand, it seems." He put his arm through Troy's and closed his hand round hers. "Let's go indoors, shall we? Here's Fox, darling, come for a nice bucolic rest. Can we give him a bed?"

Troy pulled herself together and greeted Inspector Fox. Presently she was able to give them a coherent account of the evening's tragedy. When she had finished, Alleyn said,

"Poor little Bates. He was a nice little bloke." He put his hand on Troy's. "You need a drink," he said, "and so, by the way, do we."

While he was getting the drinks he asked quite casually, "You've had a shock and a beastly one at that, but there's something else, isn't there?"

"Yes," Troy swallowed hard, "there is. They're all saying it's an accident."

"Yes?"

"And, Rory, I don't think it is."

Mr. Fox cleared his throat. "Fancy," he said.

"Suicide?" Alleyn suggested, bringing her drink to her.

"No. Certainly not."

"A bit of rough stuff, then?"

"You sound as if you're asking about the sort of weather we've been having."

"Well, darling, you don't expect Fox and me to go into hysterics. Why not an accident?"

"He knew all about the other accidents, he *knew* it was dangerous. And then the oddness of it, Rory. To leave the Harvest Festival service and climb the tower in the dark, carrying that enormous Bible!"

"And he was hell-bent on tracing these Hadets?"

"Yes. He kept saying you'd be interested. He actually brought a copy of the entries for you."

"Have you got it?"

She found it for him. "The selected texts," he said, "are pretty rum, aren't they, Br'er Fox?" and handed it over.

"Very vindictive," said Mr. Fox.

"Mr. Bates thought it was in your line," Troy said.

"The devil he did! What's been done about this?"

"The village policeman was in the church. They sent for the doctor. And—well, you see, Mr. Bates had talked a lot about you and they hope you'll be able to tell them something about him—whom they should get in touch with and so on."

"Have they moved him?"

"They weren't going to until the doctor had seen him."

Alleyn pulled his wife's ear and looked at Fox. "Do you fancy a stroll through the village, Foxkin?"

"There's a lovely moon," Fox said bitterly and got to his feet.

The moon was high in the heavens when they came to the base of the tower and it shone on a group of four men—the rector, Richard De'ath, Edward Pilbrow, and Sergeant Botting, the village constable. When they saw Alleyn and Fox, they separated and revealed a fifth, who was kneeling by the body of Timothy Bates.

"Kind of you to come," the rector said, shaking hands with Alleyn. "And a great relief to all of us."

Their manner indicated that Alleyn's arrival would remove a sense of personal responsibility. "If you'd like to have a look—?" the doctor said.

The broken body lay huddled on its side. The head rested on the open Bible. The right hand, rigid in cadaveric spasm, clutched a torn page. Alleyn knelt and Fox came closer with the torch. At the top of the page Alleyn saw the word Ezekiel and a little farther down, Chapter 12.

Using the tip of his finger Alleyn straightened the page. "Look," he said, and pointed to the thirteenth verse. "*My net also will I spread upon him and he shall be taken in my snare.*"

The words had been faintly underlined in mauve.

Alleyn stood up and looked round the circle of faces.

"Well," the doctor said, "we'd better see about moving him."

Alleyn said, "I don't think he should be moved just yet."

"Not!" the rector cried out. "But surely—to leave him like this—I mean, after this terrible accident—"

"It has yet to be proved," Alleyn said, "that it was an accident."

There was a sharp sound from Richard De'ath.

"—and I fancy," Alleyn went on, glancing at De'ath, "that it's going to take quite a lot of proving."

After that, events, as Fox observed with resignation, took the course that was to be expected. The local Superintendent said that under the circumstances it would be silly not to ask Alleyn to carry on, the Chief Constable agreed, and appropriate instructions came through from Scotland Yard. The rest of the night was spent in routine procedure. The body having been photographed and the Bible set aside for fingerprinting, both were removed and arrangements put in hand for the inquest.

At dawn Alleyn and Fox climbed the tower. The winding stair brought them to an extremely narrow doorway through which they saw the countryside lying vaporous in the faint light. Fox was about to go through to the balcony when Alleyn stopped him and pointed to the door jambs. They were covered with a growth of stonecrop.

About three feet from the floor this had been brushed off over a space of perhaps four inches and fragments of the microscopic plant hung from the scars. From among these, on either side, Alleyn removed morsels of dark-colored thread. "And here," he sighed, "as sure as fate, we go again. O Lord, O Lord!"

They stepped through to the balcony and there was a sudden whirr and beating of wings as a company of pigeons flew out of the tower. The balcony was narrow and the balustrade indeed very low. "If there's any looking over," Alleyn said, "you, my dear Foxkin, may do it."

Nevertheless he leaned over the balustrade and presently knelt beside it. "Look at this. Bates rested the open Bible here—blow me down flat if he didn't! There's a powder of leather where it scraped on the stone and a fragment where it tore. It must have been moved—outward. Now, why, *why?*"

"Shoved it accidentally with his knees, then made a grab and overbalanced?"

"But why put the open Bible there? To read by moonlight? *My net also will I spread upon him and he shall be taken in my snare.* Are you going to tell me he underlined it and then dived overboard?"

"I'm not going to tell you anything," Fox grunted and then: "That old chap Edward Pilbrow's down below swabbing the stones. He looks like a beetle."

"Let him look like a rhinoceros if he wants to, but for the love of Mike don't leer over the edge—you give me the willies. Here, let's pick this stuff up before it blows away."

They salvaged the scraps of leather and put them in an envelope. Since there was nothing more to do, they went down and out through the vestry and so home to breakfast.

"Darling," Alleyn told his wife, "you've landed us with a snorter."

"Then you *do* think—?"

"There's a certain degree of fishiness. Now, see here, wouldn't *somebody* have noticed little Bates get up and go out? I know he sat all alone on the back bench, but wasn't there *someone?*"

"The rector?"

"No. I asked him. Too intent on his sermon, it seems."

"Mrs. Simpson? If she looks through her little red curtain she faces the nave."

"We'd better call on her, Fox. I'll take the opportunity to send a couple of cables to New Zealand. She's fat, jolly, keeps the shop-cum-post office, and is supposed to read all the postcards. Just your cup of tea. You're dynamite with postmistresses. Away we go."

Mrs. Simpson sat behind her counter doing a crossword puzzle and refreshing herself with licorice. She welcomed Alleyn with enthusiasm. He introduced Fox and then he retired to a corner to write out his cables.

"What a catastrophe!" Mrs. Simpson said, plunging straight into the tragedy. "Shocking! As nice a little gentleman as you'd wish to meet, Mr. Fox. Typical New Zealander. Pick him a mile away, and a friend of Mr. Alleyn's, I'm told, and if I've said it once I've said it a hundred times, Mr. Fox, they ought to have put something up to prevent it. Wire netting or a bit of ironwork; but, no, they let it go on from year to year and now see what's happened—history repeating itself and giving the village a bad name. Terrible!"

Fox bought a packet of tobacco from Mrs. Simpson and paid her a number of compliments on the layout of her shop, modulating from there into an appreciation of the village. He said that one always found such pleasant company in small communities. Mrs. Simpson was impressed and offered him a piece of licorice.

"As for pleasant company," she chuckled, "that's as may be, though by and large I suppose I mustn't grumble. I'm a cockney and a stranger here myself, Mr. Fox. Only twenty-four years and that doesn't go for anything with this lot."

"Ah," Fox said, "then you wouldn't recollect the former tragedies. Though to be sure," he added, "you wouldn't do that in any case, being much too young, if you'll excuse the liberty, Mrs. Simpson."

After this classic opening Alleyn was not surprised to hear Mrs. Simpson embark on a retrospective survey of life in Little Copplestone. She was particularly lively on Miss Hart, who, she hinted, had had her eye on Mr. Richard De'ath for many a long day.

"As far back as when Old Jimmy Wagstaff died, which was why she was so set on getting the next-door house; but Mr. De'ath never looked at anybody except Ruth Wall, and her head-over-heels in love with young Castle, which together with her falling to her destruction when feeding pigeons led Mr. De'ath to forsake religion and take to drink, which he has done something cruel ever since.

"They do say he's got a terrible temper, Mr. Fox, and

it's well known he give Old Jimmy Wagstaff a thrashing on account of straying cattle and threatened young Castle, saying if he couldn't have Ruth, nobody else would, but fair's fair and personally I've never seen him anything but nice-mannered, drunk or sober. Speak as you find's my motto and always has been, but these old maids, when they take a fancy they get it pitiful hard. You wouldn't know a word of nine letters meaning 'pale-faced lure like a sprat in a fishy story,' would you?"

Fox was speechless, but Alleyn, emerging with his cables, suggested "whitebait."

"Correct!" shouted Mrs. Simpson. "Fits like a glove. Although it's not a bit like a sprat and a quarter the size. Cheating, I call it. Still, it fits." She licked her indelible pencil and triumphantly added it to her crossword.

They managed to lead her back to Timothy Bates. Fox, professing a passionate interest in organ music, was able to extract from her that when the rector began his sermon she had in fact dimly observed someone move out of the back bench and through the doors. "He must have walked round the church and in through the vestry and little did I think he was going to his death," Mrs. Simpson said with considerable relish and a sigh like an earthquake.

"You didn't happen to hear him in the vestry?" Fox ventured, but it appeared that the door from the vestry into the organ loft was shut and Mrs. Simpson, having settled herself to enjoy the sermon with, as she shamelessly admitted, a bag of chocolates, was not in a position to notice.

Alleyn gave her his two cables: the first to Timothy Bates's partner in New Zealand and the second to one of his own colleagues in that country asking for any available information about relatives of the late William James Wagstaff of Little Copplestone, Kent, possibly resident in New Zealand after 1921, and of any persons of the name of Peter Rook Hadet or Naomi Balbus Hadet.

Mrs. Simpson agitatedly checked over the cables, professional etiquette and burning curiosity struggling together in her enormous bosom. She restrained herself, however, merely observing that an event of this sort set you thinking, didn't it?

"And no doubt," Alleyn said as they walked up the lane, "she'll be telling her customers that the next stop's bloodhounds and manacles."

"Quite a tidy armful of lady, isn't she, Mr. Alleyn?" Fox calmly rejoined.

The inquest was at 10:20 in the smoking room of the Star and Garter. With half an hour in hand, Alleyn and Fox visited the churchyard. Alleyn gave particular attention to the headstones of Old Jimmy Wagstaff, Ruth Wall, and Simon Castle. "No mention of the month or day," he said. And after a moment: "I wonder. We must ask the rector."

"No need to ask the rector," said a voice behind them. It was Miss Hart. She must have come soundlessly across the soft turf. Her air was truculent. "Though why," she said, "it should be of interest, I'm sure I don't know. Ruth Wall died on August thirteenth, 1921. It was a Saturday."

"You've a remarkable memory," Alleyn observed.

"Not as good as it sounds. That Saturday afternoon I came to do the flowers in the church. I found her and I'm not likely ever to forget it. Young Castle went the same way almost a month later. September twelfth. In my opinion there was never a more glaring case of suicide. I believe," Miss Hart said harshly, "in facing facts."

"She was a beautiful girl, wasn't she?"

"I'm no judge of beauty. She set the men by the ears. *He* was a fine-looking young fellow. Fanny Wagstaff did her best to get *him*."

"Had Ruth Wall," Alleyn asked, "other admirers?"

Miss Hart didn't answer and he turned to her. Her face was blotted with an unlovely flush. "She ruined two men's lives, if you want to know. Castle and Richard De'ath," said

Miss Hart. She turned on her heel and without another word marched away.

"September twelfth," Alleyn murmured. "That would be a Monday, Br'er Fox."

"So it would," Fox agreed, after a short calculation, "so it would. Quite a coincidence."

"Or not, as the case may be. I'm going to take a gamble on this one. Come on."

They left the churchyard and walked down the lane, overtaking Edward Pilbrow on the way. He was wearing his town crier's coat and hat and carrying his bell by the clapper. He manifested great excitement when he saw them.

"Hey!" he shouted, "what's this I hear? Murder's the game, is it? What a go! Come on, gents, let's have it. Did 'e fall or was'e pushed? Hor, hor, hor! Come on."

"Not till after the inquest," Alleyn shouted.

"Do we get a look at the body?"

"Shut up," Mr. Fox bellowed suddenly.

"I got to know, haven't I? It'll be the smartest bit of crying I ever done, this will! I reckon I might get on the telly with this. 'Town crier tells old-world village death stalks the churchyard.' Hor, hor, hor!"

"Let us," Alleyn whispered, "leave this horrible old man."

They quickened their stride and arrived at the pub, to be met with covert glances and dead silence.

The smoking room was crowded for the inquest. Everybody was there, including Mrs. Simpson who sat in the back row with her candies and her crossword puzzle. It went through very quickly. The rector deposed to finding the body. Richard De'ath, sober and less truculent than usual, was questioned as to his sojourn outside the churchyard and said he'd noticed nothing unusual apart from hearing a disturbance among the pigeons roosting in the balcony. From where he stood, he said, he couldn't see the face of the tower.

An open verdict was recorded.

Alleyn had invited the rector, Miss Hart, Mrs. Simpson, Richard De'ath, and, reluctantly, Edward Pilbrow, to join him in the Bar-Parlor and had arranged with the landlord that nobody else would be admitted. The Public Bar, as a result, drove a roaring trade.

When they had all been served and the hatch closed, Alleyn walked into the middle of the room and raised his hand. It was the slightest of gestures but it secured their attention.

He said, "I think you must all realize that we are not satisfied this was an accident. The evidence against accident has been collected piecemeal from the persons in this room and I am going to put it before you. If I go wrong I want you to correct me. I ask you to do this with absolute frankness, even if you are obliged to implicate someone who you would say was the last person in the world to be capable of a crime of violence."

He waited. Pilbrow, who had come very close, had his ear cupped in his hand. The rector looked vaguely horrified. Richard De'ath suddenly gulped down his double whiskey. Miss Hart coughed over her lemonade and Mrs. Simpson avidly popped a peppermint cream in her mouth and took a swig of her port-and-raspberry.

Alleyn nodded to Fox, who laid Mr. Bates's Bible, open at the flyleaf, on the table before him.

"The case," Alleyn said, "hinges on this book. You have all seen the entries. I remind you of the recorded deaths in 1779 of the three Hadets—Stewart Shakespeare, Naomi Balbus, and Peter Rook. To each of these is attached a biblical text suggesting that they met their death by violence. There have never been any Hadets in this village and the days of the week are wrong for the given dates. They are right, however, for the year 1921 and *they fit the deaths,* all by falling from a height, of William Wagstaff, Ruth Wall, and Simon Castle.

"By analogy the Christian names agree. William suggests Shakespeare. Naomi—Ruth; Balbus—a wall. Simon—Peter; and a Rook is a Castle in chess. And Hadet," Alleyn said without emphasis, "is an anagram of Death."

"Balderdash!" Miss Hart cried out in an unrecognizable voice.

"No, it's not," said Mrs. Simpson. "It's jolly good crossword stuff."

"Wicked balderdash. Richard!"

De'ath said, "Be quiet. Let him go on."

"We believe," Alleyn said, "that these three people met their deaths by one hand. Motive is a secondary consideration, but it is present in several instances, predominantly in one. Who had cause to wish the death of these three people? Someone whom old Wagstaff had bullied and to whom he had left his money and who killed him for it. Someone who was infatuated with Simon Castle and bitterly jealous of Ruth Wall. Someone who hoped, as an heiress, to win Castle for herself and who, failing, was determined nobody else should have him. Wagstaff's orphaned niece—Fanny Wagstaff."

There were cries of relief from all but one of his hearers. He went on. "Fanny Wagstaff sold everything, disappeared, and was never heard of again in the village. But twenty-four years later she returned, and has remained here ever since."

A glass crashed to the floor and a chair overturned as the vast bulk of the postmistress rose to confront him.

"Lies! *Lies!*" screamed Mrs. Simpson.

"Did you sell everything again, before leaving New Zealand?" he asked as Fox moved forward. "Including the Bible, Miss Wagstaff?"

"But," Troy said, "how could you be so sure?"

"She was the only one who could leave her place in the church unobserved. She was the only one fat enough to rub her hips against the narrow door jambs. She uses an indelible pencil. We presume she arranged to meet Bates on the balcony, giving a cock-and-bull promise to tell him something nobody else knew about the Hadets. She indicated the text with her pencil, gave the Bible a shove, and, as he leaned out to grab it, tipped him over the edge.

"In talking about 1921 she forgot herself and described the events as if she had been there. She called Bates a typical New Zealander but gave herself out to be a Londoner. She said whitebait are only a quarter of the size of sprats. New Zealand whitebait are—English whitebait are about the same size.

"And as we've now discovered, she didn't send my cables. Of course she thought poor little Bates was hot on her tracks, especially when she learned that he'd come here to see me. She's got the kind of crossword-puzzle mind that would think up the biblical clues, and would get no end of a kick in writing them in. She's overwhelmingly conceited and vindictive."

"Still—"

"I know. Not good enough if we'd played the waiting game. But good enough to try shock tactics. We caught her off her guard and she cracked up."

"Not," Mr. Fox said, "a nice type of woman."

Alleyn strolled to the gate and looked up the lane to the church. The spire shone golden in the evening sun.

"The rector," Alleyn said, "tells me he's going to do something about the balcony."

"Mrs. Simpson, née Wagstaff," Fox remarked, "suggested wire netting."

"And she ought to know," Alleyn said, and turned back to the cottage.